MARCH 2021

D1646511

The Islandman

To Ramtines Library,
with my
compliments,

Tom Quinn

Tom
Quinn

The Islandman

Tom Quinn

www.irelandstories.com

Copyright © 2021, Tom Quinn

First Edition
First Printing, 2021 – POD

First published in 2021 by
Gent Publishing
www.ca404.com

All Rights Reserved

ISBN: 9798567038192

No part of this book may be reproduced, stored in a retrieval system, or transmitted in any form or by any means, electronic, mechanical, photocopying, recording or otherwise without the prior written permission of the copyright holder.

Acknowledgements

I want to take this opportunity to thank all of the following for assisting with the production of this book:

Maureen, who proofed and read and provided valuable insights.

Paul, who published the book and who also created the cover for it. Paul's support on every level has been indispensable.

I wish to thank Bernie Collins for her reading and feedback. She has also been a source of friendship, support, and belief, during the often painful process of creating this work in a most difficult year.

Other books by Tom Quinn

Letters to Therese (a novel) – Gent Publishing

The Traumatic Memory of the Great War 1914-1918 in Louis-Ferdinand Céline's Voyage au bout de la nuit – The Edwin Mellen Press

Contents

Part I   Inish   Page   9

Part II   Dublin   Page   119

Part III   Inish   Page   177

Epilogue   Page   254

The Islandman

"Once drinking deep of that divinest anguish

How could I seek the empty world again?"

Emily Brontë

"No man is an island."

John Donne

Part I

Inish

It was the time before the autumn equinox. It was almost night when he arrived on the island. The last light was in the west and the colours of the sunset were spreading themselves, pink, rose, a deep wine colour, and faint touches of lemon and gold, over the horizon. The ferry had drifted its way over the calmly rippling waters of the bay and was now coming to rest at the quiet quayside of the island's main village. All was calm, serene, and there was no wind. The only sound to be heard was the subdued coughing of the boat's engine, with some stray notes of birdsong that drifted lightly, melodically, on the air. The crew busied themselves wordlessly throwing ropes out to waiting hands to fasten the boat to terra firma. Above the tiny village gathered darkly on the tip of the island he made out the slender sliver of crescent moon becoming visible and in her court the bright evening star, Venus, glowing in her splendid and golden isolation. When the boat was settled against the quayside he pushed his bike in front of him on to the firm, unwavering earth of the island.

He rolled his bike up the road leading through the clustered houses of the village and then after building up some momentum he deftly swung himself high on to the saddle. He had just enough lingering light, before night completely fell, to cycle with some energy out of the village and away across the relatively flat and treeless terrain of the near island, turning after a time on to a side road which took him between a low huddle of small peat-covered hills, and then downhill to the little harbour on the south of the island above which his newly-rented cottage was located. As he approached the village he heard the high-pitched haunting cry of the curlew, so like that of a weeping woman. It was quite dark now but the lamp from his bike was strong enough to pick out the features of the road ahead of him with wild green grasses spilling over its verges and not far ahead of him he made out the cottage itself with soft electric light glowing from its windows and doorway. In the doorway stood Mary Kate, like a cottage sentinel, waiting anxiously but patiently for him.

"Hi, Mary Kate!" he hailed her as he pushed up the slight incline from the shore to the cottage.

"Harry! You're here at last! It's so great to see you!" she hailed him back.

She was a slight, middle-aged woman with short-cropped red hair and she turned about on herself with quick nervous movements. Her husband Tomás a large man with an air of strength about him stood stolidly behind her in the warm light of the cottage. He raised a welcoming hand above Mary Kate's head.

The cottage was a low single-storey whitewashed building with a narrow glass-fronted porch, that Mary Kate called a "conservatory", jutting out and around the open doorway where she now stood. The roof was almost invisible in the nearly complete darkness but he remembered from his previous visit the rough lines of concrete that went back and forth over it filling and covering the crevices where the slates were laid upon each other to protect the roof from the wind. Alongside the building there was a large pile of neatly stacked turf about twenty feet long. Mary Kate had promised him he could freely use the turf for the open fireplace in the cottage. The side walls of the building had no windows but there were windows in the bedroom to the right and in the living room to the left of the path as he walked towards the front of the house. He could smell the constant island smell of burning peat in the air, and through the living room window he saw a brightly blazing fire which Tomás no doubt had set for him. He had to admit the cottage had a warm welcoming air and he was glad to have arrived at what would be his home for the foreseeable future.

"Come in, come in, come in!" cooed Mary Kate, excitedly grabbing him by the hand and pulling him in her energetic way into the warm interior of the cottage. "Tomás has the kettle on… You'll have tea won't you?"

"I will surely!" he assented.

Tea would be welcome after his day of travel.

"How was the journey?" Tomás asked him the perennial Irish question while handing him a steaming mug.

"Great!" he answered, and added with genuine relief, "And it's so great to finally be here!"

He had found the cottage during the summer after weeks of cycling along the west coast of Ireland. He had begun his quest in Limerick before cycling northwards up through west Clare and the stony expanse of the Burren. He had visited a cave system in the Burren where, in the natural darkness of the cave, an underground waterfall falling from a high ledge, and lit brilliantly by a nearby lamp, created tiny fleeting rainbows, and sent fabulous jewels of brightly glittering water drops cascading through the air.

He thought it was one of the most beautiful things he had ever seen. The luminous rushing fall of water with its dazzling scattered jewels and rainbow colours would remain fiercely radiant in his mind and imagination for a very long time, indeed for all of his life. He had sheltered a couple of nights in Kinvara in a simple holiday hostel run by a young local man with a gorgeously animated red-haired American girlfriend while a lightning-charged storm rumbled ferociously overhead. Next, he rode out along the Connemara coast from Galway City settling in another hostel in Carna where he swam on unusually hot summer days in the exquisite cold of the crystal-clear Atlantic. After visiting Roundstone and Clifden he swung back across country through Recess and Maam Cross continuing on towards the broad isthmus separating Lough Corrib and Lough Mask, all the while looking out for the elusive country cottage he would make his home. He stayed some time in a hostel in Cong where it was so busy he had to sleep on the floor in an extra room the owners had made available. He spent the evening drinking green-tinted *"Crème de Menthe"* with a young French woman, Christine Delaforêt, he remembered her name, who later, by coincidence, slept next to him in her sleeping bag and in the depth of the night climbed on him with unheralded hot embraces and kisses. When he pushed his fingers into her thighs she rolled away from him into a deeper silence and sleep. He thought she had been sleeping all the time but wasn't sure. He left early in the morning without disturbing anyone, picking his steps gingerly over the sleeping bodies on the floor, a deep embarrassment rolling through his soul.

He journeyed west again before turning north through the mountain-held glistening valley of Lough Inagh with the purple-heather flanks and the sparkling quartzite of the Twelve Bens gleaming down upon the glittering lake. He stayed on Killary Harbour listening to tales of German submarines that had sheltered there during storms at sea in World War Two. He cycled head bowed in heavy rain through the tiny village of Leenane and up through the mystical light of Delphi and along the shores of Doolough where the sun returned in great bright swathes of pure crystalline light sweeping through the valley. In Westport he drank pints of Guinness with a local man about his own age who seemed to spend all his time in the pub next to the glowing turf fires alight even in the middle of the summer, which was to be fair a typically cold damp Irish summer overall.

"There's an island," the local man told him, as if imparting a secret only he knew. "You have to take the ferry to get there... But it's a nice quiet place and yet big enough with a few small villages... There are a couple of mountains, and some nice beaches, there's one truly spectacular beach, there's a castle a pirate queen owned, and there's a deserted village from the famine times… It's a few miles off the coast. You'd be very alone there!"

His brother, a few years older than he was, joined him by car in Westport and one morning at dawn they drove to the holy mountain of Croagh Patrick and climbed to the summit. They dropped on their hands and knees as they scrambled over the loose scree covering the peaked summit of the mountain to a small whitewashed church from where, sitting with their backs against the wall, they surveyed the vast expanse of the Atlantic strewn, it appeared, with a thousand small islands. In the middle-distance a shadowy triangle of emerald-green island, called Grace Island on the map, rose high out of the ocean, and beyond it a larger island with two high peaks loomed, looking for all the world like a new continent to the west. This was to be his island. Inish it was called.

"I'll drive you there," his brother offered.

"There's no bridge," Harry explained. "There's just a ferry."

He could tell that his brother was frustrated that he had not already found, long before he reached Westport, the isolated cottage he had promised himself to live in somewhere in the west of Ireland.

"We'll drive to the ferry and take it across," his brother said with a hint of impatience. "You can make enquiries locally then about a cottage to rent."

They did just that. They drove the thirty miles or so to the coast and caught the ferry to Inish. They stopped at the main village, Killeaden, and his brother physically pushed him into a bread shop where the owner, a tall thin dark-skinned man with dark curled hair and wearing a jacket and waistcoat, told him, "I know Mary Kate has a cottage". As it turned out Mary Kate's brother, Frank, had some time before left the cottage and the island for England. The cottage was now empty, sitting about one hundred feet above the rugged shore of the island's southern reaches and looking towards the high-peaked triangle of green island he had seen from the sacred summit of Croagh Patrick. The cottage was the first place he had properly looked at on his journey but it seemed adequate. There were a few neighbours he thought he might become friendly with but apart from that it was suitably remote. The village had a church and a pub and little more. Although there was no bridge to the island you could bring a car over by ferry if you wanted to and there was plenty of traffic criss-crossing the island's narrow roads. Mary Kate and Tomás drove him and his brother to the cottage which he had already decided to take even before he saw it. It was small, compact and comfortable, it was out of the way, and sitting just a few dozen steps from the sea he could hear the rhythmic roll of the Atlantic waves, and the soft swishing of her skirts, at all times. His brother shook his head doubtfully when he told him he had decided to stay.

"It's going to be rough in winter!" he warned him. "You are going to be so isolated!"

"That's what I want," he said.

He had told everyone he was going to write books, but really he didn't think he was going to write, or even to do anything at all. He simply wanted to be alone. He wanted to forget.

That night back in Westport he shared a meal and some pints with his brother. Even though it was still mid-summer the wind had risen and was howling around the building, the sky was a cold grey, and a scattering of rain drops flew against the windows of the building. They were glad of the fire blazing near them.

"I know it's what you want," his brother said, "but it's going to be very inhospitable when the winter comes along."

He added, "Remember if you want, if ever you want, you can come to us…"

He meant to his home, to his wife and their children, where they lived in the heart of the Irish midlands.

"I know," Harry answered. "I appreciate that. I'll remember…"

But he had no intention of remembering.

The evening grew colder, darker, wetter. The fire took a tighter, more comforting hold on them. His brother asked him about his weeks of cycling. He wanted to know what the highlights were. At first Harry talked a little about the beauty of the scenery he had cycled through, about the vast and lunar Burren with its cracked and broken limestone slabs, its collapsed sunken limestone pits, its eerily twisted hazel trees sentinelling the landscape, and the cave he had visited with the iridescent waterfall scattering its jewels of light. He mentioned the fierce electrical storm above the hostel in Kinvara, he described in detail and with enthusiasm the gorgeous red-haired American woman working there, he evoked the exquisitely cold brightly sunlit water of the beach at Carna, the thick rain over Killary and Leenane, the mystical light of Delphi, and the luminous swathes of crystal light sweeping through Doolough valley. And then he began to talk of a couple of things that he had found remarkable but perhaps were not what his brother was expecting.

In Limerick city, he told his brother, he had gone walking along the river. A young boy and a teenage girl were ambling along carelessly in front of him while turning and casting curious smiling glances back at him. Eventually the young boy broke free and approached him, "Would you like to sleep with my sister?" he asked with a cheeky smile. The girl too was smiling invitingly. He wasn't sure if it was a joke but if so it was a surprising joke for such youngsters. Eventually he passed them and walked nonchalantly away from them, the boy still calling after him with his salacious offer, the girl seemingly compliant. A middle-aged woman then approached him with an air of alarm. "You shouldn't be out here!" she warned him. "If the local boys see you're a stranger they might hurt you!" Heeding her warning he decided to walk back into the city but, as he was walking close to a high wall not far from the castle, a hail of large stones was flung down upon him, one stone whizzing audibly past his head. "Good Christ!" his brother protested. There was more, he assured his brother. In the centre of town as night was falling a cavalcade of young men and boys came galloping along the main street on horseback, there must have been at least twenty of them. They scattered among the traffic and even rode on to the pavements causing people on foot to throw themselves into the shelter of any available shopfronts. "It was like the Wild West," he told his brother. His brother looked amazed and said "I don't believe it!" Just then coincidentally a person sitting at a nearby table opened his newspaper revealing a front page headline which read, "Youths ride wild horses through centre of Limerick". You see, I told you so, he said to his brother.

There was something else he hesitated to tell his brother, because it seemed not just a little morbid, but perhaps insignificant and pointless to tell it, but it was an event on his journey nonetheless. Cycling up through Clare he had come across a stricken crow in the middle of the road. It had obviously been hit by a passing car and it could no longer fly to safety but was moving about erratically on the road. At first he continued to cycle and then moved by curiosity as much as pity he dismounted and watched the bird for a time. It seemed in some pain and perhaps some terror. Eventually he went to it and gathered it up, its wings making helpless fluttering movements in his hands. He didn't know what to do but decided at last to go to the nearest house. A rather unsettled nervous older woman came to the door and listened intently as he explained how he had found the distressed crow. Understanding that he wanted her to help the bird she at first looked unhappy and even irritated but then softened towards him and said, "My son is the very same, he would do the very same, he hates to see birds or animals or any living thing suffer!" She fetched a cardboard box and he placed the crow gently inside where it ceased its frightened movements. There was blood on his hands and also he could see blood spreading through the black wings of the broken creature. "Can I wash my hands?" he asked the woman and she showed him to the bathroom. "My son will look after him when he gets home," she assured him. "Don't worry! He's very kind…" He thanked her and left. A few days later he phoned her to ask about the crow. "There was no hope for it," the woman told him with some bluntness. "My son could see that straight away… No hope…So he wrung its neck! It was the best thing… The bird didn't even know it was having its neck wrung… Dead before it knew it!" The brutality of the image swept over him but recognising its inevitability he thanked the woman and hung up. It had been a hopeless worthless act of rescue.

There was one other thing he briefly thought of telling his brother but he couldn't bring himself to do it. It was about the French woman in Cong, the one he had shared the "*Crème de Menthe*" with and who had slept beside him on the floor of the hostel and later climbed on top of him in the darkness with a torrent of embraces and a rain of kisses on his face and mouth. His brother watched him closely as he became silent and sank back into himself remembering her sudden nocturnal romantic assault, her impassioned embrace and fevered torrid kisses. And how she had finally turned away from him in her apparent sleep.

"I think I know what you're thinking about," his brother said quietly.

But he didn't.

After he had agreed with Mary Kate that he would rent the cottage for at least a year Harry returned to Dublin where he ended his rental agreement for his own apartment there, sent all of his belongings for safe-keeping to his brother's house, and whiled away the weeks until it was time to take his bike again and go to the island. In mid-September then, the train from Heuston Station took him across the island of Ireland all the way to Westport from where he cycled until he reached the ferry and made his way over the quiet water towards the furthest lamplit remotenesses of Inish and his new island home.

He woke to his first morning on the island with bright sunlight streaming through the windows and the sound of the ocean rising and falling near the cottage. It was a pleasant September day and the sun felt warm on his skin when he stepped outside. Above him there was a scattering of houses to the north of the village, and below him sweeping down to the harbour, more houses, finally gathering in a huddle within the circle of low treeless hills that sheltered the tiny community. On the road rising from the harbour itself he could see, on the highest point, the twin satellites of the small grey church and next to it the village pub. Almost all of the houses in the village were painted white but the pub was painted a conspicuous blue and it advertised bed and breakfast rooms upstairs. Most of the houses had slanted slated roofs with characteristic rough lines of cement or tar following the edges of the slates, to protect them in high wind, but many houses had flat roofs, some with canvas and tar over them, as if hunkered down out of the tearing wind which along the coast here was a constant menace.

In front of his cottage there were a number of green fields in which sheep grazed, but beyond the fields the ground became rugged and inhospitable as it retreated away towards the most southerly point of the island. A rough stony path led along the rocky shore and about a mile distant he could see what looked like a low wooden structure sitting close to the edge of the sea. Turning his gaze back towards the village he saw a short stony beach reaching across from the near shoreline to a narrow headland with a whitewashed two-storey house sitting on a small field of green. On the far side of the headland there was a fine beach of golden sand bright in the sunshine and on which fuming lines of white foam ran ahead of the turbulent waves of the wild Atlantic. Turning to gaze away from the sea he saw on all sides brown treeless hills rise away from the coast and tumble gently back towards the inner island. The island was notable for its lack of trees. The land here was almost all peat blanketed in low rough grasses and heathers which in bright daylight looked a burnt brownish colour but which in dull damp conditions sometimes had an ochre hue. Along the road that ran in front of his cottage there were bright orange sprinkles of wild monbretia and in the hedgerows the blood-red tears of drooping fuchsia blossoms.

After breakfast he decided to go for a walk and to explore a little. He set out first along the deserted rocky shore, its large craggy stones blackened in places and in others covered in colonies of deep-yellow lichen. A few feet from the path on his right there were low walls of stacked stones along which lines of barbed wire fencing ran from wooden post to wooden post to border the fields where the sheep grazed. Stray tufts of creamy sheep's wool caught on the wire fluttered in the gentle breeze blowing over the flat terrain from the sea. In the distance the high triangular emerald island to the south was already at this time a long block of featureless green shadow lying across the silver ocean. After about a mile of walking he came to the low wooden structure which was very clearly a house, perhaps better described as a cabin or shack, with a porch, a door, and windows, but it was difficult to tell from the outside if it had ever been finished or lived in. The windows were without glass and turbid wings of torn and tattered plastic sheeting hung from them moving ever so slightly in the almost non-existent breeze. The roof was also wooden but only very gradually slanted to a high point in the middle as if it only aspired to being a roof. The whole structure had a broken-down air of abandonment, desolation, and emptiness. He considered walking to it and exploring it inside but looking back towards the village he wondered if, being observed, it was a good idea to go poking his nose in perhaps where it didn't belong, certainly not on this his first day living on the island, so he decided to walk on and leave the strange house for another day.

A little beyond the house the rough path ended and he was now walking on wet spongy ground with a mixture of tough mosses and wild grasses growing from it. He had to skirt a number of rain-filled hollows to reach the rocky shore again as it swung to the right away from the house and towards a new higher headland. Out to sea he saw cormorants standing tall on rugged rocks, or skimming swiftly the surface of the water. He followed upwards over the soft wet earth, his feet sinking in the mosses, grasses, and heathers, climbing steadily toward the highest point of the headland from where he had sweeping views of the ocean, the distant mountains of the mainland, and the island of Inish itself. He now climbed further along what was really a cliff edge dropping steeply and even dangerously towards the rolling sea below. He was all alone up here on the dizzying height. There were just a few loose sheep here and there, and at one point a couple of red-legged red-billed birds resembling crows glided balletically close to him. They were choughs, sailing past, their call fragmented and bitter. Spread out now in front of him he could see the western half of the island backed by two solidly emphatic peaks, the highest one to the north of the island, Carrigmore, and the other away to the extreme west, Sleevebeg. In front of the peaks and bordering the sea there was a long stretch of golden beach backed by a wavering line of white houses and beyond the houses there was a substantial lake glittering in the sunlight. The island was bigger than he had at first believed and he realised it was perhaps too big to explore on foot and would indeed take more than a few days of cycling to visit in its entirety. The weather was set fair for the next week and he looked forward to getting to know his new island home.

He had reached the highest point of his cliff walk and while it was possible to continue straight ahead he turned back and walked down the grassy track he had followed until he once again reached the shoreline and found himself walking past the abandoned-looking wooden house. Soon he had reached, below his own cottage, the rocky beach stretching across to the headland with the two-storey house he had seen earlier, standing on its field of grassy green. Crossing the beach he encountered an older grey-haired man with a dark heavy jacket and a stick also out walking. They raised their hands to each other and nodded their heads in greeting.

"What lovely weather," Harry addressed the older man tentatively, adding, as there had been persistent rain for some days in Dublin, "I believe there's non-stop rain in Dublin!"

The old man who had at first seemed friendly shook his head with vigorous disgruntlement.

"They may as well have the rain," he said sternly, "seeing as they have everything else up there!"

Having delivered himself of this meteorological or social commentary he strode away hastily, stamping his way unevenly across the stony beach.

On the narrow grassy headland the stony beach led to Harry saw another grey-haired man standing at the back of the two-storey house there. He was a small wiry man with a merry twinkle in his eyes. It was clear he had observed and enjoyed the recent brusque exchange on the beach.

"Welcome to Dughrá! You've met crotchety Jack, I see!" he said with a laugh, holding his hand out in welcome.

Harry took the proffered hand with immediate fondness for the old man.

"I'm Paddy!" the wiry grey-haired man continued enthusiastically, "and you must be the fellow mad enough to come to live alone in the cottage beyond, you're very welcome! What shall I be calling you?"

"Harry will do," Harry said. "Pleased to meet you Paddy…"

"Come inside and meet my wife, Joy!" Paddy invited, and Harry followed him around to the side of the house where they entered through a minuscule whitewashed porch, strewn and hung with small craft items made, it appeared, from mainly seashells, into the darkened interior of the building where a tall slim slightly-bowed woman with short-cropped white hair was pouring boiling water into a porcelain tea pot.

"Great timing," Paddy approved. "You can't beat the cup of tea!"

"Oh who is this person?" Joy asked with a lively air of curiosity.

She had lively blue eyes and spoke with a clear and musical English accent.

"Harry has come to live with us!" Paddy told her.

She looked quizzically at Harry.

"Are you sure that's a good idea?" she asked him. "It's very quiet here you know…"

"Ah sure it's peace and quiet I'm after," Harry said.

"But why have you come here?" she persisted. "Aren't you a little young to be already retreating from the real world? Have you been banished here? Are you an exiled prince?"

She clearly had a lively imagination to go with her lively manner. He shrugged his shoulders accepting a cup of steaming tea from her, ignoring the bowl of sugar she pushed towards him.

"Oh, I just need a change of scene for a time," he told her.

"Oh we'll get to the bottom of your mystery before long!" she promised him. "We like a good mystery, Paddy, don't we?"

Paddy nodded his assent with the same wry grin and merry twinkle with which he had welcomed Harry.

Harry spent almost an hour sitting over tea with them. They pried but in a gentle way. He didn't mind sharing his information with them, up to a certain point. He told them about his decision to live in splendid isolation in the west of Ireland and how he had cycled from Limerick through Clare, Galway, Connemara and Mayo until finally his brother had expelled him from the car in Killeaden and he had learned about Mary Kate's cottage. He hinted he was here to do some self-exploration, he might try some writing. Paddy perked up at this.

19

"Philosophy, or fiction?" he asked.

"Well I have very little philosophy to offer," Harry answered. "Maybe a few short stories, maybe a novel…"

Paddy seemed suddenly deflated.

"Imagined stories can't compete with philosophical speculation," he said, and continued, "Is life worth the living of it, now that's a great subject…"

"Novels can ask and answer that question too," Joy told him.

"Are you a philosopher then?" Harry asked Paddy.

"He is when he has a pint of Guinness in his hand!" Joy responded in her sprightly manner.

"True! We are all philosophers then!" Paddy agreed with a self-disparaging grin.

"You will have to come to tea some Sunday afternoon," Joy said. "Bill and Jane will be here… Bill's a retired civil servant who has written and published several novels while living here on the island… You will enjoy meeting him and his wife. And they will enjoy meeting you!"

So a plan was agreed that he would visit with said Bill and Jane some Sunday.

During his stay with them he learned a little about Joy and Paddy. Joy had been born on the far side of the ocean in the Caribbean. She had left home while still a young woman to live in England where she had worked as a cook. Paddy like many of the men from the island had spent decades working in different jobs around England. Eventually they had met and he had wooed and married her before attracting her back to live on Inish.

"So you too have suffered banishment to this place," Harry said jokingly to her.

"An exiled princess trapped in the lair of the Island Magician!" Paddy declared.

Joy laughed assuring him, "There are worse fates!"

"Worse fates than are dreamt of in your philosophy!" Paddy announced, adding, "Or in your stories, Harry... I dare say..."

They were a nice couple and Harry was instantly charmed by them.

"You will be one of the younger people among the island population," Paddy told him. "Almost everyone leaves here between the ages of eighteen and seventy... Once school is done they go, flying like the wild geese to England, Australia, or Ameri-kay!"

"Sometimes they return with a wife!" Joy interrupted with a smile.

"Sometimes they bring a wife home and leave her here," Paddy said. "They return home every once in a while to fill her up with a child to bear in the autumn... There are a lot of women here raising children for distant husbands walking the remote highways and byways of perfidious Albion!"

"Many don't return to live here until they have retired from work, or living," Joy told him.

"Some never come back," Paddy concluded ominously.

Before he left them Harry had one question he wanted to ask.

"The abandoned cabin down the shore, what is it?"

Their faces darkened and they became silent for a time.

"Ah that was poor Jean!" Joy said with unusual sweetness but also sadness in her voice.

"A lovely American woman!" Paddy put in. "It was her dream to live here and she had the wooden house built out there at the end of the shore... She was with us a few short months only... when..."

He had obvious trouble telling the story. Joy took over.

"She had a heart attack," she said quietly. "Right here with us in this house... We were all having tea together with Bill and Jane. Her family came from America and took her back home with them. Somewhere in the Midwest we believe."

After a long pause she added, "It was about a year ago… We haven't heard from her since… We haven't heard anything… We hope she's ok… She was a really beautiful woman…"

"It's a pity you missed her," Paddy resumed. "Two strangers in exile you'd have had things in common…"

"Is it ok to go inside her house?" he asked.

"That's up to you," Joy said. "Just be careful, it might be haunted…"

"Rats!" Paddy hissed. "There's nothing haunting there but rats… Broken dreams… And sad memories… that's all…"

As he was leaving, with the sunlight still falling warmly over the village, Paddy drew him aside into a small glasshouse built against the southern side of the house facing the sea.

"Did you notice Joy's little crafts and trinkets, shells and stuff?" he asked. "She sells them to the odd stray tourist who makes it here… But this here is my pride and joy!"

He pointed to a thick cluster of vines climbing the wall of the house. Here and there tight firm bunches of light green grapes were visible resplendent in the sunlight falling into the glasshouse.

"I make wine with these!" Paddy said.

"No, not possible!" Harry protested.

"Yes, possible!" Paddy countered. "You forget I am the Island Magician!"

"You will have to invite me to the first tasting!" Harry said.

"Consider yourself invited!"

Before returning to his cottage Harry walked on the sandy beach on the far side of Joy and Paddy's home. Small buff-coloured birds busied themselves foraging along the line of the seawater. Sandpipers. And sturdier black and white birds with orange legs and bills also ran along the water's edge. Oystercatchers. He did not see any curlew but from time to time the fleeting shadow of a cormorant raced above the swelling waves. On his way back to his cottage he stopped at the small post office where a young woman was working.

"They told me all the young people had left the island!" he said with surprise.

"You've no idea how much pressure they put me under to leave," she said. "What are you doing here? they constantly ask… As if it is some sort of taboo to remain here after you finish school…"

"Don't you want to see the world?" he asked her.

"If it's so great what are you doing here?!" she replied sharply.

He explained that he was going to be living in Mary Kate's cottage, so if she received post for him she'd know where to find him.

"It'll be lonely up there on your own," she said with apparent compassion.

"That's what I'm looking for," he told her, told himself.

She had dark hair and bright blue eyes. She was of medium but stocky build and might have been described as plain, but looked at with any attention she was not unattractive. She said her name was Kathleen. He left her and walked back on the road towards his cottage. As he arrived at his gate he met a woman about his own age walking down towards him with a black Labrador dog at her heels. She had shoulder-length brown hair, dark but lively blue eyes, and she held her hand out straight to him with a friendly winning smile on her face. She was slim and taller than Kathleen and she was wearing a cosy padded jacket and denim jeans over flat comfortable-looking walking shoes.

"Hi, I'm Clare!" she introduced herself brightly.

He was taken aback by her forthright introduction and the shock of her name but reached out to take and shake her hand and told her his name.

"I live in the next cottage up!" she told him.

"You're English!" he observed

"Good observation!" she congratulated him. "My husband is a local… He picked me up in England and brought me back here to rear his brood… I have five kids! He's traipsing around England as I speak!"

"I believe it's a common fate for women in these parts!" he laughed.

"There are worse fates!" she said, echoing Joy.

They stood together in silence for a while.

"It'll be great to have you in the house as we walk by after dark," Clare said. "I never liked going by with the house in darkness… It'll be like a protection now with your lights on!"

"I'll do my best," he said. "But I've never seen protection as one of my fortes…"

"Oh you can work on it," she reassured him, and then wheeled back towards her own house, a fairly modern-looking bungalow, pointing it out.

"If you ever need anything that's where I am… I hope you won't be bothered by the children… or the dog…"

"I hope you will be happy to have me as a neighbour," he said, "lighting your path after dark…"

"I'm happy about it already!" she assured him turning back to walk to her own house, casting a hearty "See you!" to him as she walked away.

"How do you spell your name?" he called after her.

"C-L-A-R-E!" she called back. "Like the county…"

"Good!" he said, nodding with approval, though for the life of her she couldn't understand why.

The day was still warm with sunlight falling on the front of the house and the porch. He could feel however the slightest of chills, even some dampness, inside the house from a lack of fires over the summer months. It was the kind of cottage in this part of Ireland where fires needed to be lit every day of the year to keep the dampness of sea and rain at bay. He gathered some turf from the stack alongside the house and placed the sods neatly in the fireplace above some coiled ropes of paper and kindling left the previous day by Mary Kate. He lit the fire he had built with the aid of some firelighters and matches. While the fire was taking he settled in the porch gathering the late-afternoon warmth of the sun around him like a cosy coat. Through the windows he was looking out on the green fields, the low stone walls and wire fencing, the vast shining ocean, and the rocky shoreline stretching all the way to Jean's broken dream and sad memory of a home about a mile away on the tip of the island. He sat there for the rest of the day, stirring himself only to rebuild the fire as it burned down. He sat with a book to appear to be reading for the benefit of anyone passing. A tall young man strode past and waved as did some laughing children he took to be Clare's kids. He wasn't reading, he just sat watching the changing light over the fields, the sea, the shore, and Jean's house sinking ever so gradually into the darkness of evening. While the cloud thickened towards nightfall there was still enough light in the sky to produce a colourful sunset of bright pink and rose-red colours. It was the time of the autumn equinox he suddenly remembered, day and night equal all over the world no matter where you were. When the sunset was gone and the darkness had settled over the island he closed up the book he had not been reading and moved to his bedroom and his bed. He lay on his bed still in his clothes and stared for a very long time into the deepening darkness of the ceiling... Some hours later, his eyes still fixed on the ceiling, dreamless sleep came and swept him away unawares.

Life on the island was quiet and in the very early days as he established himself there were few incidents of any note, however there was one which with hindsight took on a vaguely premonitory value. He had settled quickly into a routine and most days he walked along the shoreline past Jean's house. He was sure here not to encounter anyone and so to be able to walk and wander in peace. One day near the abandoned wooden house he noticed a sheep standing motionlessly. This seemed strange as normally sheep would run away in fright when anyone approached but this one stood perfectly still and did not skip away from him. Returning from his walk he was surprised to see the sheep in exactly the same place.

A couple of days later walking again along the shore he was surprised to see the same sheep, as far as he could tell, in exactly the same place, and again it didn't move as he approached. He decided to look more closely and as he drew close the sheep began to tilt away from him but seemed unable to move away. It danced around in agitation as he came up to it and he was now near enough to see that the animal was caught up in some barbed wire which was hanging loose from some nearby fencing. With the animal kicking and leaning away from him he began to pull the wire out of the wool in which it was deeply entangled. The sheep had obviously tried to free itself but had only succeeded in deepening the grip of the barbed wire which had embedded itself even more and had even cut through the wool into its skin. Now in its efforts to escape Harry it jumped on to the low stone wall along which the fence ran. Harry had no choice but to stand on the unstable wall whose stones rocked under his feet and made it hard for him to keep his balance. The sheep spun around in a circle and soon had Harry's legs wrapped in the jagged wire. Unsteady on his feet, balanced precariously on the wall, afraid too he was going to fall, Harry needed to twist and turn as the sheep twisted and turned, but he managed to stay upright. Unsure of where the start or end of the barbed wire was he pulled hard at it while all the time the sheep fought, pushed, and tilted against him, pulling away from him and then twisting back around him. Harry followed the line of wire under the sheep's belly and around its legs pulling thick tufts of wool away as he struggled to release it and he began to see spots of blood appear where the animal's skin was torn. The struggle continued ceaselessly for about fifteen minutes and then the end of the wire miraculously appeared in his hands so that he was now able to unwind it from the wool and flesh of the sheep in a purposeful methodical way. Quickly now he spilled the wire out of his hands and within a couple of minutes the sheep was free and skipping away into the nearest field. Harry's hands had been cut in the effort of tugging the wire away but not too deeply. He brushed the few spots of blood away on his jeans which were also torn here and there. He felt very tired after his effort and he decided to return to the cottage. As he strode away he felt completely irrationally that someone was watching him from inside Jean's house. It made no sense. He was certain there was no one there. But the sensation of being watched still sent a shiver along his spine. Crazy, he told himself.

For many days during late September there was still warm sunshine over the island. A few mornings after the "episode", as he called it, with the sheep, Harry decided to go on an exploratory cycling trip. He directed his bicycle away from the heart of the village and rode up past Clare's bungalow turning inland at the base of the long hill whose cliff-edge crest he had walked along on his first full day on the island. After about twenty minutes of cycling he came to the main road through the island and turned westwards towards the townland he had seen from the cliff-edge with its long stretch of white houses strewn out along the golden line of beach in front of it. The name of the townland was Kill, an old Gaelic word perhaps deriving from a church. Another derivation was woodland but, as there were no trees on the island, church it must most likely be. The island was quiet so early and there were very few people stirring. Those out and about raised a hand in salutation to anyone who passed. From nearly every house plumes of fragrant peat smoke rose slowly through the air. Beyond the houses there was a large lake brightly rippling in the light breezes of the morning. Close to the lake he saw a flock of slender black and white elegantly crested birds he knew were called Lapwings. They looked to Harry like trim tufted gentlemen wearing dinner jackets. Their call was shrill and piercing. Harry heard distress in it. Further away, beyond the glittering lake, he could see a long line of broken stone houses on a hillside. He cycled around the lake and made his way to the ruined houses.

After about fifteen minutes of cycling away from the townland he came to the old deserted village strewn on the lower slopes of the island's highest mountain, Carrigmore. He climbed up over the rough grassy ground to reach the first of the empty buildings. The first house was small, built with unmortared stones of various sizes. There seemed to be just one room with a single doorway and one small window. The floor was overgrown with grass and weeds and mosses and there was moss on the stones. There was no roof, and looking along the scattered line of houses stretching away to the west of the island he could see that there were no roofs on any of the buildings but that they seemed to follow vague lines as if separated by uneven irregular streets. In the stillness and quiet of the sunlit morning there was an eerie ghostliness over the abandoned scene, like a secret desolation within the heart of all he could see. He began slowly to move westwards from house to house. There must have been at least a hundred. The population of the village in its heyday must have been five hundred or more, maybe a thousand. Some of the houses he saw had two doors, with one on either side of the small dwellings, as if to enter by one and leave by another, and he also noticed here and there small spaces perhaps for rooms, and space for a hearth. In some of the houses a shallow gutter dividing the house in two ran along the floor to the doorway. He imagined animals may have been kept indoors along with the families, and the gutter would have served to drain away waste, perhaps that of the animals. In the fields above the houses he saw shallow ridges running beneath the grass. He had been told as he cycled through the west of Ireland in the summer that these ridges visible in very many places had been used to grow potatoes. An information panel at the foot of the hill told him that the village dated from before the famine. In the years following the famine it had ceased to exist through desertion, emigration, abandonment, or some form of exile in any case. Nonetheless, until the mid-twentieth century some of the houses had been used as summer dwellings or shelters by families with cattle grazing on the hillside. Right now there was nothing only the desert of stone, the moss, the light breezes, the warm touch of golden sunlight, and the lasting mystery of all that had been, and was here no more. He felt a slow quiet movement of loss growing in him as he made his way back down the hillside to find his bike and cycle away from the abandoned and empty pastures of the past.

Reaching the townland of Kill again he swung further west on the long road through the village passing a café, a restaurant, a pub or two, and a number of guesthouses, one he noted called "The Emerald", all closed this early in the day. Leaving the village the road began to climb high on the island's second mountain, Sleevebeg. It was a steep climb and in a couple of places he had to dismount and continue on foot. When he reached the highest point of the road the views were spectacular not just back over the route he had cycled but down in front of him where the road uncoiled towards a short but wonderful beach of gold. This had to be the "truly spectacular beach" mentioned by the mysterious interlocutor in Westport who had first spoken to him about the island. He let the bike carry him downhill sweeping into the tight bends and hastening towards the broad parking area above the beach where he settled the bike against a low stone wall and walked down on to the beach itself enjoying the firm but yielding pressure of the sand under his feet. It was a breathtaking beach enclosed by high hills all around and swept by high curling waves of green-gold falling and breaking on it. A few derelict buildings stood mysteriously behind him on the hillside and he wondered what they had been. Here and there too on the hillside there were large scars visible as if the earth had been gouged by some machinery in that place. Leaving any burgeoning speculation aside, he threw his clothes off in an untidy heap on the sand and plunged into the rolling surf. Like in Connemara, the water was exquisitely cold and made him sigh in its shocking embrace as the green-gold of the waves covered and possessed him. Out of the water he ran in short quick steps along the beach his skin glistening in the sunlight and the warmth slowly returning to his body. He had only been a short time living on the island but this now felt like a green-golden baptism, an icy inauguration, which he experienced deep down as a bright acceptance of his untoward presence on the edge of his country and his continent, the edge of the western world. "I am the new Playboy of the Western World!" he called out loudly to the deserted beach, while laughing to himself. He added quietly, inwardly, self-mockingly, "some Playboy!"… What was he actually in his new island state, but a capsized and marooned traveller, abandoned and lonely, fleeing his memories, exiled from his own life? He was not a "Playboy" of the western or of any world. He was Robinson Crusoe d'Amour. Exiled, marooned, loveless.

After he had warmed up, dried off, and dressed again, he sat on a grassy knoll above the beach eating some banana sandwiches and drinking hot tea from a flask. Leaving, he needed to trek back up the mountainside pushing his bike in front of him until he reached again the highest point above the bay and from there he let the bike roll down inland terrifically fast back through the long townland of Kill stretched out along the line of golden beach and glimmering sea. He traversed the entire island all the way to Killeaden where he called to talk awhile with Mary Kate and Tomás and shopped for some food. From Killeaden he took the coastal road along the eastern flank of the island with views towards the mainland and its mountain ranges and eventually further south towards the emerald triangle of Grace Island falling into shadow as the sun circled behind it. On the most prominent part of the coast towards the mainland he came upon a rugged rectangle of ruined medieval castle rising high above the sea. He settled his bike against a low stone wall and walked through a rusted metal gateway and along a broken track to the dilapidated building. A plaque on the outside announced it as the onetime castle of a local pirate queen who had sown strife along the western seaboard of Ireland during the time of Elizabeth I. He was able to go inside and even follow some steps up to a higher floor from where intruding himself into a breach in the wall he could climb a narrow winding staircase to the uneven battlements. The views of Killeaden and the near island, the broad stretch of sea he had come across on the ferry, and the mountainous terrain of the mainland, including the cone-shaped holy mountain of Patrick, were vast and breathtaking. The pirate queen would have commanded an extensive geography from here, perhaps with a robust ship moored nearby, ready to launch against any intruder sighted upon her territory of land and wave. He was to learn later that she had many castles strewn along the mainland and its attendant islands, including one on the emerald triangle of Grace Island to the south, the heart of her domain.

From the castle he continued along the spectacular coastal route back to his cottage waving to Paddy, who was tending to his vines, as he arrived in the village. His new home was already familiar territory, the cluster of houses held by the upturned palms of the surrounding treeless hills, the few green fields with the grazing sheep, the rugged coastline stretching away south from his cottage, and in the dim distance Jean's ruined dream of a home sitting in isolation upon the broken shoreline. It was now late afternoon but there was still warm sunshine flooding the porch of his cottage. He stirred his fire to life adding fresh dry sods of turf before settling in a chair inside the porch. He held a book in front of him which he wasn't reading but rather he sat in complete quiet and restfulness letting the sun fill him with warmth through the glass. The tall thin youngish man went by and waved, as did an older man leaning upon a stick, and Clare also walked past with the black Labrador and a couple of her kids. She shot him a lovely bright smile while the kids examined him with an Irish mixture of curiosity and shyness. Later he made himself a pot of stew with the provisions bought in Killeaden, and ate it washed down with a glass of neat whiskey. The sunset spilled a reddish glow over the sea and he watched it fade before a three-quarter moon, bright and yellow, became visible, near which the bright planet Venus shone like a lantern. As dusk deepened he heard the lonely weeping curlew cry.

His mind was empty of thoughts and his heart of feeling as he lay once again to sleep on his dishevelled bed. With no lamp lit he stared into the deepening darkness of the ceiling while images of the day reappeared in his mind's eye. He saw again the long townland of houses following the line of golden sand to the west of the island. He saw the glittering lake with its rippling waters at the foot of the highest mountain. He saw the hundred broken houses strewn in a wretched chain of abandoned stone over the deserted hillside. He saw the stunning bay and beach in the westernmost part of the island, of his country, and of his continent. Next stop Ameri-kay! He saw again the tall stone castle of the medieval pirate queen and the dominant views of the world it commanded. He saw the village quiet in the sunlight as he returned to the cottage. He saw Jean's isolated wooden cabin under the rose and pinkish tints of the sunset turning to blood-red and then darkness. He saw the moon rise and the vivid gleam of Venus in the west. He heard the curlew weeping. The images of the day unfolded slowly in his mind as he lay there without thought, impulse, or direction, other than sleep. All in all it felt like it had been a good day, even for someone in exile. Robinson Crusoe d'Amour. At a certain point some hours later without his ever stirring a wave of sleep traversed him and carried him into another complete darkness without dreams.

The weather held good into October and warm sunlight was general over the island. On the first Sunday of the month he waited until the crowd had dispersed after Mass before making his way for the first time to the pub next door to the church. The locals were surprised to see him but warmly welcoming and they all exchanged pleasantries together. He noticed Kathleen there sitting with an older woman he assumed was her mother. She gave him a brief nod of recognition but nothing more, not even the ghost of a smile. Paddy was there wearing a broad hat with corks bobbing from the brim. Over a pint, standing together in the middle of the pub, he invited Harry to call to the two-storey house in the afternoon to meet the writer, Bill, and his wife, Jane.

"Is your wine ready for drinking yet?" Harry asked him.

"It won't be long now!" Paddy assured him. "*Chateau Páidí* is on its way…"

A tall strong-looking man approached them with a very young boy held high in his arms.

"So you're the writer! *An Scríbhneoir!*" the man acclaimed Harry in Gaelic while stretching out a hand to shake.

Harry smiled to himself at how readily that little fiction had spread wings.

"I suppose I am," Harry accepted, with a self-effacing smile.

"Well there's no shortage of them about," the man said, swinging the child down to the floor as he left them as quickly as he had arrived.

"Sure where would we be without words?" Paddy said.

"There are writers in love with silence," Harry reminded him.

"Well silence is a hard thing to get a story out of," Paddy said, slurping his Guinness.

He did not prolong his stay in the pub but set out to walk along the shore away from his cottage. He had spent some time exploring different pathways and possibilities of walks around the village. There were the beaches to walk on, the sandy one and the stony one, but both of them were short. There were three roads in and out of the village but on each road he was sure to meet traffic or people walking while really he was seeking solitude. There was the possibility of striking over the boggy ground on the hillsides to reach their distant summits but walking there just felt wayward and unsatisfactory to him. He was most comfortable following the track along the rocky shoreline which led to Jean's house, always on the lookout for some distressed sheep, or one entangled as before in cruel and cutting barbed wire. Each time he stopped involuntarily in front of Jean's abandoned house, as if it was appealing to him to enter, but he hadn't yet worked up the courage to go inside. He didn't know if he ever would. Something about the house caused a sliver of fear in him. It reminded him of a scene from an old black and white film he had seen as a child in the cinema, a scene recalled only too vividly. In the film, the house appeared empty to a woman who approached it. She called and looked through the windows but there was no answer. Eventually she went inside. After a protracted moment with the camera fixed motionlessly on the front of the house a prolonged shrill scream was heard from inside. The scene had terrified him and was one of the very few moments of childhood cinema that had remained with him and haunted him into adulthood. He deplored his imagination which conjured the scream again to spill from the desperate isolation and silence of Jean's home. All he could remember of the film was the woman entering the house and the scream that followed. That was the sum total of his terror. If there was anything else to remember he was glad he could not recall it. He realised it was going to take him some effort to enter Jean's house, if ever, before shaking his head doubtfully and continuing on his shoreline walk.

The shoreline was the least visited of the surrounding area by the locals so he was able to amble in total quiet aware at the same time that he could be observed distantly from perhaps any point in the village, but happy too knowing he would be untroubled by anyone coming along and engaging him in conversation. It actually cost him a lot of effort to talk with anyone. Even minor exchanges sometimes left him feeling exhausted. At the same time he did not venture overly far on this walk conscious that he needed to be in Paddy and Joy's for the famous afternoon tea and the introduction to the island's resident writer. It was a social duty he could not avoid. As it turned out the afternoon proved very affable and he enjoyed it more than he had expected. Bill was a tall and energetic retired civil servant, his wife was a short, dark-haired woman with soft blue eyes and a warm manner. Both of them enjoyed conversation, new company, and both of them showed ready interest in him. The pretext that Harry had come to the island to write excited them and he needed to work hard not to disabuse them.

"No, no, I've written nothing yet," he said. "This is really an experiment… I may write nothing at all. We'll see!"

Joy was happy to have a newcomer to display and promoted him assiduously as a writer, "*An Scríbhneoir*".

"I am not sure that isolation is a good thing for a writer," Bill warned him.

Bill had only begun to write since retirement from the civil service and retreat to the island. He specialised, by his own admission, in cheap horror novels, the kind you pick up in airports before boarding a long flight, or to take on an idle vacation. He had produced a number of novels that had sold well enough and he resented that the better newspapers would not review them or take them seriously. Together they ran a guesthouse called "The Emerald" which Harry had seen when cycling some days previously through the townland of Kill. Bill and Jane promptly invited him to visit and even to stay.

"You just have to watch out for the ghosts, demons, and monsters!" Paddy warned him with a laugh. "Their place is full of them!"

"Don't worry, they're all enclosed in book covers!" Bill reassured him.

Joy who was particularly enjoying the conviviality of the occasion had baked some warm scones which she presented to be drenched in butter and jam. Bill was a good conversationalist and had many stories to tell of his time in the civil service but also of exotic journeys he had undertaken with Jane. They had no children and had been ardent travellers especially to Africa. Some of his stories made Harry feel queasy.

"I saw a lion take down a young zebra and devour it while it was still alive and kicking... I saw a crocodile drown a wildebeest between its jaws..." Bill recounted darkly.

"The dark continent!" was Paddy's ominous contribution.

"You knew Jean?" Harry discreetly asked the couple.

"That is a very unfortunate story," Bill said with genuine sadness. "She should never have been allowed to build out on the deserted shoreline like that... Even in the summer it can be desolate and lonely. I think that had a lot to do with her heart attack."

"But she was a lovely woman," Jane reminded everyone and everyone agreed.

"And beautiful too," Paddy said with a melancholy air.

"What was her history?" Harry persisted.

"We never really knew that," Bill explained. "She was an attractive, smiling, bright, retired woman with family back home in the States... She just said she was retired, from teaching or something or other, and she wanted to live here... She said it was the end of the world and there was nowhere else for her to go. There's no doubt she was fleeing something. A broken relationship, marriage, or bereavement... Or something haunting her. Or maybe it really was just a dream she was chasing... which is what she always told us... that living here at the end of the world was her dream."

"Maybe she was here like our new friend to write as well," Paddy said.

"It's a pity you didn't get to meet her," Bill told Harry.

"Well maybe in a sense I have," Harry responded. "But anyway I can't allow myself to be haunted by someone I have never truly met..."

Bill grew more animated at this.

"You know the parents here tell the children to avoid the rocky shoreline between the village and Jean's house... They are really afraid of them falling into the sea, but they tell them there's a ghost."

"And now maybe there is," Jane said with mock solemnity.

"There's a story for you," Joy said to Bill.

"Or for our new writer friend here," Bill deflected the comment to Harry.

"But is there no news of her?" Harry asked. "She went home but she is probably still alive... There's no ghost without a corpse I believe."

"I think if she is still alive, we will someday hear from her," Joy said.

"She'll be back someday to taste some of Chateau Paddy's brew!" Bill scoffed.

"But we do miss her," Jane said sadly. "She came here with so much hope. She was a good friend for the time she was here. She visited us in 'The Emerald'. There is an emptiness after her, we all feel it..."

She looked meaningfully at Bill as if asking him to confirm what she had said. He nodded. They all became silent then for a time. Eventually, to lighten the mood, Harry told his story about rescuing the sheep from the barbed wire near Jean's house. They enjoyed the story and their surprise at it soon turned to laughter as he displayed the slight wounds, now almost healed, the barbed wire had inflicted on his hands.

"It's like some kind of sheepish stigmata!" Paddy joked.

Paddy got an amused dreamy look in his eye as he wove a humorous tale from the episode.

"The island sheep will all be assembled now in the field begging to hear the tale again from the mouth of its leading sheep protagonist of how some unknown but gentle human sacrificed himself to save an unfortunate one of their own entangled in the harsh and unforgiving wire from slow cruel and painful death in the savage wildernesses of this remote isle so inhospitable to the sheep population in general!"

They all laughed.

"They'll want to put a statue up to you outside Jean's house!" Paddy roared. "With long strands of wickedly barbed wire in your hands… And a prostrate grateful sheep gazing adoringly up at you from your feet…"

In the evening sitting in the porch Harry could not take his eyes off Jean's cottage being absorbed into the deepening darkness of the dying sunset. At first it glistened within the broad spread of burnished golden light, and then it faded into the vivid pinks and deep reds of the sunset's fiercest moments, before a velvet fall of light and dark blues closed over it, until eventually it was absorbed into total darkness. For a moment he imagined he could see a lamp close to the house, perhaps even inside it, but then he realised it was just a bright star low on the horizon shining through one of the windows. He sat for hours in a darkness which kept him unseen, like a ghost himself, to anyone passing. He heard the curlew's plaintive cry. He saw Clare walking by, throwing quick short curious glances at the cottage. He was glad his fire was ablaze and the living room lights were lit. She wouldn't find the road so lonely then. And then when he was least expecting it something strange happened. He heard the high-pitched wincing of his gate being opened and a low dark figure came walking towards him. His heart beat a little faster and he felt a sudden apprehension as the shadow drew close to him. He reached his hand up to switch on the light in the porch and as it flooded the garden area outside the figure lifted her face to him. It was Kathleen.

The moment she stepped inside the porch Kathleen shot out her fingers to flick the light switch off and instantly as the darkness wrapped around them she had her arms about his shoulders and was pulling herself up on him to kiss the flesh exposed by the open collar of his shirt, his neck, his face and eyes, and his mouth. Her arms pulled him close and tight to her and her kisses on his mouth were firm and irrepudiable. They wrestled for some time in darkness before eventually she briefly breathlessly released him and he began to protest. She closed his mouth with her raised hand and said with absolute determination.

"Don't send me away or even turn me away. Don't even think about it. I'm not going!"

She drew him then into the house and into the bedroom which was also deep in darkness. She pulled and dragged at his clothes until she had him naked sitting on the edge of the bed and then she spilled hastily out of her own clothes casting her sweater and blouse away, unhooking her bra to release gently swinging soft white breasts, kicking her shoes, jeans, and panties away along the floor.

"God it's lonely here..." she whimpered pushing him back on the bed and clambering on top of him.

She pulled his hand down and pushed it into her thighs.

"I'm so tired of touching myself there all the time... I want a beautiful man to do it... I want you to do it!"

She spread herself wide as he opened the folds of skin within her thighs, and he mewled with her as her oil surged and spread over his fingertips. She rolled around his caressing fingers with a succession of sweet moans.

"Stick them in!" she said with urgency. "Stick them in me..."

She held his hand firmly between her legs while his fingers moved in and out of her wetness. From time to time she jerked his hand closer so that his fingers entered harder and deeper inside her.

"Oh God," she said then... and repeated, "Oh God..." As she pushed him flat and climbed on top of him.

She pushed her fingers into his mouth so he could say nothing to her, only grunt and groan and moan as he sucked all four of her fingers which she stretched and curled all the way to his throat as if she were trying to claw something out of him. She began to rub her crotch on him, hoisting herself to his chest and chin, and then sliding down him over his belly, thighs and legs. She repeated this over and over and he imagined long glistening lines of sticky silver all down his body like trails made by some gastropod. At times she pressed her middle down on distinct parts of his body and pressed and rubbed herself there with greater intent. And then she climbed and kneeled above his mouth and pressed down hard on his tongue moving in a rocking rhythm on his open lips which were drenched with her. After a time she began to shake with mounting pleasure and at the point where it seemed she could contain herself no more she slid back down his body to find his penis with her hand and direct it inside her. She shook wildly on him, with unrelenting intensity, for a long long time, in which his own pleasure raced unstoppably towards hers. At the very limit of endurance and postponement she opened wide over him and expelled all the pleasure she contained in an overwhelming tidal rush which reminded him of the green-gold power of the sea he had immersed himself in some days before. Only now it was deep dark night and she came not like a bright cold green-gold sea but in a warm flood of silk and velvet blues, violet, indigo, cobalt, cerulean, sapphire, ultramarine… and he thought helplessly of lapis lazuli… sweeping over him. She was the aftermath of sunset he had just witnessed made woman. She was the velvet fall of light and dark blues. She was the aftermath of sunset made complete and utter and desperate pleasure.

Her love-making, if you could call it that, was incessant. She rose and fell on him mouth hands thighs in wave upon rising falling wave until the first grey light of dawn came to the window, and then she closed the curtains only to fall back into bed with him and finally sleep for a couple of hours her arms bound tightly about him while he slept astounded and exhausted beside her. In the morning when he woke she was gone. He could not believe what had happened. He asked himself "did it happen?" But his incredulity was answered by various scratches and bites strewn over his skin and even some bruising on parts of his body and an unanswerable ache in much of his limbs. Even his tongue felt limp and sore, and his penis still sticky from her looked beaten and broken from the combat. The bed was a mess with damp stains all over, and when he knelt to smell the sheets he could definitely catch her odour on them, a strange mixture of sweetness and bitterness like a fish fresh from the sea. Finally picking his own clothes up from the floor he found her panties rolled in a soft pink bundle beneath the bed. When he pulled the bundle open, like opening a flower, he saw in the fabric playful little sheep being chased by a number of sheepdogs. He read her name printed on a label inside, Kathleen Hartigan, and an added word, "Hostage". A couple of hours later he went outside and looked down towards the post office where he saw her unlocking the building and entering to begin her day's work. He shook his head again with disbelief. He had been just a few weeks on the island and this had happened. He shouldn't have let it happen. He wasn't there for that, he wasn't there to live or love, or for sex, or for anything. He was there to disappear, to become a ghost. And he wasn't going to let anything or anyone interfere with that.

After breakfast he went cycling again turning north past Clare's house to ride away from the village and following the road at the bottom of the cliff-edged hill as far as the main road through the island. By doing this he avoided cycling in front of the post office and kept the odd sense of embarrassment he felt at bay. It reminded him of the early morning he had fled from the French girl in Cong, the *"Crème de Menthe"* girl, Christine Delaforêt, who had also embraced him in the night, only this time things had gone much further. His life on the island had taken an extraordinary turn and he did not know if it was for good or bad. He thought it was not what he would have chosen, not as it had happened anyway. What did he know about Kathleen after all, other than what he had discovered in the night, that she was a ruthless and even brutal lover? She had torn pleasure from him in an irresistible but ultimately painful way. He had been taken by her. He thought of a coarse word he would not allow himself to use. A bigger problem might be admitting to himself that he had enjoyed it. And finding out what to do next. If there was to be a next. It was suddenly a time for reflection. But right now his thoughts, such as they were, were scattered and purposeless. Kathleen had broken him open and thrown everything inside him into wild disarray.

When he reached the main road he swung back right towards Killeaden and then turned left after a couple of miles to visit the north of the island. He reached the small village of Carrigdúbh on the northern shore from which a path rose to the summit of the island's highest mountain, Carrigmore. Leaving his bike in the backyard of the village pub he began to follow the trail all the way up. The path was rough, uneven and difficult, but he pushed himself pitilessly step after step until he reached the top, at the very end scrambling on his hands and knees over loose stone to attain the jagged peak. The view was vast but, unlike the views the island disclosed to the south and west, which were full of warm greens and golds and glittering seas, the northern prospect was flat and bleak, with various cold blues splashed with savage whites. Most of the north of the island seemed to fall in sharp steep cliff formations down from the peak he was standing on. This was where the great Golden Eagles the island had once been famed for had made their eyrie. This was their abandoned world. No bird now ruled the air here. Apart from the small village he had climbed up from, which was gathered like a tiny fist around its harbour, there was no sign of any habitation or life on this side of the island. The land was rugged, bare, and inhospitable. The ocean was cold and vast sweeping away to infinite horizons broken by rocks but without islands. The distant mainland to the north was also flat and bare, with no touch of highland or mountains as far as he could see. In the furthest distance he imagined he could see stacked clouds waiting to bring new weather systems down from the north. It was October now and the weather was due to change. Some people were calling the recent warm spell an "Indian Summer". It was typical of Ireland for a cold damp grey summer to deliver a warm bright swan song at the end of its days. He knew in the weeks if not days ahead colder wetter conditions and perhaps even a storm or two were inevitable. The days would also shorten and with a seasonal time change soon due his time on the island was about to descend into a general darkness. He felt tired from his climb and after standing for a while to gaze out over the comfortless northern sea and landscapes he sat down on a rough bare stone on the mountain top and, letting his face fall into his raised hands, he began to sob quietly with a sudden despair.

He did not know how long he had been on the mountain but eventually he began to feel some cold. The descent hurt his legs at every step and it seemed an interminable time before he reached his bike again. He cycled again to Killeaden to buy some food and took the coastal route again past the castle of the pirate queen. He imagined her standing on the castle battlements, looking out over her sea domain, plotting her forays and attacks against the ships of the English Queen. He noticed the post office was closed as he passed back through the village and up the slight incline to his cottage. He almost expected to find Kathleen waiting for him but there was of course no one waiting at the cottage, only the usual emptiness. From a cottage next to Clare's a small old man leaning on a stick emerged to amble towards him. He waved the stick. Harry wasn't sure whether to interpret it as a greeting or a threat. The old man whose back was curved gently above the stick with which he picked his steps gingerly smiled as he drew closer.

"Do you know the island now?" he asked in a rasping tone.

"I'm starting to," said Harry, wondering what it was to "know" the island.

"Ay, it's small enough, and big enough," the man said cryptically.

Harry knew the man lived with his sister, who was far more sprightly than the man was. He saw her regularly flitting in and out of the house or passing on the road and they had exchanged greetings. The pair were part of the predominating older population on the island who had left it after school, and after a lifetime of travel and work outside of Ireland had returned for their retirement and their pension.

"You brought the good weather to us," the old man told him. "We're thankful to you for that!"

"I can't guarantee we'll keep it," Harry said. "Don't blame me when the winter comes!"

Harry was at home just a half hour when a knock came to his door. It was Paddy offering two freshly caught shining silver-blue mackerel.

"How do I cook them?" Harry asked, unused to handling fresh fish.

Paddy told him just to fry them in a little butter.

"And do they need to be cleaned?" Harry persisted, looking for help.

"Oh Lord," Paddy said, with some good-humoured exasperation. "You city folk..."

With a sharp knife Harry gave him Paddy slit the raw fish open and spilled their intestines on the grass in front of the cottage. He chopped the heads away and sliced each of the fish in two offering them again to Harry who took them.

"Can I give you something for them?" Harry felt he needed to offer something.

"I want you on the bog with me someday," Paddy said. "I need to get the last of my turf in before the weather turns bad..."

Harry agreed and watched Paddy walking away towards the stony beach he would cross to get home. Where Paddy had stood a mess of fish gut and flesh was scattered on the grass, the clean bright green of the blades now streaked with dark and bloody stains. Later, Harry fried the fish in butter and the strongly-flavoured brown flesh was delicious to eat. As darkness fell he took up his station in the porch and sat quietly looking out towards the sea and Jean's cottage fading from view. Clare walked past again looking towards the cottage without seeing him and he felt a quiet and somewhat fearful anticipation wondering if the scene from the previous night when the gate creaked open and Kathleen appeared on the darkened path to the cottage would reenact itself. But in the briefest of moments Clare had vanished, and no Kathleen appeared like a ghost from the darkness, and there was no one now but himself alone it seemed in the whole wide abandoned world. He sat up late staring emptily into the darkness (was he hoping Kathleen would come?) before retreating to bed and another night of dreamless sleep. Before he slept he heard dogs barking.

He had thought nothing of the dogs barking until the morning brought bad news. A sturdily-built but tall and grim-faced young farmer he recognised as the same one who had spoken to him in the pub, calling him "*An Scríbhneoir*", came knocking on his door.

"Did you hear nothing last night?" he asked.

Harry was at a loss.

"Nothing," he confirmed. "Why?"

The farmer's language was thickly larded with foul words.

"Dogs attacked my sheep. They drove them out of the field and on to the rocks... A good many of them are dead, others as good as dead..."

"I'm sorry," Harry sympathised, and added, "I did hear some barking... I thought it was a local dog, maybe Clare's Labrador I thought..."

But he hadn't really thought anything.

The farmer swung his head from side to side with disbelief.

"I can't believe no one heard anything..." he protested. "I don't mind you, you're a newcomer... but they should have heard... they should have known what was happening..."

His eyes filled with repressed tears and he shook his head again in disbelief and bitterness before turning away to leave. Harry followed behind him as he strode down to the shore. He didn't have to go far before he saw the bloody remains of about a dozen sheep strewn on the black rocks of the shoreline. Even in death the animals had the dumb uncomprehending look that sheep have, but in the violence of their end that look had resolved itself into a fixed image of helpless terror. The farmer had a couple of men to help him drag the bodies up from the rocks and he heaped them in the back of a small truck he had parked nearby. The scene reminded Harry of scenes of slaughter, of humans as well as animals, he had seen on television or in film. In death the helplessness of the creatures seemed infinite, and replete with horror. He felt a terrible pang of distress rise and fill his chest, squeezing around his heart.

"I'm really sorry," he repeated to the young farmer. "Next time I'll know..."

The farmer shook his head grimly, silently, as if any kind of expression was suddenly beyond him, before stepping brusquely into the van and driving away with his broken and bloodied beasts heaped behind him. Clare and the old man with the walking stick were standing in front of the cottage. They all agreed with each other that it was terrible, what had happened, the poor sheep, the savage dogs. Nature. No one had heard anything. They had all been sleeping. How awful. Life on the island and perhaps across the whole world and all of life itself was suddenly awful. They exchanged looks of helpless dismay with each other. There was nothing anyone could do except feel terrible about what had happened and utter impotent words of pain.

Later that morning Harry decided that he should have had some post. He realised it was perhaps an unsubtle strategy to see Kathleen but he decided to walk down to the post office and ask her if any post had arrived for him. When he entered the post office there was only Kathleen there. She looked at him without saying anything and without any sign of welcome or warmth, or even recognition.

"I was wondering if there was any post for me?" he asked hesitantly.

"You'd have it if there was," she answered him sharply and began to busy herself with objects he could not see below her counter.

He waited a little while without saying anything. She looked up again.

"Is there something else?"

He began uncertainly, and truly at a loss for words. He felt so awkward speaking. His words sounded ridiculous echoing back to him.

"I just thought after your visit you might prove more civil…"

"What visit?" she asked sternly.

He felt he should turn and leave at this stage but his feet would not move and he heard disembodied words floating from his mouth.

"After you came to the cottage and we were together…"

She laughed with a hard, dry, dismissive laughter.

"I know you're a writer," she said, "but you sure have one hell of an imagination…"

"You spent the night with me," he persisted stupidly. "We made love!"

"Are you mad?" she asked, with an air of genuine disbelief, her eyes and mouth wide open.

He no longer knew what to say. With an effort he twisted around on his feet and left the post office. He trudged back to the cottage hardly able to lift his feet. When he walked into his bedroom he saw the soft bundle of pink underwear he had found under the bed after she had left him. He placed the bundle in his pocket and walked back the half-mile again to the post office. Kathleen said nothing as he entered again. He took the bundle of fabric from his pocket and placed it on the counter in front of her.

"I thought you might like to have these back," he said quietly.

She picked them up and opened them out in her hands revealing the playful sheep and dogs. They looked very small in her hands.

"What child did you steal these from?" she asked him.

"I believe they're yours," he said without conviction.

She tossed the panties to one side and then quickly undid the button and zip of her jeans lowering them in front of him to reveal a shiny pair of black lace panties.

"In case you are wondering," she said, with a knowing smirk, "this is the kind of underwear I like…"

He stood looking as she pulled the jeans back up to her waist and zipped and buttoned them again.

"Tell me when you are having a birthday and I will send them to you as a present you can play with… While you dream about the night we made love together."

"I don't know why you are like this," he protested without force.

She replied nothing, but just shot him a look of utter dismissal, almost contempt.

He turned to leave once again.

"I know what happened," he told her, stepping away.

"Are you going to write a novel about it?" she sang after him.

The last words he heard her saying were,

"You sad fool!"

Back in the cottage he undressed and examined his body carefully to detect the scratches, bites, and even bruises he had noticed on the morning she had left him. The scratches and bites were all but imperceptible, and the couple of bruises he found could have been caused by knocking against any solid object. He suddenly wasn't sure of himself or of his reality at all. He sat in the porch with a book open in his hands. He wasn't reading but anyone passing would think he was. He was aware of some people going by but he feigned being absorbed in his book and did not acknowledge them. He was troubled by what had happened but he didn't know how to address it. He was sure he had made love to Kathleen a few nights before. She had come to him, thrown herself upon him, made love to him all night with a violently insatiable appetite. It had been absolutely physical and real. And now for her own reasons she was denying it. But he knew it had happened, as much as he knew anything had ever happened. If his experience with Kathleen that night had not been real, he concluded, then he himself and the life he lived might not be real either. But he knew it had happened. Of course it had happened. He was certain of it. What strange game then was she playing?...

That night another event occurred. He had just lain down in bed when he heard dogs barking. He got up quickly, threw on his clothes, and went outside into the darkness. The sky was black with cloud, there was no moon or starlight, and at first he could see almost nothing at all, but while his eyes adjusted to the darkness he followed the barking for a few hundred yards along the shore. And then he saw dashing out of the darkness in the nearest field some sheep running in terror with the dogs scampering behind them. There were two or three dogs. He climbed on the wall of the field, spread his arms wide, and shouted at the top of his lungs forcing the sheep to turn around and the dogs to whirl around after them. It was no good as the dogs were undeterred in their attack and continued to chase the sheep. He jumped back down from the wall and ran down the road to the first cottage below him where there were lights showing. He knocked hard on the door, shouting "Help Help Help!" to get a response. The door opened and the grey-haired man he had seen on the beach whom Paddy had called "Crotchety Jack" appeared.

"The dogs are attacking the sheep!" Harry panted, out of breath.

"I'll get the owner!" Jack said shutting the door behind him and moving away at a half-shuffling run into the dark.

Harry went back to the field where the sheep were still running frantically around with the dogs in hot pursuit. It was like some savage animalistic dance. He wondered what the dogs were trying to do, were they trying to tire out the sheep before viciously attacking them? Or trying to direct them back towards the shoreline where they could dash them down on the rocks again? Or just playing a prolonged game of death with them? At least Harry's presence at the seaward end of the field kept the dogs from driving the sheep out of it and towards the fatal shore. Within minutes there was an unknown man at his side with a shotgun under his arm. The man began striding into the field. As Harry followed him he felt a slight trepidation that maybe he shouldn't be there. As he advanced behind the first man he could make out two more men appearing at the top of the field, one he thought was the grim young farmer who owned the sheep. These two men also had shotguns. The sheep and dogs were encircled by the men but Harry noticed how the dogs, aware now of the men, had given up the chase and had begun to slink low along the ground to the edge of the field. There was a shout from one of the men and the dogs broke into a run. A second later there was a sudden loud roar from one of the guns and the man near Harry instantly fell over clutching his side and crying out in pain. Harry rushed to him to stand over him sprawled on his back and clutching his side as blood spilled from his wound. In a moment the farmer and his companion, their shotguns tucked under their arms, were standing over the stricken man who was groaning in pain. Even shaken as he was Harry had to admit it had been terribly poor shooting.

"We have to get him to a doctor," the farmer said firmly, and without waiting they unceremoniously hoisted him and staggered along with him to the road where the farmer's van was parked. They laid him down on the flat back of the van where the dead sheep had been heaped the day before. He had already lost consciousness and was motionless and quiet. Harry wondered if he wasn't already dead. He had all the appearance of it.

"I'm going to kill those... dogs and their... owner!" the farmer swore as, along with his still able-bodied companion, he swung into the vehicle, switched on the ignition and, as the lamps of the truck flooded the darkness in front of them, sped away.

Harry walked back to the cottage and again saw the old neighbour leaning on his stick outside his cottage and Clare standing close to him.

"We will have to stop meeting like this," Harry couldn't resist saying.

"What's happened now?" Clare asked.

"Some dogs attacked the sheep..." Harry said. "The men came after the dogs with guns but one of the men got shot..."

"Oh that's terrible!" he heard an alarmed Clare say.

Before he entered the cottage he looked up at the sky to see that the clouds were now broken, as if the blast of gunfire had also torn their flesh open, but where the wound was made, instead of blood pouring out, the sky was gushing bright stars, sparkling and brilliant. He kept the image of the starry heavens in his mind as still dressed in his clothes he slipped under the bedcovers and becoming quickly warm began to fall irresistibly into a heavy and exhausted sleep. He could still hear before he slept the sound of the dogs barking, the awful release of the shotgun, the distressed cry of the fallen man, but he knew it was only memory, echoing quietly in him as he sank into dreamless slumber. There was nothing to be afraid of, nothing at all.

The next morning the grim-faced young farmer, looking less grim now, called with a gift of a bottle of Irish whiskey as a reward for what Harry had done to save the sheep. He had caught up with the dogs on the road and he had dispatched them, all three of them, he said with grim satisfaction. He didn't say if he had dispatched the owner. The shot man had not sustained a serious wound and was recovering at home, also with the help of some good Irish whiskey. Harry wondered to himself if the wounded man had been taken to the doctor before or after the dogs had been tracked down and killed. The farmer stretched his hand forward to him.

"I never introduced myself," he said, "I'm Peter... Peter Goode... I'm really grateful for what you did... saving the sheep..."

As he had done in the pub, Harry accepted his hand, it was strong and firm, rough from constant hard work on the farm and land.

"Harry," he said. "Glad to be of service."

That night sitting in the darkness of the porch he opened and dispatched, to use Peter's word, half of the bottle of whiskey. It warmed him, made his head muzzy, and eventually made him fall asleep in the porch. He woke in the early hours of the morning, his body cramped and uncomfortable, with cold starlight filling the sky above him. It was like following a pathway of stars to his bed, with at the end of it only complete and embracing but such welcome darkness.

A few days later there was what was probably the warmest day of the untoward Indian summer. Paddy called mid-morning to ask for his help with the turf. They walked together on the road out of the village before striding across the peat-covered hillside with its rough covering of wild grasses until they reached a stretch of bare brown bog. There were already a couple of men there working, either cutting fresh sods of turf and stacking them in small neat pyramids to dry in the sun, or moving already dried turf on to sturdy wheelbarrows ready to be carted away to shelter. A track fell away back from the exposed peatland to where a truck was waiting its open platform already half-full with plastic bags brimming with brown-black sods.

"This is how we work," Paddy told him. "Everyone lends a hand to help his neighbour. I'll return the favour on another day…"

The work was carried out with a great sense of ease and without any urgency. Paddy began by calling a tea break. The men stood around drinking their tea poured from a battered aluminium pot into old chipped mugs while chatting and soaking up the warm sun on their faces. They talked about the weather, a perennial Irish topic of conversation, and Paddy held forth heaping disdain on the weather forecasters.

"Why do they say the weather will 'disimprove'?" he complained. "What does it mean? Why can't they just tell us the weather will 'worsen'?"

"Maybe they mean 'disapprove'," one of the men suggested.

"Well then, 'disapprove' of what?" Paddy objected.

"Well, of you for a start," the other man said grinning.

Paddy's conversation was thick with the terminology of meteorological forecasts. He spoke at length about high and low pressure, about weak fronts and cold fronts, about wind strengths and rain quantities, and several times mentioned "the Bay of Biscay", and the "Gulf Stream".

"All of Ireland is washed by the Gulf Stream!" Harry contributed, offering what he believed was a quotation from James Joyce.

"I hope you wash more than Joyce did!" Paddy admonished him, while showing too his own store of literary reference.

It seemed to Harry that the object of being on the bog was company and talk. He was sure any worthwhile cutting or gathering of turf had already been done and it seemed to him the men were only there to pass the time. He wondered indeed why he was wanted there when after a few desultory exchanges about events or people, all unknown to him, the subject of the attack on the sheep came up and, of course, the shooting of the man in the field. Harry was a direct witness whose account was particularly sought.

"Well I think I had better plead 'the Fifth'," Harry said laughing.

And yet he told them what he knew which was no more than what they already knew. If fact they knew more than he did as they knew the names of all the persons involved. They even knew the owner of the dogs and could tell Harry that he had been roughly manhandled by Peter Goode. He was suing Goode, they claimed, for the shooting of the dogs. Goode was suing him for the slaughter of the sheep. The shot man was not suing anybody. It was all part of island life, Paddy told him, and he expected it soon to enter the local folklore. They learned nothing new from Harry but they enjoyed hearing his account of what had happened.

"After this latest sheep-saving exploit, and having freed the poor animal caught in the barbed wire, you will definitely be entered among the saviours or worshipped deities of the sheep world," Paddy assured him.

"And who will enter me?" Harry asked.

"Well of course the island congregation of sheep will!" was the quick response. "Along with their sheepish associates worldwide!"

Harry realised that for the time being he had achieved an unsought for prominence in the life of the island. He hoped it would not last long.

"It's time to get back to work!" Paddy ordered all of a sudden as if they had all been dawdling, apart from himself, over their tea, and for a couple of hours the work went on busily until another tea break was called for, and this time sandwiches were produced.

After another couple of hours work in the afternoon Paddy decided their activity should finish and while the men drove away in the truck heaped now with plastic bags full of turf, Harry walked back slowly to the village with Paddy. Harry wanted information so after a pause he asked,

"What about Kathleen in the post office?"

"What about her?" Paddy countered without enthusiasm.

"Well, shouldn't she have left the island for England or America?"

"Well she should but she can't," Paddy told him.

"And why is that?" Harry wondered.

"She has a child," Paddy said flatly.

Harry knew now he needed to be delicate.

"And is there a father, a husband even?" he asked.

"Well there must be a father," Paddy said. "Every child has a father is what I've heard… But there's no husband and there never was one…"

"Is the father still around?" Harry couldn't help probing.

Paddy stopped on the hillside and looked down over the village and the sea all bright with golden sunlight.

"Since you're so interested," he said, "the father lived in the cottage you're living in and the child was probably conceived in the bed you're sleeping in…"

Harry came quickly to the only possible conclusion.

"Mary Kate's brother then… What happened to him?"

Paddy had started walking now but faster as if he wanted to get home more quickly or simply to end the troublesome interrogation.

"Well it's a small island and there was a great scandal, and Mary Kate's brother, or Frank to call him by his name, was filled with shame and deserted the island, the girl he got pregnant, and his small baby… He barely waited for it to be born… He was gone soon after… He vanished overnight… like a ghost…"

"There are a lot of ghosts on the island," Harry said.

"There are," Paddy said, closing the conversation quietly.

They walked the rest of the way back to the village in silence. Before they said goodbye and parted ways Paddy turned to Harry.

"Don't be thinking too much about Kathleen," he said. "She has her own ways about her... And you'd get lost pretty quickly in them..."

Harry said nothing but thought that perhaps he was lost already. He walked back to his cottage passing alone in front of the post office. He saw Kathleen busy inside but she did not look at him. He concluded to himself that his adventure with her was already over. He needed to stop thinking about her and he needed to find his way out of her "ways", whatever they were. Perhaps she was just lonely. She had said, "God it's lonely here!" as she first embraced him that night. It was better now to go on as if nothing had happened. But what if she called to the cottage again some dark lonely night? Well he would know better the next time... But deep down inside he couldn't even be sure if there had been a first time. For some time even before Kathleen he had felt unsure of his own reality. He tried to think his way to first premises. He was living on the island. He was living in the cottage. Kathleen had come to him and slept with him. The island was real. Paddy and Joy were real. He was real. Kathleen was real. He couldn't believe he was even thinking these things. As soon as he arrived at the cottage he poured himself a glass of whiskey and drank it straight. The whiskey burned in his throat and chest. The whiskey was real.

While many of his days were isolated and quiet, punctuated only by walks or cycles, and random conversational exchanges with his neighbours, he had to admit his first month or so on the island had brought its fair share of events and surprises. For a couple of weeks after the sheep had been attacked nothing of note occurred. He had some letters, one from his brother announcing a visit, and one from a Norwegian friend also writing to say he would call with his wife, but neither specified a date for their appearance. His days had settled into a quiet but constant routine. On fine days he would cycle to different parts of the island, he had climbed the mountains, he had walked the beaches, and he had returned once or twice to the deserted village. At least once a week he would cycle to Killeaden to replenish his store of food. He called regularly on Paddy and Joy for brief exchanges and Paddy sometimes called to him with offerings of freshly filleted fish. Clare had called a couple of times and had even sat in the porch one day to share some tea with him. He liked her, her body was lithe and easy, her attitude and movements relaxed, and her voice had a soft musical quality that pleased him, as if there was a constant song in her. A couple of times her older children breezed in to chat giddily with him before leaving as quickly as they had come, warned by their mother not to bother him. He met "Crotchety Jack" on occasion while walking on the beach where he sometimes went to gather wood to start his fire with and they had very curtailed conversation where Harry, while often summoning the weather, good or bad, painstakingly avoided any references to Dublin. He got to know the tall thin young man he had often seen walking past the cottage. His name was John but his conversation was limited to evocations of series and characters on television that Harry knew nothing about. It was clear that John's life was limited to walking around the village, or watching his television series. It was a life without horizons beyond the village or the confines of television but he seemed contented and was always friendly. The old bent-over man with the stick would occasionally also stop outside the cottage gate to deliver succinct judgements about the state of the village, the world, and the weather. One day while talking with Harry he gazed with a look of secret wisdom at a lemon-gold sunset and pointing his stick at it forecast a certain continuation of the long spell of fine weather. Two days later rain and wind took hold of the island and beat it relentlessly for an entire week. The man's sprightly sister always had a cheery greeting and a smile when he encountered her but she never delivered herself of any sententious judgements on the weather or anything at all and her conversation was committedly monosyllabic as she fleetingly passed him by. She was a woman who when you encountered her always seemed glad to see you and to be fleeing you at the same time. Harry guessed it was some kind of native reticence or shyness, or perhaps she just had nothing to say. In all his time on the island he would never have a real conversation with her, or anything more than an exchange of one or two words. He only ever saw Kathleen in the distance as she came and went at the post office but still he remained puzzled by her and that night she had come to him. In the early evenings he settled in the porch to watch the sunset if there was one, or he would simply stare into the encroaching darkness if the sky was filled with cloud. He sat with a book in his lap but which he never read. When he looked down at the cover of the book it was always the same. He told himself he should choose another book, if only for the sake of appearances.

He spent almost all of his time alone and sat for long hours in the porch with the book he pretended to read. He became very absent-minded sitting there. In fact since coming to the island he found it harder and harder to keep any focus on his thoughts or actions and this appeared to be exacerbated the more time he spent alone. Once when Clare called she asked him what he was reading and he had to examine the cover of the book to say what it was.

"A German book," he showed her, holding the book up.

"Steppenwolf," she read from the cover with apparent interest. "'For Mad People Only'… Oh Lord, what's that about?"

He had read the book many years before and it had impressed him so while he had forgotten almost everything about the story and characters he could still hazard an opinion.

"Oh one of those intensely gloomy German novels," he told her. "There's madness in it alright, and suicide, murder, and a lot of disturbing things… But ultimately it's hopeful! There are even some beautiful women and a love affair or two… I think it all ends happily!"

"Thank goodness for that!" Clare laughed. "Is that the kind of thing you're writing?"

Everyone had accepted his writer imposture as his *"raison d'être"* for being on the island. He had even installed a small mechanical typewriter on the table in the porch on which to the incurious eye he appeared to be tapping out long lines of interesting narrative, but which he was really using to teach himself basic typing skills. Most of what he produced was gobbledygook, long unpunctuated sentences of mangled potential words that looked more like Polish, or some consonant-ridden Eastern European language, than English. The distorted indecipherable words and sentences often made him smile. They were like a secret language of his exclusion from the world. He had never really had any intention to write and all that he did really write were random words or phrases jotted down by pen in a small notebook he kept. It was really like a diary. Each day he would write the date and then some of the events of the day. Some days he wrote simple observations such as "sunshine today", or "rain and wind today", "the sea so quiet", "a sunset stained with blood", or "stars in the sky", or "no stars", or "Clare visited". Sometimes, but very seldom, his observations would be more substantial. On the day the time changed from summer to winter he wrote,

"The island floats like a mirage on the ocean. It is real and the people here are real, but it often feels unreal. I sometimes think it will suddenly disappear in front of my eyes while I am watching it. It will disappear and everything in it will disappear along with it. Including myself. As if we were all some kind of fiction, fantasy, or dream."

After this untoward and lengthy observation he wrote on the same page,

"Very true. The island, the ocean, all the people… and myself included… we will all one day disappear… But, nonetheless… Maybe I am too much on my own here."

He reminded himself of the caretaker from the Jack Nicholson film "The Shining".

He was seated in the porch one afternoon when an unknown blonde women pushed open the cottage gate and walked hesitantly towards him. He remained seated when she stepped into the open doorway of the porch. She was about his own age and he noticed how the sunlight dazzled in the bright gold of her hair and pooled in the smiling warmth of her green-gold eyes.

"I'm really sorry," she began in a noticeably American accent, "but my car has just gone off the road... Is there any way of getting a recovery vehicle out here?"

"I've no phone," he explained, standing up, "but let me try to help you."

He walked with her the few hundred yards to where the front wheel of her car had sunk down in the soft verge of the road. He suggested she walk to the post office from where she could phone the local garage for help. When he saw her hesitation he said he would accompany her. As they walked he appreciated the light grace of her body at his side and a pleasant feeling of subtle warmth that emanated from her. After a short while they came upon two men working in a field. One of them was Peter Goode.

"Feel like helping a damsel in distress, Peter?" Harry asked.

Peter and his companion were only too glad of distraction. They bundled into Peter's car and drove the short distance to where the American woman's car was stranded. Using a strong rope tied between the cars Peter was able to pull her stricken car back from the soft earth it had sunk into.

"Can I offer him some money?" the woman asked Harry.

"There's no need," Harry told her. "They're glad to help... They now have a story to tell."

"Maybe I could buy you a drink?" she said to Peter. "I'm staying up at the pub..."

"Gladly," Peter responded. "But I have a day's work to finish."

"Later this evening then?" she asked.

Peter looked pleased and nodded acceptance. She was an attractive woman and it was unlikely she ever had men turn down her offers to buy them drink.

"You too," she offered, turning to Harry, and he was struck again by the bright warm green-gold of her eyes peering into his.

"I'll be there," Harry assured her, pleased too like Peter to be asked.

"Later this evening then," she said offering her hand to each of them in turn.

"Done deal!" Peter said with enthusiasm as she left.

He turned then to Harry and added good-humouredly, "Let's not fight over her!"

All day Harry thought about the American woman. He walked out along the shoreline past Jean's house and continued over the rising headland to walk again along the steep cliff edge with its spectacular views of the island. He had been several weeks on the island and he knew it well now and could not only pick out in the distance the string of broken stone houses that formed the deserted village but also believed he could make out "The Emerald" guesthouse where Bill and Jane lived in the townland of Kill. The day was bright and the air high on the cliff edge filled him with a kind of exaltation in which his thoughts of the American woman mixed. Her golden hair with the sunlight in it, her green-gold eyes, the memory of her light and graceful movements, all danced brightly and warmly in him, causing him to look forward keenly to seeing her again. Her name he learned that evening was Helen.

They had a nice evening together talking quietly in one of the lowlit corners of the pub close to the fire, the men drinking Guinness, Helen sipping at a white wine. They talked about where she came from in the States which she described as an "outpost of the wild Midwest", but then she laughed and said it was more like "the mild Midwest". She complained about her accent but both men found it very winning and told her so. They asked her about her travels in Ireland and she was happy to talk about her journey. She had landed by plane in Shannon, rented a car, and driven north through many of the places Harry had been to during the summer as he had cycled north from Limerick on his quest for an isolated rural cottage to live in. They enthused together over the Burren and Connemara, and Helen had even made it to Cong.

"My mother loved 'The Quiet Man' movie," she confided.

"The Quiet Man" with John Wayne and Maureen O'Hara had been filmed in Cong. It had felt like a pilgrimage to her to go there.

They told her stories about the island and Harry's escapades with the sheep were produced for her entertainment. Harry's heart skipped a beat when Peter announced he had to go. He was driving to Dublin early in the morning. He shook Helen's hand, wished her well on her travels, and hoped that she would return to the island someday soon. She promised she would. Harry felt his chest filling with warm pleasure as he found himself sitting alone with her. Determined to prolong the pleasure of being near her he ordered more drink, without asking her if she wanted more.

"You'll get me drunk!" she laughed.

"No, never!" he insisted. "I know you wild Midwest girls can hold your liquor!"

"But the 'mild' Midwest ones not so good!" she countered.

As she spoke to him her eyes never left his face and he could feel her gaze physically pierce his own blue eyes as if entering into him like fine bright rays of enquiry, as if she were gazing into his soul. And yet as she spoke she grew more serious and shadow veiled her eyes and voice as she began to confide in him.

"The real reason I've come here," she said, "is to visit that old broken down cabin out on the headland..."

He felt he knew why before she said it.

"It belonged to my mother... Jean... Perhaps you knew her?"

"I only came to live here a short while ago," he explained. "I know people who knew her... She had a heart attack in the house of some friends. They said her family came to take her back to the States."

"Yes," she said, "my brother and uncle... But they only visited Westport where Jean was in hospital after the heart attack... And then they took her home... No one got to visit Inish... I'm the first to come here to the island... I've been to talk already with Paddy and Joy... And Bill and Jane... They tell me she was happy here. And that they miss her..."

"How is Jean?" he asked her quietly.

The response seemed inevitable.

"She died shortly after returning home..."

After a long pause she continued, "I think I needed to come here just to be at peace with her ghost…"

She reached her hand out to lightly touch his arm.

"Have you been inside the house?"

"No," he confessed. "I've wanted to… but I hadn't the nerve really… I'm not sure I'm up to other people's broken dreams… Or hearts… I'm not sure I have room in my life for a ghost."

"Will you go inside with me?" she asked in an earnestly pleading voice.

"Sure," he said, feeling that he had no choice, feeling that finally the secrets of the haunted house on the shore would be revealed to him and that he would learn if it was truly empty or if some presence lingered there.

"I'll call to you in the morning," she said tremulously. "We can go to the house together then."

He could tell it was something she was eager to do, and yet that she was feeling some reluctance for the task. He felt it too. Neither of them had any idea what the house held in store for them.

The next morning as arranged she called to the cottage and together they walked along the shore towards Jean's house. It was another day of bright warm sunshine but the warmth of the sun was amplified and expanded for him by the warmth he felt at Helen's presence walking by his side. As the sun filled her hair and eyes with a dazzling brightness he felt as if every step she took beside him reverberated through him and set up a rhythm inside him he instantly realised was intimately connected to the inner movement of her heart and blood, and the intimate rhythm of her heart and mind. He wanted to keep her by his side for as long as he could. They stood uncertainly outside the house before entering.

"It looks so sad, so desolate," Helen said on the edge of tears. "I can't imagine inside… the emptiness…"

"Let's do this," he said walking determinedly towards the door, which opened for him without resistance.

The inside of Jean's house was truly sad, desolate and empty. The few spartan items of furniture looked as if they had been haphazardly shoved about and then left in no particular order. There was dust everywhere and a dingy light through the plastic sheeting over the windows fell in shabby folds on the dust. There was a raised and curtained mezzanine area with just a few steps up to it and a bed still unmade from when Jean had last slept there with some books and tattered magazines scattered around it. There were no electrical appliances other than some lamps powered by a small electrical generator. A small gas stove seemed to be how Jean had done her cooking. There was a radio which when he switched it on remained silent. In spite of the warm dry weather for most of the recent weeks the place felt damp and cold and comfortless. They spoke in subdued whispers as they looked around and then Helen let a sudden piercing scream as she opened a chest beneath the steps. He stepped quickly towards her and at the same time she jumped towards him so that in a split second he was holding her trembling body in his arms.

"Something in the box," she said, pointing at it.

He released her from his arms and she stood a few feet back from the stairs. He opened the chest in time to see a grey rat scurrying through a hole in the back of it. It slipped then in a single dark fluid moment through a crack in the floorboards.

"A rat," he told her with distaste. "Paddy said the place is haunted by rats!"

He bowed down into the box to see what it contained. It seemed to be just loose sheets of torn or scrunched papers scrawled over in a large hand. He picked a handful up and began to read them but dropped them quickly into the box again and closed it.

"Anything interesting?" Helen asked, but she seemed to have lost all interest in the chest and what it might contain and was stepping away to explore other corners of the house.

He followed her and they rummaged through cupboards and drawers which only contained the detritus of a life that had ended in sadness there. They explored in silence. There really seemed nothing to be said. At one point as he moved around her he noticed tears, silent too, falling on her cheeks. After a few minutes they decided to leave the house to its own irretrievable abandonment. The day seemed to have grown quickly cold while they were in the house and Helen shivered as she looked out over the vastness of the ocean rippling with golden light all the way to the horizon. In spite of its vast luminosity, stripped of its warmth the sea had become bleak and the land cold and inhospitable.

"I can't believe my mother ever thought she could be happy here," Helen said as they walked away.

When they reached his cottage she accompanied him inside and sat with him. She asked him why he had come to the island and he trotted out the by now well-established pretext.

"I'm 'an Scríbhneoir'," he told her using the Gaelic words. "The 'scrivener'... The 'writer'..."

"What are you writing?" she asked him.

"Oh just words," he said, Hamlet-style. And of course it was true. Just words. Words words words.

"What are you going to do now?" he asked, and her eyes filling again with tears she gave the answer he would most have wished for.

"Well, after that dismal experience visiting Mom's house I think I would like to see the rest of the island..."

She hesitated a little before adding, "Will you accompany me?"

He felt his chest fill with warm pleasure again.

"Let's go!" he said with a broad grin of undisguised enthusiasm.

The day grew brighter and warmer and the grim shadows of their visit to the house fell away as their mood improved. They travelled in her car. She drove as he directed. He took her through the long townland by the sea to walk together on the edge of the glittering lake. They continued then to the deserted village on the hillside.

"It looks like Mom was part of a long tradition here," Helen said sadly as she walked among the broken houses and tumbled stones.

They went then to the beautiful beach in the westernmost part of the island. They were the only people there. She surprised him after they had walked a little in the sheltered warmth of the bay by throwing her clothes off and rushing in bra and panties only into the green-gold tumult of the waves. He hesitated a little but finally he threw his own clothes off and rushed into the water flinging himself headlong and with a loud excited yell towards her. They bobbed around in the rolling ocean, speechlessly, breathlessly, gasping as each cold wave struck and tumbled them. When they emerged from the sea they ran lightly along the beach. She was fitter and faster than he was and ran at a constant pace ahead of him. He had leisure running behind her to observe her closely. Her hair shone with gathered sunlight. Each frozen drop of water was like a bright jewel on her magnolia-white skin. She laughed as she ran with a free musical laughter that delighted him. She seemed so full of life. It seemed so easy for her to be happy. Walking, or running, on air, on light. He ran along behind her, and though he reached out his hands to touch and hold her, she was always out of reach. She seemed to have a perfect unattainability that would always be beyond him as they ran. Her hair was a dazzling gold, her eyes were a vibrant green-gold, her magnolia-white skin was covered in glistering jewels of ice-cold Atlantic water. In the golden bright sunlight she looked like a Venus emerged from the rolling lace-edged sea. When finally they stopped running he had no breath for speech and she too was panting lightly with no words to offer him. Then she began to shake with subdued laughter.

"It's the end of the world here," she said finally, "but it really is one of the most beautiful places I have ever been. Perhaps Mom did find a promise of happiness here. It just never became real..."

He could not get over how directly she looked at him, looked into him. Her green-gold eyes pierced the cold blue of his eyes and descended inside him in a movement he could physically feel, like tangible rays of inquisitive searching light, as if she was seeking the secret of him, or his soul. It unsettled him but pleased him at the same time.

They left the beach and drove the entire length of the island back east towards Killeaden where they stopped to pick up a couple of bottles of white wine. Chablis, she had told him she liked, and Chablis he found. She smiled approvingly when she saw the bottles.

"Looks like we won't be spending the evening in the pub!" she said.

They took the coast road back to the village but stopped at the castle of the pirate queen. Together they climbed the crooked stairs to the battlements and Helen stood there for a long time silently, looking out over the vistas of land and sea. He watched her in her concentration and abstraction sink into herself and apparently away from him and the present world they occupied. She became for a time all reverie. She could have been the pirate queen herself, he thought, looking at her from behind her, swept as she was by the fading sunlight, her strong back, her golden hair, her quiet stately bearing, her eyes fixed upon her domain, her heart pondering the manifold destinies of herself and her world. He recalled the tale of how the sons of the pirate queen had been taken prisoner by the English. The pirate queen had sailed up the Thames to face the English Queen in her Greenwich palace garden. The two ladies had walked in the garden talking in Latin phrases. The pirate queen wanted her sons back. Whatever else she had done the pirate queen had fought for life he supposed even when sowing death in battle. She had had no suicidal dreams, no desire to give up life, any other or her own. Her only desire was to make the world and life in the image she desired. And she would have expressed this in the Latin she held in common with the English Queen. "Give me back my sons," she would have demanded. And the Virgin Queen, who was without sons, or daughters for that matter, and who knew nothing of being a mother, would have nodded in womanly understanding. Yes, the power in the pirate queen was the power of life, of life, and nothing more. Or if there was more, it must have been also love. Love of life, love for her sons. Love for the troubled western world she alone could dominate and make subject to her image.

He shook this romantic vision from himself and called Helen out of her reverie. Helen no doubt had been thinking of another mother, her own, whose destiny had called her to the westernmost island of the world, and who had left her dreams there, broken and bloodied. They arrived at the cottage as the sunset was losing its golden colours to a dark and bloody red. Night was not long in coming. They sat and drank Chablis and their conversation was easy and relaxed and laced with soft laughter. They sat side by side on a couch in the living room and little by little as they drank and talked in the dancing light of the turf fire over their bodies he slipped down little by little closer to her. Eventually, as if he sensed some tacit invitation, he began to touch her and to move his hands lightly over her clothes.

"Is it ok to touch you?" he asked her.

"Yes, it's ok," she said quietly.

He kissed her for a long time on her soft moist mouth, their tongues melding, while his hands brushed her inner thighs in a light rhythm, before he raised her sweater high and eased her full ripe white breasts from her bra taking her raised nipples in his mouth to lick and suck, squeezing her breasts gently all the time with his hands.

"Do you like this?" he asked her.

"I like it, I like it..." she responded warmly.

She now began pulling his clothes away, unbuttoning his jeans, unzipping him, using her hands and feet to push the material down to his heels.

"I want to have you inside me!" she said with sudden determination.

She lay under him and pulled him towards her. He caressed her thighs first with his tongue, then played there with his penis in the slick folds of her skin, before she drew him down into her, her full white breasts pillowing his movements upon her, her warm moist mouth devouring him greedily. As they rolled and twisted about each other, her body rose against and fell away from him in warm wet sensational surges, grasping him greedily in a succession of rising falling embracing waves. As he moved in and out of her, and surged increasingly inside her, her mouth caressing him, her feet rising and falling on the backs of his legs, her arms embracing him lightly, tightly, warmly, the touch of her everywhere like satin or silk on his skin, he felt the whole bright day spent with her resolve itself into a sudden clear and pristine harmony that swept irresistibly through him. And as he came at last in an exquisite torrent inside her he felt something he recognised as complete sensual happiness, and embraced and held it as a stranger who had been too long distant for what seemed in the moment a desperate lifetime. In all of his being there surged a tremendous and sensational carnal gratitude.

"Oh thank you oh thank you oh thank you!" he said falling falling falling falling falling deep down into the tender embrace of her body.

And as he fell fell fell fell fell he heard her coming under him in a prolonged spate of musical sighs that faded finally to a deepest silence. They slept together like babes in each other's arms and when he woke first in the morning he shed quiet but real tears that his bed held an astonishing beauty such as hers. She looked "angelic", he told himself, lying there beside him, and on her face as she slept there was an angelic smile.

Later that morning she collected her things from the pub. She was returning to the States and he accompanied her to the ferry in Killeaden. They said little on the road but he stroked her leg and arm all the time with his fingertips. The journey by car was far too short and there was very little waiting time when they reached the ferry. Before they arrived there, still stroking her arm and leg, he said,

"You could stay, you know…"

She smiled indulgently at him before saying to him with a tangible sadness in her voice.

"And spend my days looking out on the ruin of my mother's existence here?… Under those sinister blood-red sunsets?…"

"The sunsets are sometimes golden," he countered, but her expression remained unpersuaded.

She surprised him then by saying in an upbeat manner.

"You could come to the States!"

His heart skipped a beat but he didn't know how to respond. It was like being offered a trip to Mars.

"It's a whole other world out there," he said, regretting each word as he spoke them. "I am struggling to survive where I am…"

Before she boarded the ferry they stood close by the car and they embraced.

"Try to be happy!" she urged him tenderly.

"Am I not happy?" he quizzed her.

"At least stop being so tormented!" she said with a gentle admonitory laugh.

Her green-gold eyes pierced him and it was as if she could see the hard stone of unfathomable sadness at the heart of him. Was his torment so visible? At least to her…

"I wish I could make you happy now before I leave," she said in real earnest.

"The last two days have been like a miracle," he said.

"Yes they have," she said, her eyes filled with green-gold light.

"Thank you!" he said.

"Thank you!" she said, kissing him on the mouth, her arms drawing him to her and holding him tightly to her body as if she never wanted to let him go.

"It was nice!" she said in parting, beaming a golden smile at him.

"Yes, it was nice!" he said.

He held her as if he never wanted to let her go. And then he let her go. And then she left.

He watched the ferry pull away from the quay and as he walked away he realised that every iota of his being wanted to turn back in her direction and to follow her while each step forward took him somewhere he did not wish to go. He was only a short distance from the village when he doubled up at the side of the road with a sudden vast surge of despair through him. "Oh Christ!" he protested bitterly. "Oh Christ!"

Falling to his knees he dropped his face into his raised and plaintive hands. How could he have forgotten? They had not exchanged contact details. He did not know how to get in touch with her, no address, no phone number, he did not even know the name of the town where she lived, or the State... All he knew was that she lived somewhere in the "wild Midwest". Or came from there... Maybe she lived elsewhere. But she knew where he lived, didn't she? She could get in touch. He had no phone but perhaps she would write. Perhaps. Or perhaps she was gone forever. Perhaps he would never hear from her or see her again. Not in this entire lifetime. Oh God!... What did he know about her life back home? Maybe she had someone waiting for her, some lover, even a husband... Maybe she had forgotten him already. Those wild American Midwest girls. What were two days of holiday dalliance to her? He curled up in the high grass at the side of the road his hands still covering his face, a bitter grief biting hard in him, a sea of desolation rising in him. He realised that in the moment overcome by loss he had been reduced to a pathetic, helpless child who had lost his mother. He had become an idiot rolling at the side of the road, inconsolable in his grief.

With some effort he picked himself up and walked haltingly along the road until he came to the castle of the pirate queen. Quickly he climbed, half-running, to the battlements. He was in time to see in the distance the ferry making its way towards the mainland. He could see only the boat but impulsively he stood high on the nearest battlement and waved his arms above his head, calling her name silently to the departing world, "Helen!... Helen!... Helen!..." He hoped that she could see him. He strained his eyes trying to catch the movement of a figure, any figure, on the boat, or arms raised and waving in response to his, or some semaphore signal of dazzling sunlight in her hair flashing brightly on the ocean air. But there was nothing nothing nothing... She had well and truly gone. But still he waved and continued to wave his arms high in the air, hoping against hope, that somehow she would see him from the furthest distances before the boat became little more than a speck on the sea and disappeared from view, and still he hoped against hope, that seeing him she would know he was still there on the island, and that he wanted, and that he waited, for her to return. He would think of her now always as the pirate queen of his heart. His broken and breaking heart.

It took him a couple of hours to walk all the way back to the village but when he got there he saw Paddy dragging a small wooden boat across the beach to the sea. Paddy waved to summon him down and Harry threw his weight behind the boat to edge it into the water.

"Come with me," Paddy invited him. "I'm going out to the island beyond…"

Harry did not want to miss the opportunity to familiarise himself with the green island he had only seen mostly in shadow on his horizon to the south. Its name was Grace Island and he felt he could do with some grace today. Paddy rowed the boat with a steady lift and fall of oars cutting into the water which seemed to flow swiftly beneath them. It took almost an hour of steady rowing to cut across the ocean to the green triangle of island like a small pointed mountain set on the sea and while Paddy, in tune with his deep steady breathing, rolled the oars back and forth, Harry scanned the far coast of the mainland for any sign of the ferry that had carried Helen away or an impossible sighting of her car slipping quickly along the coast road back south to Shannon and America. As they approached the island he could make out a lighthouse above a high cliff face and white birds wheeling gracefully through the air. "Gannets!" Paddy informed him. Eventually they pulled into a quiet harbour on the north of the island where a friend of Paddy's was waiting with some fishing pots, nets, and equipment Paddy needed. The friend's small grey van sat on the road above the harbour.

"Hey Tim," Paddy hailed him, "fancy giving my friend here a quick tour of the island?"

There always seemed time on these western islands to follow whatever whims or possibilities appeared out of the blue and Tim with a curt nod and a smile was only too happy to oblige. The three men sat side by side in the front of the van and Tim spun the vehicle away from the tiny harbour towards the island's mountainous interior. There was really only one small mountain, the shadowy emerald one which dominated Harry's views seawards from his cottage on Inish. The mountain swept from its lowest point on the east of the island, over rough green fields intersected by dry stone walls, to shoot up sharply and steeply over the entire western end of the island to reach a high point on which a slender metal mast was raised, surrounded by a high wire fence and gate.

It was a small island and it did not take long for Tim to spin the van around to its most salient landmarks. There weren't many of these on the island but they were notable nonetheless. First of all, situated in the extreme north-east of the island close to where they had come ashore there was the lighthouse Harry had seen from the boat arriving. It was not a functioning lighthouse, Tim explained. It had been decommissioned for some years but there were ambitious plans to make it into a guesthouse. Racing south down the eastern edge of the island they came in the extreme south-east to the small village of Ballymore scattered around the island's main harbour at the closest point of the island to the far mainland. A ferry called in and out of here and Harry felt an irrepressible pang thinking of Helen who had sailed away from him, perhaps forever, just a few hours earlier.

"Only a couple of hundred people live here," Tim said. "A bit of fishing and a bit of tourism keeps us going…"

"Ay, and a bit of drinking!" Paddy added acerbically.

Not far from the main harbour, raised up on a rocky headland to its western side, there was a ruined medieval castle like the one on Inish. It was another stronghold of the pirate queen. Grace Island had been her principal fortress, Tim insisted. They stopped and walked around and inside the ruined building. The façade was divided up by narrow defensive slits and two chimneys protruded above it. Inside was an empty shell, the floors and staircases had been torn away, and there was no way to reach the circling stone stairway on the first floor to climb to the summit. Though Paddy suggested Harry could stand on Tim's shoulders as a way of doing it.

"This island is where the pirate queen was born, grew to womanhood, got married, and after she died she was buried here too!" Tim said with blunt pride.

"And she haunts the place as well!" Paddy said with a grimace. "Sure she loves playing tricks on any of the lads who've been drinking if they happen by late at night!"

"Come on," said Tim, growing in his enthusiasm, "I'll show you where she sleeps in peace…"

"Her fighting days are long done!" commented Paddy.

Following the southern coastal road westwards they came after a few minutes to an old abbey of crumbling stone surrounded by a vast field of gravestones. Tim explained in his shambling island voice that the abbey had been built by Cistercian monks in the twelfth century. Most proudly he announced that it had been the site of baptism, marriage, and burial of the famous pirate queen. They stopped briefly to amble through the ruin and

Tim and Paddy pointed out with quiet but slightly competitive enthusiasm dim medieval murals representing heraldic creatures, such as griffons and dragons, as well as curious human figures and interesting architectural features, delicate traceries, or the strikingly narrow pointed gothic windows rising high in the walls like slender unlit candles. They came at last to an interior wall with some fine medieval tracery and a plaque with the words *"Terra Maris Potens"* above a canopied tomb, the reputed last resting place of the pirate queen.

"Here she lies!" Tim said touching the tomb reverently with his hand.

"Her last dominion!" was Paddy's echoing commentary.

Harry said nothing but he was deeply impressed and moved by the remoteness, simplicity, and also the dilapidation of the pirate queen's final resting place. Apart from the plaque above her there was nothing to suggest glory in the living of her life or in the conquests she had made of her world. She had gone from movement to rest, from speech to silence, and only silence now could speak her, silence and the cold damp grey stone which circumscribed all that she had ever been.

Silently the three men made their way back to Tim's van. They drove finally to the highest point of the island for magnificent sunlit views, and as they drove along roads splashed here and there with the bright orange of monbretia, heavy with the blood-red of fuchsia, and thick with golden gorse, Harry spotted on the rising slopes of the mountain the now familiar ancient potato ridges known as "lazy beds", the arduous labour of the long ago struggling to live and the long-since dead. Tim pointed out some ruined stone cottages.

"Famine cottages!" he said.

The whole of the west of Ireland Harry realised had been for over a century past a geography of abandonment, desertion, exile, and of course death. There were two kinds of death perhaps. Either you died on the spot from hunger or disease and you remained where you died, sinking into the soil of your birthplace until you were swallowed and forgotten by it, or you fled from your fate, leaving everything that had existed in you for your entire lifetime, family, home, friends, work, in the place which you had left behind in your desperate bid for survival. There had been a lot of both kinds of death in these landscapes left to only memory and ghosts, the ruined and empty remains of houses, cottages, cabins, fields, villages and townlands, and entire worlds from which people had disappeared, leaving only desperate traces, like these famine cottages, while they themselves were never to be encountered or seen again.

"Most of the people of that time lived in mud huts," Paddy offered with some seriousness now. "Over the years and before too long the rain and wind washed away their dwelling places. Anything of them written on the landscape was soon eroded and erased."

"Terrible times, terrible times!" Tim muttered as they reached the summit of the mountain and came to a halt under the modern communications mast.

"What is the hill called?" Harry asked.

"The Big Hill!" Tim and Paddy chimed in together in sudden good humour.

"*An Cnoc Mór*," Paddy translated into his native Gaelic. "Knockmore!"

Harry looked out over the vast ocean spectacle of the islanded western world.

"And what does "*Terra Maris Potens*" mean?" he asked.

There was no way Paddy would allow Tim to beat him to the answer.

"Power over Land and Sea!" he announced with great ceremony before Tim could even open his mouth.

Harry strode away from the two men to where he could gaze out alone over the island, the ocean, and the distant mountainous mainland, dominated by Patrick's holy mountain. It struck him, without putting it into words, but it was his sense of it, how the historical and the spiritual and the everyday overlapped here, to make a broad palimpsest of beauty, exaltation, and sorrow. He could see below him on Grace the ruined abbey and castle, the town scattered about its harbour, and the now distant tower of the disused lighthouse above its rugged cliff. He could see too his own island of Inish and could pick out his own tiny village of Dughrá on its southern edge with the cottage he lived in on its nearest shore. He could barely make out Jean's house, its drab brown wooden structure camouflaged against the deep browns of the surrounding wild grasses and peatland. He strained to see if he could make out the distant shape of the pirate queen's castle on Inish but he realised it was impossible not because of distance but because it was simply, he recognised, out of view. And yet he strove in his imagination to see it standing proud at the sea's edge, and he strove further to see Helen again as she climbed in front of him, her waist swaying and her hips graceful and dancing, weaving her way on the spiral staircase to the battlements where she stood lost in reverie gazing out upon the sea and land she had held perhaps, in that instant of abstraction or dreaming, power over. In his mind's eye he saw the dazzling gold of her hair, the piercing green-gold of her lovely eyes, and the pure white magnolia flesh of her face, around the moist warm tender pink blossom of her mouth. He spoke but so quietly, as if in near silent prayer, so that the two men would not hear him, invoking Helen and his desire for her.

"Oh Helen, please come back, come back, come back, come back, please come back!"

She had not been in his life long enough. He would have loved her to have shared this day and this visit to Grace Island with him, to have shared this day of grace with him. She would have loved it, they would have loved it together, and being together would have been so beautiful, sharing a world he suddenly saw transfigured by beauty. By beauty, exaltation, and sorrow. His thoughts were interrupted by Tim who pointed him towards the west of the island where a heavy square block of a building with square windows could be seen on an elevated site overlooking the sea.

"Signal Tower from Napoleon's day," Tim told him. "The British built them. They feared invasion by the French..."

This islanded western world seemed so remote from the affairs of the world of power, conquest, and major wars, but that was an illusion. History had struck its blows here as hard as in the deepest hinterlands of the continent. Harry shuddered to think of French battleships sailing into these furthest-removed reaches of Europe and the signals sent in haste from the tower to warn of their approach.

"The Spanish Armada came here in the fifteen hundreds," Tim said, adding gloomily, "The sailors washed up on shore were slaughtered by the locals..."

"A very nice one hundred thousand welcomes," Paddy said. "And now let's go home..."

Out on the ocean once again in Paddy's small boat they were viewed close to the harbour by a party of bobbing grey seals who watched with quiet interest as they sailed away, and about half way across to Inish a school of dolphins began to swim with the boat. Paddy was excited by the dolphins and worked his oars with even greater vigour as if to race them. Leaning over the edge of the boat Harry could almost touch the backs of some of the fish as they shot to the surface and sped past him. When they leapt the spray from their flesh made fleeting rainbows appear that he also felt he could reach out and grasp in his hands, but they were gone before his fingers could touch them.

As they approached Inish, Paddy pointed towards the west of the island where Kim Bay lay.

"They used to catch basking sharks out there," he said. "There are still the ruins of some factory buildings. The oil from their liver was very sought after… It was a big industry here in the fifties!"

Harry remembered the derelict buildings at Kim Bay, so that was what they were, remnants of the island's past glory as a haunt of the basking shark.

"And of course they mined the lovely purple amethyst there too, all gone now, apart from a few fragments!" Paddy continued.

Harry recalled the scars he had seen on the earth at Kim, the remnants he now understood of the old mining for the lovely purple stone. Amethyst, it was the birthstone for February. Helen had said she was born in February. He wanted to share that with her. He wanted to give her Amethyst. Was it too late?... Too late for Amethyst?...

With a final poetic flourish Paddy waved an arm towards the high clear summit of Carrigmore.

"That's where the Golden Eagle reigned," he said. "The pirate queen ruled over land and sea, the Eagle triumphed over the mountains and the sky."

When they arrived back on Inish Harry helped Paddy unload the boat and then drag it high on the beach out of reach of the tides. They worked in silence but before Harry left Paddy said to him,

"You got on well with the American woman I think…"

"Jean's daughter…" Harry responded hesitantly. "I went to the cabin with her and showed her the island…"

Paddy stared at him with a knowing look but said nothing. Finally as Harry was walking away, he added,

"She's a beautiful woman just like her mother…"

"Well, like her mother, she's been and gone now," Harry shot back.

"You'll have to call soon and sample my wine!" Paddy shouted before Harry had walked too far from him.

Harry waved his assent before continuing on the road up to his cottage. It had been a long day and he hadn't eaten since breakfast. He warmed some leftover stew for himself and ate it with chunks of brown soda bread. He washed it down with the leftover Chablis he had shared with Helen. Later he sat in the porch and watched one of the sinister blood-red sunsets Helen had invoked. It settled as she had suggested over Jean's house and little by little as it turned to deepest black it swallowed the house and all it contained, including its memories, at least he imagined it did, for the duration of that night. Before going to bed he went through the cottage and touched all the objects Helen had touched no matter how fleetingly. He cradled her glass lovingly in his hands and touched the rim with his lips. He ran his hands over the couch on which they had made love and tried to imagine her body under his touch. When he lay in bed he made love fervently to her, driving his imagination into every nook and cranny of her that he had owned the night before, and as he came in a sensational release tainted with deep sadness, he called her name into the oppressive darkness above him. As he fell back from the peak of his fantasy sleep caught him and carried him away in an instant but for the first time since coming to the island his sleep was not dreamless. Instead he had vivid dreams of a startlingly real nature. The invented incidents and figures of his imagination populated his dreaming with a clarity which contradicted their unreality, but as he woke they immediately dissipated and after an instant he failed to grasp anything of them other than that in his sleep they had appeared to be so real, so vital, so incontrovertible. The result was that his remaining sleep was troubled and broken. When he fully woke in the morning he already on waking felt exhausted and his mood was disconsolate. In the mid-morning he dragged himself to the porch where he sat with a pot of tea he constantly replenished and the book with "For Mad People Only" written across it lying in his lap. He sat all day and stared at the world before him, the long line of craggy shore, the waves falling on the jagged stones, Jean's house floating in a hazy grey light, and beyond it the vast gleaming ocean and the distant shadowed triangle of Grace Island. He heard the lonely cry of the curlew like that of a disconsolate woman. He sat again the next day in the porch, and the next, and the next, until an entire week had passed. He did nothing, he read nothing, he wrote nothing, he thought nothing. He merely sat and stared at the scenes in front of his eyes as if mesmerised and pinned down physically by them. But all the while he felt inside his unmoving body a sea of sadness drowning his heart and the most complete loneliness he had ever felt, like a solid wall he stood facing, or like some immense wave of the sea towering over him, and which he could not penetrate or emerge from. At night he slept profoundly, helplessly, and without dreams. In the mornings he rose slowly, reluctantly, to take his position again in the porch and stare out upon what was now his entire world and which could not have appeared more bereft, or more remote, beyond any redemption at all that he could imagine that might come its way, or his way. It was a dead world. A dead world. His, he realised with some fatality, was a dead world.

One day finally he roused himself and made himself walk to Jean's house. There was something he needed to do there. It was unchanged of course since his visit with Helen, with a thick layer of dust over everything and the same dishevelled appearance, the same mingling smells of damp and decay in the atmosphere. Unhesitatingly he made his way to the chest he had pushed back into the corner beneath the wooden stairs and he opened it. He was relieved there was no horrid animal scurrying about among the papers deep in the bottom of the box. Little by little he pulled everything out of the box, the loose sheets of paper with the large handwriting, and beneath these pages he found photographs. There was some little sign of damage from the damp condition of the house but otherwise the pages and photographs were perfectly intact. He made a neat pile of them and put them in a shoulder bag he had been carrying and returned with it to the cottage.

In the cottage he separated the pages and pictures into two piles. He then spread the photographs one by one on the floor of the living room inspecting each one carefully as he did so. They were remarkable. Many of the photos were of the island and village, most of them featured the headland where Jean had chosen to live and there were several of Jean's house under construction. Looking closely at these he could pick out among the men working on the building Peter Goode. He didn't recognise anyone else though it seemed to be the same group of men in all of the pictures, perhaps a team working under Peter's direction. There were photos too of Paddy and Joy, and Bill and Jane, and of most interest in some of the photos there was a blonde woman beyond middle-age who could only be Jean herself. Although older than Helen the likeness was remarkable. It was more than just mother and daughter, the two might have been twins but at different ages, perhaps thirty years apart... And in Jean's eyes he saw something that Helen's did not hold, a veil of shadow or sadness, and even something like fear, a haunted look visible beneath even the brightest of smiles. There were also a small number of photos which had obviously been taken in the States. For the most part there was nobody in these pictures, just places. There was a house among woods, and there was a lake. A couple of pictures were of Jean, standing on the porch of the house, or by the lake. She looked younger, if anything with a greater resemblance to Helen. The resemblance was really extraordinary. It even occurred to Harry to begin with that he might be looking at pictures of Helen but he realised it couldn't be and he brushed the idea away. He wondered why Jean was alone in the pictures from the States few as they were. Someone had obviously held the camera so she wasn't alone when they were taken. And why was there nothing more? No pictures of family, or friends, or of Helen? Had she just kept these pictures of some lakeside cabin trip for some particular reason? But then why were there no pictures of the person who was with her, the one taking the photos? The more he looked at these pictures from back home the more he became aware of the loneliness surrounding Jean. After a while he saw her immersed and perhaps drowning in the isolation and remoteness of her beautiful surroundings, the cabin, the woods, the lake. Did he detect lovelessness? He certainly began to sense it, and to feel it. Had Jean come here to the edge of the western world to escape all that? But surely she would have found it all here just as it had existed back home? All the extreme geography of desolation... Or had she wanted to journey to the end of it? To reach the extremity of her condition here on the edge of the western world... And perhaps be finished with it. If so the lonely headland in the corner of the island where she had settled was not a landscape of hope, but of beyond hope. And as he already knew, her poor sad heart had not been able for it.

He turned his attention now to the loose sheets of paper with the large handwriting. In fact the pages were covered in what was really no more than a vast untidy scrawl that bordered on the childish and illiterate. There were no names. There was only a fearsome "I" and a "you" terribly subject to that "I", but nothing more. He looked for dates or signatures but he found none, so he had no idea what order to put the pages in. In any case they all resembled each other as if they might even be one single piece of writing. Like the photos he laid the pages out one by one on the living room floor. They were all written in the same handwriting and it was obvious they were from the same person but he had no idea who that person could be. At first he considered that Jean herself might have written them and that they might have formed some fragments of a fantasy or book but it became quickly clear that the pages were addressed and directed towards her in the most uninhibitedly abusive manner. They were unrelentingly sexual and detailed every possible animalistic variation that could be inflicted on a woman by a man. There was more than brutality. There was a kind of perverse Sadean exultation which bordered, one could surmise, on the insane. He could not imagine by any stretch of his imagination that Jean could have written them. If she did she must have been on the verge of madness, or at the very least the most violent and painful sexual despair. The two things perhaps existed close to each other.

When he had been in the house with Helen and after she had opened and jumped away from the chest, frightened by the scurrying rat, he had lifted up some of the pages to inspect them. The large and grotesquely-scribbled words had immediately leapt out even given the dim drab light of the house and the position of the chest beneath the stairs. In an instant he had picked out words of such extreme crudity and ugliness that he had let them fall back to the floor of the chest and shut it up. Helen had not noticed and after being startled by the rat she gave the chest a wide berth busying herself well away from it. He had considered what to do. The letters, he thought of them as letters, were in Jean's house and were her property. They now belonged to Helen. He thought he should share the find with her. At the same time he thought it was impossible to do so. The fragments he had read had shocked him. He did not want to shock, distress, or sadden Helen. He had decided to come back for the letters another day and look more closely at them. Already he felt glad he had allowed Helen to leave the island without carrying away with her the excoriating coarseness of these scrawled epistles.

He read the pages now with close attention. There were about twenty pages, scrawled on both sides, with the large twisted handwriting filling each page with just a dozen or so sentences, looking for all the world to him like the grotesque handwriting of a demented or demonic child. Each page and indeed each word was filled with what he could only think of as deranged sexual intent. He read reluctantly, haltingly, as the language filled him with horror and despair. The words were those most commonly used in everyday conversation as sexual expletives but here those same words were relentlessly and unrestrainedly specific in their fierce sexual determination. They read like an assault coming from the mind of some retarded pornographer. Much of what he read would have been more appropriate to the fetid surrounds of public toilet walls or perhaps in the foul atmosphere of some asylum for the degenerate, only that here they went far beyond those confines, because here they had a direct and defenceless object to assail, and that was Jean.

Who had written to her like this? And what was her relationship to that person? Did she even know the man? Were these vile and violent missives directed at her as fantasies or threats? Could she have solicited, encouraged, wanted them, treasured them? He couldn't imagine it. But why then did she keep them in the chest with the photographs? They didn't belong together. Or did they in some way? Did the letters somehow serve as a counterpoint to what the photos displayed? A hidden dimension of them, stowed away in the extremity of Jean's being, her soul? He was bewildered. He told himself the letters had to represent an assault on Jean. They would have been terrifying in any circumstances, to any woman, but to a woman isolated and cornered on the distant headland far from the village, far from her native home, they would surely have been charged with overwhelming horror. Harry came quickly to the only conclusion he could accept about the letters. Someone on the island and perhaps in the village had written them to Jean as vile fantasies or threats. She had kept them perhaps as evidence. He wondered if she had spoken to anyone about them, perhaps shown them to the police? He quickly shuttered his mind against any other kind of speculation. After all Jean was Helen's mother. Although he was aware that the human being was spectacularly unpredictable in its wayward and wild longings and behaviours, it was beyond him to imagine even without having known her that Jean had descended into any kind of perversity here on the island or even before she came here. He imagined her as a brave soul establishing herself here on the edge of the continent and prepared to withstand any adversity, even the most crude and grotesque, and the most threatening to her independence and integrity and safety as a woman. But by the time he had finished reading the letters he was himself utterly exhausted and despairing. He had looked over the edge of his western world into something deeply dark and disturbed, and what was more, it was so close at hand, tangibly present in the letters, that he could reach out and touch it. He felt both his heart and his head throbbing with desperation. He resolved to probe a little with Paddy when next he saw him. And then he just lay there, exhausted and unthinking, supine on the living room floor, arms spread wide, and sprawled without knowing it over the photos and letters as if he and they were some kind of novel and pitiless crucifix.

A few days later his Norwegian friend called. His name was Nick and Harry had met him years before when working during the summer as a nursing aide in a Dublin convalescent home where Nick's father was residing. They had liked each other and had kept in touch but rarely saw each other. Hearing that Harry had moved to Inish had prompted Nick and his wife to make the journey to visit him. Nick was a published writer of philosophical novels set routinely in remote snowbound mountainous Norwegian fastnesses. His novels were thrillers with a philosophical and sometimes occult leaning. His most popular, bestselling book was called "The Frozen Waterfall". It was about a lone university professor of philosophy who had stumbled on a terrible crime, a murder, for witnessing which he was now on the run pursued by a gang of international assassins intent on killing him. After the philosopher protagonist takes refuge behind a frozen waterfall in the midst of a vertiginous Norwegian mountain range almost the entire novel is taken up with philosophical speculation on the origins and meaning of existence while the protagonist cycles painstakingly through the entire evolution of the Tai Chi "form", with only occasional forays from the cave to hunt or gather food, the occasion for much dwelling on the beauty and cruelty of nature. The chapters were delivered in the form of "meditations" each one reaching a certain moral conclusion, a definitive statement about life, its manifestations and its intentions, while the protagonist awaits his fate, which is prefigured as inescapable violent death. When spring comes and the waterfall melts the assassins catch up with the professor in hiding and the novel provides a spectacularly violent and bloody denouement, the sensational nature of which had catapulted the thriller into the bestseller charts. The novel had also made philosophical discussion briefly fashionable in the cafés of Oslo and other Norwegian towns and cities. There had also been a boom in tourist visits to the region where the novel and its frozen waterfall were located. The philosopher protagonist had emerged not unscathed but vibrantly and indeed heroically alive from the cataclysmic finale of the novel and there were ongoing rumours of a film adaptation and a sequel.

Nick had come to Inish with his tall, athletic, long-haired, and stunningly beautiful blonde Norwegian wife, Anna. They had been married for almost thirty years and Nick loved to tell the story of how he had met her, aged twenty, in an Oslo street. After an hour of conversation she had invited him to her twenty-first birthday party in her Oslo flat. When every other guest had left he had stayed, was how Nick put it. They were very much in love and were very seldom apart. Harry felt that Nick suffered from a deep uncertainty and anxiety about life, and that the constant presence of Anna gave him a protecting shelter which allowed him to live, and to write.
"Without Anna," Nick once told him, "I'd have been dead long ago…"

Nick and Anna had travelled from Oslo to the west of Ireland by jeep. It was not unusual for them to undertake such long journeys. Sometimes they would drive from Oslo to the southernmost outposts of Europe sleeping in the jeep parked at the side of the road, or in random camping sites, or deep in secretive woodlands. To reach Ireland they had taken the ferry from Norway to Denmark and driven through Germany, Belgium, and France, to arrive finally at Calais, where another ferry awaited to take them to Dover. They had continued from Dover across England into Wales and from Holyhead on the Welsh coast to Dublin by ferry and on to Connacht, Ireland's westernmost province, and the county of Mayo. Finally they had crossed by ferry to the island of Inish, driven out of the quiet village of Killeaden, and followed the short coastal route to Harry's cottage. Without any possibility of telephone communication they had arrived unexpectedly, Harry awaking one morning to find them sitting in their jeep outside his cottage. He had had no contact with anyone for a couple of weeks and was glad to see Nick and Anna who hugged him and demanded copious coffees and a semblance of breakfast as soon as he emerged from his slumbers and his surprise to greet and welcome them.

As well as his writing pursuits, Nick was also something of an amateur psychic. He relentlessly pursued the "unseen" and the "unknown", and he often wove stories of the "supernatural" or "immaterial" into his novels. No sooner had he finished breakfast than he was exploring the cottage, deploying a couple of cheap electrical measuring instruments he always carried with him, attending to any shift in atmosphere, vibration, or temperature, that might signal ghostly or occult presences. Harry made a quick mental note to introduce him to the island's resident writer, Bill, who of course had his own interest and fascination in the same realm of the mysterious.

"Have you found anything yet?" Harry asked. "You know it is only in the night that things go bump…"

"There's definitely something here!" Nick assured him. "And I will definitely continue my researches after nightfall…"

Leaving the cottage they stopped briefly at Joy and Paddy's house. Joy was delighted always to meet new visitors, and especially now such interesting ones all the way from Norway. She quizzed them on life in Norway gathering all the information she could from them about their cold northern existence.

"Joy was born in the Caribbean," Harry explained. "She's a child of the sun… You cold Nordic creatures are so exotic to her!"

Paddy was instantly besotted with the soaring Nordic beauty of Anna and he took her by the hand to inspect his vines. The greenhouse was warm in the gathered sunlight. Anna listened disbelieving to Paddy's extravagant claims of successful viniculture.

"The grapes are long harvested!" he told her. "Come back in a couple of weeks and we'll be having our first tastings!"

With Anna at the wheel of the jeep, Harry guided them around the island, stopping at all the places he had been with Helen just a few weeks previously. Helen he thought of already as a star faded below the line of the horizon yet he could not help feeling a pang of emotion as he returned to the places he had walked with her, the deserted village with its broken abandoned houses, the ruined castle of the pirate queen, and the spectacular radiant gold of Kim beach where he had jogged behind her wanting to reach out and sweep the glistening diamonds of seawater covering her skin into his open palms. At the deserted village and in the castle Nick busied himself with his instruments, strolling about with one in each hand, trying to pick up evidence of forces past or present that might be within an electrical meter reading of us. He's trying to do with those things, Harry considered, what the rest of us do with our hearts and minds, constantly reaching out to touch and grasp all that is intangible in our world, to grasp, hold, understand, and perhaps even to keep it, whatever it is. He repented later, recognising that Nick's mind, and undoubtedly his heart too, was constantly active and searching, and that he was embarked on an unending quest for evidence and meaning lurking within or beyond the material presence of the world. Harry thought of Nick's mind as a huge question mark placed against the Universe. He's not running away from or fleeing anything, Nick told himself. He's not afraid. If anything perhaps the unseen unknown forces of the world were afraid of and fleeing him, fearful of his detection, and of his conquest of them.

"It's the skeleton of a village," Nick said. "The wind has carried away everything that is not stone... There's just stone here... and moss..."

Harry remembered reading a German writer who, writing of the west of Ireland, had said moss was the "plant of forsakenness". It certainly seemed true here.

"There must have been about five hundred people or more living here once," Nick continued.

He gazed out over the gleaming ocean.

"Where are they now?" he asked.

"Liverpool, Manchester, London, New York..." Harry provided the names.

"Diaspora people," Nick said quietly with a rueful shake of his head. "The lost Irish. Scattered on the wind."

On Kim beach Nick left his instruments in the jeep to stroll on the golden sand with his arm around Anna's waist. Late in the year the days were much shorter now and colder but still bright with golden sunlight and Nick and Anna cut a romantic picture as they strolled quietly along the lace-bordered green-gold of the waves curling and splashing at their feet. Harry sat on a grassy knoll above the beach and with eyes wide open saw Helen again, laughing and running, in bra and panties, along the beach, her wavy hair tossed bright with dazzling gold, her magnolia-white skin glittering with thousands of tiny drops of jewelled seawater. You see, there are always ghosts, he said to himself. But this one, like some others, is only here for me... Only his eyes, only his mind, only his heart could perceive her. Helen was his private, personal, living, ghost. She lived in him.

They stopped to visit with Bill and Jane at the "Emerald" guesthouse. Nick was excited by the size and age of the building and the complexity of its scattered arrangement of rooms and the puzzling meanderings of its corridors which sometimes appeared to lead nowhere but nearly always led to spacious and well-appointed old-fashioned guestrooms. Bill and Nick were on immediate great terms, they talked animatedly about writing, and Bill displayed for Nick the garish volumes of his ghost, monster, and demon-ridden island novels, before inviting him to explore the guesthouse from top to bottom with his electrical measuring instruments. Jane and Anna also melded seamlessly into warm conversation over tea made by Jane, while the men's voices could be heard drifting from different parts of the house as their supernatural exploration continued.

"We hear you've become quite a recluse," Jane said turning the conversation to Harry.

"Oh he's probably too busy writing his great novel of island life!" Bill exclaimed returning to the room with Nick behind him.

Nick shot Harry a strange look of inquiry.

"Oh, you know," Harry began to explain, "the days are so short now, and it's been cold... I don't get out so much... And then down the shore I seldom see anybody... I guess people don't see me either... I'm not a recluse. I only seem like one."

"You see no one and no one sees you! You are a ghost, Harry!" Jane laughed.

They returned to the village as the sun was setting. It was one of those deep blood-red sunsets evoked by Helen, settling in ever deeper darker colours of nightfall over Jean's distant home, until everything was obliterated, home, shore, sea, the horizon was the first thing to be fully eroded by darkness and to disappear. Harry rustled together a quick stew and they sat eating it with chunks of bread and washed it down with some full-bodied strongly-flavoured red wine Nick and Anna had brought with them. Harry sipped at the wine savouring the dense wash of its flavours over his palate and welling warmly in his throat. Afterwards they sat by the smoking turf fire in the living room, Nick and Anna together on the couch, where Harry had made love to Helen, while Harry sat in an armchair close to the fireplace. Mischievously, Harry wanted to ask Nick if he could sense any lingering vibration of his love-making to Helen emanating from the couch. But he realised Nick was switched off his ghost-hunting right now, and was simply in relaxation mode. Like his vision of Helen running on the beach, any vibrations there were existed for Harry alone. There was so much of his existence, of his experience, and of his memory, Harry thought, that was there to be captured, remembered, and held by him alone. And that must go for every living person, he felt. People were full of so much that could not be detected from the outside, not even by a mind or spirit reader, and no matter what battery of measuring instruments was arrayed against them these inward hidden things resisted clear perception, interpretation, description. He laughed inwardly at his own musings. Maybe he should start writing, he told himself, start putting things down... He might find he had things to say.

Just then Nick broke abruptly into his hidden thoughts.

"What's this about you writing? I didn't know you wrote..."

Harry carefully gathered his response.

"Well, you know, it's ostensibly my '*raison d'être*' for being here. If I tell people I'm writing they don't ask awkward questions..."

"But you're not a writer," Nick said almost accusingly. "And you're not writing... Nothing! I can sense it... Not a word!"

"Well," Harry protested feebly, "I have written some small things... a few words..."

"But why have you come here?" Nick didn't let him elaborate.

Harry responded with a long silence.

"Let him be, won't you!" Anna interrupted with a smile. "This is the end of the world here... Harry didn't expect you to follow him here with your questions. He came here to get away from questions! You're just annoying him..."

"I'm sorry," Nick said, "but I seem to need answers to everything."

Nick and Anna, exhausted from their journey and from the long day visiting the island, went to bed early. They slept in the only bedroom, in Harry's bed, while Harry lay awake on some bundled blankets in front of the turf fire. Harry heard their quietly delicate efforts at love-making before they slept. He thought it was poignant and it moved him. He was glad they were close and happy. He was glad they had each other. Harry lay awake long enough to hear the wind rising forcefully before he slept. It sometimes happened like this, the wind would rise deep in the night and sweep like an ocean of sound over the island. It sometimes became a constant rushing booming sound over the cottage and in his earliest days on the island, before Harry had gotten used to it, he had feared the wind would blow the windows in, or rip the roof away. He was glad Nick and Anna were sleeping and hoped the wind would not disturb them. He had been listening for an hour or more to the great squall of noise around him when with a sudden movement he reached up and caught a corner of the wind with his hand allowing it to pull him upwards and carry him flying forward in a spinning spiralling movement towards the deepest sleep he had known in a long long time. He was in an instant dead to the world.

The next morning when he woke the wind was still. All he could hear was the mesmerising rhythm of the sea as it came and went brushing the shore with its movement. When he entered the kitchen he was surprised to find Nick standing in the middle of the floor, perfectly unmoving, his face white as a sheet.

"I've seen a ghost!" Nick said with an air of real seriousness.

Harry gave an involuntary snort of laughter.

"Come on!" he cajoled Nick. "No jokes..."

"No, no," Nick insisted, "I've seen a ghost!"

Harry noticed Nick's hands were trembling. Quietly, calmly, he made some tea and they sat in the living room. Nick cupped his mug in his hands and stared with a lost, dismayed expression, at the steam curling upwards from the tea.

"It was a woman," Nick then said in a low secretive voice. "A very distressed woman…"

Harry said nothing for a while, struggling inwardly with his native incredulity and with his fears.

"Ok," he asked, "what kind of woman? Young, old, big, small, fat, thin, blonde or dark? What colour were her eyes?"

"I can't say," Nick replied. "I woke with that incredible roar of the wind around the house… I was stupidly afraid the window would get blown into the room… I don't know why but I got up to close the curtain… There was complete darkness… I had the fabric of the curtain in my hand when a face appeared in the window… The darkness concealed her features but her eyes looked straight at me… with a kind of desperate longing… And then she reached her hand out as if looking for mine… as if to draw me to her… as if calling me to her…"

Despite his effort at cold objectivity Harry felt a shiver rise along his spine to the back of his neck. Nick's voice continued to tremble as he spoke and his hands now shook as he sipped from the steaming mug of tea.

"Why was she calling you to her?" Harry asked. "What did she want from you?"

"I think she wanted me to help her…" Nick said, looking at Harry with a pitiful look of needing help himself.

"Could it have been a real person?" Harry asked.

"In that wind? At that late hour? It must have been four or five in the morning…"

"What happened next?" Harry asked.

"I didn't know what I was doing," Nick said. "I swept the curtain closed… It was automatic… With the curtain closed she wasn't there any longer… I felt terrible about shutting her out but I hadn't the courage to open the curtain again... I went back to bed... Anna was still sleeping... The wind was still rushing with that incredible deafening noise over the house... I tried to sleep but I couldn't... I felt so bad..."

"Why did you feel so bad?" Harry asked.

Nick hesitated a long while before answering.

"I did nothing to help her," he said finally with an air of deep regret. "She came to me looking for help. I didn't help..."

Harry had a sudden idea. He got up and walked to a drawer, opened it and took out some photos. He returned to Nick and placed the photos on his lap.

"Look at those," he said.

As Nick picked his way through the pictures Harry pointed to Jean in each one she appeared in.

"Was it her?" he asked each time, pointing again and again. "Was it her?"

Nick examined the photos carefully.

"I can't say," he said, "only..."

"Only what?" Harry asked.

"Looking at these pictures I feel the same sense of sadness, and helplessness, I felt last night when she appeared in front of me..."

"Do you think it could have been her?" Harry persisted, beginning to think there could be something in the notion of a real ghost.

Harry returned to the drawer and took from it the sheets of paper with the large grotesque childish handwriting.

"What about these?" he asked, holding them out to Nick.

Nick read them slowly.

"Good God," he said, with some revulsion, "did you write these?"

"No, of course not…" Harry said. "But do you think there is a connection between them and the woman in the photos?"

"Yes," Nick said emphatically.

"What is it?"

"Well they were written for her…"

"Strange deranged love letters of some sort?"

"Yes, very much so…"

"And who wrote them then?"

Nick sat with his eyes closed holding photos and papers together in his hands. After a long considered silence he then said,

"The man who lived here before you!"

It was like a blow to Harry. He gasped for breath and it was a long time before he could speak. In the meantime Anna came into the room looking wide awake, bright and cheerful. Her smile faded when she saw how grave the men looked. She tried to take the photos and pages from Nick's hands. He held them tightly.

"They're not for you," he warned her.

While Harry fixed breakfast for everyone, Nick went outside the house with his measuring instruments, spending a long time kneeling at the window of the room he had slept in. When he returned he shook his head.

"Nothing," he admitted. "Not a trace…"

"Maybe it was just a bad dream," Harry suggested.

"It wasn't a dream."

"Maybe it was a real woman then…"

"Oh, did you have an interesting female visitor during the night?" Anna chimed in with a laugh.

"Yes indeed," Nick said. "One of my habitual paranormal paramours…"

"Do you get a lot of them?" Harry asked with real curiosity.

"No!" Nick reassured him. "I've never experienced anything quite like this…"

Nick and Anna stayed on the island for several days. There was no recurrence of the vision of the first night and they did not talk about it. Before Nick left, Harry did take him along the shore to Jean's house which Nick explored with his instruments picking up what he called "very little activity". Harry told him about Jean.

"It's odd," Nick confessed. "I'm not getting any electromagnetic variations but I find myself consumed by feelings of distress and sadness here… I feel like I'm drowning in sadness… It's not like any manifestation of hidden forces… It's more like an assault on my heart. As if my heart has become the detecting instrument for whatever took place here."

The weather held good and over the next few days Nick and Anna made some solitary forays around the island. They returned to talk with Paddy and Joy and also stopped at the "Emerald" to be entertained by Bill and Jane. Harry remained in the cottage sitting in the porch with his book on his lap. Occasionally he went walking along the shore past Jean's house, but when he invited Nick to accompany him the invitation was studiously declined.

"I need to protect myself from all that sorrow," Nick said.

Anna laughed telling Harry how Nick now kept the curtains in their bedroom closed all the time even during the day.

"I thought he wouldn't rest until he had chased her down and caught her in his net of instruments," Harry said. "Especially after her appeal to him."

"He says he has caught her in his heart and that's enough… He says her 'reconciliations', as he calls it, are not with him… Though he plans to write a book about the experience."

The time came for them to leave and Harry stood close to the jeep as they prepared to go. Nick caught him by the arm before leaving.

"You're not a writer," he admonished him. "Don't pretend!"

They had been good company during their stay. Harry felt some loneliness as the jeep pulled away, turned a nearby corner, and disappeared from view. A minute later he saw, on the far side of the village, the jeep rising swiftly on the road following the Atlantic coastal route to Killeaden. In the sky above the cottage a lone seagull soared and shrieked like a lost soul.

Harry was troubled by the irrational fear that something terrible had happened to Helen and that perhaps she was the woman at the window. For several nights, like some desperate Heathcliff, he slept in the room keeping the curtain open at all times. Once or twice in the middle of the night he got up to stand for long intervals at the window but beheld no vision. He wondered if the face could have been Kathleen's, but why the arm and hand reaching out, pleading? He knew or believed nothing could have happened to Helen. If there was a ghost it had to be Jean. Jean had suffered here on the island. Her dreams and her heart, her life, had been broken. Or if not Jean then some other ghost. Blonde or dark. Harry remembered his initial question to Bill. Blonde or dark. Here he was on the edge of the western world, isolated, lonely, heartbroken, and aware that any number of ghosts might come to haunt him. Or at least one or two he could think of. Over the next few nights he slept dreamlessly and finally all thoughts of hauntings faded from his mind. One day the postman in his van stopped outside with a postcard from Nick and Anna representing vast high and dangerous cliffs in the south of Ireland. They expressed thanks for their visit and said how happy they had been to see him before signing off with a question Harry considered flippant, "Any further ghostly sightings?" It seemed as if far away from the island and the cottage Nick had shed his fear and his sorrow, if not his curiosity. A second postcard arrived from Dublin about a week later. There were only four words written across it. *"The woman was dark."*

It was now December and Harry had been almost three months on the island. The days had shortened as the solstice approached and there were fewer and fewer of the bright sunny days he had enjoyed so much of in the weeks that had followed the equinox and beyond. The days were often dull now and when there was constant cloud or sometimes prolonged rain the island seemed to float in a permanent semi-darkness in which the electric light in the houses remained bright all day like sentinelling enshrouded beacons. Harry often went early to bed and slept until late in the morning. He noticed his skin had lost its oaken hue from exposure to the sun in summer and had become white, as white as magnolia. Most mornings on waking he roused his dormant fire to life, stirring the live embers out of the cloak of ash which had preserved them during the night. He would place some fresh dry sods on the embers and return to bed while waiting for the turf to produce lively flame to warm the house. He had little appetite in the midwinter, nibbling a crust of bread and drinking some hot tea for breakfast, surviving on tepid meat stews in the evenings. Each night however he drank a glass or two of red wine or burning whiskey. He preferred the stronger whiskey flavours and was not unknown to overindulge. During the days if the weather remained dry, but sometimes too on days of lighter rain, he would escape on brief forays to walk along the shore as far as Jean's house. At least once a week he would seize the occasion of clement weather to cycle to Killeaden for messages. There was a mobile shop too, a van which would pull up outside his cottage once a week, and he could get small items from it. Another van brought library books and another functioned as a bank. Harry needed neither of these. Clare looked in a couple of times a week to ask him if he needed anything. Sometimes she stayed for tea. They had grown used to each other and it was not unusual for them to sit drinking their tea in silence.

"My husband says he can't make it home for Christmas," she told him quietly one day.

"That's a pity," he sympathised. "What is it? Work?"

After a short pause she answered him,

"Too many September babies I think…"

Her voice had an air of sad resignation. Her voice had the soft texture of delicate green moss on sun-warmed stone.

He rarely saw her children. There were five. The eldest was a young teenage girl, the youngest a boy just starting school. Earlier in the year before the bad weather he would see them walking past on the road talking and laughing amongst themselves. Now if he saw them at all they were hurrying past in the falling rain or to escape the encroaching darkness. There was no talk, no laughter, just a flurry of huddled shadows as if blown by the wind.

The wind was his real adversary. Harry could cope on windless days, or days of light breezes, with the pinching cold and the frequent soft persistent rains, but the more than occasional strong winds that rushed from the Atlantic to buffet him as he walked or cycled often persuaded him to stay indoors where, sitting in his porch with his book on his lap, "For Mad People Only", tapping pointlessly at the small typewriter, or making desultory formless handwritten notes in his notebook, he would watch for long intervals the grey liquid veils of rain falling down the window panes. When the winds rose high they would sometimes drown the cottage in a sea of sound where nothing else could be heard. On a couple of occasions the wind howled as it had the night Nick and Anna had arrived. It sometimes seemed as if doors and windows might be blown in, or the roof torn away. He was by now a seasoned Islandman and wasn't as alarmed by it as he had been when he had first experienced it. He did however fear that some lapel of wall or roofing might be torn loose from the building but so far no damage had been done. If it happened it happened. Hopefully the cottage would continue to stand intact against the Atlantic as it had always done since being built here on the shoulder of the ocean. Below him the high waves rolled white-capped against the village as if to wash it. Its noise was the one sure constant on the island. Its noise varied in volume and intensity but it was always there day in day out like an unceasing rhythmic voice driven by the pulse of all the Universe as if it were its relentless heartbeat, a long-drawn out, soughing, but constant heartbeat.

One day of respite when the winds fell, the rain ceased, and bright sunlight returned, he cycled to "The Emerald" to spend a couple of hours with Bill and Jane. They had scones and tea together and then Jane left to drive to Killeaden to do some shopping, leaving the two men alone.

"How is the great novel going?" Bill asked him somewhat sceptically.

"Oh you know, inspiration takes time," Harry answered defensively.

"Your friend Nick says you're not writing, just pretending…"

"Nick doesn't know what is being written in my brain and in my heart…"

"You know," Bill said with a note of concern in his voice. "You don't have to be creating a novel… Writing can help with a lot of things."

"Like what?"

Bill took his time before responding.

"Oh, everything really. Dreams, bad dreams, fears... terrors... love... lost love... sorrow..."

He looked knowingly at Harry before continuing.

"We all feel you are running away from something..."

"Maybe so," Harry said dismissively.

Bill took out some of his novels to show Harry.

"These stories help me survive here, especially in the isolation and darkness of winter."

Harry examined the garish covers with a show of interest.

"What do all these errant spirits, ghosts, demons, monsters, represent?" he asked.

"All the things buried in us," Bill replied, as if it was an answer he had had long practice giving.

Harry opened his shoulder bag and began to pull photos and scrawled sheets of paper out. He handed everything to Bill.

"I'm looking for some answers," he said.

Bill fed the photos and pages through his hands pausing from time to time to look more closely at a picture, or to scrutinise more intently one of the written pages.

"Poor Jean," he mumbled quietly a couple of times gazing at the pictures. "She was so beautiful... so full of life... of hope... dreams..."

He showed little reaction to the violence of the written pages.

"You don't seem shocked," Harry said.

"I'm the writer of horror, remember," Bill reminded him.

"Well then, writer of horror," Harry asked, "what do you think of these?"

"I think you've stumbled on one of the island's secrets," Bill told him. "I think it was inevitable that you would do so, living in that cottage of yours..."

Harry began to offer some of his own conclusions.

"Did Mary Kate's brother create problems for Jean?"

Bill sighed and sought where to begin. He began to hesitantly explain.

"He helped her to begin with... And some of us thought they were getting involved. But then there was someone else too..."

"Peter Goode?" Harry anticipated.

Bill looked surprised at first but then forged on.

"Yes. One day there was a confrontation on the lawn in front of the cottage... Frank threatened Peter with a sickle he had... Peter pointed a shotgun at him. They were threatening to kill each other. It looked like they would spill each other's guts out on the grass there. They said they were going to. They meant it."

"So did Peter shoot him?"

"No, but Frank left the island... Peter would have shot him."

"So was Peter also involved with Jean?"

Bill reflected on this.

"Some say he was, but I don't think so... It's complicated..."

"Could both men have been involved with Jean?"

"Maybe... I don't know... Perhaps there was no involvement at all with either man. Jean was ultimately an independent reserved strong woman... But she was alone. The edge of the western world is not always an easy place to be. She may just have been trying to manage their attentions..."

"Yes, but then Frank grew tired of being managed, he got out of control and began to write those terrible pages."

The two men sat in silence for a time.

"What if I asked Peter?" Harry suggested.

"I suppose you could ask Peter," Bill said, "but I wouldn't..."

"Why not?"

"It's the island..." Bill told him. "We have to leave people their secrets... their privacy if you prefer..."

"So Peter was defending Jean, we can at least assume that?"

"Yes we can!" Bill confirmed.

Harry took his time before continuing.

"I have something else I want to ask," he said.

Bill looked with curiosity at him, "What is it?"

Harry plunged in where he really feared to go.

"Kathleen called to me one evening... as it was getting dark... You know her? From the post office."

"Ah," Bill said knowingly.

It was neither a question nor an affirmation, it was simply an acknowledgement.

"She denied afterwards that she had come to me. She seemed to think I might have imagined it!"

"Well, did you?" Bill asked.

Harry sighed with frustration.

"Of course not..."

"So what do you want to know now?" Bill asked coyly.

"Maybe you can tell me what's going on?"

"I have to disappoint you," Bill said resignedly, "but I can't…"

Harry considered this for a time before he persisted.

"Is there any connection with what we've just been talking about?"

Bill shot him a quizzical look.

"I mean," explained Harry, "was there any connection between Kathleen, Frank, Peter, and even Jean?"

"I don't believe there was any connection between Kathleen and Jean…" Bill said, adding quickly, "she didn't write those pages if that's what you mean…"

"I think we know Frank in his wisdom wrote those," Harry said.

"I always had him down for a psychopath," Bill spat out. "I'm glad Peter drove him out… I only shudder to think what he's up to now wherever he is."

"Perhaps the two men had more than Jean between them?" Harry asked.

"Do you mean Kathleen?" Bill asked.

"Do you know?" Harry responded with a question.

Bill sat in silence for a long time, then emitting a prolonged sigh, he conceded,

"It was well-known Kathleen was sleeping with both men… Everyone thinks that's what they were fighting about in front of the cottage. Only I knew the argument was over Jean."

"How did you know?" Harry asked.

After a long considered silence Bill told him,

"Because Jean told me."

"Ok," Harry went on, "and did she tell you about Frank's literary efforts?"

Bill nodded.

"Peter Goode did us all a favour getting him away from the island."

Harry laughed.

"So Peter saved both women from the fire-breathing dragon... That's good! No pun intended..."

"It was for the best," Bill told him. "The island is better off without Frank..."

"And what after?" Harry wondered. "Jean's heart broke under the strain... She returned home to die. Are Peter and Kathleen still together?"

"I don't really know," Bill said. "I think they see each other from time to time... They have to."

"Why so?"

"Peter is the father of Kathleen's child," Bill told him.

Harry absorbed this before continuing.

"Paddy says Frank fathered the child. He seems pretty sure of it."

"I know... but I don't think so..."

"Why not?"

Raising an eyebrow, Bill answered,

"I just don't think he was capable. You can see it in the letters. There's so much impotent rage."

There was no tension between the two men as Harry was leaving. Harry was glad of the information he had gleaned. They shook hands warmly.

"Thanks for clearing things up for me..." Harry said.

"You've learned a lot since you came here," Bill told him. "You know half the island folklore by now..."

"I'll have to learn the other half," Harry said mounting his bicycle.

"I'm not sure that's such a good idea," Bill said.

Bill caught the handlebars of the bike to stop him leaving.

"Just don't imagine things about Jean," he admonished. "I don't believe she had any close involvement with either man, apart from perhaps a few friendly words... or whatever business she needed done with them."

Harry understood there was more to come. He put his feet down firmly on the ground, realising this could take a little time.

"I wish you could have known Jean," Bill said, his voice full of warmth and sadness. "She was a beautiful woman, blonde, bright, radiant, with remarkable green-gold eyes... piercing... She graced the island with her beauty. She lit us up. She lit me up. She made your village and all of Inish radiant and lovely. The island was so much more beautiful with Jean here. Goodness, you saw her daughter... Helen is the living image of Jean, but younger. I don't think I ever saw a more beautiful woman than Jean."

Harry could hear the great depth of love, and the great intensity of being in love, flowing like a river within Bill's words, a river of love for Jean, flowing through the world, flowing through Bill.

"The saddest moment in my life was holding her in my arms in Paddy and Joy's when her beautiful heart broke... I wanted her so much to go on living. I willed her so much to go on living as I held her dying."

Harry saw tears in the eyes of the writer of horror. He raised his hand to grasp and squeeze Bill's shoulder, conscious of the frailty and inadequacy of the hackneyed male gesture.

A quiet sob broke through Bill's troubled words.

"I realised as I held her in my arms how much I loved her... And how cruelly in one fell swoop all that love was being swept out of this world, as Jean and her dreams were also being swept out of this world... out of my world... I had known her such a little time. And here I was holding her as life was taking her away from me... Oh I know she returned home to die...But right then, holding her as her heart gave way, I knew I was holding her death in my arms! The end of her life... the end of our life..."

He sobbed and could not speak then gasped.

"That's what life gave me of Jean... What a privilege... And what heartbreak..."

Harry saw the darkness advancing over the island but made no move to go.

"Ah Christ!" Bill swore. "I think you're the only one now who knows!"

"I won't tell," Harry said, suddenly feeling terribly sorry for the older man. "Your secret is safe with me..."

Bill wiped his tears away with the back of his hand.

"You know," he said, his voice still broken, "maybe the ghosts and demons and monsters allow me to escape the difficulty, cruelty and pain of simply being human... Maybe that's what they represent."

Harry did not respond. Bill continued,

"I wrote recently in one of my stories," Bill said, "how we are born out of nothing and return to nothing... And in between we meet and connect with random people... people we encounter haphazardly... We grow close... Helplessly, we sink ourselves in them... Our desires... Our emotions... Our love... We give ourselves or lose ourselves to others. We become attached to them, so deeply attached. We call it love. And then it's all so cruelly broken. It's taken away. By life, or by death... And we are left face to face with the nothing, the no more, that comes after, in life, or in death... We live and love with all our incredible unstoppable human intensity... And in the end we reap loss, separation, pain, grief, heartbreak... So much that is proper to the human, and which we are all, without seeking it, born to... And in the end there comes the ultimate heartbreak of annihilation. We are annihilated. Our life... our love... our everything..."

"But it's not a horror story," Harry offered. "Or is it?"

"No, no, it's not!" Bill said, gathering himself together. "It's a human story... All too human!"

The two men stood in silence for a while as the darkness gathered, and then Bill concluded,

"I console myself sometimes by thinking, or by telling myself, that that is why Jean came here to the extreme edge of the western world with nowhere left to go... I think she might have come here to die in my arms. To be gathered into and to die in the arms of someone who loved her."

"Perhaps that was her dream," Harry said.

Harry cycled fast to get back to the cottage before sunset and darkness. As he shot down the road past the church and pub into the village there was still some bright golden sunlight lingering in the western sky. There were some showers at sea and his heart leapt to see a rainbow suddenly forming and then another and then another until in the last dying rays of the sun and caught in the prismatic patterning of the rain a spectacular triple rainbow was arched across the ocean. His breath taken away, Harry had to dismount from his bike and he walked slowly all the way to the cottage, never taking his eyes off the bright triple bridge of rainbow. As he steadied his bike against the wall of the cottage and turned to look back at the scene, the sun was absorbed by the bright line of the horizon and shielded by thickening cloud. The rainbows dissipated and disappeared in an instant as brief as the dark space between two heartbeats. He stood watching for a long time as the entire scene was consumed by nightfall. In his heart there was a perfect blend of sadness and wonder. Spontaneously, and without words, he offered a quick prayer to Jean, who had graced village and island with her beauty, and he joined it to another for Bill, who had loved her so much, and who had lost her so completely.

He was surprised a few days later by the arrival late in the evening of his brother. It was one of the wilder nights with an opaque blanket of dark thrown over the island, tumultuous winds, and great turbid wings of torrential rain sweeping over sea and land. The sea was in uproar and high white waves crashed on to the road below the cottage. His brother struggled out of the car holding on hard to the door which swung forcefully to and away from him in the buffeting wind.

"I thought I'd try to get to see you before Christmas!" he shouted.

Inside the cottage they settled around the blazing turf fire and after a preliminary tea Harry poured two large glasses of burning Irish whiskey. As the fire warmed him and the whiskey filled his mouth and throat with warm flavours his brother, now sheltered from the storm, made low noises of quiet satisfaction.

"I was at a work meeting in Westport," he explained. "I thought I'd pop up here... I don't think the storm was forecast. It caught me by surprise!"

The two brothers had not been in touch since Harry had come to live on the island. There had just been a letter from his brother announcing vaguely a possible visit. And now he was here. It was a nice surprise.

"So tell me about it," his brother encouraged him. "How has island life been treating you?"

It reminded Harry of the time they had sat on another wild night by a fire in the pub in Westport and he had told his brother about his cycle trip through the west coast of Ireland in search of a cottage. As he recounted now his adventures on the island he recalled in parallel, in the silence of his mind, the young girl and her brother walking by the Shannon, the wild horses charging through the streets of Limerick, the vast bare sun-warmed stones of the Burren, the opulent waterfall rich with fleeting rainbows, luminous and glittering with jewels, in its underground cave system, the hot sun on the beach at Carna, the exquisite cold of the green-gold Atlantic he swam in, the animatedly gorgeous red-haired American girl in the Kinvara hostel (on yet another night of storm, crazy and electrical), the heavy veils of rain as he cycled around Killary Harbour, the mysterious light-filled ambiance of Delphi, and the pure translucent sunlight sweeping through Doolough Valley. He recalled too, darkly, the wounded crow he had rescued from the road and how blood had run through its black feathers on to his fingers. How later he heard its neck had been wrung by the son of the woman he had left the bird with. He recalled too with some bitter-sweetness, although he had not spoken about it with his brother, the young French woman who had clambered on top of him during the night in Cong. It was all only a few months ago and yet he understood that all the vastness of time now stood between him and these things, these places, and these people, and that in the future they would only be part of him in so much and for as long as memory could hold them, if indeed it could hold them. If he wanted it to hold them.

His brother was enthralled by Harry's stories of the island, his description of the landscape, the mountains and beaches, the deserted village, and the castle of the pirate queen. Harry told him about his adventures saving sheep and his sole day on the bog with Paddy. He spun out the tale of the boat trip to Grace Island and the guided tour from Tim, aided and abetted by Paddy. He told him about Paddy and Joy, about Bill and Jane, and the visit of Nick and Anna. After some hesitation he told his brother about the ghost Nick had seen but they both laughed it off as an oddness on the part of Nick, some ragged illusion of broken sleep. Reinforced by whiskey they felt they had nothing to fear from extraneous spirits. Harry told his brother about Jean's house, and Jean's sad fate, but he said nothing of his found trove of photos or the pages written by Frank, or anything of what he had learned from Bill. Nor did he mention Helen, except to say that Jean's daughter had visited the island. And he said nothing at all about Kathleen. He said nothing either of the many long days when he sat in the porch doing nothing, thinking nothing, staring blankly down the shore towards Jean's derelict cabin, waiting for sunset and nightfall with a book he never read on his lap, tapping out senseless sequences on the typewriter, or filling his notebook with disjointed words and pointless phrases.

It was late at night but Harry had kept the fire glowing. The wind was still howling around the house and the rain continued to pulse like a snare drum on the windows. They had finished a whole bottle of whiskey. When he caught his brother yawning Harry counselled sleep,

"Perchance to dream!" his brother said.

As he had done with Nick and Anna, Harry ceded the bedroom to his brother and stretched himself out on cushions pillaged from the living room couch to lie in front of the turf fire. His mind was full of all that he had been talking about but as he lay watching the sods of turf collapse in bursts of sudden flame upon themselves the noise of wind and rain melded to wash the images that had arisen from his mind. His last thoughts were those unspoken ones of Kathleen and Helen. It was impossible to share these things. His three months on the island had brought many extraordinary things but the encounters with Kathleen and Helen had been outlandish and inexplicable, and as such were better left unsaid. They asked too many questions that couldn't be answered. He felt he couldn't even grasp them with his mind, or his heart. He tried to but the effort instantly fatigued and emptied him and he fell, trying to catch hold of the immaterial air and light, into another deep and dreamless sleep. The next day the wild weather had abated and the morning was sunny and mild.

"No ghosts?" Harry inquired when his brother appeared for breakfast, bleary eyed from his deep sleep and the residue of so much whiskey.

"No ghosts!" his brother said with a wry but relieved smile.

Harry offered his brother the by now ritual tour of the island. To begin with he introduced his brother to Paddy and Joy. Paddy told him he could enjoy the season's first offering of "Chateau Paddy" if he stayed on for Christmas.

"I think I had better stay home with my family," the brother resisted.

Joy commented on how alike they were in spite of the six-year age difference separating them.

"You are definitely peas from the same pod," she asserted.

"People always mistake me for him," Harry told her with some jaundice. "It galls me that he looks as young as I do…"

"Or that you look as old as he does!" Paddy teased him.

With some pride and emotion Joy produced a large heart-shaped black seed from her native Caribbean which she had found that morning washed up on the sandy beach near her house. She could not believe the seed had drifted all the way, like the flotsam of some remembered dream, across the Atlantic. She produced an old black and white picture of herself as a young girl standing in a sun-drenched tree with some friends. She pointed herself out dressed in a simple white dress. In the picture she was holding one of the heart-shaped seeds in her hand as if it were a biscuit. Her other hand clung to a straggling vine that climbed above her head.

"That's me! The climbing plant I'm clinging to is the one which produces the heart-shaped seed… The plant climbs up the tree to reach the light. It spreads across the canopy. It forms bridges in the air!"

The seed was like a message from home to her, a heartfelt message.

"I grew up on one side of the Atlantic, climbing trees in the tropical forest of the new world... Here I am now on the western edge of the old world, on an island without trees. My native island speaks to my heart through its heart, from one end of the world to the other."

She pointed to the ocean.

"If I take one step from here..." she said wistfully, "I'll find myself back where I started!"

"Well let's not go back to where we started, whatever we do!" Paddy discouraged her.

"I really detest the notion of life going around in circles," Paddy told the brothers as he accompanied them to their car.

As they were leaving he remembered.

"I want to see you here on Christmas Eve," he told Harry. "Bill and Jane will be here... You will get to taste the latest vintage!"

Harry guided his brother along the now familiar touristic route he offered his visitors taking him along the Atlantic coast to the castle of the pirate queen, cutting straight through the island then from Killeaden to the long townland of Kill with the beach at its feet, then past the glittering lake on the way to the deserted village, and then on to spectacular Kim beach where they walked kicking the golden sand up at each step. They stopped later at the "Emerald" before returning to the village. Late in the afternoon they drove through a semi-darkness of returning rain, the wild grasses glowing orange with their strange inner light.

"That's an unusual effect," his brother commented. "The way the grasses and the entire landscape glows with that orange light... It's eerie, almost ghostly to be honest."

"It's the gloom and the rain together over the peat," Harry offered.

At least that's what he thought it was, but he really couldn't explain it.

Night was falling when they stopped at the village pub. The few locals who were there, each one with a pint of Guinness before him, were surprised to see Harry.

"Jesus, Harry!" one said with rough humour. "We could understand you not going to the church, but not visiting the pub! None of us could believe that…"

It was true he had only been a couple of times to the pub and never to the church. But how was he to explain to them that he couldn't find what he was looking for there. He had not come to the island to socialise, but to forget. How did you tell people that? I want to be alone… It sounded absurd. Forgetting, by its nature, was something you could not talk about.

"Ah sure he's too busy with his books," another excused him, without any hint of mockery. "Writing is a tough trade… It's lonesome being *an Scríbhneoir!*"

"There's always been a tradition of writing on the island," the publican proudly proclaimed.

He cast his eyes out forlornly over the few men gathered at the bar, before adding,

"Apart from one or two illiterates!"

As soon as they reached the cottage Harry built up a blazing mound of peat and poured two liberal glasses of whiskey.

"Well you do seem to be very well settled in here," his brother admitted. "I wasn't sure you could stick it…"

"Did you come here to rescue me?" Harry asked.

"I did wonder if you'd like to come home…"

"This is home. The island is home."

"I thought you might like to spend Christmas with us… In the midlands. With Máiread and the kids."

"I want to be here…" Harry reassured him.

His brother cast around lost for words.

"But why?" he said with a sudden brusqueness. "Why? You can't bury yourself here…"

Harry let a sigh of impatience but said nothing. He knew his brother was only voicing his concern for him. There was a long silence. Harry replenished the glasses of whiskey. They sat shifting their eyes from the fiery liquid they sometimes swirled in the glass and the crackling flames among the black sods of burning peat. Outside the night was total and opaque. The wind was quiet however as was the sea. The only sound was the rain whispering over the window panes. Then suddenly almost as if he hadn't intended to say it his brother blurted out,

"You can't bring back the dead you know!"

Harry felt an involuntary piercing of his soul.

"No, well then, in that case, maybe the only choice is to go and join them…"

A look of dread flashed over his brother's face.

"Jesus, Harry! Where can you go from here? What will you do?"

Harry felt a sudden overwhelming wave of emotion rise and fall over him. He struggled to contain it as it threatened to capsize or to drown him.

"Where else is there to go, what more is there to do," he asked gazing into the collapsing fire, "when you have driven yourself to the western edge of the world, other than to go over the edge of it?"

He saw tears in his brother's eyes, silvery-red, gleaming with reflected flame.

"It's ok," Harry said, reaching out instinctively to reassure him. "It'll be ok…"

After a long pause, he added,

"I'm ok… I just need to rid myself of every thought, every feeling… every desire… every dream… every memory… When I've gotten all that out of myself I'll be a new man…"

"It is terrible to see you suffering like this!" his brother cried out, and added, pleading with Harry,

"I wish you would come home with me!"

There was desperation in his voice.

"I will, someday," Harry said.

But he didn't believe it, and nor did his brother.

The next morning Harry sat by his brother as he drove to the ferry waiting at Killeaden. They said little on parting but hugged each other warmly and Harry waited to watch the ferry pull away. His life seemed to be full of painful partings these days. After the ferry had gone he started on the long walk along the coast back to Dughrá. After a couple of miles he reached the castle of the pirate queen and recalled out of the blue Helen's blond tresses and green-gold eyes, along with the tender musicality of her American voice. She had sailed like a pirate through his own dark heart but he had thought so little of her, he realised, in the past few weeks. He recalled Bill's words in "The Emerald" about losing everything we become humanly connected to in some inevitable fatal cruel annihilation. He would forget Helen too, he thought, inevitably, effortlessly, it had already begun, without his even noticing. Some things you forget without even trying, forgetting just comes to claim them. Some things are harder to forget, they stick in you. Some things you want to forget but they won't let you. You try with your bare hands to tear them out of body, heart, mind, and soul.... But you can't. You end up needing to take the knife to them. But as the knife tears out the unforgetting unforgiving living material of the heart mind and soul of you it risks tearing your life away too. But maybe that's just as well. Because... Because maybe without the part of you that won't forget there is nothing left for you to live for. You have cut away all that was essential in you. And annihilation has come early to sit in your soul. Or in what used to be the receptacle of your soul.

Harry followed the coast and eventually came to the highest point on the Atlantic route with perhaps the most spectacular views anywhere on the island. Below him small green islands were strewn on the white-streaked green-gold of the ocean. In the distance the emerald green of Grace Island's steeply-sided triangle of mountain looked diminished in its veils of shadow. Night could come quickly in the island's deep midwinter and Harry hurried his step to get home before sunset. Once back at the cottage he poured some whiskey and sat in the porch. He switched no lights on. He saw Clare and her children flitting past like vague shadows. He regretted not having left a light burning for them. He turned the living room light on and kicked the fire to a low constant flame. He returned then to the porch to gaze out at the erosion of his world in deepening darkness. He remembered his words to his brother. What more is there to do when you have reached the western edge of the world than to go over the edge? He finished his thought with the words he had left unspoken for his brother. What more is there to do than go over the edge, into death itself? He sat then with his face in his hands, hidden and unseen in the darkness, weeping without tears.

It was Christmas Eve. After a simple breakfast of bread and tea and a stroll down the shore past Jean's cabin, Harry walked back up through the village to the pub which had been decked for Christmas with glowing colourful lights both inside and out. The pub was exceptionally busy, warm with a blazing fire and also the crush of so many bodies close together. A tepid haze redolent of peat detached itself from the damp clothes of the tightly-packed group to mingle with the smells of freely-flowing alcohol, beer, whiskey, and wine. Many of the faces were unknown to Harry and he presumed that they were emigrants returned home for Christmas, but everyone had a greeting for everyone. As the pubs closed traditionally on Christmas Day everyone was trying to renew contact on the eve while not allowing the last few hours of alcohol consumption on licenced premises to slip away without profit. Harry wriggled about between the bodies only stopping to talk for a time with one or two he was familiar with before coming to rest alongside Paddy who was wearing his cowboy hat with the corks bobbing from the brim, a pint of creamy Guinness held firmly in his grasp. Harry grabbed a pint of his own from the bar and drank thirstily from it. Directly behind Paddy, he was surprised to see close to the fire Kathleen seated with a small boy playing at her feet. Kathleen did not raise her eyes towards him and seemed entirely oblivious of his presence. Peter Goode stood over mother and child watching both of them intently. He had his back to Harry and did not see him.

"Ah sure now you couldn't miss Christmas on the island, could you?" the publican shouted from behind the bar to Harry.

"Not for the world!" Harry confirmed, raising his glass up.

"*Sláinte 's saol, agus Nollaig shona!*" Paddy sang, dashing the two glasses together. "To good health and long life, and a very happy Christmas!"

At Christmas time, when the island filled up with returned emigrants from all corners of the globe, its traditions of warm welcome and hospitality reached their zenith. Just the day before, Mary Kate and Tomás had called to leave Harry a hamper of Christmas food. Alongside homemade bread, baked by Mary Kate herself, as Tomás announced proudly, there were potatoes, sausages, rashers, and eggs, some sprouts, a jar of cranberry jelly, another of mustard, a generous cut of baked ham, and some cooked turkey breast, an entire Christmas dinner in other words, the whole crowned with a bottle of red wine and another of whiskey, and the '*coup de grace*' of a plump and rich-looking Christmas pudding, again the produce of Mary Kate's hands and heart, as Tomás declared.

"We hope you won't be too lonely here over the Christmas," Mary Kate said with an anxious look on her face.

"You know you're welcome to join us!" Tomás repeated enthusiastically.

"Oh I have an invitation from Paddy and Joy," Harry said, knowing Mary Kate and Tomás would be busy that day with family visits, and not specifying that his own invitation from Paddy and Joy was for the eve and not for Christmas Day itself.

"Maybe next year!" he added with a smile.

Mary Kate looked contentedly at him.

"The island will never send you away!" she promised him.

"I've no plans to leave," Harry assured her.

After a round of desultory conversations with people around him, some of whom he knew, some he didn't, he prepared to leave for Paddy and Joy's.

"You must come up to see us more often, *Scríbhneoir*," the publican shouted after him as he was going.

He followed Paddy, who had already left - "to set the world to rights," he had said - down the hill to the two-storey house on its grassy headland. It was simply but colourfully decorated for Christmas. Garlands swayed from the mantelpiece and over the doors. A small tree with globes of light stood in a corner of the sitting room, at its summit a bright golden star. Bill and Jane arrived and Joy bustled around with plates laden with sandwiches and offered mugs of tea. Their conversation was pleasantly incoherent and entirely inconsequential and Jean was never mentioned. After darkness fell, Paddy appeared with a clear bottle of some hay-coloured liquid.

"Is this what you intend to poison us with?" Bill teased him.

"*Chateauneuf de Paddy*," Paddy said cheerily. "The latest vintage!"

"Now, Paddy," Harry protested, "I saw grapes on the vine when I arrived here in September… There is no way you could produce a proper wine in three months…"

Paddy grinned knowingly to himself but said nothing.

"An earlier harvest perhaps?" Jane suggested holding her glass out on hearing the cork popped.

"I think Paddy freezes the grapes from the previous year!" Bill claimed.

But no one would ever know the secrets of Paddy's homemade wine which had acceptable flavours of lemon and honey, and something more.

"This is a fortified wine!" Bill pronounced, with tones of accusation.

"It's got the usual Paddy spirit!" Jane laughed.

"It's very good!" Harry said, genuinely enjoying it. "*Chapeau!*"

Paddy took a bow, doffing an imaginary cap. He had known the wine would be as always a great success.

"It's hard to believe, isn't it?" Bill summoned their attention. "Here we are on the edge of the western world, out on the cliff end of Europe, enduring in splendid isolation these cold, grey and damp northern climes, and we're drinking a wine to rival the dining salons of Paris... Rome... or Hellenic Athens!"

"Have it your own way," said Paddy raising his glass, "but I propose a toast..."

He raised his glass and they all followed suit. He glanced first towards Harry,

"Here's to your continued presence and contentment among us, young man, and continued success in your writing endeavours!" he toasted, before swinging his glass around to embrace the entire company. "And here's to the continued good health and happiness of all here gathered under this roof and about this miraculous nectar... nectar of Paddy... Happy Christmas one and all!"

They all wished each other a happy Christmas and drank from their glasses.

"I'll drink to Paddy's nectar!" Bill said with enthusiasm.

"It's more important to drink *of* it, than to drink *to* it!" Paddy rebuked him with customary wryness.

"I shall do that!" Bill promised, raising his glass delicately to his mouth.

Late in the evening Harry made his way back to his cottage. He heard the lonely call of the curlew lamenting the darkness. He sprang a couple of lights on and opened the embers of the fire below fresh turf which came to quick warm fiery life. He poured himself a glass of whiskey and took up his usual position sitting in the porch. He had been there for about an hour when a shadow passed nimbly and silently through the gate. It was a woman. His heart skipped a fearful beat as he thought irrationally that it could be Kathleen. He was relieved to see Clare walking towards him, a bottle of wine tucked under her arm, and a bright smile on her face. He flicked the light switch and she was bathed in sudden light. She was of medium build, slim, light brown hair, a soft mouth and sensitive blue eyes in a neatly proportioned face warm with smiles. He had only ever seen her in jeans and boots but now she was wearing a dress of a light sky blue fabric under a denim jacket with silver buttons. Her shoes were silver-coloured and light, he noticed her feet and legs were bare. She wore no jewellery apart from her wedding and engagement rings. She had lightly touched her mouth with lipstick. She was an attractive woman. For the first time they hugged, his hands on her shoulders, as she held the wine towards him.

"Just a little something for Christmas," she said.

He lightly kissed her lips when hugging and they tasted sweet.

Inside they sat in the living room, she close to the fire, on a cushioned chair, and he sat on the couch away from it. He poured the wine and they sipped it while talking quietly with long intervals between their speech, as if there was no hurry for anything to be said.

"So your husband hasn't made it home then?" Harry asked.

"I didn't expect him," she said. "For a long time I felt he wouldn't come this year…"

"You must miss him."

She paused to sip some wine and savoured it at length before answering.

"It's hard on the children," she said at last.

Another pause followed and then looking directly at Harry she said,

"I stopped missing him some time ago…"

They had been talking for about an hour. She had asked him about his life before coming to the island. He distracted her with the story of his cycle through the west of Ireland during the summer looking for a cottage and how he had finally come to Dughrá. He even told her about drinking "*Crème de Menthe*" with the French girl in Cong and how she had clambered on top of him during the night. He admitted how he had slipped away full of embarrassment in the early morning.

"I hope you don't slip away with embarrassment from every young lady's advances," Clare said, raising her glass to form a shining question, a gleam of mischief in her eye.

"Well," he said, "I try to be courteous…"

He wondered how long Clare was intending to stay. She had already been for over an hour. He wondered about her kids. Her glass was almost empty and he expected her to go but instead she raised the glass to him again.

"Fill me up won't you," she commanded.

He filled both glasses and realised that Clare was probably drinking more than she normally would.

"I wanted to ask you something personal," she said quietly in an almost conspiratorial fashion.

He waited but she said nothing.

"Go on!" he encouraged her.

"I saw you with Kathleen!" she said.

His heart beat hard in his chest.

"What?" he mumbled with disbelief.

"I couldn't sleep that night… I came down here. I sometimes do that when I can't sleep. I walk down here to look at the cottage in darkness."

She paused and drank deeply from her wine before continuing.

"I can't sleep... I think about you here... on your own... or so I thought... So I get up... I walk down here... I look at the cottage... I think about you... I've been doing it for a long time... Almost since you got here."

Harry's heart was beating hard and fast. But it wasn't just Clare, it was Kathleen too.

"So you saw Kathleen? You saw Kathleen with me?"

"I saw everything!" Clare said, her blue eyes opened darkly wide with meaning.

"Kathleen says it never happened," Harry told her. "She says I imagined it..."

"It happened!" Clare reassured him with the intensity of conviction. "I'd swear to it in court..."

"I hope that won't be needed!"

"Well, if you doubt your own reality so much..." Clare teased him.

Harry had more questions for her.

"And did you come here when the American woman was with me?"

"Yes. I saw her. I saw you with her," Clare admitted with just a hint of shamefaced reticence.

"And did you come here when my Norwegian friends were here?"

"Yes. I saw them."

Harry wondered if he might have caught his ghost. They sat in silence and he was aware of the time passing, that it was getting late. Clare reached over from her chair and tossed some turf on the fire.

"What about your kids?" Harry asked.

"The older girl is sitting them," she told him without concern. "The younger ones are already sleeping..."

She paused again, before asking him, hesitantly, reluctantly,

"Do you want me to leave?"

"Not at all," he said. "Quite the opposite!"

She sat up alertly.

"What's the opposite?" she asked him.

It was his turn to look directly at her leaning forward with expectation from her chair. He said nothing but drank in the firelight flickering on the pale skin of her neck and legs. The light ran over her skin like warm sunlight over polished stones in the bed of some stream gleaming with summer. Saying nothing Clare placed her glass on the ground in front of the fire where the red light danced in its shining surfaces and added deeper warmer tints to the purple wine. Slowly with a look of inner absorption she quietly twisted her rings from her finger and placed them next to the glass before the fire. He watched then, enrapt, as very slowly, slipping her feet out of her light, silver shoes, she lifted them up to the edge of the chair, raising her knees to the level of her shoulders. And then with a slow sedulous motion she caught the edge of her dress and began to lift it over her knees revealing the naked heart of her body where a diamond of open, thrillingly exposed flesh summoned him to her.

"*Sláinte 's saol, agus Nollaig shona*," she whispered with a quiet and oh so beautifully musical peal of laughter as he fell to his knees and crawled helplessly towards her.

When he reached her, feeling the heat of the fire burn his skin, he pressed hard with his lips on her moist and tender flesh and he thrust with a wild and ecstatic tongue into the open diamond exposed for him, offering a sensational silken doorway through which he entered her body. He felt her hands taking the back of his head to clasp him ever more tightly to her, pulling him ever deeper inside. Very soon he was lost and falling falling falling in a magnificent perfumed swooning in which his mind and thoughts, his desires and dreams, were obliterated. Oh the perfume of her skin! He clung desperately to her waist hips and thighs, hands slipping helplessly along the smooth alabaster surfaces of her body. He was like a man clinging to the sides of a boat as the ocean claimed him. He could not win against the ocean. He knew it. Little by little he began to loosen his grasp, and to let go. He dropped down then into an ocean of sweetness. He could see nothing but darkness, and could feel or taste nothing beyond the moist flesh that filled his mouth and drowned his throat with its sensational and golden juices. He felt finally some sudden fatal annihilation rising swiftly to embrace and swallow him. And all he could hear was her voice repeating over him a softly sweet and irresistible incantation, inviting him to,

"Let go… let go… let go…"

He did let go and melting into Clare he became nothing. It was a midnight of transformation. He could not remember when he had last felt such pleasure and such peace. But oh yes, he could remember. Spilling out of the darkness of memory, out of some deep dark pool of forgetting, it was a long time ago, or so it seemed, it was Dublin, it was Christmas Eve, and back then he had clung too to alabaster surfaces from which his hands slipped, back then he had swooned too in perfumed magnificence, back then he had also drowned in an ocean of sweetness, and back then mind and thoughts, desires and dreams were obliterated, and back then he had fallen towards some swift and fatal annihilation. And back then he had "let go… let go… let go…"

Letting go he slipped away from Clare, from himself, and from everything he had ever known. The last thing he was aware of as he let himself go more completely than he had ever done in the past was a single word blossoming from the heart of Clare's quiet and musical laughter,

"*Chapeau!*" she said.

And in the narrow interval of those two musical syllables of sound Harry succumbed and was gone like a flash, utterly consumed, as if he had never existed.

His annihilation was complete.

He was nothing.

Part II

Dublin

A friend had left Dublin and had invited him to occupy his newly-vacant spacious high-ceilinged apartment by the sea in Monkstown, where he could swim and sunbathe, which he did and enjoyed. It was a new scene and a new freedom. The new apartment was upstairs at the back of the building with views out over gardens and a hospital residence for nurses. The nurses rarely closed their curtains so that he had clear views into their lives when not on the wards. Usually he just saw them moving around, or sitting in the window, reading, watching tv, or applying make-up. On occasion, with some music apparently playing in the background, one or other of them would break into more or less elegant or disjointed dance moves. Quite frequently he saw them dress or undress. At first when this happened he would move out of sight so as not to be observed observing them, but after a time he resolved to remain in the high window of his apartment and simply look without concealment. None of the nurses showed any interest in him and remained unfazed as if unaware of his presence. Once or twice he raised his hand to a particularly attractive nurse, acknowledging her opulent nakedness, but his overture always went unreciprocated. He thought of the nurses' residence as a kind of bright Eden or Paradise from which he was excluded, a world of warmly attractive female flesh, eminently desirable, and utterly unattainable. He enjoyed observing this Edenic world but felt a certain sadness that he could never touch or enter it, other than with his eyes.

He had been living for a good number of years in Dublin having moved to college there after secondary school. His school years had been undistinguished, he had shown only a slight proclivity for English and languages in general and his teachers had pushed him towards a degree in translation. After college he survived on random assignments from different translation companies, either working from home, or moving from company to company and from office to office for days and sometimes weeks on a freelance basis. The documents he translated were nearly all exclusively concerned with burgeoning information technologies and their associated domains and had no real "human" (as he thought of it) interest or content. To get beyond the purely technical scope of these texts he wrote slender pieces for free local distribution newspapers mainly on social occasions of note, events and parties, the opening of new businesses, cinema and theatre reviews, and so on. Occasionally he interviewed people involved in amateur drama, or who featured in local small-scale Irish tv series, but also on a number of occasions he had gotten to talk to more notable personages from Irish stage and screen, both big and small. Over the years he had published thousands of small pieces which had helped to build him a portfolio and supplement his income without ever making his name known or in any way notable. He was, like most people, perfectly marginal and anonymous. He had little or no social circle, few acquaintances, and few interactions with the world around him. His life and his world sometimes seemed cut off from the outside. He was very much like an island, very much like someone marooned on an island.

His habits were quiet and contained. As a teenager he had kept to himself and was very much the stay at home type who did not follow his peers into experimentation with smoking, drinking, or girls. While one or two girls showed interest in him he had had no girlfriends during his school years but preferred to sit at home reading novels during all of his spare time. His favourite writer was James Joyce, and his favourite film was "One Flew Over The Cuckoo's Nest". After school, on weekends, and during school holidays, he worked in a local supermarket, packing bags at the checkouts, stocking shelves, or manning food counters, fruit and veg, or meat. He got on well with staff and customers and he worked hard and efficiently but he counted the minutes all the same until he could get home, isolate himself in his sitting room or bedroom, and simply read with a book held in his hands. His parents wanted him to continue after school in the supermarket and dreamed that he could one day rise to be an "assistant manager". He desperately wanted to escape that fate, the supermarket was like a cloud shadowing him, and so he colluded assiduously with his teachers' attempts to get him to college. His older brother had left home six years earlier and was working on construction projects nationwide. They had not been close while he was growing up and they rarely saw each other. The brother had his own life and was recently married and starting a family in another part of the country. Harry grew up practically alone.

He liked Dublin. He liked the new freedom of the city and he made some friends in college. He inevitably went out with a couple of girls without ever really becoming close. On a beach weekend away with one of them, encouraged and guided by her, he had had his first full sexual experience and while he enjoyed it he felt he could take it or leave it. He never took the first step with women and to be honest they never seemed overly-interested in him. As one girl in school had told his mother, "Harry is too quiet, too nice..." It didn't bother him. In college his few relationships fizzled out generally after a few weeks or at most months, the girls just seemed to lose interest and to move on to less quiet, not so nice pastures. As a translator he worked more and more from home and his occasional office stints rarely allowed him the time to become involved with anyone.

And yet over the years he grew used to brief explorations with different women and got used to sharing their beds and caressing their bodies and being caressed by them in a casual and non-committal way. These relationships would generally just end without any great declaration of intent, just sometimes the voice of a girlfriend would take on an accusatory air telling him that she had "nothing to expect from him" or that he should "make more of an effort". It sounded sometimes as if these young women were disappointed in him on every level.

"You're happier with your books," one told him.

Adding bitterly, "You're happier with nothing at all! You don't appreciate life, you don't appreciate love! You don't appreciate me!"

Time slipped by. His parents died when he was in his twenties, his father suddenly, and his mother after a short illness. He was sad of course and disappointed for them that he had not become the "supermarket assistant manager" they had wanted him to be. There was just himself and his brother now. It was about as little family as you could wish to have. He had been over a decade in Dublin and he was already in his thirties when he was offered the vacant flat in Monkstown to the south of the city, on the coast. At the time he had not been involved with anyone for a number of years and so perhaps took a deeper interest than he might have in the bodies of the young nurses who undressed for him (well he began to think of it as "for him") at all hours of the day and evening. Sometimes while he watched them he felt a warm movement ripple through his body stirring him in ways he had never really been aware of before. He even wondered if "voyeurism" might not be his "thing", but dismissed the thought. After all, how was he expected not to see what was in front of his eyes. The apartment building itself was quiet. He saw and heard almost nothing of his fellow-tenants other than vague comings and goings. Only sometimes in the evening or early night there was over his head the rhythmic creaking sound of a bed being plied by lovers. And once or twice he thought he could catch the high songlike sound of a woman's voice fraught with pleasure. These things were small, his swimming and sunbathing, the nurses dressing and undressing for him, the lovers rhythmic dance in the nighttime, the woman song of pleasure, but he understood, he could feel it, that they were operating some shift in him that was both strange and new.

The move to Monkstown marked a change in him, literally a kind of seachange. The apartment was just a few hundred yards above the sea and often during the day and evening he would walk downhill to the bay. Even though he had been living in Dublin for over a decade this was his first time to live by the sea. Monkstown was an affluent area and the tall houses were impressive. The area was popular with bathers especially around the old Martello Tower dating from Napoleonic times. In the early eighteen hundreds the British had built about sixty of these towers around the coast to defend Ireland from invasion by the French. They had never been used in anger and most now were either abandoned or transformed into museums, galleries, cafés, or dwelling places. The most famous one was the tower James Joyce had briefly lived in, in nineteen hundred and four, which stood just a few miles south of Monkstown close to a pristine little harbour known as Sandycove.

It was the start of September some weeks before the equinox when Harry moved to Monkstown and yet another grey cold damp Irish summer had given way at the death to successive days of febrile late summer sunshine people often called an "Indian summer". It was not too late for him to swim by the tower in Monkstown but also he began to take the time to walk along the coast through Blackrock and Dunlaoghaire as far as Sandycove where he could swim also under Joyce's tower in the bathing area known as the "Forty Foot", which famously appears in the first pages of Joyce's "Ulysses". In theory, and for the most part in practice also, the area was reserved for "Gentlemen", and so on days of warm sunshine, of which there was a late prolonged burst, it was possible to sunbathe naked on the exposed rock slightly away from the bathing zone. This was a new experience for Harry and he quickly learned to bask in the sun's heat and appreciate how it touched and warmed the different parts of his body. As the sun warmed his flesh he began to think in a very pleasant way about the nurses undressing in the hospital residence and often he had to turn on his stomach to pursue his inner contemplation of them without causing an offence to public decency. His favourite time to visit the "Forty Foot" was mid-afternoon when he had finished his translation work and he could swim and then laze in the sun until it sank in a great blazing ball of orange colour over the city visible to the west. Northwards across the bay Harry could see, like a silently sleeping giant, the great prostrate bulk of Howth Head, with its coves and bays, its stony beaches, its high cliffs, its lighthouse perched at its eastern end, and from where he lay, his body still warm and vibrant with imagining, he could see stretching over the vast openness of the bay an infinity of blue-pink-gold sky that dissolved the horizons of his mind. As he walked home observing a massive full moon rise in the evening sky he felt the pleasant warmth of the sun still lingering in his skin and for the first time really in his life he was aware of his body as a receptacle of sensation and pleasure which reverberated excitedly with every brushing movement it made through the silken night air. He began to look with a keener interest and a burgeoning hunger at the women who passed him on his walk, some in lightly dancing summer clothes, some in revealing bikinis, their skin deeply-browned and smooth, as they swung bags overflowing with their discarded clothes upon their hips. Back in the apartment he kept the lights off so that he could now stand naked in the darkness of his window while observing the nurses taking their clothes off, "for him". He began to feel an exciting hunger for them and would grow erect as he watched them. Sometimes he waited for his bed and the beginning of his dreams to revisit them, slipping them out of their clothes to run his body to and fro over their bodies. But sometimes as he stood watching in the darkness of the tall window his body hurt with a desire demanding to be expelled from him and which with a helpless gesture or two he could instantly release before falling to his knees with an exquisitely unendurable burning sensation in the heart of him, and the turbulent and inchoate vowels of unstoppable moans bubbling barbarously from his mouth like a broken brook.

In the day now as he worked at home he always had some of his attention turned to the windows of the nurses' residence, always watchful for the appearance of some nurse in her room, peeling her clothes off in the window, slipping out of bra and panties to stand opulently and obliviously naked in front of him. It became a constant distraction but still he forced himself to focus on his translation work and get it finished. He went down then in the mid-afternoon to the sea and while to begin with he might dip and swim below the tower nearest to him in Monkstown he ultimately preferred to walk to Sandycove where at the "Forty Foot" he would lie naked on the rough exposed and lichened stone, letting the sun go so far as to burn his body to a deep reddish-brown colour while his mind sank luxuriously into sustained reveries of sweet sweet sweet lust and febrile defilements... Later in the evening he would hurry home with a rising anticipation in his body of the ongoing cascade of ritual revelation pouring from the brightly-lit windows of the nurses' residence. And of all the conclusions he could come to while he watched. After just a month of living in the new apartment, of walking, and swimming in the bay, of lying naked under the burning sun, Harry had discovered unprecedented new states of mind, body and imagination, within himself. He had become a sexual being with a new vital sexual hunger falling like waves of the sea upon the soft and burning edges of his body. The new full moon held its one eye wide open in bright and surprised speculation. While Harry in his darkened window fell to his knees, again and again and again and again, in his most intense and exquisite attitudes of prayer.

Then above his head one night, while he was kneeling in his prayer, a volley of loud shouting, the clashing voices of a man and a woman, roared through the quiet of the apartment block and a sudden loud report like a gunshot ripped through the evening. That gunshot tore his world open.

Without thinking Harry dashed out on to the stairway only to be pushed back forcefully by the outstretched arm of a burly male rushing downstairs past him. In the surprise and confusion he barely glimpsed the large shadowy man rushing downstairs and away from him. He was caught in two minds about which way to turn, whether he should follow the figure fleeing downstairs and out of the building or whether he should go upstairs to see what had happened there. He chose to go up. There was a turning in the stairs so at first he could not see what was waiting for him, but when he went around the turning he found himself face to face with a woman dressed in a bright pink dressing gown standing at the top of the stairs. The woman had long raven-black hair, her eyes were a deep intense blue, there were glistening silent tears streaming down her face, her body was shaking, and her feet were bare. Below him Harry could hear other tenants coming out of their rooms to investigate the stairwell.

"Is everything ok?" someone shouted up.

"Is everything ok?" Harry asked the woman almost in a whisper.

She nodded but with a look of shock and fear in her face.

"Everything's ok!" Harry shouted back downstairs and after a moment he heard bodies retreating slowly into apartments and doors being discreetly closed.

Harry advanced closer to the woman until he was standing one step below her on the stairs.

"Can I help you?" he asked quietly.

Before he could finish she threw her arms around his shoulders and, her body trembling and shaking in helpless waves against his, she began to sob softly into his neck. He folded his arms around her and held her while she continued to sob. After a minute or two the sobbing ceased and her body became still, she pulled gently away from him and began to wipe her tears from her face. She looked at him now as if seeing him for the first time. She smiled a light fleeting smile which Harry took to be strangely apologetic or embarrassed, and then she turned away and walked back through the open door of her apartment without closing it behind her. Not really knowing what he should do, Harry followed into her apartment. He cast his eyes quickly around noticing the dishevelled bed, a chintzy armchair, and two half-empty glasses of red wine on a small table close to the window. There had been an argument but little sign of disorder in the apartment. Then he noticed on one of the walls a framed picture of an ocean sunset whose glass was smashed and the image of the sun, in the midst of a blood-red sky, as if it was bleeding from its wound, had been torn by some impact. Without having been asked he began to pick up the pieces of glass that had fallen on the couch and on the floor below the picture. As he searched carefully for the smallest pieces embedded in the carpet she knelt beside him to also pick at and retrieve the last scattered slivers of broken glass.

"My Atlantic dream," she said, in the softest of musical voices. "I was always saying how much I wanted to live in a cottage by the sea and watch the sunsets there..."

Harry for the instant didn't know what to respond. Eventually they seemed to have gathered all the tiny pieces and they stood to face each other, their upturned hands full of broken glass. She was shorter than Harry by several inches, was of slim but strong and full build, and she looked up at him with those intense blue eyes which seemed to say something to him he could not interpret. He wondered if she was going to put her arms around his shoulders again, and he felt he wanted to fold her in his own arms again, but he couldn't do that, could he?... Certainly not with the shards of glass in his hands. Together they threw the shattered glass into a nearby wastebasket where the pieces clattered together like some broken music.

"I heard what sounded like a gunshot," he said with a questioning tone.

She nodded but as she did so she turned away from him. She picked up one of the glasses of wine and sipped from it, pursing her lips and then smacking them.

"You mustn't tell," she said then. "My boyfriend has a gun... He got a little trigger happy. I guess he never liked my sunset picture..."

Later she would tell him how it had always been her dream from very young to live in a cottage on Ireland's Atlantic coast, on some island somewhere perhaps, if only for a few months, a year perhaps, or longer.

"Shouldn't he be reported?" Harry asked with concern.

"No, please," she pleaded. "No reports. He's a Guard... He's not supposed to have a weapon, never mind fire one... It could end his career..."

"But is he dangerous? I mean he just fired at you..."

"I think it was probably an accident," she reassured him. "I think he was aiming at the picture... I don't think he really intended pulling the trigger..."

"Even so!" Harry protested. "He could have killed you!"

Harry began to feel he had no right to probe her with questions. He thought maybe it was time to go.

"Listen," he said, "my name is Harry. I'm in the apartment just below you... I work a lot from home so if I can ever be of any assistance... for anything... Please don't hesitate!"

He was aware even as he said it of the wealth of involuntary meaning that lurked behind "for anything".

"I appreciate that," she told him, closing the dressing gown more tightly around her body and walking a step or two behind him to the door.

"I think I'll be ok," she told him softly as she shut the door after him.

It was late and while he could not sleep he stretched out in his bed looking at the ceiling above him. In his few weeks in the new Monkstown apartment he had not been aware at all of any presence above him other than the occasional music a bed had made under straining lovers and the high-pitched faraway woman's voice he sometimes caught spiralling through the air as it spun loose in pleasure. He had hardly given a thought to these infrequent sounds in any case typical of life in apartment blocks like the one he was living in. He had been much more moved and interested and absorbed in the visual feast provided by the nurses in their distant and inaccessible Eden. But now while he lay unsleeping beneath her he could see in his mind's eye the woman with long raven-black hair and intense deeply blue eyes whose voice he had heard singing in the night. Now he listened intently for any sound or movement from her. Now he felt he would never be able to stop listening, or to stop thinking about her. It must have been past midnight when he heard a quiet almost inaudible knocking on his door. He opened and she was there still wrapped in the pink dressing gown.

"I don't want to sleep in my apartment tonight," she said. "I can't sleep there..."

He let her in and settling a spare duvet and a couple of spare pillows on the floor he told her he would sleep there and that she could sleep in his bed.

She insisted on his remaining in his bed and that she would sleep on the floor and after some light mutual dissent he let her have her way. So she curled on the floor and became instantly quiet as if sleeping. He laid awake another while thinking about the intense blue of her eyes. He had never seen eyes quite like hers, like a deep dark fascinating sea. He sought for words to describe them. He thought of their colour as an opulence of silk and velvet blues, violet, indigo, cobalt, cerulean, sapphire, ultramarine… and he thought helplessly of the precious treasure of lapis lazuli. Her eyes were like lapis lazuli. Oh God, how would he sleep? He was mad… He was crazy about her already. After a time and just before he did sleep he heard her voice like a fleeting ringing of crystal in the night saying,

"I'm Claire by the way!"

"How do you spell it?" he asked sleepily.

"C-L-A-I-R-E!" she told him, spelling each letter out distinctly.

"Good," he said.

In the morning when he woke Claire was lying sleeping peacefully in his arms.

Claire quickly became part of him in a way no one ever had. While they quickly became close they did not immediately establish a full physical intimacy, indeed not for a long time. Sometimes they would share a glass of wine and sometimes she would creep into his bed to spend the night with him, but it was to be a couple of months before they made love, even while more than once or twice she allowed her fingers to tangle and play teasingly in the tufts of hair below his waist, or her lips lingered warmly on his mouth before he slept. They got to know each other little by little through conversation, and they laughed retailing stories of the nurses open divesting of their clothes in the rooms opposite, like a "gaggle of would-be strippers", Claire said dismissively. Now that Claire was in his life his interest in the nurses faded and he became all but indifferent to them. Sometimes Claire dressed or undressed in front of him, slipping her clothes away from her milk-white skin, giving him knowing looks that admitted her awareness of the full beauty of her own body which while on the smaller, slighter side, possessed a tremendously potent voluptuous quality. He would become erect watching her, and he was never reticent about letting her see his response, but he never made any move to possess her bodily, nor she him. It was as if they were both waiting for some electric moment of final consummation which would come in its own good time. And it did.

He felt things with her he had never felt with any woman. It was far beyond mere attraction or desire. When he thought about it and tried to describe it he fell upon words like "magnetism" or "gravity". He thought of her perhaps as a dark blue planet drawing him in, and around which he was now revolving. She certainly exercised a "pull" on him, and held a "sway" over him. She was a lively sometimes playful conversationalist but sometimes she would linger over long silences in which he felt himself more and more absorbed, sinking deeper and deeper into her until, lost in an area beyond words or even understanding, he floated helplessly in her atmosphere, not knowing any longer where or what he was, but feeling only the most complete contentment he had ever felt close to a woman. She was playful too in other ways, in teasing ways. She would kiss him out of the blue pushing her tongue deep into his throat. Sometimes in her pink dressing gown, or when wearing loose blouses and skirts, she would turn in such a way that the fabric of the blouse or gown fell away from her breasts, or kick her legs up revealing parts of her lower body to him in exciting sporadic flashes. She often laughed when she did this as if acknowledging the delicious surprises the normally hidden parts of her body were delivering to him. Sometimes out of the blue she would stand and undress in front of him casting her clothes off in "would-be-stripper-mode" for his delight. She would finish with a laugh and a flourish of her arms above her head before climbing into bed to sleep in his arms, her head upon his chest while she dreamed. He wondered what the nurses in their distant residence made of these extravagant displays. Did they stop to watch? Were they envious? Did they wish sorely to have a man within a heartbeat of them, whose warm excited body they could reach just by stretching out an arm, or to dance and undress for with the same sudden flourish of laughter and arms extended in playful presentation above their heads? He thought Claire might be doing it not so much to please him or herself but as an act of revenge against the diurnal and nocturnal rituals of undressing the nurses had imposed, whether intended or not, on the two of them. He knew too it was her way of preparing him for the moment when inevitably, finally, fatally, she would invite him fully into her body where, he had no doubt about this, she would sensationally ravish and fiercely competently devour him. In the meantime there were questions to be answered.

"What about your boyfriend? Is he coming back?"

She told him about Frank, she said his name was Frank. He was a local policeman, a Guard, she had met him when he came to the building to investigate a burglary. She liked him, she said. She was always partial to a man in uniform. She liked his air of strength. And he had good hands. The rest of him was good too, she smiled when she told Harry this. They had been going out for a little over a year. He told her that he loved her but then she discovered he was sleeping with other women. He had the advantage of the uniform, his strength, and his good hands, and the rest of him. And he took it. The advantage. She didn't really mind the women so much, after all he returned again and again to her, and she liked his company, his dark brooding eyes, his deep voice, and the movement of his body in hers when they made love. But then she became aware of a wayward, violent, frightening quality in him. At first it expressed itself in foul words he used when making love to her. And then he began to hurt her. Gently, even playfully, at first, but later with more physical intent, slapping her hard, punching her, and tightening his hands around her throat, while he rained sexual swear words down upon her. She began to be afraid of him. Sometimes he put his hands over her eyes and mouth while he ransacked her physically. When she asked him to stop or to be more gentle he became more brutal. There were fits and bursts of temper. He began to break things in the apartment. He stopped wanting to go out with her, to be out with her. All he wanted to do was… her. Their love-making became more and more like an assault. All he seemed to want to do was attack her, beat her, and ransack her, while smearing her with the most vile and crazed poetry she had ever heard. And then there was the gun. He produced it one evening and little by little made it part of their sexual combats. He pushed it into her mouth and into her thighs. He made her play with it in her mouth and thighs. He hit her with it but not so hard. He cursed and insulted her and told her he would shoot her. He made her play "Russian roulette" with it… Did Harry know that game? A stupid game. She was never sure if the gun held a bullet or not. She was lucky she hadn't blown her… head off. She laughed at this. It was a stupid game. She did resist him. They had terrible rows and she asked him again and again to leave but he always returned. And she always accepted him back. Even knowing he was probably playing out the same scenarios with other women. Was she afraid? She was afraid that maybe she was starting to like it. The violent, painful humiliations, the abusive language, and the intrusions of his worst instincts on every part of her female body. She was afraid that it was starting to be what she wanted. The night Harry had met her, the night of the gunshot that had torn his world open, she had broken. She refused to let him touch her. He had tried to but she had pushed him away. They had fought together and the gun had gone off by accident, she was sure of that, by accident. He panicked and fled. If the police came and he was found not only to have an illegal weapon but to have used it his career would be over. He did well to clear out as quickly as he did. And then Harry came to her rescue. Her Knight in Shining Armour. Her gentle, quiet, good Knight. Knight Harry.

"It sounds to me like he'll be back," Harry said sceptically.

"No he won't," she said with firmness.

"What makes you so sure?"

She hesitated.

"Well, he has other perhaps more pliable playthings you know…"

"Yes, maybe so," Harry accepted, "but he has only one you…"

She hesitated again before answering.

"No," she said, shaking her raven-black hair in negation, "he's not coming back…"

"Why then?" Harry persisted.

She said then with determination,

"If he comes back I'll kill him…"

And then after one final hesitation but with the same determination as before she added, looking firmly into Harry's eyes, telling him,

"Or you will…"

Before long, Harry was totally besotted with Claire. He looked forward at all times to seeing her. Like he did, she worked randomly, finding bits and pieces of work here and there. A strikingly good-looking woman she normally worked on low-key modelling assignments or working as an "extra" in advertising or on tv series.

"I've not seen you in anything," Harry said.

"Well, I've not done any big stuff," she laughed. "And the make-up department always makes me look like an ugly sister or cousin…"

"I can't believe that!" he protested.

"Oh trust me!" she said.

Harry was surprised all the same that he had not seen her in any of her magazine or tv appearances no matter how transient as, after all, it was an aspect of his metier to follow the media. On the other hand he hated magazine and television culture. They were like everyday cultural atomic bombs as far as he was concerned. But then again if you had to earn your living from them as he did, outside of his translating work, perhaps they were a necessary evil, and could be tolerated. In any case, as they say, "beggars can't be choosers".

Claire took a ready interest in his work, especially his reviews and interviews with people strutting the stage or silver screens.

"I know him! I know her!" she would often say excitedly, stumbling across an interview with some lesser light of stage and screen.

As he was at home so often translating, and as she was at home so often between assignments, almost all the time in fact, she would often sit with him while he worked translating texts from French and Spanish into English. Sometimes she would stand looking over his shoulder which never bothered him, in fact he liked it. From time to time she'd ask him about the text, what was it about, what was that word, what did it mean?

"I did French in school," she said. "Let me see if I can translate that sentence!"

And by dint of trial and error, of guesswork, stopping and starting, while Harry was infinitely patient with her, she would often arrive at the correct outcome.

"Wow," Harry said, impressed. "*Chapeau!*"

"What does that mean?" she asked him, pleased with what she sensed was a compliment.

"It literally means 'hat'," Harry explained. "It's like doffing your hat in admiration..."

He made the gesture of lifting an imaginary hat from his head and bowing slightly forward. She laughed. She was so often ready and free with her laughter. It seemed to come easy to her. He thought she must be happy.

"Oh, I do like it when you doff!" she said.

Harry continued,

"It's like saying 'well done', 'great job', 'you're beautiful'..."

And as she giggled like a little girl he pulled her to him, sat her on his lap, and kissed avidly the silken skin of her neck and shoulder blades.

" '*Échancrure*' is one of my favourite French words," he told her.

"What does that mean?" she asked.

He traced the V-line of her dressing gown from her shoulders to her breasts.

"It could be this," he told her. "This revealing V-shape..."

And then he dipped his fingers into her cleavage, caressing ever so gently her silken skin.

"Or it could be this," he said, "this inviting separation, calling men to you... calling men to fill you up..."

And finally, he lowered his hand into her thighs pushing his fingers gently into the fabric that covered her body there.

"Or it could be this moist ravine, like a secret ravishing diamond of flesh in the middle of you, a silken or velvet doorway... that opens for the one man you allow to enter..."

When he said that he saw a rose-coloured flush of emotion swirl beneath her milk-white skin. He had never gone so far with her. In fact he had never truly touched or spoken to any woman the way he now did with Claire. He felt his voice become soft, fragile and brittle, and he thought it was going to break. He sighed with relief when he reached the end of his speech and could be silent. He held her warmly against his body. He left his hand lying in the hollow of her lap, and she settled against him cradling her head in the crook of his neck. After a while she said,

"I'm so glad I met you Harry…"

Like Harry she had not distinguished herself in school and did not get the grades she needed to attend college. With hindsight she thought she might have done Arts or Literature, after all she did like reading, and not just any old books. She had read everything by Thomas Mann, and had a passion for Heinrich Hesse, especially his "Steppenwolf" novel which, much read, was always to be seen in one corner or another of her apartment.

"I think I like it so much because I identify with it…" she told Harry with real conviction.

"Deeply unhappy, mad, suicidal?" Harry quizzed her playfully.

"Yes, that's me," she answered.

One evening lying in his arms after long minutes of silence she said quietly to him,

"I've always wanted to go out with someone called Harry…"

And after a pause she added,

"I think we might be made for each other…"

Of course she hadn't come from nowhere. She had been born and grew up in a town near the coast to the north of Dublin. She had been reasonably happy there, it was a small town where little happened but it was her world, and it was close to the sea, and she was happy with her horizons. She had always liked being near the sea. When she moved to Dublin she always chose to be close to the bay. She loved Monkstown. She had a family back home, as she called it, but her attractive mother (she claimed she got her good looks from her mother) had died when she was a young child, some random ugly illness, leaving her in the care of a taciturn brooding father who showed her little affection or interest. She sometimes went to visit him but as he only sat in silence not responding to her the visits had become less and less frequent. She had a couple of brothers and a sister. She said the one sister lived with her father but she had never really developed what she called a proper relationship with her. The sister, perhaps purposely, was usually elsewhere when she called. Both brothers had left Ireland for America. One of them was working as a policeman there, but she had no contact with either of them. With sadness in her voice and a tear or two she told him about a third, younger brother, Gerard, whom she had been incredibly fond of, but shortly after the death of her mother he had drowned in the river when he was only four, as if he had wanted to go join his mother, that's what people said, even the priest. He had been a "beatific" little boy, her Gerard. He inspired everyone with his "blessed" nature, the nuns said he was a "saint". She loved him, everyone did. She worshipped him. She had been minding him but somehow he got away. He ran to the river, which he loved, and he fell in. She had gotten in after him but some neighbour pulled her out. When Gerard was recovered just a few hundred yards downriver he was already a lifeless doll in the arms of the man who carried him to her father. Nothing was ever the same she said for any of them. There was what she called "a shadow of tragedy" on the family, on the town, on all their lives.

"I think it will always be there!" she said.

"Do you blame yourself?" he asked, biting his lip as he instantly regretted the question.

"I am to blame!" she told him looking up helplessly at him, as if pleading to be helped. "I am to blame… It's all because of me…"

He held her more tightly in his arms, not knowing what to say, while she went on darkly,

"All the death and sadness in the world is because of me… I'm the shadow of tragedy on us all!"

He saw her almost every day and she quickly became the centre of everything to him. He realised that for the first time in his life he had fallen "in love". His pulse quickened to think of her and to see her and hold her in his arms was Heaven to him. He remembered, sometimes shooting a casual disinterested glance towards the nurses' residence, how he had once thought hopelessly of that world as an Eden or Paradise that he could never enter or touch. But now Claire was in his arms an Eden or Paradise he could embrace and hold tightly to him. And still two months after meeting, despite a constant pattern of touches, caresses, and kisses, and while their bodies were familiar and sweet to each other, and their words constantly sought myriad penetrations and fulfilments, each in the other, they had not made love together. Harry didn't question it. He knew the time would come. He had once heard someone say that the most exciting part of love-making was the time spent "climbing the stairs", the "anticipation". Without dwelling on it he understood he was now in that time of "anticipation" and it filled him with a wild and constant intoxication that ran warmly through every moment, every word, and every gesture of his time with Claire.

In their first weeks together and well into October the untoward hot sun of the Indian summer accompanied them as they walked together on the coast.

"How beautiful it is, how beautiful it all is!" Claire would exclaim looking out over the expanse of bay towards the sleeping giant of Howth Head.

She made an extravagant display of taking deep breaths of the iodine-charged air. He would match her, standing face to face with her, filling his lungs to the maximum, with each breath pushing his chest out further towards her, and she would do the same, waving her outstretched arms wildly at her sides, which he would copy, and then they would dance as they exerted their lungs even further and drew in ever more sea air until they were full to bursting and even their cheeks were full and round with the salty air of the bay, and finally, fatally, they would blast all that air out towards each other's faces, still waving their arms, still dancing on the spot, while dissolving in helpless laughter. He felt so helpless with her, and so happy. Here they were, both grown adults, and yet to casual bystanders looking at them they must have appeared like teenagers or even children lost in their own silliness, as if being together, being by the sea together, had simply gone to their heads. Crazy youngsters.

He had not touched her inside, had not entered her, with fingers, tongue or penis, he had not come inside her in the ultimate expression of sexual union he so wanted, they both so wanted, but it would happen, they both knew it would happen, when one day he heard himself saying to her,

"I had no idea you were coming behind everything else... everything else that has ever happened to me..."

She wrapped herself around his waist and chest and he felt her heart beating rapidly against his.

"I am so glad of everything, everything that has brought me here to you..." he told her.

"I am so glad of everything, everything that has brought me here to you..." she echoed.

They walked together to Sandycove where after swimming in the deep cold water they stretched out naked together on the lichened stone. She admired how his burnished skin glowed golden brown all over in the sunlight. Her skin was still milky-white but gleamed with a thousand jewels of sea water before the sun burned them away. He played with his fingers on her belly and breasts trying to gather up the watery jewels into his palms but only succeeding in dissolving them. She giggled like a school girl as he tried hopelessly to grab clusters of these bright sea diamonds into his hands.

"Is this some kind of smash and grab?" she asked in mock stern amusement.

Some older men their faces taut with disapproval approached. One who appeared to be leading them said,

"This is a gentleman's bathing area. Ladies are not admitted."

Harry didn't know if it was expressly or haphazardly done but as Claire sat up in surprise her legs swung open towards the group of men exposing her fully to their shocked gaze. Immediately they backed away as if some scalding substance had been thrown towards them.

"They're like devils running from holy water," Harry scoffed, as Claire lay back in a more modest pose.

They had only a week or ten days of the unwonted hot weather but for the remaining days they chose a spot more distant from moral opprobrium to lie down and sunbathe in. The team of male "prohibitionists" who had earlier visited disapproval upon them never reappeared. Indeed, encouraged by the presence of Claire a couple of other women began to sunbathe fully unclothed nearby.

"What have you started?" Harry asked.

"If only the nuns could see me!" Claire laughed. She was a convent girl.

Both of them felt free and innocent, without a care in the world. Neither of them worked, preferring to spend almost all of their time together. Claire said she had taken the phone "off the hook", meaning no one could contact her with work assignments. Harry too turned down any work offered him. He simply didn't care whether he worked or not. He just wanted to be with Claire. He would think of work, they would both think of work, when the time came, whenever the time came. Right now, as is often the case with lovers living their own early miracle, was all that mattered. The rest of time was somewhere over the rainbow, beyond the horizon, lost in space… in the cold futile spaces without a heartbeat. As mid-October established itself and became truly autumnal they were surprised by rain and had to run for cover. Their days of naked dalliance at the "Forty Foot", their "smash and grab" days, were at an end.

After those first weeks in October the weather settled into a typical Irish pattern of cooler conditions with scattered showers. They still went for walks finding places for teas, coffees, or drinks, when the rain fell. They promised each other that in the following spring they would holiday together "on the continent".

"I've never been anywhere," Claire told him. "I'd love to see those places... Germany, Switzerland, Italy..."

She was very excited by the idea.

"We'll burn right up!" she said. "We'll lie naked in the sun... We'll seek out forty degrees... Your golden skin will burst into flame... My milky skin will boil alive..."

"Your poor white skin!" he sympathised.

Claire always enthused about the beauty of Dublin Bay.

"I sometimes think it must be one of the most beautiful places in the world!" she said repeatedly, her eyes wide and full with wonderment.

One day of showers as they walked home she gasped and pointed in silent astonishment out over the sunlit bay. A rainbow bright and intense with colour had formed. As he followed the line of her pointing fingers he gasped as a second rainbow formed above the first one. And then, unbelievably, as they both watched a third rainbow rose higher than the first two. The sky was magically transformed by them. It was like a series of bridges bright with colours above the vast reach of the bay. It almost felt as if they could rush to run on them. It felt as if the fabulous bridges were inviting, even calling, them. Claire accepted the invitation. She danced a joyous dance, waving her outstretched arms, singing a wordless childish song of glee, her eyes flashing bright with light and life and unsubdued happiness. He couldn't hold her now as she danced her dance. He could only watch as inevitably she kicked her shoes off and ran to gambol at the water's edge, throwing her arms high and kicking her feet up, singing her wordless childlike song and laughing all the while, as she danced beneath the triple arch of rainbows. He was filled with a blessed harmony as he watched her, and yet he was aware of a current of fear underlying his incredible happiness. He was afraid she was going to run into the sea and lose herself in its waves trying to swim to reach the triple-tiara of rainbow still high over the bay. He was afraid she was going to lose herself out there in "one of the most beautiful places in the world", and that she would never return. The thought really occurred to him and the fear was also real that she was going to rush out into the waves and drown there, drown herself there. He was afraid suddenly that she was going to rush out into the bay to drown like her beatific little brother, Gerard, had drowned, and that she too would go to join her mother, that she wanted to join her mother. He was afraid but before his fear could rise like a tsunami to overwhelm his incredible happiness she returned with that superb crystalline girlish laughter of hers to rush into his arms, like a dancing wave of the sea he thought, where he held her like a dancing wave of happiness or love he thought, never fearing that she herself might overwhelm his incredible happiness, and he with it, in the dancing, drowning, movement of her own incredible happiness. Incredible happiness. He held her then tighter than he had ever held anyone or anything. He determined never to let her go. Never let go... never ever... let go... let go...

That night an immense yellow full moon rose above the nurses' residence where no rooms were lit or nurses were seen but just the shadowy bulk of the long building appeared under the great yellow immensity of the bright full yellow moon. Claire sat in the tall window of Harry's apartment, her arms wrapped around her knees, and she watched intently as the moon rose high in the sky, diminishing in size as it did so. She said little just gazed endlessly out on the "big bright blind yellow eye" as she called it as it climbed the darkness as if it were a ladder.

"Just think," she told him, "this is our first full moon... Just look at how crazy and beautiful, beautiful and crazy it is... this big yellow moon..."

Later she said,

"Is it watching us? Does it see us? Does it care? Does it care about us? Or is it simply big, bright, beautiful, but blind, and crazy... And so totally indifferent to our lives and our hearts?"

She said it with such sadness that it moved him. He had not seen her in a mood like this, as if she had slipped off her blessed bridges of happiness and was now drowning in a sea of despondency. He thought that now perhaps was the time to take her and penetrate and love her, but still he waited. The time would come, he told himself, it would come... And Claire herself would announce it. He was certain of that.

On the fourteenth of November they celebrated his birthday with a meal and some wine in a pub looking out over the bay. He wanted it to be a sort of belated dual celebration as he had missed her birthday on the fourteenth of September, before he had met her or even known of her existence (how could that be?) and he wanted to "catch up, make up", he told her. They drank a lot of Prosecco and a lot of strong red wine after, far too much for the relatively small portions of food they had eaten. He had to support Claire as, not as able as he was to withstand so much alcohol, she staggered on the road climbing back to their building. He laid her down to sleep drunkenly in his bed and he sat the entire night watching over her, attentive to her every breath, sigh, and restless movement, loving her as he had never loved anyone before. He had never felt anything like this. It was so deep, so profound. He wasn't satisfied just to love her as she was now, the companion of his days, or sleeping drunkenly in his bed like this. He wanted to love all of her. He wanted his love to reach out its arms so vastly wide and embrace every single moment of her existence from conception, through birth, childhood, and all of her early womanhood to where she was now, and on beyond any sense of "now", towards everything of her life that was to come, and beyond that too, whatever was beyond that. He wanted with every iota of his being to love every iota of her being, past, present, and future... And all the timeless reaches before and after past, present, and future, in all the spaces of time and space, or negation of time and space, with or without a heartbeat. With or without a heartbeat.

They spent their first and what was to be their only Christmas together. It was not an important date or day to either of them, neither had any strength of spiritual affiliation, but a learned traditional frisson going all the way back to childhood was still undeniable and they felt a rising excitement as the day approached. They walked through Monkstown, Blackrock, and Dunlaoghaire to savour the seasonal atmosphere and enjoy the strings of coloured lights over the streets and the warm conviviality of the restaurants and pubs. In one of the pubs, as the last drinks were being served on Christmas Eve, the publican (he must have been inebriated) climbed high on to the bar above the packed crowd, raising his glass and calling out loudly in some kind of irrepressibly drunken-sounding blessing,

"*Sláinte 's saol, agus Nollaig Shona daoibh!*"

Claire, despite having done her compulsory Irish at school, didn't understand the words and so Harry explained their meaning and painstakingly recreated them with emphasis on each and every syllable until she had grasped them and they could say them together perfectly in tandem, face to face, forehead touching forehead, beneath the babble of voices around them. There was a full Christmas moon as they strolled arm and arm to his apartment. Harry couldn't remember ever having seen a full moon at Christmas before. Maybe he just hadn't noticed. There were lots of things he mustn't have noticed. But now, big and bright, blind and crazy, crazy and blind, it filled him full with wonderment. Claire sat in the deep armchair close to a fire he had lit in the little-used fireplace. It wasn't needed, but this was Christmas, and while it was not terribly cold outside, Christmas and its traditions deserved a fire. He poured some wine and they linked arms and drank from the glasses at the same time, face to face, forehead to forehead, eyes lost in eyes. He then gave her a gift he had had specially made for her. It was a piece of silver representing the moon on whose lower half was carved a rising wave of the sea. Sitting in the cradle of the wave and perfectly placed in the heart of the moon there was a beautiful intensely blue sapphire, her birth stone. She gasped when she saw it and sat gazing at it lying on the palm of her hand for a long time before asking him to tie it on its silver chain around her neck. She was wearing a light blue dress which matched the stone well. Her legs were bare and on her feet she wore a light pair of silver shoes, not really appropriate for midwinter, but they suited the festive mood of Christmas. After he had placed the chain and medallion around her neck she asked him to stand back to admire her which he gladly did. She said she would always wear it from now on. She would never take it off. And she never did.

And then as he watched her it was his turn to gasp as she raised her silver-clad feet up to the cushion edge of the armchair, pulling her knees up high to her shoulders, and with a slow sedulous movement of her hands lifted the light blue edge of her skirt to expose the open diamond of flesh, like a silken or velvet doorway, at the heart of her body. Every iota of Harry spun in dizzying circles, like some kind of intense inner molecular confusion right through him, as she said quietly summoning him to her,

"*Sláinte 's saol, agus Nollaig shona!*"

And he fell to his knees and crawled hopelessly to her until his mouth burned at the touch of her flesh and closed exquisitely over the moist and tender doorway at the heart of her, doorway to ecstasies, as his head, heart, and soul (he called it his soul) spun wildly, as if they were going to separate centrifugally from him, soul from being, from self perhaps, and everything became a blur of sound and sense as he rocked to and fro with his tongue deep inside her and her hands pulling him deeper and deeper inside her until he felt he was slipping and sliding without any hold on the smooth edges of her alabaster magnolia milk-white thighs hips waist and breasts, and he thought he might be drowning, like a capsized man clutching hopelessly at the edges of a boat he could not use to rescue himself, until she saved him from drowning, by pulling him up from between her thighs, so wet with his slaver (he was a slave to her) and her own juices, and directed his painfully hardened penis down into the profound heart of her, where he began to float upon the dancing waves of her body, and felt her breasts mouth eyes and thighs again all fill his mouth and throat at the same time so that he was filled with her, all of her, while she was filled with him, all of him, until in one sweeping swathe of brilliant crystalline light, that could not be held back from or for anything, as if it were all of the infinite brightness of everything subsumed into one golden moment of perfect and irresistible union, he felt himself jolt and shudder liquescent into her, all of him into all of her, while she battered him in a succession of jolting shuddering waves, all of her rising and falling and falling and rising to all of him, and he became her and she became him, in a way he had never experienced before, or dreamed of, or imagined before, until he felt he was no longer himself, but only an infinite ecstatic crazy blindness, so sensational, so exquisite, embraced by her, as she was embraced by him, transformed in each other, until she let him fall from her like a swooning staggering helpless drunken man, drowned first then freed from drowning, by her in both instances. The last word she said to him as he fell was,

"*Chapeau!*"

As if he was the translation of her and she of him… into a single French word meaning "hat".

"I take off my hat to you!"

"I take off my hat to you!"

"I doff myself…"

"I doff myself…"

Claire doffed. Harry doffed. He would never be the same person again.

From now on they were like one sexual being. Now that their bodies were open cities to each other they became tireless and insatiable for every pleasure they could exhaust and which could exhaust them. For a time the rest of their world disappeared from view.

"We're like an island," Claire said to him one day. "We've become an island..."

"An island in the Atlantic?" he suggested, pointing to the blood-red sunset picture.

"My Islandman!" she called him.

And he did feel stranded in her, marooned, but it was a more beautiful abandonment than anything he could ever have dreamed or imagined. They had become the entire substance of each other and their days. They saw no one and kept the phones off the hook. They continued to go out on their walks by the bay, on some days they even threw their clothes off and immersed themselves vigorously if briefly, and with exaggerated shouts of joy, in the cold waves. They visited pubs and restaurants for meals, and of course they shopped, life was still life, hunger was still hunger, but morning noon afternoon evening and night, they couldn't say for how long, because their sexual pleasure melted time, as it melted them, they resumed and continued their fervid love-making, with an all-consuming thirst or hunger, which eroded and wiped away everything else that existed, and left only their two bodies, that felt like one body, balanced on the most exquisite and timeless extremities of flesh, in the most fiery and transcendent of physical embraces.

Harry was not oblivious. He was not the type to become entirely insane and forget all his realities. He was not, he reassured himself, the "taking leave of his senses" type. He thought about things. He thought about them. He asked himself how long this intense sexual absorption in each other could go on for. He didn't want it to end but he felt at the same time it couldn't go on forever, weeks and perhaps months, but not forever. He had never heard of such a case, not even in the novels he had read, or films he had seen. But right now they had both abandoned work and neither was earning any money. He had some savings and tried to calculate how long that would last, if they were frugal, and didn't splurge on extravagances like expensive meals out or on holidays, but they still had to live, to pay the rent, to buy food, drink, fuel for the fire. He even thought about the possibilities they would have to borrow money from the bank or from his brother. He had no close friends he could ask money from and anyway it would never be enough. And Claire seemed to have no one. He had not met a single friend of hers since getting to know her and she did not speak of any, just later a friend of her schooldays now living in Germany. She seemed to have no contact whatsoever with family, and she never had work. He did not know if she had savings and he never asked, he was never going to discuss money with her if he could help it. But she was paying her own rent, wasn't she? And she was supporting herself before she met him, unless it was her boyfriend, the one who had yelled and fired the shot before running from the house, perhaps he had been paying for everything, perhaps he still was. She did have money. He had seen her pull notes from her purse or bag at times and she often insisted on paying for drinks or a meal. Money, he hated to have to think about it. Money was not love, money was anti-love, against love. But he came up with best and worst case scenarios. He assumed Claire had little or nothing, so he simply calculated his own amount of savings and added to it the likely loans he could get from the bank, by lying about working, or from his brother, who had his own family to support and so perhaps could offer very little. He wondered if he could also ask for something from social welfare or one of the charity organisations but that would be a last resort. This however was the best scenario. Pulling together all these possibilities meant they could survive for a year at most. But what a year that would be of being together all of the time, of tireless insatiable transcendent lovemaking, of being in love, as he was so deeply, profoundly, infinitely with Claire, his love without precedent. In the worst case scenario there would be only his savings to live on. At best six or seven months. His heart sank. But he felt ashamed of himself for even thinking of it, for thinking about money, for doing these inner calculations. He never said a word to Claire. He just continued to embrace her and pierce her and move and spill in her as continuously and exquisitely, morning noon afternoon evening night, as he could sustain, as she could sustain, embracing and holding him, piercing each other, being one body shuddering and jolting together, in perfect unstoppable irresistible movements of transcendence. They were addicted to each other and the sensations they gave each other. They told each other constantly, repeatedly, throughout their most torrid embraces, to "let go"… "let go"… But in their bodies hearts minds and souls they felt they could never, would never, ever, "let go"… certainly not of each other… "Can't stop, won't stop," Harry used to say as he made love to Claire and climaxed inside her. Letting go. Letting go had so many sides and angles to it. You could never really tell just what "letting go" might mean.

Harry knew when the time came they would discuss their "material needs" and find a solution. They could quite simply return to work, he to his translations and newspaper or magazine pieces, she to her modelling or work as an "extra" on tv or in advertising. It was simple, wasn't it? They would do whatever they needed to but until then they would simply remain so deeply in love and they would in all the hours Heaven gave fervently embrace and plough each other like a boat plying a rough sea or some strong animal turning up a field, crazily, blindly, to exhaustion, if exhaustion ever came. But something else pulled at Harry's mind. As far as he knew they weren't using any "protection" in their lovemaking. He assumed Claire was on the pill, after all she had had a boyfriend before him, hadn't he heard them punishing the springs of the bed above him often enough. He had never been forthright about sexual matters, he had grown up with a native shyness, he had always let women take the initiative, and so he was reluctant to broach the matter. He did on a couple of occasions ask her quietly if she was taking "the pill" but she only tossed her head back with a dismissive laugh and asked him, "Don't you think we would make a beautiful baby?" He felt any child of Claire's would be beautiful and he was ready to be the father of that child. He thought about it, he knew he needed to think about it. He had never thought of being a father, he had never thought about having a child, he had never felt he wanted to. He knew he had taken risks in the past with women he had made love to, but he always assumed if a problem arose a solution would be found. He always assumed the woman would know what she was doing or what to do. But many of his intimacies with women had been sporadic, one-night stands, or several-night stands at a push, or a matter of a few weeks or a couple of months at most, where lovemaking was often intermittent or marginal, and so the chances of creating a pregnancy were reduced, though he had known someone who the first time he had ever made love, in the high ecstasy and uncertainty of losing his virginity, had made his girlfriend pregnant and eventually become a father. Harry's odds right now he figured were all on the side of the baby. He was now making love to Claire, spilling himself inside her several times a day, filling the heart of her body with the bright pool of his sperm, over and over and over and over. She was awash with him. If they were both fertile, and he had to assume they both were, there could only be one outcome, if Claire was not doing anything to prevent it. And yet as he watched her, following her with his eyes as she moved naked around the apartment, her full voluptuous body wavering like a magnolia flower upon a windblown branch, or when he caressed the infinite white silk of her skin with his fingertips, or when he held her in his arms, gazing in her sapphire eyes as he shuddered and jolted upon her, he felt that he would readily accept any outcome borne by their two bodies and their two hearts. If there was to be a child, so be it. If it was to be Claire's child, with her intense blue eyes, her raven-black hair, her silken magnolia skin, and her infinitely tender and joyous heart, he would love it as he loved her, boy or girl, and as fully embrace it as he embraced its mother. In a few short words, keeping his thoughts secret from Claire, he considered all that their immediate future might bring and he was ready for it. In fact, he felt that all of these troubling thoughts were simply inevitably the labour pains of the future being born or realised inside of them, inside of who or what they were becoming, and what finally they would be. He refused to be afraid.

In the early spring, as the weather began to warm up again through lengthening days, Harry made a bold decision. Instead of waiting indefinitely he decided to book flights to the continent. Claire had said she had one good friend from her convent days who was now living in the south of Germany on the shores of Lake Constance. They could fly to Zurich, cross the lake by ferry to spend some days with the friend and her husband, and then turn back down south into Switzerland and Italy. They wouldn't go as far as Rome but could visit Verona, Bologna, Florence, and Cinque Terre, before returning home. When he told Claire, he had never seen her so excited. Until then her entire horizons had been bound by her home town and by Dublin and now she was going to see Germany, Switzerland, and Italy. It was a whole new world beginning. She contacted her friend, Belinda, who was happy to have them stay for as long as they wished. They decided they would spend a week or so with her and a further four to five weeks in Italy, mainly in Florence and Cinque Terre. Harry booked return flights to Zurich. Claire wanted to pay her share, but Harry insisted on paying for everything. They flew to Zurich on April the first. It was April Fools' Day and Harry felt that was appropriate.

"We're Heaven's fools," he told Claire.

"I hope Heaven will always look after us!" Claire said, warmly embracing him.

"We're Heaven's blind and crazy fools!" Harry laughed happily.

"We're Heaven's blind and crazy... fools!" she yelled at him.

He knew she was very excited but it was the first time he had heard her using a swear word with real intent and it shocked him a little. And it was the first time she had yelled at him and he was shaken by that too.

It was the trip of a lifetime for both of them. Harry had spent time in France and Spain when doing his translation degree and he had used the time to make forays into Germany, Austria, Switzerland, and Italy. He knew Rome, Vienna, Lucerne, and Berlin, none of which were places on their itinerary but they were at least places on the map he could use to cling to and help his orientation. He also had the linguistic advantage of knowing, as well as French, a smattering of words in German and Italian, in fact he could read quite well in Italian. Claire had not been anywhere outside of Ireland and her very rudimentary schoolgirl French would be of no help to her in the countries she was visiting but she knew Harry was going to guide her and that he would take care of everything. She just had to let herself go, she told him. "Go with the flow," he said. "I've been doing that since I met you," she told him. They were going to have a wonderful time.

When they arrived by ferry in Constance, Belinda was waiting with her two young daughters. Harry was surprised by her. Claire had kept no photographs of her so he hadn't known what to expect and he was more than a little taken aback to see a buxom thick-haired blonde with big bright eyes stepping forward to greet them in a bright haze of golden sunshine. Her eyes and her skin too were golden and in her light summer clothes her richly tanned breasts swung voluptuously inside her blouse each time she stooped down to attend to one of her girls. Harry felt instantly that here was a woman who knew the immense attraction she had for men and who was happy to exercise it. He felt from the very beginning she was setting out to subdue him and he felt, from the very beginning, so susceptible. He was attracted to her, he couldn't help it, especially when she stood close to him, as she quite often did, and he could feel the warmth of her body brushing his and he could smell warm musky scents rising from her silky brown skin. Her soft voice too brushed him, and she said his name often, each time as if it was a caress. *Oh Harry.* Every time he looked at her he felt a shock of desire for her but he maintained a calm, cool demeanour until he was alone with Claire in their holiday bedroom when with little ceremony and no words of desire or love he threw her back on the bed and took her, summarily releasing the desire and frustration Belinda had provoked in him into Claire's supine and helpless body. He felt some relief afterwards.

"Wow, that's a new departure!" Claire said.

He had never taken her without tenderness before.

"That's the way Frankie liked to do it!" she told him, her tone even and without emotion.

"Do you want me to be sorry?" he asked her with just a hint of bitterness. "Should I apologise?"

"No," she said. "I only want you to be happy... Go with the flow... Let go... I can tell you needed that..."

He said nothing but bit his lip regretfully. He changed his clothes to get ready for dinner but all the while Belinda was like a rocket flying through his mind. In the bathroom he leaned his forehead against the cold mirror above the wash basin and released a stream of silent sexual swear words. Oh Heaven, he told himself, I don't know if I can cope with this. But he did. Just about.

They had a tasty German dinner of sausage, sauerkraut and beers. The children were spending the night with neighbours. Belinda's husband, Hermann, was a tall solidly-built man with very few words and a constantly grim expression. He had spent years as a child in a post-war refugee camp, Belinda told them. Hermann had very little English and only occasionally smiled or nodded approval where it seemed appropriate. Harry and Claire decided to retire early and because there was a streetlamp outside Hermann had pulled the wooden shutters tightly closed on their windows, blocking out all the light. They were tired and were lying down in total darkness when the door of the bedroom opened and Harry saw a quietly laughing Belinda slip along a shaft of electric light into the room. Belinda shut the door to restore the total darkness again and she sat on the edge of the bed. Claire sat up and Harry heard the two women laughing quietly together and then launch into quiet, mainly whispered conversation. Lying on the bed he could see nothing at all in the darkness and was only vaguely aware of the relationship of their voices to each other. He was not sure who was sitting where.

"Is Harry sleeping?" Belinda asked.

"I don't think so!" Claire giggled.

They were like two schoolgirls enjoying a secret midnight tryst.

Harry lay perfectly still even when he felt the duvet being pulled away from his naked body. He wanted to say something, emit some murmur of protest, but when he opened his mouth, as if spellbound, no words came out. Shortly after, as Belinda and Claire continued to talk and giggle, he couldn't even begin to discern or follow their words, he felt a hand descending over his stomach to grasp his penis and begin to lightly stroke it. He became excited but continued to lie perfectly still and unmoving as the hand tightened its grip and stroked him with increasing intent. Who was doing this to him? Was it Claire? Could it be Belinda? Sometimes there was an interval when the caressing hand withdrew before returning. He wondered if the two friends were working in tandem. Could they be? Whatever was happening in the total darkness of the room he put his hand over his mouth to suppress any moans of pleasure rising from his throat. He was not enjoying what was happening, it felt like a torment, as if he was a plaything of the two women, but it was a sweet torment, quickly becoming an ecstasy, as the pumping hand or hands became firmer and faster with strengthened determination and he felt the melted silver moonlight of his testicles and penis rush to a frenzied head and spurt and spill messily on the now gently stroking hand and on the broad hot plain of his belly. He had managed to remain unmoving and perfectly silent during the entire performance, but he realised that whichever of the two women was caressing him, the other could not fail to be aware of what was being done to him, and so was a participant in the act, by stealth if not directly. The two friends had dissolved in inchoate laughter at this stage and he could pull the duvet back over his thighs and belly. In a little while, Belinda opened the bedroom door on another shaft of sudden electric light and she was brightly illuminated and then gone. Claire lay down beside him and wrapped her arms around him.

"Oh I love you so much, Harry!" she said and within minutes she was gently snoring.

While Claire slept the house grew vibrant with the sound of Belinda and Hermann making love. Their room was not far and Harry fancied he could feel the reverberations of their lovemaking in his own bed and throughout the structure of the wooden house close to the lake. Hermann's groans and grunts were firm, workmanlike and functional, but Belinda's voice as she was tupped rose with a golden vibrancy high above their bed, rooms, house, and any silent listeners, to sing in the nighttime itself, like a bird singing a delirious song to the moon. Harry thought he would never forget the highest pitch of her pleasure when her voice stretched infinitely over him before breaking as it came washing down on him like wave upon wave of melted silver moonlight.

In the morning Claire said,

"They can only make love when the children are away."

"I thought you were sleeping," he said.

"Oh, you know," she countered, waving her hands as if it were some integral part of her argument, "you know, I always know what's going on..."

Later she produced a handful of cream-coloured thick-rubbered condoms as if it were some delightful treasure.

"Belinda wants us to have a good time," she said with a conspiratorial smile.

He finally asked the question that was on his mind,

"Last night in the darkness was that you touching me or was it her?"

Claire sank into quiet helpless laughter.

"Oh Belinda hasn't changed," she said at last. "Oh Belinda's never changed."

But she never gave an answer to the question.

The weather continued sunny and warm all week. Hermann worked, apart from some days over the weekends when they drove to Meersburg, Friedrichshafen, and Lindau. Once they drove across the border into the Austrian Alps where they walked and sat for lunch at a mountainside restaurant with sweeping views of the neighbouring peaks and valleys. On the weekdays when Hermann was working they visited towns and villages closer to home but almost every day stopped at the lake where they could sunbathe naked in the sun. The south of Germany was not like Ireland and no coterie of protesting males ever came forward to admonish or banish the ladies. Each day the colour of Harry's skin deepened, and also Belinda's grew richer, though Claire's white skin seemed invincible even under the hot German sun. He wondered if she would develop a tan at all on their five to six-week continental holiday. Belinda was a tight taut ball of sumptuous golden flesh. She was completely free with her body and had no inhibition being naked in front of Harry. For his part he was anything but immune to her charms and sometimes felt so excited near her he was afraid he would spontaneously ejaculate. His necessary stratagem was to lie on his belly and appear to be sleeping. Once when he did this he felt a finger running down his spine to the small of his back. He knew Claire was swimming in the lake and so it must be Belinda touching him. He played dead. He didn't want to, but he did. Once when he knew Claire was a distance away in the lake he propped himself on his elbows to gaze upon a sleeping Belinda, or perhaps she was only pretending. She was just inches away from him, her skin beaded with golden drops of sweat, the moist crevice of her thighs gleaming in the sunlight. He wanted to reach out and open her thighs and unfurl the moist folds of flesh over the diamonded heart of her body. He wanted to touch and caress and kiss her there and he felt she would readily accept his caresses but struggling with himself he dug his fingers into the earth, he closed his eyes (oh it was so hard to do!), and he lay back face down to take up his sleeping pose ready for when Claire returned.

All week the two school friends were very close, spending long secluded hours alone together. Sometimes Harry went for walks or cycles to let them enjoy their solitude together. One day Claire said,

"She likes you, you know…"

"I guess so," Harry said.

"I don't mind, you know…" Claire said.

"I'll be glad when we leave for Switzerland," Harry said, meaning it.

He tried to avoid being alone with Belinda but he inevitably found himself alone with her whether at the lake or in the house. One evening late in the week Claire went to sleep in her room but asked Harry first to help Belinda prepare dinner, while Hermann was visiting a neighbour with the girls. Harry obliged happy enough to chop onions and peel potatoes while Belinda threw the meal together. Belinda that evening was wearing a beige sleeveless dress which just covered her thighs, with a long bright golden chain around her waist. She was barefoot and danced silently around Harry as she prepared the meal. They worked in silence but Harry took note of how often Belinda moved around him often close enough to brush against him. After about ten minutes she looked at him sternly without saying anything. Harry became embarrassed, lost his composure, and babbled weakly,

"What? What is it?"

She smiled a patient smile at his lack of understanding,

"*Du hast einen schönen Schwanz*, Harry!" she said with quiet intensity.

Despite his feeble German he believed he knew the meaning of the words but he babbled again,

"What? What?..."

She laughed quietly and repeated,

"You have a nice cock, Harry. You have a really nice cock!"

He didn't even know what he was doing. He had her in his arms and lifted her to sit on the counter top among the sliced vegetables, the chopping knives, and saucepans. He was kissing her face and neck and tearing at her dress. He squeezed her breasts so hard she cried out. He tore with his hands at her thighs, she opened them and, wearing no panties, he could feel her wet on his fingertips. Somehow, expertly, she had his "nice cock" out of his pants and in her hands pulling it towards her. He tore at the golden chain around her waist and it came away. And then he heard Belinda saying in that high musical voice of hers,

"Oh Claire... we thought you were sleeping..."

He swivelled around to see Claire standing just feet away, her face empty of expression.

"Nothing happened!" he said to her.

"I can see that," she said.

"Dinner will be ready in another half hour," Belinda sang.

"I'll just go back to bed for half an hour then," Claire said flatly, turning away.

Harry followed her. He lay on the bed beside her, he took her in his arms. After a while she turned to him, she kissed him on the eyes, the mouth, the neck, and then opened his shirt over his chest and kissed and sucked his nipples, and then she opened his pants and slid down him until she had his penis in her mouth and was sucking him in a slobbery frenzy. He let her do what she wanted with him and after a while he came inside her. She took him by the shoulders and pulled herself up to lie on top of him.

"Harry I love you. I love you so much. I don't ever want to be without you!"

"I have no idea what's going on," Harry reacted. "I have no idea... Are you women trying to drive me mad?"

A little while later, he told her,

"I'm really sorry we came here…"

"I'm not," Claire said. "I knew it was going to be like this… Nothing matters. I just want everyone to be happy…"

"I just want you to be happy, Claire," he told her.

"I just want you to be happy, Harry," she said.

They were suddenly talking about their happiness as if they had lost it or were in danger of losing it. It was the first time the spectre of unhappiness had arisen between them.

They enjoyed a perfectly normal dinner together with both Claire and Belinda and even Hermann in animated form, while Harry's mood had become resolutely gloomy. After dinner the two female friends retired to a spare bedroom and talked and laughed into the small hours while Harry and Hermann sat on the veranda under the waxing moon and talked football and drank beers solidly. Hermann was a lifelong and passionate fan of Bayern Munich and recounted, in a mixture of broken but enthusiastic English and German, every successful League campaign and trophy win for Harry's benefit. He even sang fragments of the most popular fan songs. Harry wondered what the "girls" were talking about. He would always wonder about it.

On their last evening they ate out in a restaurant, Harry treating the hosts. Towards the end of the meal Harry found himself alone again with Belinda.

"I'm so glad Claire found you, Harry," Belinda told him. "She's so in love with you… I can't believe anyone could be so much in love…"

"You don't?" Harry quizzed her, and instantly regretted the question.

"Oh, you know, Hermann!" Belinda said, shaking her blonde curls with frustration. Shaking with laughter she then gave some abrupt grunts and groans that Harry understood perfectly.

"Oh it's just," Belinda continued, her voice light and disingenuous, "it's just that Claire used to be so unhappy when we were teenage schoolgirls together…"

Harry found he was being drawn deeper than he wanted to into Belinda's desire or determination to talk about Claire. He didn't really want to hear anything Belinda had to say. He suspected that behind everything there was a selfish, self-serving, ulterior motive. He didn't trust her. He didn't know if she was truthful. And yet, against his own better sense, he found himself responding to her.

"I believe there was some tragedy in her background... some shadows," he said, "but I believe she enjoyed growing up in your town..."

Belinda was enlivened by his response.

"Oh we had fun, such fun," Belinda said and burst into subdued laughter again shaking in her seat. "We were crazy girls! I couldn't tell you, Harry, and the fun... the things... I couldn't tell you!"

She covered her mouth and eyes with her hands laughing behind them.

"Please don't!" Harry urged her.

But then as they both saw Claire returning to the table, Belinda said quickly and quietly to him, loud enough for just him to hear,

"Except deep down... deep down..."

"Well?" Harry now prompted her, feeling a sudden unreasonable sense of urgency to know "deep down"... "What?"

"Deep down," Belinda answered, "Claire was the unhappiest person I have ever known..."

He never had time to ask her about this. The next day they boarded the ferry back to Switzerland. When they were saying goodbye Belinda stretched up and kissed him full on the mouth. They smiled regretfully at each other.

"Take care of Claire," she said with depth of feeling. "Love her all you can!"

For a long time, until they could no longer distinguish her golden figure standing on the shore of the vast lake, they watched her diminish in the increasing distance. Harry thought or imagined he had seen an infinite sorrow of parting in her expression as they left. It seemed to him as if Belinda herself might be the "unhappiest person".

"I'm so glad to be out of there in one piece," Harry said, not sure if he was still "in one piece", or if they were still in "one piece".

"She liked you," Claire said brightly. "She said she was sorry she didn't succeed in getting you inside her... She said she normally enjoys more success with men!"

"Does she have affairs?" Harry asked.

"She has lots of offers," Claire told him. "I'm sure she's accepted one or two. You know she's very open... And so is Hermann. They go to parties. You know... sex parties... swinging... all that..."

"She didn't learn that in the convent," Harry laughed, but at the same time felt slightly shocked.

"Oh the convent," Claire told him, also laughing, "that's why us girls are the way we are..."

Halfway across the lake she said to him, fixing his eyes with her intense blue gaze,

"I really wouldn't have minded if you had slept with her... I really wouldn't... She's a friend. A wild and sexy and fun friend... You'd have liked it!"

She said it, it seemed, with total conviction and sincerity, but as she said it Harry could only recall the utter emptiness of her expression that evening in the kitchen as she stood just feet away watching his erect penis quivering in Belinda's hands, and the broken golden chain Belinda had worn around her waist, dangling limply from his fingers.

Claire was never the same again. It was as if some slight avalanche had started in her during their time in Belinda's house which, while its effects were now small but noticeable, would steadily grow to have a terrible effect. When he thought hard about it Harry could identify three moments when she could have changed, when the landslide could have begun. There was that first evening when they arrived at Belinda's chalet and overexcited by Belinda he had taken Claire brutally, without feeling. It was the time she had said to him, "That's the way Frankie liked to do it!" The second and perhaps the most significant time was when she had found him with Belinda, when they were preparing the meal together, when all the expression drained from her features and she looked so lost, so lost, so lost. The third time was that same evening when lying in bed shortly after making love they had talked about wanting to be happy, and a spectre of unhappiness had risen unnoticed between them. With hindsight he felt he had never gotten her back after that. Happiness, as they had known it, was gone. Until those moments they had existed in a perfect shell of mutual happiness, in their own world, their own islanded world. He had cogitated at length on the possible challenges of their future life together, how to survive on love alone, what would happen if Claire got pregnant, but he had never considered the impact there might be once they opened up to allow the world outside their love to enter inside and disrupt it. And now the outside world had irrupted and something, but something essential in them, to them, had been lost. Until Belinda, every movement, thought, gesture, expression, he had seen in Claire had been filled with her native warmth and positive energy, what he thought of as "happy" energy, a "loving" energy. But now from time to time he saw that native happiness slipping away and that empty "expressionless" look take its place, an "unhappy" look, but he hadn't the courage to call it an "unloving" look, and yet it was far far far from a look of love. He had identified those moments visiting Belinda when he thought the change had operated in Claire, but he also wondered, and he would never ever know the answer to this, if there were other moments, when she was alone with Belinda when some essential transformation was taking place through their interaction. It occurred to him that maybe revisiting Belinda, Claire had returned in some way to the stages of her girlhood in her small town and that amidst the "crazy, fun things" she had rediscovered there, she had also rediscovered the "unhappiest person" Belinda had described her as, the one who cast the "shadow of tragedy" on all the world, and on everyone. Much later Harry wanted to write to Belinda to ask her. And much later he wanted to return to the south of Germany to see her and ask her face to face. But he never did. It was one of those big little things in life that would never get answered.

The first inkling he had something was wrong was in Lugano where they spent a night. On a beautiful warm evening basking in the rosy glow of a lingering sunset they walked by the shimmering lake and sat to eat dinner in a lakeside restaurant. Claire was quiet all evening and, normally an avid eater, she barely touched her food. She didn't drink much either and yet as they walked back to their hotel he felt her stagger lightly against him, once, twice, then three times. He thought she was playing a little game with him but when he pushed her back he noticed how sad and tearful her face looked. He felt immediate concern for her.

"Are you missing Belinda?" he asked her.

"No," she said, her voice trembling slightly. "I'm missing something, but it's not Belinda... I'm missing something but I don't know what it is... I thought I had everything with you, Harry... but I'm missing something..."

Harry stopped and put his arms tightly around her pulling her close to him.

"You do have everything with me," he told her. "I'm going to make sure of it... I am going to give you everything... everything I can..."

They made love with an especial fervour that night. Harry realised how constrained he had been under Belinda's roof and, while even deep in his lovemaking Belinda flashed like forked golden lightning in his brain, he penetrated Claire as deeply as he could, seeking to dissolve his recent temptations, seeking once more to fully lose himself in her.

"Can't stop, won't stop," he promised her, sighing above her, while he beat with a tremendous rhythm against her thighs until he had broken her and she melted in a flood of pleasure-wracked moans and tears like a drowning woman within his arms. She had never wept during their lovemaking before. In fact he had not seen tears since the fateful night of the gunshot when she had held him and sobbed on his shoulder standing outside her apartment, he one step below her, she one step above him, on the stairwell, the gunshot that had brought them together.

"What's wrong?" he asked, truly alarmed at her collapse into tears.

She pulled him down hard upon her to kiss his eyes and mouth, his penis sliding even deeper into her.

"Oh Harry, it's just that I'm so happy," she said. "Am I too happy?"

There were tears again in Florence when she stopped dead in her tracks in front of Michelangelo's unfinished "Slaves", immense vigorous figures struggling to emerge from the stone in which they remain, forever trapped in a perpetual desperate effort to escape imprisonment, suffering, or of becoming. She stood silently before the massive statues and simply cried. Harry was so moved he was unable to reach out to touch her but could only watch as the tears streamed down her cheeks. Eventually one of the invigilators stepped towards her,

"Va bene, Signora? Sucede qualcosa?"

Claire, understanding that the attendant was concerned about her, smiled reassuringly in response and wiped her tears away. Harry took her by the hand and they walked a short distance to a restaurant on a corner in the centre of town, right behind the famous medieval octagonal Baptistery where they drank Prosecco sitting in the afternoon sun. Claire was quiet, and Harry tried to distract her with stories about the Baptistery, the Duomo, and the Giotto bell tower, all of which they could see from the front of the restaurant. He told her how Michelangelo had dubbed the gilded doors of the Baptistery the "Gates of Paradise", which did make her laugh for some reason, aided perhaps by the Prosecco. Later he took her to see his favourite work, the Cellini "Perseus" in the *"Loggia dei Lanzi"* in front of the city's town hall. She gasped when she saw the muscular naked helmeted figure, sword in hand, holding the severed head of the snake-haired Medusa high in the air.

"Creating this almost cost Cellini his life," Harry told her. "But making it made him immortal... Cellini is Perseus here, announcing his own conquest of death!"

"You can be very serious sometimes, Harry!" she chided him with a laugh. "You almost sound like a professor... But a handsome one... And I like you very much."

He was happy to see her smile and laugh again. But they never ever talked about her tears in front of the Michelangelo "Slaves".

Harry thought she would love all of the Italian food on offer, pasta, pizza, gelato, but she rarely ate more than a half-bowl of pasta for lunch or dinner, or occasionally a panino with some Prosecco. She drank little overall but sometimes after drinking she would become quiet, expressionless or absent, and if she drank more than a couple of glasses he often had to hold and steady her as they walked in the street. They continued to make love as often if not more than before, and with more intent. Sometimes it seemed to Harry they were striving to wipe away the memory of Belinda (or at least he was, but why did he think of the "Gates of Paradise" when Belinda entered his mind?) like a golden stain on them but their essential fiercely determined desire for each other was undeniable. Every time Harry felt desire for Claire he took her. She was an open city and he had established a kind of sexual carte blanche over her, his island. One afternoon, with the windows of their "*Pensione*" room open on an inner courtyard, Harry bent Claire over on her knees on the bed and belaboured her with a violent but exalted robustness. Even as he heard women's voices floating across the air of the courtyard he did not cease his frenetic rhythm but instead increased it. Glancing over his shoulder he saw two blonde women he thought could be Dutch watching him at work. One of them bit her lip as his eyes caught hers, the other woman raised her fingers to her mouth and blew him a kiss. A little while later the two women discreetly closed the shutters on their room, both waving him a tender goodbye. The disappearance of the two Dutch women released him and he whipped himself to a crescendo which caused Claire to writhe and moan with pleasure as she beat the carved wooden frame of the bed with her hands. Harry sometimes felt aggrieved at the fierceness of his own assaults on Claire, but when he held back she often came to him, spreading her thighs and drawing him towards her. Often she would caress him with her mouth and hands before climbing on him and riding him to sensational conclusions sometimes as swift, wild, and brutal as his most extravagant effusions. Once when she came, beating his face and chest with her hanging raven locks she cried out over and over,

"I'm in Italy! I'm in Italy! I'm in Italy!"

And as he devoured her breasts and held her heartbeat like some wild bird of ecstasy in his hands he felt the already familiar union of their two bodies come seamlessly together in what seemed to him a golden eternal and unbreakable togetherness.

After Florence they travelled north to the Ligurian coast and to the five villages known as Cinque Terre. Before visiting the famous coastal villages they stayed in La Spezia. Harry wanted to visit the "Gulf of Poets" and see where Byron and Shelley had been. They took a boat to Portovenere, the "Port of Venus" Harry explained to Claire, and visited the light-filled green-gold grotto associated with Byron and from where he had swum, legend had it, across the "Gulf of Venus" to San Terenzo, five miles away, to visit Shelley. They walked to the promontory church of Saint Peter which Harry told her had once been a temple to the Goddess of Love. They loved Portovenere with its brightly coloured buildings and they lunched in the centre of town close to the jetty. Harry heartily scoffed some local mussels and stuffed octopus, but Claire, despite his encouragement, was still eating poorly and merely picked at a salad mostly left uneaten. Another day they journeyed south of La Spezia to Venere Azzurra, Lerici, and San Terenzo to see where Shelly had lived and drowned and been cremated. Claire did not know the poets Byron or Shelley well, "so romantic, so tragic", as Harry told her. She had read Mary Shelley's "Frankenstein" as a teenager she said. She had fallen in love with the monster, she joked. That night making love he called her his "Portovenere" as he knelt and feasted on her thighs, drinking insatiably from her. He called her also his "Venere Azzurra". He wasn't sure of the derivation of the name but Claire stretched open and under him on the Gulf of Poets was, he told her, his "Blue Venus", his "Lapis Lazuli Venus". She called him her "Frankenstein". It was not quite the same thing, he protested, a little upset at the joke.

Before moving to Cinque Terre proper they took the train to Riomaggiore and walked together on the path known as the Via dell' Amore, the "Path of Love". They even bought from a small souvenir store one of the small golden locks to fasten on the railings along the pathway. With a marker Harry drew a simple heart with an arrow through it on the lock and above the heart a crescent moon with a bright star. He wrote their names linking them together at the H and C so that they were entwined. The lock is still there today if you wish to go to see it.

"What do you think love is?" Claire asked him as they watched a golden red sunset flood the sky and ocean with colour.

"I think it's like genius," Harry answered.

"What do you mean?"

"I think it's one percent inspiration, and ninety nine percent perspiration," Harry told her.

"I think it's the opposite," Claire said. "I think it's ninety nine percent inspiration and only one percent perspiration."

"So you think it's almost entirely a matter of inspiration?" he asked.

She hummed her response, affirmative.

"Well I suppose the end result is the same either way," Harry concluded, professorially, intruding his hands beneath her clothes.

In Cinque Terre, they based themselves in Monterosso al Mare, staying in a hotel high on a hillside overlooking the Mediterranean. They stayed for a week. In the mornings they visited the other Cinque Terre towns, before returning to lie on the sandy beach at Monterosso. Italy was more conservative than Germany and when Harry tried to sunbathe naked some youngsters gathered to heckle him. He ignored the kids but later a policeman arrived on a scooter and vociferated fiercely, threatening to put Harry in jail. Harry felt at this stage that naked discretion was the better part of naked valour and resigned himself to sunbathing in his swimwear. At one end of the beach a tortured stone figure twisted up over an outcrop of broken stone. The locals called it "the Giant". They drifted down closer to it away from the busier more exposed areas of the beach.

"It reminds me of Michelangelo's 'Slaves' in Florence," Claire said casually, but with sadness in her voice.

It was the only time that the Michelangelo "Slaves" were ever mentioned. Each day as they lay on the sand or bathed close to the shore the "Giant" gazed down upon them while twisting his body in ever more desperate efforts to break free and escape his imprisonment. Harry imagined the giant escaping but noted that having only one leg he wouldn't get far.

"And he has no arms!" Claire said sounding appalled.

"Well, then," Harry judged, but not devoid of sympathy. "He can stay trapped in his imprisoning stone, or he can fall in the ocean and drown…"

"Isn't that like being caught between the Devil and the deep blue sea?"

"Yes," Harry agreed. "Literally, between a rock… And a hard place!"

It was mid-April and the weather had become unseasonably hot. Already in Florence there had been sudden great electrical storms over the city with vast peals of thunder crashing down upon the rooftops. The storms continued on the coast and there were many dashes made to escape sudden torrential downpours. It was a long slow arduous climb from the town to their hillside hotel. The hotel was adequate and their room was simply furnished with the wall paint and furnishings all done in various shades of terracotta. Late one night to avoid the cacophony produced by their bedsprings, Harry put Claire kneeling on the floor while he made love to her from behind. A storm erupted and the lights went out, the room being illuminated now only by successive lightning strikes, all blues, violets, purples. Maybe it was the elevation on the hillside but the thunder was much louder than usual and seemed to descend right above the building, shaking it with its tremendous roar. It was deafening. The room shook and the floor under their knees trembled with it. As he moved rhythmically in and out of Claire he saw her body come and go in the wild chiaroscuro of the lightning flashes, now illumined and visible, streaked with blues, violets, purples, now plunged in a total blackness in which he could only feel the silken tenderness of her flesh warm and wet against his penis and thighs, impossibly sweet under the hands that clasped and fastened her to him. Her black hair shook wildly above the torrid stream of her moans, covering and eventually stemming them. When he was certain she was satisfied he let himself flow blissfully freely into her, and saw in his mind the "Giant" above the beach breaking his bonds and flying above the waves towards some hidden goal. A naked inviting Belinda, open wide for him, flashed golden in his mind.

"Are you the thunder and lightning, Harry?" Claire asked him as he lifted her and laid her supine upon the bed.

"No," he answered, "but I think I might be the silence and darkness in between."

But, like with many things, he had no idea what he meant by that.

"No, Harry," Claire said quietly as she drifted to sleep. "I think that might be me..."

On their last day in Monterosso Claire had an unfortunate accident. They had decided to spend all day on the beach but had ventured further away to find a more secluded area for their sunbathing. They had had to clamber over some rocks to get there and returning, with Harry walking ahead of Claire, he suddenly heard her cry out as she fell. She had fallen helplessly face down on the rough edges of the rock. She was hurt and distressed and he had to lift her and help her over the remaining boulders to where they could sit on the beach. Under her chin was badly swollen and bruised (blue violet purple) as were her elbows, hands, and knees. She was shaking and tears streamed down her face. He had become used to her tears, so many tears, on this continental journey.

"We have to get you cleaned up," Harry said tenderly.

It was difficult to walk up to the hotel as Claire continued to tremble and weep all the way. Eventually Harry hailed a passing taxi. In their room he bathed the wounded spots, pulling away the torn skin and washing away blood and dirt. From Reception he got some antiseptic cream and some sticking plasters. Claire looked ridiculous with so many bright stripes and patches of pink on her arms and legs and face and she refused to go anywhere that evening to eat. He brought her some bread and cheese and olives which she barely touched. A lot of the time she seemed to be sleeping but sometimes when he looked at her he noticed her body shaking with repressed sobs beneath the blanket. Lying beside her that night he wanted to hold her but she struggled away from him saying that it "hurt too much".

From Monterosso al Mare they travelled to Genoa and Milan before heading north to Verona. The pre-Easter full moon had been and gone and in Genoa they witnessed the religious processions of Holy Week. Claire had never seen or imagined anything like the spectacle offered, the serried ranks of participants candles in hand, the sacred statues swaying on their raised, shoulder-supported, platforms, the funereal dirges, the sinister hooded Penitents.

"It's spooky," she whispered to Harry, as she gazed fascinated upon the figures marching in step, the statues swaying above them.

Harry watched her very closely, her eyes transfixed by the spectacle of gloom and suffering.

"It's like the memory of some everlasting haunting," she said to him. "It's like a dark shadow or stain that can never be removed… No matter how hard they try…"

He felt tears might not be far away again, but she held back and restrained them. She gave him a wry smile on the edge of pity and weeping.

"Where to next, Harry?"

They continued to Milan with its cathedral of pink stone, and Verona with its spectacular amphitheatre. They liked Verona but had to leave over the weekend as all the hotels and pensiones were booked solid. They fled to Brescia, and as was now their custom, Claire sat at the train station while Harry found somewhere for them to stay. He didn't need to go far before readily finding a small slightly shabby room in a hotel near the station. Claire didn't like it but insisted she would "make do". During the night however, a loud scuffling on the narrow stairwell woke them and when Harry opened the room door they could see Italian policemen unceremoniously escorting some untidily dressed women downstairs and out of the building. Harry quickly shut and locked the door.

"You brought me to a brothel!" Claire accused him. "You brought me to sleep in a brothel!"

"I'm not sure," Harry tried to excuse himself, still not clear what he had seen on the stairwell.

But Claire insisted and returned to the fray frequently over the coming days. She sounded mainly good-humoured about it but at the same time there was a trace of annoyance and even accusation as if he had shown her some ineradicable disrespect. The following day early they found another better hotel in Brescia but Claire was anxious now to move on to the final destination of their journey, Lake Iseo, and the town of Sulzano. Iseo was the smallest and quietest of the main northern Italian lakes. They stayed in a very conservative lakeside hotel and made friends briefly with a strong looking Dutchman and his blonde English girlfriend. They had drinks together but the Dutchman ignored his girlfriend who looked withdrawn and unhappy most of the time. There was obviously something wrong, some disharmony. Most days the two couples' paths crossed in or near the hotel and the Dutchman was always walking a few steps in front of his girlfriend, who continued to look unhappy, distanced and estranged.

"What do you think is going on there?" Harry asked Claire. "She doesn't look happy!"

"I think she's madly in love with him," Claire snapped back.

"Ok," Harry said, appeasing her, "I was just wondering…"

But he noted the sharpness of her tone and it hurt him.

In the middle of the lake there was an island called Monte Isola they could ferry out to. They spent all the remaining days of their holiday there. They found a grassy verge to sunbathe on, close to a restaurant where they could have lunch. Harry swam all the time in the lake and by the end of the week not only was his body incredibly deeply bronzed but he carried the warm glistening touch of the lake in every pore. Claire said she loved making love to his body with all its new glistening bronzed warmth, like making love to the sun, the air, the mountains, and the lake itself, she said. It was like making love to Nature, she said, but she used a brutal word to say "making love". She seemed happy most of the time and remained an energetic lover but more and more she fell into deep absences, often sitting half an evening with him with that expressionless look on her face, the same lost look he had first seen in Belinda's kitchen. One evening sitting over dinner with him in the hotel dining room she asked him with sudden cheery animation,

"How do you say 'I don't want to go home!' in Italian?"

He wasn't sure but thought it might be something like,

"*Non voglio tornare a casa!*"

She spent most of the evening learning and repeating the words as if she had nothing else to say. Finally she said to him,

"But we have to go home, Harry, don't we? I mean everyone has to go home…"

"Maybe we could come and live here sometime," Harry suggested, wondering if they could and if they would be happy here. "It just needs a little planning…"

"Oh I don't want to plan anything!" Claire protested. "Let's not plan!"

"What about your cottage on the Atlantic?"

"Oh that too, Harry! We can do that too…"

"But without planning of course…"

They laughed happily together.

During the very last nights there was another full moon and Claire loved to sit and watch its yellowy light glistening on the mountains, the island, and the water.

"Italy is beautiful in the moonlight," she sighed.

"Oh isn't everywhere?" Harry said, not thinking about it.

"Oh you don't understand anything," Claire impatiently reprimanded him.

They flew home from Milan to Dublin, Harry drinking the complimentary red wines the stewardesses ferried to him, Claire gazing out the window at the cloudscapes below.

"So this is the world," she said at one point to Harry, and she laughed, adding, "I had no idea!"

She cried a little when they arrived home but she seemed to quickly settle and they returned seamlessly to their old lives, days of idleness and constant lovemaking, four or five times throughout the day and night. Her skin had not boiled like milk in the hot continental sun but neither had it picked up any glints of bronze or gold or even pink. Harry travelled every inch of it with his eyes and tongue trying to find any hint of tan but there was nothing. She did taste of the lake he told her but she had not really spent much time in the water and he was exaggerating. On the other hand, Harry had carried a layer of lake home with him just under his skin, but it quickly began to fade. He regretted the seeping of the lake and sun from his skin until he could no longer feel them as a tangible sensation in his flesh but at the same time being at home with Claire completely compensated him. It wasn't long before he had sunk into her body like a familiar addiction and all he felt he wanted was to make love to her endlessly and to wrap his body and his voice around hers in a wild and unceasing intoxication and celebration of their singular amorous sweetness. Their lovemaking was prolonged and exquisite and after a time they became so absorbed in the physical efflorescence of each other in and around each other that if began to feel as if they had never been away. Harry told himself he was infinitely deeply in love with her and he believed it. If this loss of oneself through desire in the deepest substance of another was not love, then what could it be? And then he noticed, at first dispassionately, but later it troubled him, that she was spending increasing amounts of time in her own apartment. He never challenged her about it, he simply accepted it, and anyway it was a very gradual process, and she still spent all of her nights with him, just for an hour here and there during the day or evening she would vanish into her own apartment and leave him alone before eventually returning. At the same time she talked about renting one or other of the apartments so that they could live in just one and earn some money from the rental of the other. He had paid for all of their holiday but he wondered if she could be short of money. And yet the idea made sense. She said she was looking for a tenant, but he saw no evidence of this "looking". Once or twice she even said she had people coming to look at her apartment and even left him ostensibly to show it to them, but again he never saw or heard anyone calling. And then she began to spend more time away from him, and he wondered, while they seemed to be making love with more fervour than ever, he could not help wondering, if he was beginning to lose her. Or had he already begun to lose her some considerable time before.

Claire not only seemed to be withdrawing and spending more time away from Harry but she was less willing to accompany him on his walks in the sun. Since returning in mid-May from Italy the weather in Dublin had been dry and warm and Harry had been eager to return to the "Forty Foot" to swim there and to sunbathe naked. He expected Claire to accompany him but increasingly she urged him to go on his own. He didn't want to. He still wanted to be with her all the time. All the time. But he yielded to her promptings and so would walk all the way through Blackrock and Dunlaoghaire to Sandycove to swim and lie naked in the sun there. He was often four or five hours away from her during the day. Sometimes when he returned she would fall on him and devour him. She said she loved sucking his "golden cock". She seemed to still have the same fierce sexual thirst that he had, her desire even seemed, as it always had done, to topple over his and to demolish it. But at other times he returned to an empty apartment. On occasion she only came to him when it was time for bed. Harry knew that away from Claire, either in his apartment or walking by the bay, or no matter where he found himself or what he found himself doing, his only thought and desire was for her. Belinda had even slipped from this mind, he was so glad about that, but Claire was a constant feeling of loving, lusting, wanting, needing that could not be stilled... And away from her he sometimes felt crazy with missing her... One day when she did walk to the sea with him he threw his arms out over the expanse of bay with ferry boats dotted in the distance and the sleeping giant of Howth Head resting upon the horizon.

"This is the extent of my missing you!" he told her.

"But I'm here with you!" she said, laughing.

"Yes, but when you are not here with me..." he said. "When I'm alone without you..."

"Oh, silly!" she said.

"I want you to always be with me, Claire!" he told her and he meant it.

Once he said to her,

"I don't think I can live without you!"

He felt and meant every word. But while his feelings for her seemed to grow and grow to absorb him more and more, he couldn't help wondering what she felt deep down. He asked himself if she felt the same way about him as he did about her. One day he caught her gazing at him for a long time without saying anything.

"What is it?" he asked breaking the spell.

"I don't think I can live without you!" she said with an earnestness that was heartbreaking.

And yet her absences grew and grew and grew… Not only the times she disappeared to her own apartment, sometimes telling him she had people coming who were interested in renting it, but also when she was with him, when she would become silent and withdrawn, her gaze inward or expressionless, those incredible blue eyes turned away into an inner blankness. Once early on she had joked with him that when he looked at her it felt as if he was gazing into her soul. But he had always felt that she was the one gazing into his soul. And now with her eyes turned inside her it felt as if she was gazing into her own soul. What was she seeing there? What was it? It was a question he asked her more and more. She seemed transfixed by her own increasing unhappiness.

"Oh Harry," she said one day with an air of desperation that startled him, "sometimes I feel like I am trapped in stone and can't get out… Do you see how awful it would be to be trapped in stone?"

One day when she had left to go to the shops he decided to visit her apartment. He didn't ask himself why he was doing it, the impulse simply came to him and he followed it. The apartment looked as it always had done, there was nothing of note, no untidiness, no disarray. He noted the blood-red Atlantic sunset on the wall. He saw the Hermann Hesse novel "Steppenwolf" on a small table with a lamp and alongside it a notebook with a cover of intertwined dark, green and golden leaves. He glanced inside the notebook and saw there were handwritten notes but he refrained from reading them. It was a step too far. He accepted that by being alone in her apartment like this he was invading Claire's privacy, but he was only prepared to go so far. If there was always to be something unknowable in her for him then so be it, he would have to live with that, and pay for it too if he had to. He began to look in her presses and drawers where he found mainly clothes. He picked some of her lighter clothes up and ran them through his fingers. He lowered his face to pick up her scents and her warmth from them. He loved touching her things, anything that had been next to her skin was beautiful to him, and moved him to great tenderness. In the bathroom there were the expected toiletries and nothing else of real interest until, in a cabinet under the washbasin, nestling under some washcloths, rolls of cotton wool and bandages, he found some boxes of medicines, pills. He didn't know Claire had been taking any kind of medication, it surprised him. He wrote the names of the medicines on a piece of paper and tucked it into his wallet. He didn't recognise the names of any of the medicines and wondered what they were for. He opened one or two boxes to see if there were descriptions inside but he found nothing.

A couple of days later, out on one of his walks, he dropped into a pharmacy in Blackrock. He hoped he would find a quiet pharmacy and a friendly, pliant pharmacist, and he did. He produced the list of medicines.

"I wonder if you could tell me what these are for?" he asked.

The pharmacist studied the list nodding with recognition as his eyes travelled down it.

"It's quite a cocktail," he said.

"Yes, but what for?" Harry asked. "Is it a pleasant or unpleasant cocktail?"

The pharmacist hesitated as if unsure if he should be answering the question but in the end, maybe it was Harry's affable trustworthy nature that swayed him, he seemed to decide in Harry's favour.

"These drugs are used in the treatment of a whole range of mental difficulties," he said. "They are used for anxiety, depression, schizophrenia…"

"Are they given as a temporary treatment, or something more long-lasting?"

"You mean chronic," the pharmacist said. "Someone on these drugs usually needs them for long periods or even all of the time…"

For the first time Harry felt real fear and dread come to settle in his mind, and in his heart. He returned to the apartment, conscious that he was dragging his feet behind him and that he could barely walk. He had no idea what to do next. He couldn't confront Claire about the medicines, but could he even talk to her about them? She was lying on the bed as if she had been sleeping when he got back. She was surprised to see him return so soon from his walk.

"You didn't get to the 'Forty Foot' then?" she commented.

"No," he said, "I wanted to be here with you…"

"But it's such a lovely day, Harry!"

"It is a lovely day... But it's a lovely here with you too..."

He sat on the bed beside her and looked intently at the milk-whiteness of her skin, her raven black hair, and the wild intense sapphire of her eyes. He sensed the warm scents rising from her body to envelop him and he felt his entire body heart mind and soul swept by a swathe of profound tenderness far stronger than anything he had felt so far for her. He felt himself filling with love for her, filling to the brim, it was uncontainable, he began to tremble with it.

"Oh Harry," she said, reaching a white hand up to brush a single tear away from his cheek. "Oh Harry what is it?..."

He struggled with the words and blurted them out, but with the greatest intensity of feeling, that to him sounded inchoate and inadequate.

"I just want to love you, Claire. I want to love all of you, all of your life. I want to love you so much and to be happy with you, and for you to be happy with me. I want to love all of you, all of your life, from beginning to end, from before the beginning, and after the end. I want to hold you as a baby and love you. I want to love the child you were, the girl you were, and the woman you have become, and will become. I want to hold you as the babe you were and gather your first cries into my heart. I want to hold you in the last moments of your life and to gather your dying breath into my mouth. And I want to love every moment of you in between, between birth and death. I want to gather all of your life into my heart and hold it there. I want every moment of you to be and to feel loved by me. Every moment, every happiness, every sorrow, and everything before and after and in between... every heartbeat and all the space between heartbeats... and all that there is in the space where there are no heartbeats... I want my loving you to have no boundaries or horizons in this world or beyond it, or in this life or beyond it... I want my love for you to be all-encompassing and forever, Claire... I want it to never end... I want it to have no beginning and no end... Golden... Eternal..."

Without saying a word Claire sat up and put her arms around him and held him tightly. They sat for a long time in each other's embrace. They could feel each other's heart beating against their own heart, and they felt time like a bright clear stream trickle down between them. At last Claire said,

"We will never stop loving each other, Harry! It's you and me now until the end of time..."

"We won't end there," he said. "Time can run to its own end... You and I... we'll never stop..."

"Can't stop! Won't stop!" she laughed, echoing words he used sometimes when in the greatest intensity of making love to her, when physically he was unleashed and unable to cease his movements on and in her, through her.

They laughed together, and then cried together, and then she pulled him down and they lay and slept together without making love. In the evening darkness a bright yellow moon appeared at their window Claire leapt up.

"I have to run, Harry... There's someone coming to look at the apartment..."

But it was surely too late, Harry thought, for anyone to be calling. But she was gone, running from the apartment, he heard her feet racing on the stairs, and she didn't return until deep in the night when he was sleeping.

He couldn't figure out what was going on, he couldn't see, but he felt he needed to do or say something. Claire was becoming increasingly erratic. Those moments when she became absent, withdrawn, gazing inwardly with that expressionless look on her face, became more frequent. She encouraged him to be on his own, or would run to her own apartment, away from him, saying there was someone calling who might rent. She continued to eat and drink little, but even after one glass of wine or beer she seemed uncertain in her speech and on her feet, stumbling so that he had to hold her when they walked, or sinking physically into herself as if suddenly deflated. She spent more and more time away from him but still returned to spend each night in his arms. They made love as avidly as ever, in fact even more so, and their lovemaking was heightened and intensified by what he recognised was a sharp edge of desperation that seemed to wash over them like a wave even when drowning in their most sensationally exquisite moments. If anything Claire acted with more desire than he did. It was more likely to be her whose hands, mouth and thighs sought him in the nighttime, or woke him in the morning. And during the day it was often she who was first to turn from some task to start pulling his clothes away with her fingers and teeth until she was devouring him supine under her flesh in unceasing movements of wild desire, unhinged and blind.

One evening when he returned from walking in the warm evening sunshine by the bay he found her curled up in bed. She may have been sleeping, he wasn't sure, but either way she did not notice him returning to the apartment or when he sat in an armchair close to the bed. He sat and watched her with so much love for her that it felt like a pain inside him filling his heart. After a time she began to roll with abrupt movements from side to side as if her sleep was becoming disturbed and then he heard her voice, low and quiet, but full of a kind of keening distress, flowing from her in a restless, tearful, stream. He listened hard to catch what she was saying. He heard the name Gerard several times and then in a quiet crescendo she called out, piteously, "Mother... Mother... Mother..." Tears streamed down his face as he listened to her and yet he did not, as he wanted to, rush to embrace and hold her but he waited until the crisis faded, fearing that like waking a sleepwalker some elemental and damaging shock might occur. Instead he waited until she was quiet again and then lay down beside her and held her until darkness covered them and while Claire appeared to sleep through the night he lay awake staring at the darkened window panes and the ceiling at a loss to understand what was happening to their love.

A few days later he returned to the Blackrock pharmacist, finding him thankfully alone again.

"The person on that medication is my girlfriend," he explained. "She hasn't told me about it... And we haven't talked about it... But her behaviour for a couple of months now has become strange... She's become withdrawn... distant... I think she may have lost some emotional balance... I just don't know... She sometimes seems very unhappy... Trapped... Lost..."

He felt very uncertain. It was the first time he had ever tried to put into words how Claire was, how she appeared to him. It wasn't easy. The pharmacist listened with interest but without emotion and gave straightforward, simple advice.

"She needs to see her G.P.," he said. "Get her to go to her G.P. Only someone who knows her condition and her history of medication can help... It may be important to do this without delay."

He didn't know who Claire's G.P. was or if she even had one, but he knew he had to broach her behaviour before it worsened even further. So that evening for the first time he said to her,

"I think there's something wrong, Claire. I think there's something the matter with you..."

She became immediately alert and wary, sitting up abruptly.

"Wrong? Wrong? I don't like that word... 'Something the matter', I don't like that..."

"I'm sorry, Claire, I have to say something..."

"What do you think is the matter?" she asked in a reprimanding voice.

His voice breaking he rolled off the names of the drugs he had found in her bathroom cupboard. It was perhaps the worst thing he could have done. As he spoke her face turned to disbelief and dismay and anger. Before he had finished she fired a volley of swear words at him.

"How dare you?" she said. "How dare you? You have no business... How do you know those drugs are even for my use?"

She stood up and began pacing energetically about the room, waving her arms, a frantic look appearing on her face. She yelled at him, pouring coarse and scornful epithets over him. He had never seen or even imagined her like this. He stood and followed her around the room. He tried to take her in his arms but she shook him off.

"I can't believe it," she said, "I trusted you... I loved you... I thought you loved me..."

"I do love you, Claire!"

"Well then, what do you want from me?"

"I want you to be happy, Claire."

"Is that all?"

"I want you to talk to someone..."

"Who do you want me to talk to? Don't I talk to you? Isn't that enough?"

"I want you to talk to a doctor..."

At the word "doctor" she doubled up as if he had punched her in the stomach. She held herself across the waist and scrunched her facial features into an expression of utter bitterness and pain. He saw her eyes filling with tears and reddening. She began to swear again, repeating the most violent curse words over and over, her arms folded and tightening around her waist as she swung to and fro on her feet, walking quickly and erratically in one direction before swinging back, as if she was hanging loose from a cord, like some human pendulum, in another. In the end he tried to grab her to hold and quieten her but she broke from him and grabbing a couple of items of clothing she ran from the room leaving the door opened behind her. He followed her but when he got to her apartment the door was closed and she didn't respond to his knocking or his pleading with her to answer. He persisted until he heard the doors of the downstairs apartments open and voices calling, "Is there something the matter?" and, "Is it possible to be a little quieter, please?" He did not see her for a couple of days and then in the night she came and slipped in to bed beside him and made love to him. It was sweet beyond words but as he held her he felt her tears falling and running on his face neck shoulders arms and chest. And then when she had brought him to fruition and had exhausted herself in a wave over him she skipped from the bed, pulled her clothes around her, and left him. It was the last time he would see her alive.

It wasn't that night but the following night when he was sitting alone in the apartment that he heard the loud report of a gun being fired from Claire's apartment. He ran to her floor and with all his strength crashed through the locked door of her apartment. He saw her immediately in her pink dressing gown splayed back across the chintzy armchair, her arms along her sides, the blunt ugly gun still held in her fragile white hand. Around her neck the chain and medallion he had given her at Christmas, sea, moon, the sapphire blue of her eyes. He stumbled to her and knelt at her side and cried inconsolably into her lap. He knew he shouldn't but he couldn't help reaching up to put his arms around her and hold her. He ran his hand over her raven black hair, brushing it as if it were the wing of some dark bird, and his fingers came away covered in blood. He watched now as the blood ran out thickly into her hair, the deep red of the blood melding with the deep blackness of her hair. He saw thin streams of crimson begin to trickle down her neck towards her breasts. He kissed her mouth but for the first time ever there was no response. He wondered if somewhere, somehow, she could hear him and so he said to her, his voice breaking over every word, what he had felt and wanted and tried to say to her so many many many times before,

"Oh Claire, oh Claire, I will always love you. I will love you before and after time, through an eternity of Eternities, and an eternity of Eternities more. When everything is over and done with, when this world and life and time is over and done with, come what may, I will love you and go on loving you... Forever, Forever, Forever... My love for you will never end, Claire, never... never... ever... Do you hear me, Claire? Please hear me... I will never stop loving you! Never, never, ever..."

He clutched her to him so tightly as if he wanted to drag her body inside his body and make it part of his physical being.

"Time may stop," he told her. "But I won't stop... We won't stop, Claire... Can't stop... won't stop! Can't stop, won't stop!"

He wanted her to hear and to know that his love for her would never die, but as he said it, holding her as tightly as he could in his arms, he felt his heart break and come asunder within him and it felt as if he himself was dying. He heard people in the room behind him and he sobbed and cried out uncontrollably as they pulled him away from her. Looking around the room in desperation he saw through the high window the nurses' residence lit up like a ship in the night with all of its windows glowing and the nurses living their lives, sitting still, watching tv or reading, applying or removing make-up, or dancing to some unheard secret music, dressing, undressing, totally indifferent to the disaster that had befallen his world. And for which he felt there could never be any remedy, not on, under, over, or beyond this earth. Not now, not ever... Never...

Part III

Inish

It was perhaps wrong of him to do so but the day after Christmas he burned Frank's "letters", if that is what they were, to Jean. He realised that they did not belong to him and he reminded himself that Jean herself, for some reason, had kept the letters, but now they were in his possession and he wanted in this dark midwinter season to begin to bring peace to the troubled ghost-ridden world he found himself in at the cottage. He placed the sheets one by one in the fire and only when the first one had burned did he add another, and when that had burned, another. He watched as the paper twisted, curled up, blackened, and began to crumble and disappear in the purifying heart of the blaze. They were loveless letters without a single gentle word and he felt they deserved the flames. As they burned he picked out lone words that were like a dying insult to his mind and his heart, and to the memory of Jean, and even to his memory of Helen. He was glad to see those words burned from existence and to think that no one would ever read them again. He wondered if he should go and also burn down Jean's cabin but he realised that abandoned and desolate as it was it was still the enduring emblem of her presence on the western edge of the world and that while one day it would inevitably disappear right now he felt it should remain to face the rebirth of time, of the year, of the Atlantic in its winter fury, the clouds, the rain, the sunsets, and the wind sweeping through them, and sweeping too through the bright stars and visible planets that at night lay over the cabin like a shield. It was her dream and battered and broken as it was it should be allowed to find peace in its own way in the movement of time over it like an eroding tide.

It had rained heavily late on Christmas Eve and throughout that night and all day on Christmas Day. From the cottage Harry looked out over the village to see lights glowing warmly here and there while the houses huddled under the thick sheets of relentlessly falling rain. In the cottage as he sat alone drinking whiskey he became absorbed in the sweeping sound of the heavy rain on the roof and windows mixed with the tumbling rush and roar of the sea near him. He had not seen rain like this since arriving on the island in September. Each time a gust of wind came the rain seemed to flinch and fall silent a moment before returning instantly again to wash against the building. It continued raining into the night and only in the early morning as the first dull light began to seep through the clouds and mists did it begin to tail off. Saint Stephen's Day was a grey day but with hardly any rain, just that constant feeling of cold dampness in the aftermath of the downpour which, while it loved to insinuate its humid and chilling fingers into even the most carefully and cosily assembled clothing, was tolerable if you wrapped a warm sweater and jacket around you and moved briskly. The village was quiet, there wasn't a soul stirring, just thin straggling lines of smoke climbing the air above the houses and the familiar, comforting smell of the blazing peat fires. Harry followed his favoured route, walking out along the shore to the headland past Jean's cottage and climbing westward on the hillside to the high cliff path with its views towards the beach and townland of Kill. The hillside was deserted except for some scattered stray sheep and the now familiar red-legged red-billed pair of choughs who sailed on the grey air and turned balletically about each other close to Harry as he walked. In the distance the beach at Kill was swept by long unfurling lines of foaming white ocean falling from the grey cold waves of bleak midwinter. He could barely make out the lake beyond Kill and the deserted village was invisible, concealed by a veil of thick grey cloud over the middle of the island. The skirts of the island's two mountains were also dressed in veils of grey and their summits were invisible. As he walked Harry was conscious of every sound he made, the crunch of his shoes on the damp earth, the breeze as it brushed the fabric of his clothes, the stern pulsing of his breath, and within himself a constant rising sensation of pain and sadness from the depth of his being. Her name echoed over and over in his mind as if every iota of him sought her and called out for her. But as he stood finally on the highest point of the cliff edge, three hundred feet above the sea, he swung around to survey the entire solitude of the island and all that lay beyond it, and he suddenly saw himself, and felt himself, as the King of a World of Nothing. On the cusp of the solstice, the year had died, time had died, or a certain measure of time had died, and he felt as if he himself was dying. For the first time he wondered if anything could ever be reborn, or begin again, out of all this. All this where he found himself. For the first time he felt that he would have to leave the island. And that realisation only sharpened his sadness and made it more painful.

He returned to the cottage and while the weather was not clement he decided he would go cycling, he wasn't sure where, but perhaps to Killeaden to see Mary Kate and Tomás, or to "The Emerald" to talk with Bill and Jane, or maybe to the north of the island, its least hospitable extremity. As he cycled through Dughrá on the road climbing towards the church and the pub he was surprised to see some strange figures approaching over the brow of the hill. There were about eight of them and they stopped outside the door of the pub where some of the locals emerged to observe them. Harry had to dismount from his bike and he walked towards them hesitantly. He had never seen anything like it. There were six obviously male figures dressed in white robes with heavy black boots stamping the ground. Over the long robes they wore white shirts but what astonished Harry was that over their faces they wore elongated helmets of straw or wicker surmounted by what resembled a simple crown apparently made by looping single strands of straw together. Their faces were completely concealed by the primitive headdress. Their leader carried a cane and he began to bark orders in the Irish language and point out positions on the road for the others to take, hitting the ground with the tip of the cane. One of the figures carried an accordion and he now began to play it sonorously, a traditional Irish dance tune floating mellifluously over the loud rhythm of the group's stamping feet. The men now circled around each other in a kind of Irish set dance, their pattern loose and basic as they stepped awkwardly closer and shuffled stumblingly apart from each other in an eerie off-kilter group. To one side but accompanying them Harry saw a male and female couple, young enough he judged, but made up to look old in old-fashioned, worn clothing, the man with a waistcoat, jacket and hat, and smoking a pipe, the woman wearing an expansive apron, thick-lensed glasses, and a scarf tied over her hair. The apparent old timer also carried a cane and beat out the rhythm of the dance on the air while the woman swayed at his side with a hugely pleased, broadly idiotic, grin on her face. Harry saw Paddy leaning against the wall of the pub grinning and clapping his hands in time with the music and the dance.

"It's just the Strawboys come to entertain us!" Paddy shouted to him.

"Lads, '*Tá an Scríbhneoir ann*'!" Paddy encouraged the dancing group. "The Writer is here!"

As if on cue the group moved over to encircle Harry and they danced around him, creating a kind of human cage out of which he couldn't emerge.

"How do I get them to release me?" Harry asked. "Am I to give them money?"

"Oh the offer of a drink opens many a door!" Paddy promised him.

Harry hastily pulled a couple of crumpled banknotes from his pocket and offered them to the leader of the group who readily accepted them. At his barked command, the whole group then turned away from Harry and began to dance their way into the pub, the music still playing, and the old couple hobbling behind them.

"For a moment there I thought they were going to sacrifice me," Harry said, glad to be out of his bondage.

"Ay," said Paddy, "and it's been known to happen!"

"I'd better make good my escape then," Harry said, swinging himself back on to his bike.

"I hope you won't find those Strawboys in your cottage when you get back!" Paddy shouted ominously after him.

Harry felt he needed some vigorous exercise to rid himself of his troubled emotions and he cycled hard to the main road. He abandoned his plans to visit Killeaden or "The Emerald" but decided to cycle to Kim bay on the westernmost edge of the island. He realised that he wanted to be alone – wasn't that after all why he had come to Inish, to be alone, and to forget? And all he had done since he had gotten here it seemed was to remember, while the life of the island, as it had just done, had invaded, disrupted, and at times possessed him. The beach was deserted. It was the most beautiful beach Harry had ever seen but today swaddled in comfortless grey mist, which obscured its high angled sides, its golden strand and the green-gold of its waves appeared more desolate than he had ever seen them. He strode down past the old abandoned shark fishery to walk on the sand feeling at last that he was completely alone here, and feeling again that sense, as he looked out over the ocean under its thick impenetrable blanket of grey, that he was indeed the King of a World of Nothing. Monarch of all he surveyed. Monarch of Nothing. He walked to and fro on the beach trying to keep himself warm and then he noticed an abrupt change in the light and a sense of darkness drifting over the landscape from the sea and sky. As a fresh bank of mist rolled into the bay and even the little visibility there was began to vanish Harry grabbed his bike and half-ran to the top of the road where the mist was now so thick he could only see a short distance in front of him. He sat on the bike and peddling hard cycled down the steep road into Kill and through the townland. There was no one about but the lights and lamps in the houses were much more vivid now as the midwinter darkness thickened around the houses. He was afraid he would not get home before dark and so shunted on to a side road which would take him home more quickly. The road ran along the base of the hill that rose to the cliff edge and walk Harry had been on earlier that day. Cycling hard now in the thickening mist and darkness Harry could see little ahead of him apart from wild grasses springing wetly at the side of the road, and the lower slopes of the hill with its rough peatland overcoat of heathers and mosses, glowing strangely orange as it sometimes did in these gloomy conditions. Harry then heard a low deep rumbling sound like distant thunder but it wasn't thunder and it sounded very close to him. He had never heard anything like it and had no idea what it was. It was a groaning like the deep moaning sound of a wounded animal but it wasn't an animal, it was a sound big and overwhelming enough to be coming from the earth itself, to be emerging from within the dark earth itself. Harry stood perfectly still as the mist and darkness held him even more tightly in its grasp. He felt afraid and wanted to escape but he didn't know if he should continue ahead or turn back. What was happening was completely unknown and he was lost, not just to understand it, but most of all how to respond, trapped for the time being in a perfect and unbreakable immobility. And then he saw it. Sliding down the hillside like a monstrous reptile, a high thick tongue of blackened peat, as if it were a dark molten lava flow seeping from the wounded earth, rolling over and over upon itself, and seeming to carry all of the land on its back, as it rushed to engulf the road in front of Harry and continue its progress to his feet. The noise the moving earth made was now like an eruption, similar to the sound a mighty storm of wind might make if it was tearing the world asunder. The ground under Harry's feet was shaking and he realised as the high black wall of peat slid towards him that it would swallow him. Above him too on the slope of the hill high to his right he heard further voices rising from the wounded earth to join with the original voice and signal further sections of the peatland uprooting and detaching itself to begin their journey down the hillside towards where Harry was waiting. Harry shook himself from his stupor and turning his bicycle around he shot back along the road he had travelled on, watching out for further landslides, listening more than watching, fearing that the entire hill might come asunder, detach itself, and roll down upon him. He felt his fear rising inside him but he determined not to panic. He leaned his head forward into the mist and darkness and cycled furiously back to the main road, returning then on the more usual road to Dughrá. He waved down each car he passed to warn them of the avalanche and urging them to spread the word to fellow-travellers they might encounter, to neighbours, police, and local council, as soon as they reached a phone. When he reached Dughrá he told everyone there in the pub gathered around the warm turf fire and sipping their pints. The ominous Strawboys were nowhere to be seen. Harry wondered for a moment if they were waiting for him in his cottage as Paddy had suggested.

"Can you phone around to spread the word?" Harry urged the publican who rushed to the phone.

"Will you have a pint, Harry?" a voice came from near the fire.

Harry looked over to see Peter Goode.

"The island is falling to pieces, Peter," he said.

"Oh I dare say it's not the end of the world," Peter said continuing to quaff his beer.

The publican came back from the phone.

"It'll be work for Peter," he explained to Harry.

Harry cycled down to his cottage. The island was swathed now in total darkness. Harry could hear only the wind and sea but the recent sound of the earth flowing down the hillside and over the road in front of him still echoed in his hearing. At heart its sound had been a sloppy gurgling sucking sound as if its vile dark tongue was intent on sucking the life out of the world itself. It was a sound, Harry shuddered to think of it, like blood might make bubbling thickly from an ugly wound in the flesh of some dying animal. It was pitiless and inconsolable, like death itself. There were no Strawboys at the cottage, thankfully. Harry put the lights on and stirred the fire to life. He showered and had something to eat. He poured himself a glass of whiskey and sat in the porch. It was Christmas time he reminded himself, always a good excuse for drinking. He sat there for hours and had refilled his glass several times when Clare returned.

He had been wondering if she would call again. He had not seen her on Christmas Day or since the fervently exquisite hours they had spent together on Christmas Eve. He reckoned she was busy celebrating the day with her children and perhaps visiting or receiving visits from neighbours and friends. He knew she would call when she could and was only a little surprised but pleased when, with the evening now well-advanced and the rain beginning to fall again, he heard the cottage gate creak open and he looked out of the porch to see her walking along the path. She stepped into the light of the porch but continued past him into the living room. She stood in front of the fire as if for warmth, wiped some rain from her face, and brushed stray strands of hair back over her ears. She didn't, as he had half-expected, sit down, but remained standing as she turned to face him. She had an unsettled anxious look on her face. He waited for whatever she had to say.

"I can't stay long," she said with quiet emotion in her voice, "I have to get back."

He knew there was more and he waited for it.

"My husband is coming home," she told him.

He nodded. He understood what she was saying.

"He's due home any moment," she said, already moving away from the fire as if to leave.

"Will he be home for long?" Harry asked.

She stood beside him and looked fixedly in his eyes, those lovely blue eyes of hers, that reminded him so much of the other Claire, his Monkstown Claire. Her eyes searched his as his other Claire so often used to, as if she was trying to gauge his feelings, or measure the turbulence in his soul.

"He's coming home to stay, Harry. He's decided to stay. He won't be leaving again."

Harry nodded again, at a loss what to say, so everything had changed again, like this so suddenly, and his only possibility was assent. Abruptly Clare threw her arms around his waist, pulled herself close to him, and laid her head on his shoulder. He felt the warm breath of her words in the crook of his neck.

"Oh Harry, it was so beautiful... but it was only and will only ever be those few hours..."

She pulled away again to gaze into his eyes again. In her eyes there was unfathomable tenderness and the beginning of tears.

"I'm not free, Harry... I never was... Please understand!"

"I understand!" Harry told her and in an instant she had released him and she was gone.

"Don't hate me!" she said. "Please don't hate me!"

And she was gone.

He heard the gate creak open and shut again in the nighttime and at the same time he felt a real and tangible sadness fill his heart as if it was a glass filling up. It was as if every time anything was said or done his heart was emptied and refilled with painful sadnesses. He sat by the fire and stared into the flames. He felt another part of him was being consumed there but he did not believe that even fire could destroy the sorrow of his heart. After a time he gathered himself and returned to the porch where there was some blank paper and a pen. He switched on the electric light and saw himself sitting reflected in the windows of the porch, a lone figure in a rectangle of light, isolated in all of the world's darkness closing tightly about him, the King of a World of Nothing, the Islandman. He began to write, in the top right corner of the blank page, "An Scríbhneoir, Dughrá, Inish, County Mayo", and then on the left hand side under the date he wrote the address of Nick in Bygdoy Alle, Oslo. In the body of the letter before he signed off he wrote just a single question,

"Nick, the dark-haired woman you saw at the window, was her hair long? Did it fall below her shoulders?"

And he signed off with his name.

In a day or two when the post office reopened he would send it.

Of course there were questions to be answered. The Guards were called and they spoke to him. He didn't know what they had gleaned from the other tenants but he said nothing to them about his closeness to Claire. She was his upstairs neighbour and that was all. He sometimes heard her moving about that was all. He sometimes heard her voice singing in the nighttime that was all. She was unknown and destined to remain a mystery to him that was all. He tried to say as little as possible. Maybe the Guards would find out about them, about how close they were, about the trip to Germany and Italy, maybe they would suspect him of terrible things, but they weren't going to learn anything from him. He just didn't want to talk about it. And how, in the name of Heaven, could he communicate or explain to anyone what his life and death with Claire had been? All he wanted was for he himself to die. He should have taken the gun while he had the chance. He should have taken the gun and followed her wherever she had gone. He should have followed her when he had a chance. But he never had a chance, had he? Not from the first moment he had met her. Not from the moment she had put her arms around his shoulders and sobbed against his throat that first evening outside her apartment above the turning of the stairs. He had never had a chance. *Oh Claire, why did you leave me?...*

The body was removed from the apartment. The apartment was cleaned up to look as if nothing had ever happened, no trace of violent death, Claire erased, and in time new tenants came to occupy it. He would be aware of new bodies moving over the floor, and new voices sometimes rang out in the late evenings or nighttime, calling to each other or calling for each other. There was a post-mortem of course (but what was the point of that? Harry wondered), Claire's death was briefly mentioned in a couple of newspapers, and Harry read a short piece containing the funeral arrangements. She was to be buried in her home town beside her mother and her beatific little brother, Gerard, the happy little child she had so often described to him, the saintly little boy. Harry decided to go there. He couldn't really say why. He just knew that come what may his mind, his heart, and his feet were going to take him to wherever Claire was, or wherever she might be. The train took him there following the crooked line of coast to the small nondescript town north of Dublin where Claire had been conceived, born, and grown. From the little Irish he remembered from school Harry knew the town's name in Gaelic, "*Droichead*", meant bridge. In English it was called Bridgetown. From the train carriage looking out over the cold Irish Sea (all Irish seas are cold, even in high summer) Harry wondered if there was a bridge anywhere that Claire might be passing on, or one that he might use to follow her. He watched for a rainbow to form over the water, he wanted it to, but it was a warm sunny day without rain and there was no rainbow.

He sat at the back of the almost empty church while the funeral Mass was said. There were very few mourners, he realised it was just a handful of friends and neighbours of the family, there appeared to be no one, other than immediate family, with a personal connection to Claire. She had left the town many years earlier and it had mostly forgotten her, or remembered her only as a young wayward or troubled girl, if at all. He saw at the head of the group of mourners an old bowed-down man with a cane who looked as if he carried his years and his sadnesses heavily on his shoulders, and with this man helping him there was a woman, older than Claire, he judged to be her sister. There were two darkly-dressed men of about the same age who he thought must be her brothers. As the priest spoke it became clear that this indeed was the immediate family, father, sister, and brothers, forming a perfect group portrait of loss and sadness in this darkened Irish church in Bridgetown beside the sea. Harry let the droned words of the service slip by almost unnoticed by him but listened more intently when the priest began to talk in a more informal and animated way about Claire and her family. It was the time of the homily. It was mostly the standard pious stuff trotted out at weddings and funerals, what a beautiful soul Claire had been, such a happy child, and how loved she was by her family, and how difficult it would be for them, broken-hearted, to overcome her premature loss, but then in a few brief words the priest evoked the shadow of tragedy that had stalked the family, the loss of the mother at a young age to illness, and the drowning of the beatific brother Gerard, and now this third tragic loss, what he called Claire's "sad accident". For understanding and consolation, they must all look to God, and God would look to them. As Harry heard Claire's name repeated over and over and over in the priest's mournful litany he became suddenly aware that silent tears were streaming down his face. He wiped the tears away with a handkerchief and struggled bitterly to stem his weeping and achieve the level of indifference and containment he thought was the properly respectful demeanour required from a mourner. He sat through the entire ceremony with his hands lying empty in his lap, and he did not alternate his sitting, standing and kneeling, as did the other mourners, or join in any of the responses, not that he would have been able to. It had been many years since he had attended any kind of Mass and the language of piety which had filled his childhood, when for a number of years he had served at Mass, had become forgotten and unknown to him, and the consolations it promised were beyond him.

The coffin looked so small as it was carried away by the hearse. Claire could not have been so small, she must have shrunk in death. Harry followed the small group of mourners through the streets of the small town as they made their way on foot to the cemetery on its outskirts. The hole was made ready with mounds of earth to either side. Under a bright sun, now hot, the coffin was lowered. The priest continued his prayers and shook holy water over the grave, using a small rod Harry remembered, he believed correctly, was called an "aspergillum". He remembered a priest telling him that. It was part of the paraphernalia of a catholic boyhood. The blessed water being shook in the air fell in a rain of tiny droplets which caught the sun, glittered brilliantly, fleetingly, in prismatic rainbow colours, and then were gone into nothingness. Someone dropped a single white rose down upon the coffin before the gravediggers began to pile the mounds of earth on it. Without his noticing, one of the dark-suited brothers had come up beside Harry.

"There'll be soup and sandwiches back at the hotel," he offered. "It's not far... In the town... You'd be very welcome."

Looking at him more closely Harry felt a sudden surge of recognition.

"Are you Frank?" he asked him.

"Yes," the man said, offering his hand, which Harry did not take. "I'm Claire's brother..."

Harry remembered him now, the burly man pushing him back forcefully with his hand, as he rushed past him on the stairwell, that first night he had encountered Claire, following that first gunshot which had disturbed his world forever.

"Her brother?" Harry mumbled, bewildered, unable to join fact to fact.

"Yes, her brother," Frank confirmed.

"Do you remember me?" Harry asked.

"Yes, I do," Frank said, "I'd like to talk to you..."

Harry watched the mourners leaving the cemetery, the old bowed-down man leaning on his cane, uncertain in his steps, being helped by the woman he now knew was Claire's sister. Far younger than the old man was, she now looked old and bowed as he did with the same sadness.

"Sure," Harry answered. "I think you know where to find me..."

On his way back to Monkstown it happened. Harry was sitting with his head leaning against the train window. Some grey cloud had moved in over the bay and just as he was arriving home a flurry of rain fell and a colourful rainbow arched suddenly, as if it was some magic trick, over the bay from Howth to Sandycove. Harry wanted to, needed to see another, and yet another, but there was only one rainbow forming a bridge over the bay, a bridge through the troubled sky. And then it was gone. It was gone in an instant so quickly that Harry wondered if he hadn't imagined it. What did it matter anyway? A rainbow was not a bridge going anywhere. A rainbow couldn't mend a broken life or world. A rainbow couldn't mend a broken heart. A rainbow was like a literary fiction, offering hope where there was none.

About a week later Claire's brother, Frank, called to see Harry. They sat in Harry's apartment just inside the window. Frank noted with a smile the nurses coming and going in the nearby residence.

"You've got pleasant company!" he approved.

He had a small package he gave to Harry.

"I think you should have these things," he said.

There was a copy of the novel "Steppenwolf" with "For Mad People Only" written across the cover. And with it there was Claire's notebook with the green, dark, and golden leaves interlaced on its cover. Harry took them and put them to one side.

"There was a medallion with the sea and the moon... a sapphire gem..."

"We left it with her..." Frank said. "She was buried with it..."

Harry felt a dark grief about to overwhelm him but like a man clinging to a boat in a storm he held firm. He didn't let it carry him away. Not in front of Frank. He didn't slip away. Not then.

"The notebook is a kind of journal," Frank continued. "It's mostly about you..."

"Why didn't the Guards?..." Harry stumbled over his question, wondering why the police had not connected the notebook to him.

"Oh you know," Frank said, "sometimes they don't look too closely at things... And then I removed these things discreetly... I didn't want them looking too closely into Claire's heart and soul... I didn't think it was anyone's business really... That is, perhaps, apart from yours..."

"I don't understand who you are?" Harry said.

Frank remained silent. Harry continued,

"Claire said her brothers lived in the States… She said she had a boyfriend called Frank… She said he was a Gárda… that the gun was his… Before I met her I used to hear them making love in the night time… You were here the first time when the gun was fired… You ran away… Didn't you want to save her?…"

Frank began,

"I did live in the States… I was in the police force there… My brother still lives there…"

He paused wanting to leave Harry the time to absorb each piece of information, waiting to see that it had been absorbed.

"I returned to live here last year… I have a position with the Guards here… At first here in Dublin but now down the country… I tried to get close to Claire… but she had withdrawn from us in recent years… She said she didn't want me in her life and she got angry each time I tried to impose myself… The last time when I visited she flew into a rage… She produced the gun and I really thought she was going to shoot me… I ran from the building… But I didn't think at the time that she was in any danger… Or was a danger in any way to herself…"

"Well think again," Harry commented sharply, but immediately regretted it, it was unfair.

"I have friends in the Guards here," Frank continued. "I called with them just a day or two later and we searched the apartment… We couldn't find a gun… Claire said she had gotten rid of it… She had thrown it into the sea she said… She made a joke of it! Said she'd never kill me… Or herself… Said she had killed enough family members… She asked me to leave her alone to get on with her life…"

Harry couldn't blame Frank. He himself had searched Claire's apartment without finding the gun. It must have been hidden in some special place. Frank continued,

"She sounded plausible… I believed her… But I watched her from afar. I knew about you. You seemed to be making her happy. I believed you were making her happy. I let my guard down. I actually didn't see…"

Harry was more hesitant now,

"She said her boyfriend used to abuse her... play games with the gun with her... sex games... suicide games..."

Frank took a deep breath.

"Claire was very troubled. It started of course with the death of our mother and then Gerard drowning. You don't know this but she was hospitalised several times..."

"She was taking drugs... Strong drugs..."

"The drugs helped," Frank said.

"I think she might have stopped taking them when we were on holidays."

"Maybe she had begun to think she could be happy without them," Frank said.

"And men?"

"Yes," Frank responded, "there were men too. I think she had lots of boyfriends... That started before she left Droichead. There could have been some abusive ones. She was vulnerable. I think some men could have found her ready prey. There might have been a Frank. Maybe he was a Guard. Maybe he brought her the gun. There might have been someone who played games with the gun. She had to learn that from somewhere..."

"Learn what?" Harry asked him.

Frank took another deep breath.

"Russian Roulette," he said.

"Are you sure?" Harry asked.

Frank nodded.

"There's no doubt about it," he said. "She wanted the gun to decide whether she should live or die..."

Harry felt despair moving through his heart and soul. He let his face fall into his hopeless hands.

Frank's voice increasingly sombre continued to nudge at his darkness.

"In the end the gun gave the answer that maybe she wanted most..."

"But what about me?" Harry asked desperately, fighting back new irrepressible tears. "I loved her..."

"And she loved you too, Harry, that's why I'm here... I wanted you to know that..."

"But why then?"

"Maybe she loved you too much, Harry..."

"You make it sound as if I killed her... as if love killed her..."

Frank reached over and grasped Harry's shoulder.

"Harry, you have a lot to learn about Claire... It's all in her notebook... or most of it... Read it when you're ready to... You'll be surprised..."

Later that day Harry went walking by the bay but he turned away from his usual path south through Blackrock and Dunlaoghaire to Sandycove and walked instead northwards towards Sandymount, Ringsend, and the city centre. As he walked along the strand at Sandymount, remembering Joyce, he felt like some kind of desperate, desolate, Stephen Dedalus, blindly treading the beach, unseeing, listening more than seeing, trying to make sense out of the mad confusion of the world, by listening for what he could not see, for what he could never see, as his tears blinded him, utterly dominated and broken by his grief, full of mortal hopelessness. Not able to see what was in front of his eyes. "*Agenbite of inwit*". Blindness could not be a punishment for blindness. What could then? Exile? Maybe exile... In town, he walked through Saint Stephen's Green and into Grafton Street. Following his own footsteps blindly he entered one of the churches off Grafton, its interior shadowed and lit only by the light of stained glass windows and some flickering candles. After sitting in a deep silence and in an emptiness of wordless prayer for a long while he circled through the church looking blankly at the statues and the paintings. Near the door as he was leaving a darkened picture caught his eye of a pale emaciated grey old man, his upper torso bare as he appeared to struggle against a wire wrapped tightly around him. Harry thought it must be one of the church's medieval martyrs but reading a nearby plaque he realised with some surprise that the man was a far more recent local figure who had been born, lived, and died in Dublin. A patron of mortification, around his body he had wrapped chains and thick strands of barbed wire from which drops of blood fell and which had covered his flesh with ugly scars. His devotion had been fuelled by alcohol and pain and, of course, religious zeal, or obsession. He was described as a "Slave to Love", of the spiritual kind. Harry was appalled at this cruel self-inflicted punishment and compassionately wanted to reach up and pull the barbed wire away but he could not get close to the painting. He had nothing to stand on. His tears were falling bitterly again.

"Oh who did you love so much?" he asked the tortured figure. "Oh who did you love so much that you suffered this?"

Stupidly, unthinkingly, as in some reflex from his youth, he dipped his fingers in the holy water font and blessed himself as he left the church and the tortured bloodied image of the religion of love.

These days Harry spent all of his time alone. He did sometimes take walks but more often than not trying to reach the "Forty Foot" he turned away and walked back along the bay. It was one of the most beautiful places in the world, Claire had said, but all he could see now when he raised his eyes was the entire extent of his loving her, his missing her, and his grief for her. It was high summer, the weather was bright and hot, there was no rain, and there were no rainbows. He did not return to his work. He didn't read. The only book he held was Claire's "Steppenwolf". He didn't read that either. He couldn't. He had glanced inside it. There were notes scribbled in the margins that he hadn't the courage to read. But he noticed she had ringed every occurrence of the name Harry and around some of these scrawled circles she had drawn some stars and a crescent moon. He didn't look any further and so he didn't know if he was the Harry of the moon and stars, or if it was the Harry of the novel, the mad, suicidal, sex-obsessed Harry painfully learning how to live in Hesse's dream universe. Or was it both? I've found my Harry, Claire had once said. He spent most of his time sitting in his apartment. Claire's brother, Frank, called again just once. They had a drink together but said little. There was little to say. He had moved to a distant rural outpost for his police work. Harry never saw him again. Most of his time Harry spent in the apartment. He hated waking in the morning and struggled against it. At night he lay awake and stared at the ceiling, sometimes hearing his new neighbours moving about and once or twice imagining the jolting of the bed or voices singing together in sensual culminations. Most of the time he sat in the window staring blankly out. He was vaguely aware that the nurses' residence was still there with its wonted rituals but it didn't stir him to any interest. He had in the very beginning considered it as an Eden or Paradise from which he was excluded. Now he felt that sentence was perpetual, if not eternal. If the nakedness of the young women said anything at all to him it was this, "you have been abandoned by us". Sirens of the Unattainable.

Some weeks later his brother called to the apartment. Harry had been alone, so alone, all this time and could not help telling his brother what had happened. He blurted it all out. It wasn't like him to talk about his feelings, or anything to do with his heart, but he couldn't help himself. It was as if his grief needed a bridge to somewhere, to something, to someone. In the end he wept uncontrollably into his hands. His brother embraced him. Physically they had never been so close. Or emotionally.

"Oh Harry, it's terrible to see you suffering like this!"

Later when Harry became calm, his brother asked him,

"What are you going to do, Harry?"

Harry told him about the plan emerging in his mind. Claire had wanted to live where there were Atlantic sunsets, it was one of her dreams. She had spoken of living in a cottage in the west of Ireland, in some remote area, the more remote the better, near water, by a lake perhaps, or by the ocean, or even on an island, that's what he was thinking of. He would leave the apartment and journey through the west of Ireland until he found somewhere to live. He would live out his sadness there. He would wait for his broken heart to either cure or kill him. He didn't say that to his brother, but it was what he was thinking. And maybe he could start to forget, if he could ever forget.

"Will that make you happy?" his brother asked.

"I'm not thinking about happiness anymore…" Harry replied. "I'm not thinking about anything anymore… I just want to get away… to escape…"

The brother entertained his plans. Harry was determined to cycle up through the west of Ireland from Limerick to Mayo and perhaps beyond in search of a cottage where he could live. He reckoned he would know the place when he came to it. He said he would start in Limerick and travel then through the Burren and into Galway and Connemara. From Connemara he could cycle into Mayo as far as Westport and see what there was above and to the west of Westport. He didn't think he would get so far as Westport. He thought he might find somewhere in Connemara or along the coast there, or on one of the great lakes. His brother said that if Harry got as far as Westport without finding a cottage he would come to join him there and help him find a place. If it was what Harry really wanted to do?

"It sounds like a plan," he said to Harry.

"It's all I've got," Harry said, conscious of the vast reaches of remoteness and emptiness, in every sense, stretching out before and inside him.

Since Christmas and New Year, apart from his brief encounter with Clare, announcing her husband's return to the island, and the episode of the Strawboys, Harry had seen and heard from next to no one. There were greeting cards from his brother for both occasions but that was all. He stood the cards, in all their glitzy seasonal gaiety, above the fireplace which blazed constantly in the deepest heart of winter. In January, with its short dark days, the rain fell constantly and high winds swept relentlessly over the island. He seldom left the cottage apart from brief respites when he walked to the headland and sometimes climbed to the cliff edge. In the heavy rains Jean's cabin looked as if it was simply waiting to be washed away from the surface of the island into the cold devouring ocean. Sometimes he had to run for shelter to escape the showers he saw advancing in thick curtains from Grace Island. Grace Island remained for the most part hidden in mists, rains, or darknesses. When she appeared out of the blue during intermittent clearances, when bright sunlight fell upon her high green mountain, Harry thought of her as the flag and prow of an advancing pirate ship on her way to storm Inish or the distant mainland. He saw few neighbours but one day Clare's husband called. He was a tall, strong-looking (Harry while he was no authority would have said "handsome") man in his forties. He was friendly enough, shaking hands warmly with Harry, and stopping to have a drink with him. Harry poured a couple of glasses of whiskey. Clare's returned emigrant said he was glad to be back from England. There was nowhere like Inish, he said. And then of course he had a family, young kids… And then of course, there was Clare. He couldn't forget Clare. His name was Michael.

In February, after Saint Brigid's Day, the weather changed for the better. A bright warm spring day came from nowhere and happily coincided with a wedding in the church. Harry could make out the bride in her brilliant white outside the church with a small animated crowd in their finery gathered around her. Not normally curious but after almost six weeks of isolation in the cottage and piqued by curiosity about the wedding party, he decided to walk to the pub and see who was getting married. As he climbed the hill to the church and pub he almost turned away when he saw that Peter Goode and Kathleen were the happy couple. Peter was wearing a light grey suit with a white rose in his lapel. He saw Harry and beckoned him forward.

"The drinks are on me, Harry!" he shouted, pointing Harry towards the pub.

The two men shook hands warmly.

"Congratulations!" Harry said. "I wish you every happiness…"

Kathleen, veiled and wearing a dress of resplendent white, holding a neat bouquet of mixed flowers, was busy with a small boy dressed in a light grey suit of his own, matching Peter's, and also with a white rose in his lapel, who danced around her feet. A line had formed of people congratulating her with hugs and kisses. Harry found himself propelled into the line. It reminded him of when he was trapped by the Strawboys. He looked about desperately for an escape but there was none. When he got to Kathleen she leaned forward into the bright sunlight offering her cheek but she didn't seem to see him, yet he was sure she knew it was him. She had to. He pecked her lightly on both cheeks.

"I wish you every happiness," he said, his hands touching her bare shoulders.

As he turned away she launched the bouquet over him and it fell among a group of women dressed as bridesmaids in silky pink gowns who excitedly and with laughter hunted the bouquet down. One emerged triumphant wreathed in smiles and she was warmly hugged and congratulated by the others. In the pub Harry drank a pint of Guinness, but as the revelry increased, and the music started, he thought it best to leave. A low, round, bald man with an accordion stepped up to him, pulsing out some stray notes. Harry guessed it was the erstwhile accordion-playing Strawboy and he quickened his determination to flee his pursuit, the accordion music now in full flight after him.

It was an unseasonably warm day such as occur from time to time in Ireland's sometimes premature spring and Harry decided to cycle the Island. He turned around on to the back road at the foot of the hill to the west of the village to see what damage had been left by the landslide. He had heard Peter Goode had been in charge of clearing the road and he was glad to find his way unimpeded by the watery volume of peat which had slid and slurped its way down the hillside to devour the road and the neighbouring fields and which had almost devoured him. Apparently, the movement of peat had even featured on a national tv news report but not having a television Harry had not seen it. Peter Goode had been interviewed and had appealed to the county council and the national government to provide funds not only to clear the mass of displaced peat but to brace the hillside and prevent further avalanches.

"Just think," Harry had read Peter's comments in a free local newspaper left by the postman, "just think if there had been islanders out walking on the hillside at the time of the landslide, or if the hill had come down upon nearby houses, we'd be talking now, not just about the clearing of the road, but about the loss of perhaps many of our people young and old... with already so many lost to economic deprivation and emigration due to years of neglect by those who govern us..."

Harry imagined the little speech had earned Peter many a free pint in the island's pubs, but he also sensed that behind the words there was perhaps the stirring of political ambition on Peter's part to elevate himself to the status of representative and spokesperson for his island people. He was a strong farmer who could certainly fill the role of a strong leader if given the chance, or if he won it. Looking now at the hillside Harry could make out the scale of the area which had been gouged and torn by the ravenous movement of the peat. The blackened topsy-turvy earth resembled the broken and wounded skin of a moribund savage animal. The earth had been beaten and torn open. It had spilled its innards out. It looked like a blackened dead thing but Harry could not escape the impression, even in the strong sunlight now falling over the landscape, that this dead thing could quickly begin to stir and move again and recommence its devouring path towards the village and the sea. He wondered what barriers Peter or anyone else could raise up to stop the ground here uprooting and detaching itself before rushing with disaster in its teeth upon the living world.

Harry resumed his cycling in the warm sunlight turning west on the main road to the townland of Kill where he stopped at "The Emerald". He had not seen Bill and Jane since the Christmas Eve gathering around Paddy's new vintage almost two months ago. Harry was warmly welcomed and sat with the couple in the dayroom of the guesthouse, Jane offering tea and scones.

"Well how are your monsters?" Harry asked flippantly.

"Fine, fine..." Bill answered, adding a question of his own, "And how are yours?"

With warm sunlight spilling into the dayroom through open windows, they exchanged the usual pleasantries about the weather and the life of the island. There had been no visitors to the guesthouse since before Christmas but they would return Bill assured him for Saint Patrick's Day and Easter. The short dark inhospitable days of midwinter were the best for his writing, Bill said. His imagination loved darkness. They talked about the avalanche, which had been the major event on the island since Christmas, but would now undoubtedly be superseded by the news of Peter and Kathleen's wedding. Bill and Jane really appreciated Harry's first-hand account of the landslide and how he had been the one to alert the island.

"You saved us all from being engulfed by the great peat beast," Bill said with mock regret. "That could have made a great end to one of my stories..."

"It might yet!" Jane said.

"It could have made a great end to all of us," Harry contributed.

"And it might yet!" Bill concluded.

When Jane left them alone for a time the two men suddenly sank into silence and much that was unspoken passed between them. Eventually Harry asked,

"How are you?"

Bill looked at him with an immense sadness in his expression which had not been on show when Jane had sat with them.

"I can't say how much I miss her..." Bill told him in low quiet, very nearly secretive, tones, as if wanting to, needing to, hide his grief. "But it's been well over a year... I wonder if I will always feel this pain. My loss has been so profound. And I have learned that I have an only all too human heart."

He sank back into silence which Harry left unperturbed. In his own good time Bill's words returned,

"When I lie down to sleep at night I imagine she is there beside me, but she's not there, just her absence, visible, tangible, but ungraspable, like some kind of mirage... I'd love to hold her but I cannot... Each day when I wake the first thing I feel is my awareness of her and the sadness filling my heart... I am filled with a constant despair. At times I feel that I am one breath from going over the edge. At times I feel that I am one breath from dying. I am not sure if I can hold on. I think my heart is broken. I think I might die from love."

He looked fixedly at Harry, before saying with his voice full of pain,

"Have you any idea what it feels like?"

"Yes, I do..." Harry told him as Jane returned to the room with fresh tea.

She sat close to Bill and put her hand over his hand in a comforting way as if she sensed her husband had some secret pain in his mind or in his heart. She looked with a smile of gentle understanding upon the two men. Bill responded with a gentle squeeze of her hand. Harry noticed the look of desperate unhappiness recede from Bill's eyes to be replaced by his usual glinting expression of mixed alacrity and intelligence. It was a screen, he knew, for Jane's sake. He wondered if Bill could ever tell her about his love for Jean. Bill broke the silence, brushing the intensity of their previous conversation aside,

"Everything that happens to us, everything we deeply feel, Harry, informs our themes and improves our writing!"

"Are you writing, Harry?" Jane asked with genuine interest.

"Thinking about it," Harry said, shrugging his shoulders.

It was time to go. He hugged Jane goodbye and walked with Bill at his side to retrieve his bicycle.

"They say love conquers everything," Bill said as Harry was setting off, "but falling in love, being in love, the loss of love, the pain of loss... I am not sure what the possibilities of love are when faced with its hardest separations, Harry... when love encounters its most painful horizons..."

He waved Harry away on his uphill climb towards Kim Bay. Harry climbed in the sun to the highest point of the road where he left his bicycle and began hiking up the mountain towards its summit. On his way he skirted the corries, deep cold lakes that, here and there, dotted the north-facing slopes of the mountain. There was no troubling breeze and when he reached the top of the mountain with the sun still warm on his body he stood looking out over the entire island, clear today of cloud, and feasted his eyes eastward towards the distant mainland, where even the holy mountain of Croagh Patrick was visible, and southward towards Grace Island with its green triangle of mountain, and westward towards the far expanses of Iceland or North America. To the north below his feet on Sleevebeg he was surprised to see patches of ice and snow still clinging to the edge of rock hidden all year round from direct sunlight. The island rarely saw frost, ice or snow, mists and rains were its common element, but Harry realised that during the colder winter days flurries of snow had blown around these rugged heights and in sheltered spots ice and snow had gathered in the grooves and crevices to remain perhaps until the warmest days of high summer. The corries too had been sculpted by ice and snow over long millennia in the island's most inhospitable region.

Having rested he began to pick his steps downward towards Kim Bay and its golden strand gleaming in the bright sunlight. As had happened when he had walked down from the high summit of Carrigmore towards the end of the previous year, before long his legs began to ache with every step. He found it strange that his legs should hurt more with the descent than with the climb and breathed a sigh of relief to finally arrive at the beach, his legs aching. After the cycle and climb and long descent from the mountain on foot he felt an unusual exaltation rising in him, an inner excitement he had not felt in a long time, perhaps since his time in Italy with Claire, or perhaps here with Helen when she was with him. The sea was quiet on the fine windless day and it unfurled its smooth white lace in tranquil lines at his feet. Following a sudden surprising impulse he began to peel out of his clothes and when completely naked he ran quickly to the sea and plunged in. The water was ice-cold and at first he cried out in pain as the cold bit into his flesh. Then he began to swim further out into the bay with vigorously wild strokes until he felt the warmth returning to his limbs but then to get even warmer he redoubled the beating of his arms and legs propelling himself out towards the open sea. Before long he found himself at the mouth of the bay where he began to swim from side to side in long extended lengths stretching his limbs to the utmost. His body began to feel pleasantly warm as he moved to and fro in the sensuous green-gold of the quiet ocean. And then he felt something unknown touch him. It had barely troubled the water approaching him and suddenly it was there, a deep shadow dozens of feet long moving through the calm green-gold of the ocean close to him. His first thought was that it was a shark and he felt a surge of panic rush through him. The animal was immense and the sea heaved and threw him as it turned around him. He put his hand out to push its shadowy grey-black bulk away but instantly realised it was useless. He felt further powerful pulses in the water and turning saw a second fish approaching as immense as the first one, and then another, and still another, until there were three or four of the giant creatures circling around him in the bay. Another brushed against him close enough for him to feel its rubbery skin against his body and then it shot away the gold-green light of the sun in the water spilling over its shadowy flanks. As it turned away he saw its white belly flash towards him, and the pale underside of its fins treading the water. He had feared it might be a shark and at first thought it could be a basking shark but now he could see it must be a whale, its movements pushing him from side to side in the ocean and causing high waves to roll over his head. He tried to judge its length. He couldn't tell. It was at least thirty feet long. But he just couldn't tell. It was like a building or immense vessel submerged in the water next to him. And he imagined he could feel its breath and its heartbeat pulsing through him as each one approached and left him. And still they glided silently through the water turning around and around him in a constant circling movement until he struck out with his arms, panic still racing through his mind and heart, unsure if the beasts could attack him, catching the water with his fists and pulling himself forward desperate to get away from the huge creatures that, as he swam away from them, turned away from him and began to swim back towards the open sea, their dark grey bodies and the huge bulk of their heads glistening with green and gold light as they abandoned him. Within minutes, swimming as hard as he could, he reached the beach and crawled up it on his hands and knees, exhausted and out of breath. He sat on the beach leaning back on his arms waiting for the fear to run from his body, his heartbeat to steady, and his breathing to become normal, while he scanned the distant water for any sign of the gigantic fish. Nothing. It felt like he had dreamed it all. He felt he must have. And yet the feel of the animal's flesh against his own, and the play of light upon its skin, was all too vivid. The encounter was extraordinary and unbelievable but it had been real, all too real. He looked out to sea for any sign of the fish but saw nothing. And then the tension suddenly draining from him he felt himself go limp and collapse backwards on the golden sand where he lay for what seemed like a very long time, entirely naked in the warm sunlight, staring up at the infinite lapis lazuli blue of the island sky.

He cycled back to Dughrá to find the wedding had dispersed and the village was quiet in the sun. He stopped at Paddy and Joy's who were surprised but happy to see him.

"We asked ourselves if you remained among the living," Paddy told him.

He told Paddy about the huge fish he had seen. Paddy listened with polite but initial scepticism but then began to seriously consider the possibility of whales close to the island in February.

"They weren't basking sharks anyway," Paddy said. "They aren't seen here until about April... And what you described sounds very like a whale, methinks, but they are done by December and don't return until the autumn... It would be most extraordinary... But if there are any out there I want to see them...

"It would be a miracle... but I am rather fond of miracles..." he added.

The weather was promised fine again the next day and Paddy suggested they go out in the boat. As soon as it was bright they pulled out of Dughrá harbour and struck around the headland beyond Jean's cabin. They followed the coast, about a mile or two out, along past the townland of Kill and towards Kim Bay where Harry had seen the whales. For a long time they saw nothing, perhaps the fish had departed, but then Paddy, keeping his eyes peeled on the surface of the water, noticed something disturbing the surface further away towards Grace Island, just a couple of miles, and he began to push the boat in that direction.

"Thar she blows!" he cried out, and pointed toward a pair of massive flukes rising from the ocean and splashing back down.

Within minutes they were crossing the path of the whales and Paddy abandoned his oars to let the boat drift above them while he peered keenly over the edge at the swiftly moving light-dappled shadows below.

"Humpback whales!" he cried out. "Humpback whales! I've never seen anything like it…"

They watched then with silent awe as the whales shot swiftly gracefully away from them in the direction of Grace Island. And then out of the blue when the animals were still just a few hundred yards away, one after another, one two three four, they breached, flashing white and grey-black flesh, from the vastness of the ocean and flew massively majestically glistening through the golden air shedding cascades of glittering water, breaking in tiny rainbows, around them, before crashing back into the depths and disappearing.

"Humpback whales!" Paddy said, rubbing his hands, and with a glee in his eyes. "Oh wait until the boys in the pub here about this…"

Harry had had only one night of dreams since coming to the island but that night he dreamt of the huge whales swimming deep in the dark ocean singing their hauntingly beautiful melodies. That dream seemed to last for a very long time with Harry floating in it as if he were deep in a dark underwater world of plaintive submarine song. And then he had a second dream, which only lasted a short while before he woke. He dreamed of himself this time. He was standing solitary in the middle of a darkened room. He wasn't alone however. He was being observed. He appeared to be observing himself. And then some unknown, unseen person near him asked him, "How are you, Harry?" But when he answered no words formed in his mouth but just a long broken jagged trapped murmur of utmost anguish. When he woke he asked himself if he could ever be happy again, as the anguish lingered and pulsed through his heart.

The weather continued fine right up until Saint Patrick's Day. Early in March, Harry decided he was going to plant a potato garden.

"Things must be getting awful bad when you are taking up gardening!" Paddy teased him.

Undaunted Harry bought some ready-chitted seed potatoes in Killeaden, with little sprouts growing already from the blunt end of the potato. He dug up the ground behind the cottage creating long trenches between shallow mounds of earth. He placed the potatoes on the mounds and pulled up the earth around them, covering the shoots. The back garden had been neglected, possibly for years, and it had been hard work digging away its dense covering of grass and weeds. The earth itself was heavy, dark and sodden and impossible to reduce to a loose dry clay. For the most part the soil, if you could call it that, looked like the thick blobs of clay used in pottery. It took several days of work to make the potato patch but Harry in spite of his aches caused by the arduous work enjoyed being out in the warm sunlight. Word spread around the village and even people who lived at a distance from Harry went out of their way to pass his cottage and inspect his efforts. They were sceptical about Harry's intentions and joked about his prospects. One laughed and asked him if he was "going to grow grapes and make wine like Paddy does?"

"Will your potatoes be ready for the Saint Patrick's Day dinner?" another asked.

Most shook their heads with disbelief.

"You won't grow anything in that soil," one said.

Harry vowed without conviction to prove them wrong.

Clare, in denim jacket and jeans and green wellington boots, came down the road one day walking her Labrador and she stopped in the sunshine to exchange pleasantries about the garden and the weather. As she was about to go she asked him,

"How are you, Harry?"

He looked at her in silence. The question had shaken him and he was afraid to say anything. After a while she simply nodded at him and continued walking down towards the shore. He looked sadly, longingly, after her as she reached the bend in the road close to the shore and disappeared around it. He thought of how beautiful she was, and how full of life, love, and

203

desire, she was, here on the island. He wished he had been able to say something in response to her question but was afraid of only pain issuing from his chest, throat, and mouth, like in his recent dream. Every time you got close to someone it hurt so much to be torn apart. Sometimes it felt unbearable.

Later, Paddy called with some fish and to invite him for tea with Bill and Jane on Saint Patrick's Day. He walked in to inspect the potato garden and did not hide his lack of faith. As was his wonted manner, he threw the fish on the grass in front of the cottage.

"Sea bass," he said, "a great fish... But I'm sorry I couldn't catch any whale for you!"

"I catch my own whale," Harry riposted. "The fish would be nice with some of your homemade wine, Paddy..."

"Oh no," Paddy said, swinging his head and spitting to one side, "Don't you know the Strawboys drank every last drop the day after Christmas?... They got drunk and wanted to kidnap Joy on me! One of them threw her over his shoulder ready to carry her off!"

Harry laughed heartily, unexpectedly, doubling up over the handle of his spade.

"It was a hell of a fight to keep her," Paddy told him. "Now, if they had only offered money for her... or drink..."

The story of the whale sighting had travelled to Grace Island, Westport, and along the mainland, as well as the villages and towns of Inish. Paddy swore it had been reported in the national newspapers and had even received coverage on national television. Humpback whales, in February, off the coast of Mayo... Now that was news!

"Sure we're as good as heroes," Paddy said. "Come up to the pub on Saint Patrick's Day and we'll be able to wash ourselves in pints for a week..."

"I can't wait for that," Harry laughed. "I'm due a wash!"

On Saint Patrick's Day the weather changed for the worse. The day started with some pleasant sunshine but by the time Mass had finished the light began to fade to a dreary slate-grey. When the local pipe band gathered outside the church for the traditional parade through the village the first faint wisps of rain were already falling across them. As they struck up their skirling marching tunes the rain grew in intensity and as they marched down through the village it began to fall heavily upon them. Harry stepped out on to his front garden as he saw them take the shore road to his cottage. In the cottages above him, the old bowed-down man with his cap and stick came to stand on the road as the band passed, his sister watching from inside the house, and Clare and her children stood in their garden under a raised flotilla of umbrellas. The black Labrador barked sullenly at the musicians while shaking himself in the rain. Already the pipers in their moss-green jackets, pleated orange kilts, and high white stockings, were soaked in what was now a downpour. The sea and the hills and the furthest cottages were being washed from view as the rain threw a thick grey coat over them. All that stood out now on the landscape were the splashes of green and orange as the pipers turned back toward the heart of the village and the shelter of the church and pub. As they marched through the village their music came and went on the air until as they climbed the short hill to church and pub and reached their goal it quickly fell apart in disarray before disintegrating altogether in a raw sharp cacophony of broken notes. Harry saw from afar the final abandonment of music and instruments as the pipers disbanded and in one terrific rout, heads down, ran shouting in dismay into the warm dry embrace of church and pub. Meanwhile the rain was if anything falling more heavily making a crackling sizzling noise upon the island as if it were some kind of liquid grey fire.

In the afternoon Harry walked to the pub and drank a couple of pints among the crowd there. Some of the locals were interested in the sighting of the whales. He didn't tell anyone about swimming with them in Kim Bay. He was sure no one would believe him. And he was right. Paddy had told that part of the story but it was considered by all to be one of his typical embroidering extravagances, while there had been other confirmed sightings of the whales further along the coast to validate the encounter with the boat. Paddy was right about the celebratory drink however and a couple of free pints were shunted in Harry's direction on the strength of his newfound whale renown.

"I read about it alright in the newspaper," one local told him. "A mighty story it is!"

"Your heroism with the sheep is forgotten now," Paddy had commented. "Sure you can't compare a sheep to a whale!"

It wasn't a particularly cold day but against the rain the fire was set blazing and steam rose from the damp clothes of everyone there but most especially the strewn pipers with their weary disheartened expressions the plentiful drink could not dispel. The ones who had gone first into the church had changed into their dry everyday clothes and seemed happier standing with their glasses in the comforting warmth of the pub. The ones who had hurried straight into the pub seemed the most downcast sitting in the rising steam from their green white and orange clothing as if they were sitting outlandishly dressed in some kind of sauna. The rain could be heard now beating solidly on the roof and it began to drown out the voices which gradually lowered and dimmed, as if with respect for the greater force falling upon and covering them.

"It's Nature," Harry heard someone say. "What can you do?"

"Well we have more than our fair share of it here!" Harry heard someone reply.

Harry hurried down through the rain to Paddy and Joy's house. Bill and Jane were already there but saying they would leave soon as the rain was worsening and there was a possibility of flooding. In any case the first guests of the year had arrived at "The Emerald" and they should really be back there attending to business.

"A fine time they'll have on the island in this weather," Paddy grumbled unhappily.

Joy served the usual tea and sandwiches followed by scones with butter and jam all of which they praised and enjoyed with quiet satisfaction. By late afternoon there was a darkness more typical of midwinter over the island. The household lamps too seemed dimmed and ineffective against the thick dull grey light flooding in through the small windows of the cottage. Everyone's attention was on the rain and the conversation was more subdued than usual with long silences where they gazed into the fire.

"It's like being on a boat at sea!" Bill said.

"You wouldn't have that fire on a boat!" Paddy reminded him.

Paddy turned the radio on to hear the weather forecast and they sat in gloomy silence hearing a storm warning being announced. The exposed west coast and islands would be particularly badly hit. Paddy put his head in his hands saying hopelessly,

"Oh Lord, we're in for it! It's going to be a bad one..."

Bill and Jane hurried away to return to "The Emerald", while Harry strode across the stony beach to get home more quickly. He noticed the waves were higher than usual falling and rolling to his feet and beyond them a great high wall of darkness was rising up. When he reached the road he began to run for the shelter of the cottage his clothes now drenched with cold rills of rainwater running out of the fabric and down his skin. He changed out of his clothes into fresh and dry ones and sat in the porch watching the thickening gloom gather ever more tightly about the village. Clare's husband, Michael, suddenly emerged through the darkness and rain running to the front of the cottage.

"If you'd like to stay with us until the storm is passed?" he offered, but Harry declined.

He couldn't imagine what it would be like sitting all evening and perhaps passing the night with Clare, her husband, their children, and the black dog. Every time he looked at her or she at him would be a painful revelation of their closeness. It was best to stay where he was, sole captain of his ship, the last man on board, no rafts, watching the heaving seas and skies rise up to overwhelm him. He could outlast the storm on his own. He was sure of it. He would have to.

It was night when the storm hit with all its brutal force. The night had become a deep impenetrable black. The night, sea, rain, and wind, were melded together in a single dark thunderous roar which grew louder and louder as the hours passed. Harry had never experienced a night like this with the rain sweeping in torrents against the roof and walls of the cottage and the wind rushing over it, gripping its sides and shaking it, as if it were a small box it was determined to tear apart and discard on the black wings of the storm. Harry went to bed but he couldn't sleep, certain that his windows were about to be blown in on him. Eventually he moved with some bedding to the living room and made his bed in front of the fireplace. He banked up the fuel and soon had a fire blazing to lie down in front of. He hoped for sleep but understood there could be no sleep or dreams in the wild savagery of this night. By midnight the wind was like a solid object throwing itself over and over against the cottage and the heavy hammering blows it delivered sent violent vibrations through the structure. Harry had felt anxiety and trepidation since early evening but now he felt a cold movement of fear spread through him. On the edges of his mind panic settled and he had to fight to calm himself. He wondered if he should make a dash to Clare's cottage or even across the stony beach to Joy and Paddy's. But wouldn't they already be in bed, sleeping? But who could sleep on a night like this? And then there was a great crashing noise and the house shook as if was being uprooted and thrown to one side. Hesitantly, fearfully, his panic now emerging from its restraints, Harry got up and slowly made his way through the cottage wondering if some damage had been done. He feared loss of a window, or some of his roofing, or that the storm would have burst its way into the cottage, bringing with it leaks and flooding, and even overturning its contents. He feared the cottage was being capsized. There was nothing he could find inside so wherever the crashing noise had come from it was outside the cottage. He debated leaving the cottage and hesitated but eventually he took a lamp and ventured out. The wind immediately caught him as if it had grasping hands and tried to drag him away from the front of the cottage. He held tight to the walls as he shone the lamp about. He couldn't see the sea in the opaque blackness but its roar enveloped him together with that of the wind as the wind pushed, pulled, and tugged forcefully at him threatening to knock him over. The wind was veering even more strongly around the corner of the cottage and Harry realised if he stepped away from the shelter of the building itself that he risked being thrown over and tumbled hurriedly away. He clung with whatever grip he could find to the rough plaster of the walls and stuck his head forward to peer around the end of the cottage. It was dangerous. He knew a loose slate could come flying through the night to cut him open or even decapitate him, the dreadful image flashed through his mind. He feared the unprecedented violence of the storm. He wanted to rush back to the shelter of the cottage interior but he leaned back into the wind maintaining just enough balance to shine the lamp on the ground in front of him. An involuntary cry escaped him. A high white mound of fallen broken plaster from the cottage's gable end lay along the entire side of the house. Harry turned his lamp on the bare stone of the cottage where a huge sheet of plaster had been ripped away. In the light of the lamp the naked stone shone with a wet gleaming desolation. Harry wondered if the whole side of the house might come down, but he realised there was nothing he could do. He would have to wait for the storm to die down to see the full extent of the damage. In the meantime he would have to hope for the best. He struggled back to the front of the house and once inside returned to his fire and sat trembling in front of it with his bedclothes pulled up around his shoulders. Despite the blazing fire he was cold and frightened. He stared into the flames as the night seemed to grow darker and the wind stronger and the rain sounded like waves of the sea dashing against the roof and windows. He was slowly taken over by the storm. It possessed and emptied him. He became hollow, without thoughts, without feelings, only the instinct of fear survived, as he waited for an end to come. Whatever that end could be.

He didn't know how much time had passed when there was another thunderous crash, but this one did not shake the building or vibrate through it like the falling plaster had done. It sounded distant and came really with a dull and extended explosive sound which Harry thought must have been heard all over the island. He had no idea what had happened and hoped his neighbours and their houses were all safe. He could think of nothing to do except sit and watch the flames and try to contain his rising fear. And then about a half hour later he heard shouting on the road outside the cottage. He slipped out of the bedclothes and walked to the porch. Clare's husband was standing at the gate with a bright torch he was shining on the front of the house. He was shouting like a madman as the rain swept him and the wind pulled at his clothes and hair. Harry couldn't make out what he was saying and once again stepped out of the building into the light of the torch. When Michael saw Harry he shouted to him. Harry couldn't believe what he was hearing.

"We have to go to the hill, Harry! All the men are needed on the hill!"

"What the… is going on?" Harry shouted, using a rare brutal expletive.

Michael's voice was breaking as he shouted his words to Harry but Harry understood him perfectly now.

"There's been a plane crash, Harry! A plane has crashed on the hill… We have to help!"

Michael turned away and began running back hard past his own cottage and towards the hill. Harry covered his fire with ash and placed a guard over it, he didn't want the cottage burning down while he was away. He put on his warmest rainproof jacket and pulled on his wellingtons and, taking his lamp up again, strode out of the house towards the hillside. Luckily right then the wind seemed to be lessening and he was not being buffeted violently as he had been earlier. With the relenting of the wind the rain was not so strong but still it fell in a steady stream over him. Clare was standing at the gate to her house and she watched him pass. They said nothing but he saw that her eyes were fraught, full of an overwhelming anxiety, an unspoken noiseless distress, as they followed him into the darkness. As he walked towards the site of the crash, he heard a strange sad music rising in him. It was a real music like something composed and drawn out in sadness, like some plaintive weeping adagio for strings. He didn't know where the strange music was coming from, only that it was inside him. He thought of his dream of the whales deep in their ocean singing their haunting songs. He felt, listening to this strange inner symphony of his own, striding through the falling rain, that he too was like some submarine animal making his way blindly through the darkness, homeless and alone, drifting in sadness, with nowhere to go. After a short while he could see scattered over the hillside about a mile away dozens of small fires blazing. As he drew close he could see the ropes of rain brightly glowing and twisting in the fierce light of the flames. There were already a number of vehicles pulled up at the base of the hill and shadowy figures moving about. Peter Goode was there and stepped forward as he saw Harry approaching.

"We're looking for survivors!" he shouted to him. "We're looking for survivors but we don't think there can be any... We're looking for bodies then."

He pointed to the hillside where the fires continued to blaze, the ropes of rain hanging and twisting in their burning glow.

"Walk around with your light, Harry," he told him breathlessly. "If you find anything let us know... Listen as well as look... You might hear something. If you find anything just shout to us, we'll come to help you. Look for survivors or bodies... Watch out for fragments of the plane that could still be burning, hot... or cut you... Don't touch anything..."

Harry lifted up his torch and followed its light up the hill. As he climbed he carried his sad, haunting, irrepressible music inside him, it wouldn't die until he himself fell into the deepest sleep later that morning when the storm had ended. While sadness would inhabit him all his life, he would never hear that beautiful music again.

After the first appalling discoveries Harry left the crash site and wandered high to the cliff edge. He sat there dangling his feet over the three hundred foot drop to the ocean and waited until the first grey light of day began to seep into the atmosphere and he could now see below him the vast abyss of nothingness that hung over Kill bay and the west of the island. By morning the storm had passed, the wind had abated, and the rain had left only a stain of dampness in the grey light of day. As Harry walked back down the hill he saw police and army vehicles and ambulances on the road. The locals who had first arrived to search the crash site had been replaced by police and army teams spread across the hillside. Scattered here and there fragments of the wreckage still brightly burned like braziers. He saw lifeless bodies contained in bulky bags being carried down the hillside on stretchers, the stretcher-bearers staggering and stumbling under the weight. One of the police directed him away from the working teams towards the road and Harry began the long slow walk home. He was cold and his legs felt stiff and heavy. He dragged himself along. He met no one. The island had a beaten, exhausted air. Some smoke rose from chimneys here and there but otherwise nothing, no doors were open to the outside world, there wasn't a soul to be seen. Harry got to his cottage to find his electricity was out, he couldn't even boil a kettle. He poured himself a large glass of whiskey and lay down again in front of the fire he set blazing again. Before long, inevitably, irresistibly, an immense wave of sleep came crashing through him, and he capsized like a drowned man into the gathered bedding he had heaped around him.

For the next few days there was a pall of shock over the island. It had been an army helicopter that had crashed on the hillside. There had been a crew of four, all killed instantly, so the papers claimed. There had been Séan, Brian, Joe, all young men with wives, family, children. The captain was a young red-haired woman from Donegal, Julie Lacey. She was stunningly beautiful and was pictured on the front page of all the newspapers. She was unmarried and had no children, but a disconsolate boyfriend, of course, yes. She was thirty-three. She had had all her life in front of her, cruelly cut off. Harry asked for discarded newspapers from his neighbours and read all the accounts of the crash. He cut out the pictures of Julie Lacey and spread them out on his tables and furniture. He lit candles around the pictures as if he was creating some kind of shrine to her. He told himself the candles were for comfort or hope, but he had never looked for hope before, or comfort, and he felt very little of either. He told himself they were for a spirit of holiness, but he suspected they were for a spirit of love. Here was a woman he had never heard of, had never met, whose existence he had known nothing of and might indeed never have known anything of if it wasn't for the awful crash. And now, like everyone else on the island and in Ireland in general, he was exalted by her beauty and heartbroken by her loss. She was someone he did not, had never known, would never know, and yet whose presence in his life had made an inconsolable void in it at the very same time as it was made painfully, cruelly, beautifully real. A desperate unsatisfiable yearning filled him and it bore her name. He was aware that the entire country felt the same. All the deaths had caused pain and grief, but Julie Lacey's, allied to the special light and life-filled images of her startling red-haired radiance, had twisted like a cruel knife in the heart and soul of the entire nation. It seemed impossible that a life so spectacularly vital and bright and beautiful could be so entirely diminished in one tragic instant of destruction. For days, and nights, to come, Harry drank copious amounts of whiskey, read the newspaper accounts over and over again, gazed incessantly at the pictures of Julie Lacey, and cried bitter, bitter tears.

As he had asked for the newspapers, Clare called one day with some more recent ones and also gifted him a small transistor radio. Harry had lived since coming to the island without tv or radio and had hardly ever read a paper. The helicopter crash had made a crack in his world through which news from the outside began to seep through. The tragedy made the island the heartbeat of the entire country for a number of weeks. Hardly a day went by without some reference to the crash and its victims and Julie Lacey's photograph was everpresent on the front pages of the papers. Within a week the crash site had been cleared and the search teams had left the island. The bodies had been removed to Westport but a week to the day after the crash a memorial service was held in the church in Dughrá. It was the first time Harry attended Mass there. The church was full and the crowd spilled out on to the spaces around it. Photos of the crew lined the altar with brightly glowing candles around them. Colourful bouquets of flowers stood to either side of the altar. The priest spoke of tragedy, loss, death, having come to the community. It had swooped down upon them like some deadly bird of prey descending from the darkest most tormented skies, tearing pitilessly at the very heart of their world, their lives, and leaving only a terrible grief behind. A grief that would never go away, he said. There was a low ripple of suppressed sobbing through the congregation that ran too out of the church and into the crowd outside where it echoed. Harry wondered if it could ever die away now, or be contained, that sobbing.

The storm had created other talking points. Jean's house had been battered and badly damaged, timbers and roofing had been torn away. Harry saw men inspecting it. There was talk of demolishing it. The last tangible reminders of Jean's stay on the island were about to be wiped away. Soon there would be nothing of her left. Harry could do nothing about it. Deep down he accepted it. Jean's memory was a ruin now. It was better if it disappeared. It was simply another kind of death.

There had been a more untoward and spectacular consequence to the storm which brought curious visitors to the island. One thousand feet of beach close to Kill had been washed away in the storm. All of the golden sand, on which Harry had sometimes walked, had been pulled out to sea by the waves and now there were only rock pools and boulders, some as big as people. On the morning after the storm the locals had gathered in dismay to look out over their world from which a line of pure gold had been stripped away to be replaced by inhospitable pitiless stone. The newspaper and television crews when they had finished their coverage of the helicopter tragedy now turned their attention to the disappeared beach. Pictures of Julie Lacey, who with her fiery red hair and her vivacious smile seemed to encapsulate an image of magical Irish female beauty, were now accompanied on the front pages by "before" and "after" pictures of the beach around which the reporters wove words of enchantment and magic, alongside dramatic evocations of the fatality of the world itself. The reporters recalled too the recent landslide and for a while it seemed as if the island had become an apocalyptic place from which it might be better to flee. There was trouble in the face of all the island, and loss and sadness in every heart. And yet the island had never seen so many visitors. There was an economic spur as people from near and far travelled to the island to follow the trail of disaster from the crash site to the disappeared beach and then to the island's iconic deserted village. In the pubs the locals had to give or invent eye-witness accounts of the storm and accident. Paddy swore that on the night of the storm he had seen sixty foot high waves crashing down on the shore, but while he was not believed, the likelihood is that he had indeed seen them. Harry believed him. The visitors seemed to even expect direct eye-witness accounts of the desertion of the historical abandoned village from the islanders, an event which was truly lost in time. No one could definitively say why the village with its stone houses had been left. By general consensus it was because of the famine in the mid-eighteen-hundreds. Back then there had been another far graver apocalypse, and back then the people had decided to go, it was either die or go. Now in the wake of fresh disaster people were streaming to the island, disaster was the new tourism. The weather was good and having sated their appetite for the tragic the visitors flocked to the island's beaches. Kim Bay was overrun. Harry cycled there one day and wished for the whales to return to sweep the crowds away. Joy was selling lots of her handmade trinkets to visitors to Dughrá who were captivated too by the exposed site of her house on the grassy headland.

"How did you survive the storm?" Paddy was asked over and over.

"I stood in the face of it! I let it blow into my mouth! And I chewed it to bits with my teeth!" was Paddy's stock response after a time.

"I wish I had kept a few boxes of me wine to sell to the tourists!" he lamented to Harry. "Those darn Strawboys..."

A letter announced a visit from Harry's brother and he arrived a few days later exhausted after the long journey from the Irish midlands.

"God, you really are at the end of the world out here, Harry!" he complained.

For a few days and nights the brothers sat together drinking whiskey. They seldom left the cottage and they spoke little. But they were relaxed in their companionship.

On the last evening, Harry's brother tried in vain to get him to leave with him.

"Leave this God-forsaken place, Harry... Come home with me! Máireaid and the kids would love to see you... Stay with us for a time. It's time to start rebuilding your life."

Harry was impervious.

"I'm not ready to leave yet," he said. "I feel like it's my island now... I belong here..."

"You have to leave here, Harry," his brother insisted. "It's not good for you... I can see it... I can see the suffering of your soul in your face when I look at you!... I'm afraid you might have come here to die..."

"I might have," Harry said, unmoved.

The brothers stayed on good terms and didn't argue. When the time came to leave the brother said,

"Stop being a Hamlet!"

Adding, "The world is a place worth living in, Harry!"

The next morning the postman called with a letter from Nick and his answer to the question Harry had written just after Christmas, all of three months before.

"I'm so sorry it has taken all this time to write but I have not forgotten you, Harry, and I have been living with the echoes and vibrations of my time on the island with you. Or should I say the time in your cottage has continued to unfold and progress inside me like a living thing and to provide me with ongoing echoes and vibrations of my experience there.

Things have become much clearer to my inner eye and I now believe I understand much better what happened at the cottage. So, I want to try to answer your question.

I have a much clearer picture now of the woman at the window. It is as if with time and familiarity with me she has decided to show herself openly. She is a young woman (forgive me for using the present tense but she is still 'present' to me)... She is a young woman perhaps in her early thirties. She has white skin but white like milk, Harry, her skin has the brightest shine. Her hair is long and dark, but dark like a raven, Harry, it's black, black as night. But most extraordinary of all are her eyes, Harry. Her eyes are incredibly beautiful, Harry. Incredible! They are of the deepest most intense, I want to say 'precious' blue. I call them 'lapis lazuli', Harry. It is the only description that fits. Her eyes are made of lapis lazuli, more precious than gold.

The strangest thing, Harry, is that she does not speak... And yet I can hear her voice. It is a beautiful, light, musical, singing voice, quiet and beautiful, as if underwater, but high-pitched and sweet, a gorgeous female voice, it has the charm of the Siren, I feel I could drown in it... But it is so sad, Harry, so sad.

Do you remember, before I abruptly closed the curtains on her, that she reached out to me? I knew that she wanted something from me... I did not know what it was. I must admit it frightened me. But Harry she has been speaking ever since, and I have been listening listening listening ever since and I have finally heard her in that sweet, haunting, beautiful voice of hers, Harry...

She wants to be 'let in', Harry. She is asking to be 'let in'. She doesn't want to be outside, Harry, she wants to be 'inside'...

Harry, she wants to be alive, not dead."

The first page of tightly-written script ended here but there was more written on the back of the page and Harry turned it over to continue his reading.

"But there is something else too, Harry, which you need to know about. It's not this time about the woman with the raven hair and the lapis lazuli eyes... It's about the other woman, the blonde woman in the photographs, the American woman who owned the wooden shack on the shore, I think you said her name was Jean?...

I remember clearly all the photos you showed me of her. I have been looking, in my mind's eye, at these photographs almost all the time since you showed them to me. And they too began to reveal their secrets to me. The photos were taken in America some time before she left to come to Ireland. She is alone in the pictures because she is undertaking her journey alone. The person taking the pictures is not 'in the picture' because, in her heart and soul, she has already separated from him. She has a new dream she wishes to pursue. That dream is you, Harry.

That woman, with her blonde hair and green-gold eyes, Harry, came to Ireland and came to your island to find you, Harry...

Harry, she was in love with you even before she ever knew of your existence. She knew she would find you in Ireland.

This is not how the world works you will say, I can hear you, but Harry it is how the Universe works.

She came to find you Harry, at the end of the world, and she vowed that when she found you she would never let you go."

Harry let the sheet of paper fall in his lap. Nick's letter only added to the island's mysteries. It was crazy. Nick was crazy. The woman with the raven hair, the milk-white skin, the lapis lazuli eyes (why had he said "*lapis lazuli*"?). The woman who doesn't want to be dead. He believed he himself must have suggested all this to Nick during his visit either overtly, covertly, or subliminally, or whatever the word was. So there were no psychic revelations or even surprises there. Everything could be explained. As for Jean... That was even more absurd. She had come to the island, built her home, had her heart attack, returned home and died, even before he had arrived to live on the island. How could she have wanted anything of him? And if she did have her dream of him, why had her dream not been fulfilled? Or was that how the Universe worked? He must ask Nick that. Tell me, Nick. Tell me how the Universe works? And we'll see if we can make sense of all of its mad dreams and its infinite sadnesses. But he could not deny that Nick's letter had shaken him. He drank whiskey all evening. He sat in the porch watching the fall of darkness with the "Steppenwolf" novel cradled in his lap. And he wondered again if he was going to go mad, or if he was perhaps already mad. He looked out on his "Kingdom of Nothing" and wondered if, as his brother had suggested, he might die here. He remembered thinking that time earlier in the year when he had walked on the cliff that he would have to leave the island. But he reminded himself that he had nowhere to go. Under his feet there was only a vast abyss and if he got up to walk he would fall straight down into it. But he asked himself if he did fall into the abyss, what would he find there? Did he dare? Did he dare to walk? And fall? He lay in bed that night with the letter grasped tightly in his hand staring sleeplessly into the ceiling darkness. He went again and again over every word Nick had written. Did the letter contain any truth? Any possibility of truth? But finally as sleep gained him he realised he was not thinking of his Monkstown Claire, or of Jean, as he sank into the deepest darkest of dreamless sleeps, but of Helen. He had not thought of her in such a long time and now she was alive in him again, her magnolia-white skin covered in gleaming jewels of bright seawater, running before him along the golden beach at Kim. He saw, in his mind's eye, as Nick had put it, the photos of Jean before she had left America to come to Ireland. He saw the photos and the images, but he did not see Jean any longer. In her place he saw Helen. And as he thought of her his heart beat faster. And faster. And faster. Until it was knocking in him like a fist rapping on a closed door.

The next day Tomás called and began work clearing the fallen rubble from the gable end of the cottage and to replaster over the exposed stone of the building. During a break for tea the two men surveyed the potato garden Harry had made. The ground was still dark and heavy with moisture and all that had grown in the few weeks since its creation were wild grasses and flowering weeds with not a single potato sprouting up into the air and light.

"I don't think you'll get many spuds out of there," Tomás said, slurping his tea, and shaking his head more than doubtfully.

Behind them they heard the rumble of a couple of trucks along the shoreline and a little while later they could hear a loud persistent hammering and the buzzing sound of mechanical saws. Shielding his eyes from the sun Harry could make out the far-off small figures of men climbing around on the sides and roof of Jean's cabin. He noticed them pulling aside beams of timber and sheets of material, flinging them carelessly away. Over the next week Jean's dream home at the end of the world in Ireland would be broken, dismembered, dismantled, dissolved, and carted away until there was nothing left. And on the last day when it was all gone all that could be seen at the end of the shore and beyond it, above the quiet ocean, was a bright, blind and indifferent moon looking down upon the emptiness where the shack had stood, as if it had never been there at all. Where once there had been a human life lived, now there was nothing at all. Harry wondered if Jean had found anything, anything at all, of what she had come to Ireland dreaming of and looking for, before her heart decided it had had enough of dreaming and of looking for impossible things.

The island was not yet free of apocalypse. Harry had a habit now of listening to news broadcasts on the small transistor radio Clare had given him. One morning late in April he woke to hear, while still lying in his bed, the most extraordinary unimagined unimaginable news. A nuclear reactor in Eastern Europe had gone into meltdown. There had been a steam explosion inside the reactor which was now on fire. Radioactive material was being pumped out into the environment, humans and animals were dying, rivers, reservoirs, and drinking water were being contaminated. A pine forest near the reactor had turned reddish-brown and was dying. Tens of thousands of people were being evacuated from the area. The region would become a no-go, a no-human, zone. But the radioactive dust could not be contained there. Floating and carried on the air it would follow the fleeing people. It would spread into the neighbouring countryside, to neighbouring villages, towns, cities, countries, continents. The earth and sky were being poisoned and killed. The mountains, the lakes, the rivers, the seas, the islands. Harry rose from his bed stunned by the news. It seemed as if at every turn the world was preparing fresh and imminent disasters. When he looked out over the ocean Harry half-expected to see toxic clouds of radiation hovering above it, heading for land, preparing to spill poisonous rains on everything and everyone. But everything looked as it always did. On this day of nuclear cataclysm in the world there was clear bright sunshine with no clouds over the island. The sky was a pristine blue and everything looked clean, clear, pure, uncontaminated, innocent. The wind, the weather report said, was from the east.

Harry's older neighbour, bent over his supporting stick, standing on the road just outside the garden gate, peered out with narrowed eyes from under his peaked cap. He had heard the news of the disaster but had not followed the weather forecast.

"Our west winds will protect us," he said wisely, waving his cane eastwards. "The radiation will never reach Inish!"

Harry superior in his knowledge chose not to disabuse him. The poisonous cloud was coming this way, borne on winds out of the east. Over the coming weeks and months and perhaps longer, perhaps forever, tiny invisible particles laden with death would be carried across Europe to reach even the most remote hidden places, to fall like imperceptible but deadly seed to grow and destroy even in the furthest reaches at the end of the western world itself. The radiation cloud would sweep out over the ocean, it would meet barriers in some places, but where it didn't it would continue to creep forward investing all in its path with its lethal breath until an entire world might die from it. There could be no escaping. The cloud would seep into everything, land, sea, air, animals, people. And everything would inevitably crumble, decay, and die. With or without the cloud.

They were strange weeks on the island and in the entire country. The east winds continued to blow for almost a month. Every news broadcast spoke of the dangers, which no one could perfectly quantify. It would be years, decades perhaps, before the damaging impacts on environment and lives could be exactly stated for Ireland. In the meantime the site of the meltdown was the wounded heart of the world. There had been immediate deaths, dozens of them, and much sickness. The scientists from their crystal balls conjured images of deformed and dead things, young animals and babies born hellishly distorted, children and adults sickened, older people, full of malignant growths and tumours, dying before their time. No one would be safe and no one would be immune. In the reactor the fire continued to burn. The radioactive gases continued to escape. Finally they used helicopters to drop five thousand tons of sand, clay, and boron on to the flames. Eventually they would build a sarcophagus of concrete and steel around it. But it was too late. The birth of monstrous things was already stored up in the future. The scientists said that already the future had been poisoned, sickened, diseased, destined to reveal enormities, to inevitably decay and die. The future bore already an ineradicable taint, just like a living person, ill to death. Everything was now subject to meltdown, even Time.

For weeks the island was shadowed by its own and the world's misfortunes. Visitors in the early summer still came to the island in droves, stopping at the crash site, the disappeared beach, the deserted village, and still sprawled upon and swam at the beaches in the late hot afternoons. The guesthouses, restaurants, and pubs were full. And everywhere echoed to conversations brimming over with reactors, explosions, fires, radioactivity, and the myriad forms of meltdown and nuclear holocaust. Only the deserted village stood untouched, unmoved and impassive, on its hillside, but only because it was already dead, its dead stones beyond the reach of any new cataclysm. Radiation meant nothing to it. Meltdown meant nothing. Time meant nothing. Only stone and moss obtained.

By June the prevailing protecting winds had returned from the south-west to everyone's relief. The beautiful wild yellow irises had sprung to bright life by the roadsides. People were now laughing and joking, while also conscientiously remembering to deplore the receding fallout, as if it were a departing plague. Even the radio and newspapers began to set the subject aside and turn their attention elsewhere. Paddy wondered if he should harvest his grapes this year as he feared they could be poisoned. He said his wine this year, if he did make some, would be his "Fallout" vintage.

Bill was busy writing an exciting new novel about an Atlantic island overwhelmed by nuclear catastrophe in which terrifying mutants would appear. It was his "best yet", he said. Harry had given up struggling with his garden. It had only produced grasses and weeds. By early June he had let the weeds thrive and they stood insolently tall over the dismal soil where not a single edible potato had grown. Neighbours and curious passerbys joked about the failure of his enterprise. Harry resisted as best he could.

"The nuclear fallout killed my crop," he claimed.

"That's probably what caused the Irish Potato Famine too," someone said.

Even the greatest disasters had their perspective of humour.

The summer went by quickly. Harry's routines had changed. Before he rose in the morning he listened to the news on the radio. He walked more in the warm weather and despite the hordes of tourists still roaming the island he cycled almost every day and walked again to the summits of Carrigmore and Sleevebeg and walked too among the sunbathers and swimmers who added so much colour and noise to Kim Bay. While he was more occupied than he had ever been since coming to the island he began to find time weighing heavily on his hands. For the first time he began to feel what he realised was a creeping boredom. He listened more and more to the radio, he even asked Mary Kate about getting a television. He wanted to read and sent his brother a list of books he would like to have, while others he borrowed from the mobile library which pulled up weekly outside his cottage. He put "Steppenwolf" away. When the books came from his brother he sat for hours in the porch reading or outdoors in the warm sunshine. His neighbours waved and often stopped to exchange pleasantries with him. Clare's husband started to call and they would drink whiskey together sitting outdoors in the warm evenings.

"I need to get away from Clare's prattling," he sometimes said in a routine, dismissive, half-joking manner.

One evening he confided with Harry about a woman he had been with in England, and then he said,

"To be honest, Harry, there were several women... You know what it's like... being a man and all that... England can be a lonely place... Everywhere can..."

He was troubled by it but Harry's silent and apparent acquiescence seemed to comfort him.

One day as Harry walked on the stony beach he met Crotchety Jack in more than usual ill humour. Harry tried to engage him on the perennial theme of the weather, but Jack only spat a virulent response at him,

"What are you doing here?" he asked.

"Well you know I came here to write…" Harry muttered, at a loss for words.

Jack was unconvinced and stamped about a little on the stones as he spoke.

"You shouldn't be here," he said. "You're too young…"

"I'm almost forty!" Harry protested.

"You're too young!" Jack insisted. "You're wasting your time here… You're wasting your life here… The island's no good for you. Why don't you go find yourself something useful to do with yourself somewhere…"

He strode off leaving Harry to gaze wonderingly after him as he left. When Harry told Paddy the story, Paddy responded in much the same manner as Jack, albeit with much less vehemence, but equal conviction.

"Well," he said, "maybe Jack is right… Maybe you should think about getting yourself a real life somewhere…"

"You guys are ganging up on me!" Harry complained. "Anyone would think you want me to go from the island…"

"Come back like Bill when you're retired from living," Paddy said. "You'll still have time to do your writing then…"

Harry was genuinely upset by the conversations. For a couple of weeks he avoided Jack and Paddy, and did not even call to Bill. For a time Clare's husband was his only companion, and increasingly they sat in silence while drinking whiskey, and then when September was almost upon them and the weather got a little colder he saw less and less of him. As the autumn returned, Harry felt as if the island was drifting away from him, turning its back to him. He felt as if it wanted him to leave. He began to feel that he himself wanted to leave. He remembered the feeling he had had walking above the cliff looking out over his "Kingdom of Nothing". He had felt then that he must inevitably leave. And now in the wake of the disasters that had occurred that feeling was even stronger. He would soon be a year on the island. He decided to talk to Mary Kate about leaving.

It was the time of the autumn equinox again. Harry remembered arriving a year earlier on the island with the planet Venus visible in the court of the crescent moon above the island. Now there was a full moon, bright and yellow, like the moon over Lake Iseo when he had been there with Claire in what now seemed a lifetime ago, or maybe a deathtime ago. Sky, sea, and island, glistened in the yellow light which with just a little more intensity could turn to gold. Harry watched and waited for that moment, but inevitably the moon faded and vanished into the arms of the richest night hues, lovely and beautiful in their own right. The tide of the year had turned now, the summer was done, and the evenings were slipping more and more into encroaching darkness. One evening late in the month, when the moon was well on the wane, Harry felt something slip inside him, something very nearly imperceptible, like a movement of shadows parting from each other deep in his soul. He poured himself a glass of whiskey and sat in the porch with the light on. He took and opened "Steppenwolf" and began to leaf through it. It was not the first time he had done this but he had not done so in a very long time. For long hours before and during his time on the island he had sat with the book without opening it, or if he did he had not even glanced at what its pages contained. Now he felt curious again and wanted to renew contact with the words printed or those written in Claire's hand within its covers. It had, with its themes of "sadness, madness, suicide", as Harry had once put it to her, been perhaps Claire's favourite novel. He wanted to see now if it held or revealed secrets for him. It was easy to tell from the book's wear and tear how often Claire had turned its pages either to reread it entirely or seeking out her favourite passages. Harry noticed first how she had ringed with a pen every occurrence of the name "Harry" featured in the novel. Among the early pages she had written, "*I have found my own Harry!*" Her commentary was added to several episodes. When Hermione entered the story she wrote, "*I want to be Hermione!*" When Maria featured she wrote, "*I want to be Maria!*" At one point she wrote, "*I want to teach Harry to dance*" and again, "*I want to teach Harry to like music*". Later she wrote, "*I want to teach Harry to laugh!*", and later again, "*I want to teach Harry to be happy!*" In another place she wrote, "*I want to teach Harry to love!*" And later, "*I want to teach Harry to live!*" Alongside one of the novel's descriptions of exquisite and redeeming sexual pleasure she had written, "*I want it to always be like this!*" Alongside another sexual passage she had written, "*exquisite, exalted, transcendent, celestial...*" Alongside another similar passage she had written, "*I love this!*" And at every point she drew the emphatic circles around his name. On many pages shorter handwritten phrases or single words appeared, apparent interjections added to the narrative, words like, "*Oh, no, don't!*", or "*Why?*", or "*Please, Harry!*" Sometimes she had simply placed an exclamation or question mark alongside a sentence or paragraph and in some instances he saw series of suspension points, dot-dot-dot, like some kind of Morse code he couldn't decipher. Harry was never sure if the additions in Claire's hand related to him or to the central character of the novel. He didn't even know if she had made her additions before or after she had met him or, what was more likely, both before and after. At the end of the novel, beyond its final paragraphs, she had written "*The End*" and had retraced the letters several times to give it an emphatically darkened finality. A date she had added in a trembling hand fell on the day she had died. After a couple of hours sitting with the book, sipping his whiskey, Harry felt drained and exhausted. And yet he could feel deep down nameless currents moving about inside him carrying distinct emotions ferrying loss, pain, sorrow, sadness, from body to mind to heart to soul, while outside all that lay beyond him and beyond the cottage was an opaque impenetrable darkness from whence the moon and stars had been blown out, extinguished, and in whose shadow Harry alone obtained. In the darkness Harry became darkness. He felt his own desolation was now complete. But it wasn't. Not yet.

He retrieved Claire's notebook with the intertwined dark, green, and golden leaves of its cover, brushing aside the newspaper clippings and pictures of Julie Lacey which filled the drawer where he had hidden it away. He settled again in the porch and opened the notebook. He had never opened it before, since coming to the island, not once. He had never read a single word it contained. But as soon as he started reading it he realised that here was his story written by Claire, or here was their story. Here in the beginning was the moment he had entered her life. And here at the end was the "nothing ever after", the "no more", that Claire had bequeathed him. He filled his glass with whiskey again, he took a deep breath and began to read. Claire wrote to begin with in a confident happy handwriting,

"I like this new man very much. After Frank ran away I fell into his arms. I cried on his shoulder more freely than I have ever cried before, as if I could be free at last to cry with him. He held me in his arms with a lovely warmth that passed freely from him into my body. No one has ever held me like he did. I want to feel that warmth again. I want to feel his arms again. But I'm not going to rush things. I've had enough of the accidents and disasters of rushing things."

It was not a day by day or moment by moment journal, or even chronologically perfect. It was as if every so often Claire had simply felt the need to enter some thoughts into the notebook so that its style became intermittent and even erratic as it progressed. And as the strongest emotions rose in him Harry found himself unable to read it straight through, but skipped from place to place, encountering his story with

Claire in flashes that sometimes threatened to overpower him. Early on she wrote,

"At last I have my own Harry. I've always wanted a Harry. And this Harry is the kind of Harry I want. I like him very much, this Harry. He's quiet, retiring, melancholy, with airs of loneliness and sadness about him. I know he has depths and I will bring them out of him. I don't think he really has had very much experience of life, or of women, but I'll give him that too. I can give him all the experience he's ever dreamed of. I know men!"

She wrote about their early times together, the glasses of wine shared, the walks along the bay and the naked sunbathing at the "Forty Foot", also the nights she had spent in his bed. She wrote about the rainbows they had seen and how they had danced liked crazy children at the edge of the water. She wrote about her feelings for Harry during all this time, before they had become complete lovers, lost, so lost, and islanded, in each other.

"Oh sometimes I just want to grab him and make love to him so passionately. I want to surprise him, astonish him, stun him... I want to dance and throw my clothes off for him. I want to climb on him and ride him and plunder every pleasure from him. I want to teach him every form of pleasure... I want to be all the forms of pleasure a woman can be for him. I want to be Hermione or Maria for him, or both rolled into one. He can be my "Steppenwolf". I'll make him forget those nurses across the way. I'll make him forget every woman he's ever seen or heard of. Oh I'm going to be everything to him. I can see he loves me. I can see it in his eyes, how he watches me. Sometimes his eyes disappear deep into me. I can feel them seeking my soul. I told him, 'It feels like you are gazing into my soul!' He's gazing but it's a lost helpless gazing... as if he's starting to drown in me. Oh I can feel how much he loves me. I can feel it in the warmth of his body when he is close to me. I can feel it in his heartbeat under my hands. I can feel it in his gaze and in his breath and in his heartbeat. Oh it would be so easy to slip him inside me and begin to be his perfect lover... But not yet not yet not yet... There have been so many men, I've made love to hundreds of men, and it has always been too easy... far too easy... I don't want Harry to be easy. I want Harry to be right. For the first time I feel here is a man who wants to know me on the inside. To really know me, and really love me. The kind of woman I am. He doesn't just want to... me. He loves me. He wants to love me. He wants to make love to me. How could he not want that? And I am going to make it so beautiful for him... But more than anything he wants to love me. He does love me. How could he not love me? He just has no idea what's coming to him... Oh he's in for the shock of his life... yes he is..."

Some notes were randomly separate. On one page she wrote,

"The moon was so big and full tonight. I sat and watched it for a long time. It seems so bright and yet so blind and indifferent. I think she might be a crazy woman. She watches us but I don't know what she sees. I don't even know if she does see... anything... She just watches. I think she might be a crazy woman! She has a yellow face... Yellow must be the colour of crazy..."

She wrote about the night of his birthday in November and how she had gotten drunk and he had had to help her walk home, how he had put her to bed, how he had spent the night sitting watching her, caring for her, loving her.

"I am ready to give more of myself to Harry that I have ever given to anyone," she wrote, *"much more!"*

She added, *"Oh I love him so much so much, I never want to let him go. I'll never let him go! Never ever let go..."*

To this note she had added, *"Can't stop, won't stop!"*

The time he had suggested holidaying in Europe she wrote excitedly,

"We're going to Germany, to Belinda, and after that to Switzerland and to Italy, to Italia! Oh I can't wait... A whole brave new world is beginning! We will be transformed after! We will be new people!"

Later, on one otherwise blank and empty page she had written,

"I told him. I told him, I'm the reason for all the pain and sadness there is in the world. I'm the shadow of tragedy on everything. So he knows. So there's no excuse. He knows. He can run from me if he wishes. Or he can stay... Harry, please stay!"

There were small stains dotted around her words on the page. He knew they were tears that had fallen as she wrote. For the Christmas entry she had written,

"Fait accompli, we did it at last. I did it! I had prepared my surprise well. Oh Harry had his own surprise for me. He gave me the gift of a silver chain and medallion. He gave me a wave of the sea and a full moon above it. In the moon he had placed a beautiful sapphire, my blue birthstone. I loved it so much. I asked him to put it around my neck and I told him I

would always wear it. That I would never take it off. And then I delivered my own surprise. It was time. I called him to me. Harry when he crawled on his hands and knees to me had ceased to exist as someone called Harry with a life history behind him. Harry was no longer anything he had ever been up until that moment. I obliterated and annihilated him, utterly, completely, taaraa! in one exquisite fell swoop. Harry was just a bright raw new material melting in my hands. Melting in other parts of me too. I could feel Harry's flesh his body his heart his soul all melting and running into me, every crack, every crevice, every opening... I soaked him up. I completely transformed and transfigured him. He'll never be the same Harry again. We 'began' again tonight and I think we will be one person, inseparable from each other, golden and eternal, from now on. I looked at Harry when I had finished with him and I could see he was no longer there. I could see that I was no longer there either. I too had flowed into him. Every crack, every crevice, every opening... He had soaked me up. We were a new being. Our bodies minds hearts and souls had run into and disappeared into each other, to be together. It was as I had wanted it to be, exquisite... I 'doffed' Harry. And he 'doffed' me. Yes I have to admit. In spite of all my experience, all my planning, all my surprise, and all the 'doffing' I did... Harry 'doffed' me! I just want you to know, Dear Diary, that it was the most beautiful moment of my life... Harry is the most beautiful moment of my life! I never want this to end... Chapeau!..."

After Christmas was dominated by the trip to Germany, Switzerland and Italy, to begin with the months of anticipation, and later the trip itself. He skimmed the early entries and hurried to the pages where Belinda came into the picture. At first Claire's handwriting was neat and controlled as it had been all along but now he could see almost entry by entry that it began to deteriorate until by the end it had become nearly illegible. Of course there was the initial excitement about Germany and playfulness in her accounts of Belinda.

"Belinda hasn't changed I love her so much still the same fun mischievous sexy girl but there's no harm in it just the effervescence of her personality and she's so beautiful like a pillar of gold. Oh she's like one of Hesse's women. I feel like Hermione offering Maria to Harry, only I'm me offering Belinda to Harry. She likes him and flirts with him. She told me straightaway she'd like to have him. She's so bored with her husband. She told me about her affairs. Sensational! She's a real free spirit! What she does! I wish I had her courage... In the complete darkness of our bedroom we had a little fun with Harry. Oh it was like being girls again... we have a complete understanding with each other... Harry didn't know what was happening. Oh he's so innocent. But he enjoyed it. Belinda knows what men enjoy. And so do I!"

Later she wrote,

"It's funny but I feel sometimes like a fifteen year old girl with Belinda it brings me back to my teenage years in Droichead when I was in the convent and we played with boys together. We were reckless but happy. I learned so much from Belinda about boys, about sex, about life. She took me out of myself and I felt happy when I was with her. I think Belinda kept unhappiness away from me. But then she couldn't do it all the time. Oh Mother! Oh Gerard!"

This was where her handwriting began to weaken and become illegible. It recovered soon after but Harry could now follow its deterioration as he read on. Her handwriting staggered now the way she had sometimes staggered after a drink or two and he had had to hold her steady as they walked home. There were many desultory passages that anyone could have written about their visits to Meersburg, Friedrichshafen, Lindau, and the Alps. She wrote about lying naked in the sun with undisguised glee.

"I love it. I love the freedom of it. I love to look around and examine the naked bodies golden and eternal-looking in the sun. A man would be very suspect looking at naked bodies like that but a woman can do it with impunity. I love looking straight at them, those bodies, peering into their private parts, oh sometimes I want so much to reach out and touch them, all of them, caress them, bestow gorgeous wild pleasures on them with my touch, devour them... Oh Belinda and Harry look so beautiful lying close together. I want her to enjoy him, and he her! I saw him looking at her when he thought I wasn't watching. He could have been arrested for the way he looked at her. Oh I wanted to just lift him and throw him on top of her, and then watch as he ransacked her with his body. I told Belinda I wanted to watch them making love together. We laughed so much with that old private secret bold laughter of ours. She said she would try to arrange it. Oh I want to see Harry doffing her... I want to see outrageous exquisite lost pleasure in both their faces when they are stuck together! I really would love that. I want them both to be happy. And I want to witness it. Their happiness. And I want to be happy!"

But what did she want really? Harry couldn't make it out. He could take her words at face value but behind them he felt there was something else that remained unspoken and that did not match the words she was scrawling over the pages of the notebook. There was a mismatch somewhere but he just couldn't see where or what it was. There was so much he couldn't see. He had never been good at reading things. He always got people wrong in the end. He had certainly gotten Claire wrong, hadn't he? Claire was not clear. Claire was unclear. Then came the truly fateful moment.

"So I found Harry and Belinda together in the kitchen. I timed my entrance too early and they had only just begun to play with each other. Harry had hoisted Belinda on to the worktop and had spread her legs wide open, she was stroking his penis, getting him ready to enter her. Another ten seconds and it would have been done. I should have said, 'Go on! Go ahead! It's what you want, isn't it?... It's what I want! Do it! Doff each other!' But I didn't... So the whole thing fell asunder. I ran back to the bedroom and Harry followed. I felt more troubled and unhappy than I have felt in years. Oh Mother, help me! Oh Gerard, help me! I don't understand what's going on in my mind... Or in my heart... I practically assaulted Harry. I think I wanted to kill him. I think as he jolted and shuddered through the repeated climaxes I brought him to I think I wanted to kill and devour him. Finally, he lay under me broken and exhausted with pleasure, unconscious to the world. While I moved over him like an unquiet sea moaning with an anguish I could not contain. Oh I'm getting lost here... I'm getting so lost..."

Among the next entries, and before they left for Lugano, she had written,

"Belinda is telling Harry things about me, I'm sure of it. I've noticed them heads down whispering together. I imagine she's telling him stories from school, our wild Droichead days. My wild days. I didn't know what I was doing then. I still don't. But Belinda has told things before that have hurt me... What I do, what I think, what I say, is all my own business, isn't it?... I don't want anyone judging me or trying to tell me there's something wrong with me. I'm all right. Everything just feels so foreign all of a sudden. But then this is 'foreign', right?... It's Germany... We're going to Switzerland... We're going to Italy... Let's go now before someone gets hurt!"

The day they took the ferry across Lake Constance, she wrote,

"I hate leaving Belinda but we can't stay under her enchantment always. It's a pity about her and Harry, she really wanted him (she always wanted my boys! She always had them too! But she didn't have Harry!), I wouldn't have minded... I just want everyone to be happy. Most of all Harry. I want to make Harry happy. That's funny isn't it? I want so much to make Harry happy. And I can't even make myself happy. I do wonder sometimes what happiness is. Or even if it can make the difference everyone says it can. Would being happy make me happy? What a funny question that seems..."

That night in Lugano was the night she had staggered drunkenly after the meal by the lake. The only note she had made for Lugano was more or less what she had said to him there.

"I'm missing something. I don't know what it is. I thought I had everything. But something is missing. Something inside me is missing. Maybe it's never been there. Maybe I was born missing it."

The entries in the notebook were now far more succinct and far more uncertain in style and content, her words and even individual letters were beginning to crack and show signs of disintegration. She wrote about Florence and the Michelangelo "Slaves" she had cried in front of. She wrote that she had not been able to *"help herself"*.

"Later Harry showed me the city. He wanted me to see the Perseus there was in an open air 'loggia' right in the heart of town. The Perseus was nice – ummhhh! Nice! – but he was holding up a horrible Medusa with snakes writhing in her hair. I wondered if Harry was trying to tell me something. Is the Medusa me? Am I that horrible? We sat also near the Duomo and Baptistery, drinking Prosecco. Harry said the doors to the Baptistery were known as the 'Gates of Paradise'. Hah! As if there is any Paradise. Perseus didn't look the Medusa straight in the eyes, nor did Harry! But I did! If either of them had seen what I saw they'd know there is no Paradise... Or if there is, those damn gates will stay shut forever... For me anyway!"

A single sentence later said,

"Harry is all love love love... He pretends to be so full of love. But I don't think he knows anything about it. I think deep down Harry is impotent and incapable... He doesn't see..."

That must have been the time, Harry reckoned, when he had made love to her in the Florence *'Pensione'* when the Dutch women were watching. Harry sensed now that he was in the presence of a disaster looming all the time larger and larger. For some time now her tone had become embattled and aggressive, and she was beginning to question or even attack him in her writing. He hadn't seen it or if he had he hadn't paid enough attention to it. That was a crime, or even a sin, on his part. That sin would keep 'The Gates of Paradise" shut for him, and for Claire.

The scene changed now from Florence to La Spezia, the Gulf of Poets, and Cinque Terre. She wrote about their walk on the Via dell'Amore and how they placed the lock with their names on the railing along the path there.

She wrote,

"I asked Harry what love is... He said it is ninety nine percent perspiration. Maybe it is for him. But not for me. I've tried to teach Harry but I think now that he's learning nothing at all from me. He's still like a callow fourteen year old touching himself, fantasising about his first..."

Her mood seemed to brighten describing the visits to Portovenere, Venere Azzurra, Lerici, and San Terenzo on the Gulf of Poets.

"Harry is besotted with Venus," she wrote. *"Now as well as Hermione and Maria I will have to be Venus for him. I guess I can do that. I've had practice. His 'Blue Venus' he calls me, even when making love... I like it. I do love Harry so. I want to be whatever he needs me to be. I want to be whatever I can be for him. For love. I want him to truly know what love is! I want him to truly live, and truly love!"*

She loved Cinque Terre and Monterosso, but the "stone Giant" above the beach made her sombre again. She wrote,

"I wish he would just find the strength to break away and just go, escape, become something, live something... Oh for the strength to become, to live, to cease to be stone... to forget stone..."

She wrote about the terrible storm that shook their hotel with loud thunder and the crackling flashes of purple lightning, colour of amethyst, that lit up their room. Her mood changed again to become bitter and unhappy. She was a creature now of highs and lows. Reading her words Harry still couldn't understand what was going on.

"Harry ransacked me during a terrible storm. I could feel the marble floor under my hands and knees and feet vibrating from the thunder as he beat against me like a battering ram. He was furious like the first time in Belinda's, and the time in the 'Pensione' in Florence... I just let him. When he was done I asked him if he was the 'thunder and lightning'. He said he was the 'silence and darkness in between'. Oh Harry is such a child... He doesn't know anything about 'silence and darkness'. I do. I'll show him. If I can't show him what it is to be happy, I'll show him all there is to know about 'silence and darkness'..."

And then in one of the journal's most painful moments she wrote how she had fallen on the rocks on the beach and how Harry had helped her, or tried to.

"*Harry tried to help but he's not able to. He's useless that way. I'm not even sure if he could help himself. I cried so much. It was more than the shock and hurt of the fall, my fall... It was much more. Oh Mother I've been crying so much... When and where did my tears start? I seem to be so full of them... I see the river in Droichead, the one I jumped into to rescue Gerard. I think it is the river of all the tears I am destined to cry. I try to stop but it's useless... I feel like one of those 'Slaves' in Florence or the Giant above the beach here... broken, dismembered, awful... I feel trapped in stone. I can't get out. But the stone weeps! It weeps...*"

For some reason there were a couple of blank pages and then she wrote,

"*I wouldn't let Harry make love to me. He wanted to but I wouldn't let him. I told him it 'hurt'. But he has no idea where or how it hurts. And he never will.*"

They moved on to Genoa, Verona, and Brescia. Her tone was very neutral for the first two cities, just nondescript, if often incomplete, observations on the buildings, the food, and the weather. She said nothing about the religious procession at Easter she had called "spooky". In Brescia she flew into a rage, scattering coarse swear words through her sentences,

"*Harry booked us into a brothel... The police came during the night and pulled the... out... I could have been arrested! Is that all he thinks of me? Am I some kind of... in his eyes?... Oh I hate him! I will never forgive him for this! I've loved him so much and this is how he repays me!*"

Later she wrote,

"*He needs to understand that I am not a... Prostitute! I am not his... Prostitute!*"

She wrote it savagely. Harry noticed how the pen had dug into and torn the page. Oh if only he had known. But maybe she was right. He didn't know anything. He wasn't capable of knowing anything. Anymore than he was capable of loving her enough to have saved her life. More than ever he felt the uselessness she had accused him of hanging around his neck and dragging down his soul. To not to have been able to keep someone he had loved with every iota of his being alive must surely be the perfect measure of perfect, total, uselessness, the kind of uselessness that loses you a love, a life, and a world. If only he had seen... And if he had seen, would it really have made a difference?...

At first she was very positive about Sulzano and Lake Iseo. She wrote about the couple they had met and spent some time with, the Dutchman and his English girlfriend,

"Harry said he thought the English girlfriend was unhappy. He couldn't see that she is simply in love, so in love. And that guy she's with doesn't understand or appreciate the first thing about her, or how in love with him she is! He's worse than Harry. No, Harry's as bad as he is. He and Harry are just the same!"

The clouds rolled back a little, the sun shone, and her mood brightened again as they spent days relaxing on the lake island.

"Oh it's so nice to be on holiday with Harry... I love Italy so much. I love making love to him here... We can be golden and eternal here! Oh I don't want to return home. I asked Harry how to say 'I don't want to return home' in Italian. 'Non voglio tornare a casa' he says. But we have to go home, don't we? Everyone has to return home I suppose... but I don't know why. I can't for the life of me figure out why. Then Harry reminded me about my dream to live on a cottage by the Atlantic, with glorious blood-red sunsets... evening after evening after evening... Yes we'll do that. I'll do that with Harry. Just Harry and me. Together in a cottage by the Atlantic. Just us and the blood-red sunsets. Just us. So let's go home. Home is where our heart is."

Harry remembered the incredible love-making of that last sun-drenched week on the lake. And he remembered the implicit promise that they would find a cottage by the Atlantic together. And that they would be in love and happy there. What followed then was another shocking reversal in the see-sawing emotions of the notebook.

"And so we are leaving here and going back to Monkstown. It's been a hell of a journey... It's been a hell of a journey ever since I started this notebook. We've done so much, travelled so much, seen so much, learned so much... Oh but what I've learned more than anything is simply this... Harry understands nothing. He understands nothing. He doesn't understand me. He understands nothing."

As an abrupt addendum she added,

"We are going back to Monkstown. And Harry can go back to being a Monk!"

Her style shattered on returning home. There was an initial hiatus to begin with, she seemed to record nothing of their first weeks back home, and then some very random notes.

"I sent Harry on his own to the 'Forty-Foot'... He wanted me to go with him. I don't feel like going anywhere."

Later she wrote,

"I like spending more and more time in my own apartment... I don't think Harry misses me. We can still find time together."

And then one day,

"Harry came back early today. He sat by the bed and he started to cry. I don't know why. I wiped a tear away. He's silly sometimes."

She continued,

"Harry said he just wants to love me, all of me, from the beginning to the end of time... golden eternal... He was very emotional. I told him I would love him too forever, wherever there is a heartbeat, and where there is no heartbeat, as he put it... It's just you and me I told him from now until the end of time... and beyond the end of time... And I meant it. Sometimes my love for Harry rises up in me so large so powerful and so tender, like some huge overwhelming wave, I fear it will smash break and annihilate me... I often need Harry to take me in his arms at those times. I need him to love me. As he did today."

And then she wrote terrible words the meaning of which he grasped instantly,

"I've started playing the game again. I'm in my room. I play the game. The game will decide. It will decide everything."

So all the time she ran away from him to spend time alone in her own apartment, this was her game. She was letting a loaded gun decide if she should live or die, if their love would live or die. But in the end, surely she knew that the gun could only provide one outcome. She wrote,

"I can't keep you Harry... Don't you see you won't be safe with me?... I kill things... Don't you see, I always kill things?... My mother died because of me. My little brother Gerard, I let him drown. I'm afraid I will kill you

too, Harry. I'm the shadow of tragedy, Harry… on everything… I have to save you… You have to get out while you have a chance…"

He hadn't gotten out while he had a chance. He had never had a chance. Not from that first moment he had stood one step below her on the stairs and she had folded her arms around him and sobbed like a little girl into his throat. There were echoes of Harry's words in what she wrote, as is always the case with lovers. And then one last luminous blaze of brightness. Before she finished.

"I will love Harry before and after this world, this life, before and after time," she wrote. *"I will never stop loving him. There will be no end to my love, to our love… We will always be on the 'Via dell'Amore'…I will always be his 'Porto Venere', his 'Venere Azzurra', his 'Gates of Paradise'. He can come to me whenever he wants… I will always be there for him. I will always be there for him. No matter what. No matter what, this love, my love, our love, will remain."*

It moved him so much, with the most exalted feelings of tenderness and love for her, that he had ever felt, rising through him, just as her next sentence broke him and reduced him to a helplessly huddled sobbing despairing grieving mass.

"It's as if there are two Claires inside me. There's the one who hates me. And the one who loves Harry so much. One of them has to go. And I can't let the one who loves Harry go."

Her next to last words were,

"I guess the game will decide!"

The last words she wrote were,

"Can't stop, won't stop…"

The autumnal equinox was over and had taken with it the yellow full moon. The days were cooler but dry and bright. By the time the moon had waned and was gone the nights had become clear but cold, the stars diamonded the sky and the night itself was like a dark and shining beast dressed in brilliant points of silver light. Out of the blue one day unexpectedly the postman stopped with a letter from America. It was addressed to *"An Scríbhneoir, Dughrá"*. Harry knew instantly that it could only be from Helen and his hands trembled as he opened the envelope. As he read he could hear the sweet musicality of her voice, its soft sweet American tones, its profound heartfelt gentleness, sounding so full of tenderness and real love for him. She began,

"Oh Harry I am sorry it has taken so long to write. I thought at first I should forget you. My time with you on the island was so beautiful... that's the only word... But after I left Inish it seemed to me that loving you and you loving me, five thousand miles apart, would be an impossible thing... And then I got so wrapped up in my life back here in the mild wild American Midwest... and I stopped thinking about you so much... And then I didn't really know where to write or if my letter would reach you. And life just went by so quickly. And then one day I read by chance in the newspaper (one of my colleagues who knew I had been to Inish showed it to me!) how there had been a helicopter crash during a violent storm, and I realised Harry it was near the cottage, and Harry, oh Harry, my heart stopped beating... and I began to cry..."

For a moment Harry needed to stop reading. He laid the page of writing in his lap, looked out over the sunbright land and the glistening ocean, took some very deep breaths, and returned to Helen's words and the ever-deepening beauty of her voice.

"Some time later the same colleague came to me with another news story about how a beach on Inish had been swept away by the storm... And the locals were asking if their golden beach could ever return?... And Harry now I couldn't stop thinking about being on Inish with you, I couldn't stop thinking about you... And I wondered if our golden beach could ever return? Oh Harry I wanted to go to you... I could easily imagine your surprise if after flying to Shannon and driving to Mayo, after taking the ferry to Killeaden, I suddenly turned up on your doorstep... Harry as I thought about it I knew how deeply happy it would make you to see me returning... like the long lost emigrant perhaps?... I knew Harry how much you would love seeing me come back... and how warmly you would welcome me... and embrace me... and love me... But oh Harry 'tempus fugit', and my life here became so busy, my work... And again, going to you, being with you, just seemed impossible, so impossible..."

Harry took another breather. The question now was where was Helen going? The question now was what was impossible, and what was not? He read anew.

"But Harry the truth was that no matter how busy or preoccupied I was I had never forgotten you... and I had never stopped wanting you... So, one day, sitting alone in a bar, drinking a Chablis, staring into the glass of shining shimmering liquid, thinking of our evening together in the cottage, I suddenly realised, or felt, Harry, that nothing was impossible... This was love, wasn't it? Love could never ever be impossible... Not if two people loved each other so much, and wanted to be together so much... And I knew, if you were still free, Harry, you would want me to be with you... But I also knew, Harry, as I sipped my bright cold Chablis, I also knew you would want to be with me... And I thought... Just write to Harry. Tell him to come to the wild Midwest. Tell him he's got a girl waiting for him... Tell him nothing is impossible. Tell him Helen loves him and wants him. She wants to be together with him. So I am doing that, Harry. I do love you. I do want to be with you. I want you to be with me. Oh so much, Harry! Come to me! Don't delay... Don't think about it. Shut up the cottage. Close and lock the doors and windows tightly. Get to Shannon... Cycle if you have to... Get yourself on a plane... And fly to my arms..."

Harry knew there and then that he was going to do just that. He was going to leave his "Kingdom of Nothing" and fly to Helen.

"Harry, I have never stopped thinking about you, missing you, wanting you, desiring you, wishing you were here. I love you desire you lust you want you need you... Please walk away from all your torment and sadness... and please come here to me. There's so much beauty we can share. There is a river of love that flows through this world for you and it flows through me. I want to share this beautiful world with you so very much, all of it.... Please let's do it now before it's too late. Come join yourself to this mild wild Midwestern girl... You know you'll like it. You did before!"

And Harry's eyes tumbled down the last lines Helen had written, falling falling falling, to the bottom of the page, while his heart soared in his chest and began to sing his wanting lusting yearning needing for the bright unquenched gold of his mild wild Midwestern girl. And through this heartsong of want lust yearning need his love for Helen spread wings and wildly flew to and fro beating against the cage of his mind heart body and soul to escape to her and nest in her, the lovely gold of her hair, her heart, and her life.

"Come to the American Midwest and write here...
Come to the American Midwest and write on my body...
Come to the American Midwest and be the writer of my body...
Come to the American Midwest and write your future on me...
Come to the American Midwest and write the rest of your life on me...
Come to the American Midwest and write me...
Come to the American Midwest and write 'Us'...
Let's be together, Harry...
Let's be 'Us'...
Golden and Eternal..."

The day slipped by in a haze of thoughts and longing for Helen. He remembered over and over with a soaring happiness inside him every moment of their time together when he had stood so close to her he could all but hear her heartbeat. He remembered her coming to the porch looking for help with her car, he remembered the drinks in the pub, the visit to Jean's house together, he remembered how she had leaped into his arms when frightened by the rodent stirring in the chest beneath the stairs, he remembered the drive through the island, how she stood on the battlements of the pirate queen's castle, he remembered how she swam in the green-gold of Kim Bay, and how she ran in bra and panties along the golden beach, while he ran after her, trying to gather with his hands the sparkling water diamonds strewn over the glistening white of her magnolia skin. He remembered finally the evening in the cottage, drinking the cold bright Chablis, and how then they had sunk together and so deeply into each other in rhythmic movements of glorious ravishment in and through each other, bathing their bodies in what was now an intense and joyous love which could no longer be denied. He was leaving Inish. He was flying to Helen. He was going to fly to her as fast as he could.

He could not sleep that night and rising from his bed in the early morning he did something he had never done before. He left the cottage and walked down the shore towards where Jean's shack had been. There was no moon and while at first the night was pitch black, and he needed to pick his steps carefully along the well-known track, after a time his eyes adjusted and with the help also of the dazzling display of stars he could make out the contours of the island and the vast emptiness where Jean's cabin had been, where now there was nothing. As his eyes grew stronger and he could see better through the darkness he was encouraged to follow the shoreline and as he had done at the very beginning of his sojourn he followed the rising ground high on the hillside to the cliff edge where, ever so cautiously, he walked along the cliff, hearing the sea quietly mysteriously soughing three hundred feet below until he was drawn to the place where he had sat on the night of the big storm when the helicopter had crashed and Julie Lacey's beautiful life and that of her colleagues had been buried in darkness. A wave of sadness beat inside him against his dream of Helen and for a moment he thought it was going to submerge him. But then as he raised his eyes to the sky diamonded with stars something happened which took his breath away and made his heart leap.

Over his head there was a flicker of green light, at first almost like a slender scarf of green shadow waving upon the starry sky. And then as he watched the scarf unfurled to roll like a vast flag over the darkness and it began quickly to grow in intensity and brightness until it was a vast curtain spread across the darkness of the night pulsing and shimmering with vivid movements of colour, until now predominantly green, but suddenly joined by rising swathes of bright gold, like spotlights, mixing in with and joining the green from below to form a green-golden screen wavering across the entire night sky above him, strewn too with a silver brightness of infinite stars. The green-gold diamonded roof of night held him spellbound for as long as the display lasted. At first there was about fifteen minutes of the gorgeous northern light and colour floating spectrally across the heavens, and then it faded for a time, and then revived with even more colour and brightness than before. Harry's thoughts and feelings about everything were wiped away under the display. He was beyond words and speech and could only watch helplessly as the limitless beauty of the island, the sky, the world, and the Universe, gathered itself in a sweeping green-gold embrace around him, and tightened on his heart and soul. He felt as if all the beauty now gathered around him and penetrating to his very soul was ready to crush and annihilate him, or at the very least remake him completely. There was a wild joy in him but also a movement like a wild fear. Was it what people called, "Awe"?... He felt a sudden need to return to the cottage. He didn't want to wait until the display faded completely so he began walking back down the cliff towards the shore and his cottage, the noise of the sea fading behind him, but growing in front, as he walked down the hillside. As he reached the shore the noise had become a crescendo like crashing cymbals in an orchestra unleashed. After every few steps he glanced back over his shoulders to see the glorious green-gold of the Aurora rolling like waves of the sea over the canopy of night. Night, colours, and sea noises were now all one. As he turned away again and made his way hastening towards the cottage he felt an unstoppable excitement mount in him and he heard a voice rising in him, saying one single word over and over and over and over... And on and on and on and on... Life, life, life, life, life, life, life, life, life... *LIFE!*...

He felt dizzy with that one word - "*Life!*" - rushing through him carrying a wild and invincible intoxication. It made him feel weak as if he was about to fall in the darkness. He quickened his pace until, almost running, he arrived back at the cottage and as he entered there his words and his perceptions rushed back in to join with his sensations and intoxication. As he rolled in a heap into bed to sleep, and dream, he felt the absolute wonder of the world rush through him like a crazy symphony. Above all others, one word came back to him before he fell into the profoundest sleep, and it was simply, "Helen... Helen... Helen..." The brightest of words, a golden word, an eternal word... A word that was now the bright golden eternal point of light at the heart of all his dreams and wishes to live. A word that was now "Life" itself. "Life" and "Helen" were now two words that meant exactly the same thing. Like some kind of miracle. Like love.

A couple of days later he began to say goodbye to the island. He went first of all to Mary Kate and sat with her and Tomás in their house in Killeaden, drinking another mug of steaming tea just as he had when he had first arrived a little over a year ago. He had already told her some time earlier of his intention to leave the island, now he was just making it "official".

"I already have someone to take the cottage over," Mary Kate said, but he didn't ask her who it was. The cottage and the island would have their own life now, without him.

Mary Kate had tears welling in her eyes as she said goodbye to him. She was a kind and sentimental woman, given easy to tender emotions. Tomás stood stolidly behind her, her supporting rock, his hand raised waving farewell as Harry cycled away.

He had quite a round of goodbyes to say, and not just to people, but also to the island. It was a fine day of bright sunshine and so he cycled to Kim Bay and walked one last time on the golden beach there. It was a magical beach, touched by an incredible beauty. He remembered running with Helen there, trying to catch the gleaming diamonds of seawater on her white skin. He could feel a new sorrow in his heart at the thought of leaving, the sad feeling of leaving. The island had never looked so beautiful, the land shone with a bright appearance of well-being, the sky was blue pristine, the green-gold sea swelled with great foam-laced waves that unfurled and rolled at his feet with a full and resounding sigh of farewell. He didn't want it to be a "forever" farewell. He told himself, promised himself, he would return here with Helen someday. They would walk, and perhaps run, again on this enchanted beach. They would swim. Maybe they would see dolphins, or basking sharks, or whales. With Helen he felt there would always be wonders. With Helen, the beautiful magic of the world would open up for him. With Helen the world would return to its essential luminous miraculous brightness and shine for him, for them. With Helen there would be the possibility of rainbows. And bridges between earth and Heaven they would never tire of building.

He stopped at "The Emerald" and Bill and Jane were, of course, sorry that he was leaving. Bill hugged him as he said goodbye.

"You are the only one who understood my monsters," he said. "And who felt pity for them deep in their caverns!"

"We both have our caverns!" Harry said.

"Yes," said Bill. "I could see you had yours the first day we met... I knew there was something very deep. And very dark... A cavern, indeed! I hope it's better now!"

Harry considered a moment and then decided to tell him.

"On my way here, when first I came here, as I was cycling through the west of Ireland seeking a place to live, I visited show caves in the Burren where, after we had walked deep into the heart of the cave, the guide switched the lights off and we stood in complete silence and darkness. There was absolutely nothing to see, even if you put your fingers right in front of your eyes... nothing... all you had in the world at that moment was the sound of your own heartbeat... nothing else existed..."

Bill listened with great attentiveness. He nodded, encouraging Harry to go on.

"Well, the guide walked us cautiously a short distance through the darkness, until we could hear water splashing, and then he turned a single lamp on... What we saw seemed to all of us like a pure miracle of bright beautiful magic, a dream. The lamp was fixed above a small but abundant waterfall bursting out from a ledge and falling in a sweet arc into the cave. The lamp was bright and its light shone right through the stream of water illuminating every drop turning each one into a gleaming gem or diamond scattered on the darkness and adorning its edges with fleeting rainbow colours."

Harry paused before finishing his story.

"I felt very downhearted and hopeless in that cave, especially when we had to stand after they had switched the lights out in what seemed like an infinity of profound darkness at the heart of everything... But I had never expected to be so surprised by beauty as I was when the single lamp came on and turned the waterfall into the most gorgeous luminous creation I had ever seen, like a living thing of beautiful light... I won't say that I rediscovered my hope, I didn't, far from it, but I did reconnect at a very deep level within myself with beauty. I had journeyed to the deepest part of the cave. And I had found a river of light, where I believed there was only darkness. It was, I now believe, as it has come back to me often in my mind's eye, some kind of promise of redemption... if that's the word... But maybe hope, beauty, love, life, are the words... Maybe it was simply a promise of life... and possibly of love..."

The two men parted without another word, Harry taking the quick road back to Dughrá, along the base of the hillside, where the traces of its disasters had been swept away. The scars of the avalanche had been healed and the wreckage of the helicopter removed. There was no trace of injury or death on the hillside. The island itself had thrown a russet cloak over its scars. Heathers and mosses now covered the wounds of its memory. The bright orange monbretia was returned to bloom and the blood-red teardrops of the fuchsia lined every road and pathway. There was little sound to be heard, only a light rustle of breeze through the grasses, and some birdsong. Above him, high in the air, Harry spotted the fluttering wings of a skylark shedding far and wide the wild and beautiful notes of its song. From on high, they fell upon him, musical and bright.

He stopped at Clare's house. This would be the hardest part of saying goodbye. He found her home alone. They stood in the kitchen together.

"How are you?" he asked her.

"I'm ok," she said quietly and with a wry smile. "I'm adapting to my new life!"

When he told her he was leaving the island he saw a look of immediate desperation fill her face and her eyes looked about her helplessly for a wild instant. And then she stepped quickly over to him and took him in her arms sinking her face into his shoulder while her hands pulled him closer.

"Don't ever forget…" was all she said as her voice broke and trailed away leaving a sense of utter incompleteness behind.

"I won't," he promised her, kissing her eyes and tears. "How could I? You were so beautiful to me… You will always be beautiful to me… I hope you will be very happy, Clare…"

As he was leaving, she called after him, poignantly,

"I guess life is just like that, Harry!"

He turned back to her.

"Like what?"

"Oh, you know…" she said, with a wry smile, and a new light in her eyes, "comings and goings, that's all… Easy come easy go!"

But maybe it wasn't always easy, Harry thought, as he waved goodbye to her and strolled down to his cottage. Oh God, why was it so hard to leave? Was there any one of us who was made to be separate and who could tolerate it? His life seemed to be one parting after another. But wasn't everyone's? Poor Clare... He wished everything good for her. He wished that the sea and the sky and the island would always be kind to her. Along with the love of her children and her husband. Along with the whole darn kit and caboodle of Earth, Heaven, and the Universe... and all there ever was... As he reached and entered the cottage he wished that for himself too.

He decided he would finish all his goodbyes in this single day. He walked back up to the cottage where the old bowed man with his stick and cap and his sister lived. The couple looked warily at him as he told of his intention to leave. It seemed as if they were suspicious of him, as if he had some hidden ulterior motive they wondered about, but he couldn't say what it was. As he was going the old man asked him,

"Do you think the nuclear fallout will come back to get us?"

Harry shook his head doubtfully.

"The west winds will save us surely!"

And then the sister spoke up, surprising him,

"But sure something will always get us in the end," she said fatefully.

It was probably as many words as Harry had ever heard from her in his entire time on the island.

"That's for sure," Harry agreed, "something will always get us... in the end..."

Leaving their cottage he met the tall thin youngish man he had seen so often walking past his cottage. Harry stopped him to explain that he was leaving the island but the youngish man didn't seem to grasp what he was being told. He babbled to Harry about his favourite tv soaps and then after a handshake and an exchange of goodbyes Harry left him understanding that, like all others on the island, he might never see him again. In his mind he wished him well.

Paddy and Joy were next, but as Harry stepped down on to the stony beach Crotchety Jack appeared from nowhere. Harry took his courage in his hands and announced his departure.

"When you got to go, you got to go!" he said with a grin.

"Where are you off to then? Is it to Dublin?" Crotchety Jack asked him in his usual gruff discontented manner.

"No, well, maybe at first, but my ultimate goal is Amerikay!" Harry told him with a flourish.

Jack seemed to soften slightly at this news.

"Good," he said "the further the better... You'll find half this island is there before you!"

"Have you friends or family out there?" Harry asked him.

"If you meet a fellow called Jack Dempsey out there say hello to him for me!" Jack said.

"Is it the boxer?" Harry asked.

"Not at all!" Jack said impatiently. "The Jack Dempsey I'm talking of was born on this island and left it while still a teenager... We've not heard from him since... I'm his father!"

Harry nodded.

"Do you know where he lives?"

"I've heard rumours he's out west somewhere," Jack told him.

"Well, I'm heading out west," Harry said. "I'll be sure to keep an eye out for him..."

"Good!" said Jack, walking away.

After a few steps he turned back to Harry and shouted after him,

"You needn't worry about the boxer. He's dead a number of years now!"

Harry continued towards the grassy headland where Paddy and Joy's cottage stood, waving a last acknowledgement to Crotchety Jack as he went. Paddy insisted on showing him the year's crop of grapes which he said had been greatly improved by the "radiation". The grapes did indeed look especially ripe and full of bright juice.

"I didn't get to work with you on the bog this summer," Harry lamented.

"Ah sure who needs turf fires at a time like this with all the nuclear energy going around!" Paddy answered.

For some reason while they were drinking tea the conversation turned to Jean and how the cabin had been pulled apart and taken away.

"There's not a vestige of Jean left on the island," Paddy said. "I must admit I hate the idea of someone disappearing completely!"

"We won't forget her," Joy said regretfully. "I think of her every day... every day..."

"We all do," said Paddy acerbically, "but sure we won't be here forever... And who will remember her then?..."

"What about a plaque?" Harry suggested.

"And where would we hang it?" Paddy responded sceptically. "On the gate of your cottage maybe?"

Harry had said nothing to anyone about his plans to fly to Helen. He felt guilty about it but he felt it would be better to say nothing. After all how was he to know what lay ahead in America? No one could say what the future might hold... But if things turned out well he could perhaps write or send a postcard, and one day as he had told himself walking on the beach at Kim, one day perhaps he would return to Inish with Helen in tow. That would make them all sit up. Jean's daughter and "*An Scríbhneoir*". That was surely worth a plaque somewhere. Maybe on the gate of his cottage, why not?

He thought he had done all his goodbyes. Back in the cottage he had a different task. He wrote to Helen. He took a simple postcard which featured the castle stronghold of the pirate queen overlooking the sea, the very place where Helen herself had stood, the sun golden in her hair, the day they had visited the island together. "I'm on my way!" he simply wrote, sketching a childish picture of a plane flying beneath some scattered birds and stars. And then, on impulse, and thoughtlessly, carelessly, he drew a simple little heart next to the words he had written. *"I'm on my way!"* He sketched a rudimentary arrow piercing the heart and then he wrote their names together alongside the heart with both their names joined together at the initial H. Putting the finishing touches to his innocent and arbitrary, almost childlike, artwork he drew a crescent moon alongside the heart and names. And in the court of the crescent moon he placed the brightest of stars, which he knew could only be Venus. And he knew that Helen also would know.

He had intended posting the postcard from the post office in Killeaden as he was leaving the island, but out of the blue his feelings shifted and with something like remorse now in his heart he decided to bring the postcard to Kathleen to post. He hadn't seen Kathleen since the day of her wedding when she had still been cool towards him, and given their strange history, he was very uncertain about the plan, but he made up his mind to do it. He still felt some reluctance as he walked towards the post office but he managed to dominate it and kept himself firmly on his path there until he stepped inside and felt Kathleen's cold, enquiring, still hostile gaze greet him. The first thing he noticed, dropping his eyes from hers, was that she was pregnant.

"When is the baby due?" he asked involuntarily, the words speeding from his mouth.

"Any moment now!" she answered with an apparent mix of impatience and frustration.

"Is that what you called for?" she asked then in a hard voice.

He showed her the postcard.

"I just want to post this," he said.

As he was affixing the stamp to the card he told her,

"I'm leaving the island," he said. "I may never come back…"

She looked up at him but her eyes had softened instantly. She was already a new, a different Kathleen, without any trace of hardness or hostility left.

"I heard from Mary Kate you were going," she said. "Myself and Peter are thinking of taking the cottage with the children…"

She embraced her belly.

"There'll be two of them soon!"

"I know," Harry said, "I heard... Any moment now..."

She nodded.

"I'm really glad about it," Harry told her. "I'm glad the house will be lived in by a family... by a couple with children... It will bring a lot of life to it... And I hope for all of you it will be filled with happiness... great happiness... and love..."

They stood in silence for a while and then as Harry gathered himself to leave he said,

"You will have to say my goodbyes to Peter..."

As he was going she reached out and held him back.

"I want to say sorry to you," she said, "for what I did..."

The silence deepened between them and it filled with recognition and meaning.

"The loneliness can drive you mad here!" she said. "The loneliness and the desire... the desire for anything... for anything at all..."

"It's ok," Harry told her. "Believe me, I know..."

That evening Peter Goode called to say he was sorry Harry was leaving but he was glad himself to have the cottage. Clare's husband, Michael, also called. The three men sat together drinking whiskey and telling stories. Peter laughed recalling Harry's role saving the sheep, but "those damn dogs!" he spat remembering the first night of irreparable animal savagery. He said nothing about the man who had been shot, and Harry wondered if he was alive or dead. A lot had happened on the island since that night and running out of subjects they inevitably turned to the recent disasters, the landslide, the disappeared beach, the tragic death of Julie Lacey and her companions, the nuclear fallout carried to the island by the east wind.

"It hasn't been all bad," Michael reminded them. "There was your wedding, Peter! You have a new child on the way..."

Peter nodded, thoroughly pleased with himself.

"I saw some whales back in February," Harry said, not daring to say he had swum with them in Kim Bay, though it was a tale Paddy often recounted to general scepticism.

"And not so long ago I saw the most amazing display of the Northern Lights…"

"They're incredible when you see them!" both men concurred, their faces lighting up. "They're one of the island's greatest gifts to us!"

"That must be a nice way to remember the island," Peter said.

"It's one of many," Harry answered.

As they sat and drank whiskey they sank into a comfortable contented silence with each other. Over the sea the sun was setting, the men gazed upon it, the sky flooding with yellows, bright oranges, amber, and pure gold. As the copper sun's burning rim was about to disappear below the raised lip of the ocean a solitary flash of vivid green could be seen above it, instantaneous, fleeting, and perfect. Harry gasped. He had never felt the island so deeply within his heart.

It was the first of October. He left the island at twilight. Paddy had said he would drive him to catch the evening train from Westport to the Irish midlands where his brother was waiting. On the ferry crossing, as he heard the last lonely curlew call over the quiet waters, Harry stood at the back of the boat and he saw her, just like when he had arrived to Inish, Venus in the court of the crescent moon, writing once again her quintessential ethereal signature upon the eternal night sky. He gazed upon her and felt a raw excitement begin to inhabit him. She made his heart beat with hope, with desire, and with great great love for Helen. A new world and a new life was beginning for him. And for the first time in over a year he felt excited about life, about the future, about Helen, about love. Most of all he felt happy. On the drive to Westport Paddy had asked him,

"Well, what are you going to do now?"

He had thought about it a little and gave his sincere answer.

"I think I'm going to write," he said.

"But that's what you came here for," Paddy sputtered. "Didn't you write when you were here? What did you write while on Inish?"

Harry reflected on this before answering.

"Oh, I wrote a postcard!" he said finally.

"Yeah and what did that masterpiece say?" Paddy asked him.

"It said '*I'm on my way!*' That's all..."

"Well, I'm sure it spoke volumes, but it's not 'War and Peace' anyway, that's for sure!" Paddy scoffed.

"No, it's not 'War and Peace'," Harry confirmed.

He didn't tell Paddy about the sequel to his postcard which had been nestling for days now in his brain and heart, the one which read, "I'm flying to the arms of Helen!"

But Harry did really intend to write, and he knew what his story would be. It wasn't his own story however, it would be Jean's. So often he had been overcome by sadness thinking of how her dream of escape or peace or happiness had ended with her heart breaking in Dughrá, and since the destruction of her cabin and the removal of its debris from the shore his sorrow for her had taken on a keener edge. Most of all he felt he had to rescue her in some way, no matter how inadequately, from the oblivion which appeared to have claimed her. He would write about her coming to the island, about the building of her shack, the building of her dream, he would write about her loneliness, her lovelessness, her desire, and he would write about her affair with Peter (if affair it was) and her involvement with Frank. He would write about Joy and Paddy, and Bill and Jane, and all the others. Above all perhaps he would write about the island itself, its mountains, its bays, its beaches, its rugged orange landscape, and he would make it the visible substance of her dream and desire for escape, love, and happiness. Wasn't that the story of everyone? Only he knew instinctively that he would bend the truth, he would bend it very greatly, he would make it all end happily. It wasn't that he would be cheating but that there could be no happy ending here on the edge of the western world made him feel like weeping. He was not going to allow or accept that. Was it not the prerogative of the writer, any writer, but particularly one of malleable fictions, to take all the pain and losses and heartbreak of the past and redeem them? To even take death itself and redeem it? He would do that for Jean if he could. He would try. He would try to give her a story that would be the fulfilment of all she had hoped, dreamed, and ever wished for, a story which would give her the ending she had striven for. And he would make her broken heart whole and alive again. In his version of Jean's story he would ultimately (however he got there) erode and erase separation, loss, lovelessness, heartbreak, grief, death… And in their place he would put union, fulfilment, happiness, exaltation, love, life… And at the heart of all that he would put Helen, Jean's daughter, his all-conquering Pirate Queen. The finality of his fiction would be the opposite to the real outcomes that had caused so much pain, you could call it a false finality, but it would be true to the most cherished dreams of the deepest desires that the heart and world of Jean, and that his own heart and world, could hold.

It was dark now and they were still a little way from Westport. The lights of the car swept the trees along the roadside picking out the incipient autumnal colours of brown, russet, and gold. Harry felt an intense surprise as on the island there were no trees and no leaves turning to gold so there was no real feeling of autumn other than the days shortening and growing colder. Now on the road into Westport the bright yellow of Paddy's headlights seemed to clear a path for them through the darkness and along n avenue of gold. Opposite the train station in Westport, picked out in the aming neon of the streetlamps, a whole stand of trees raised a golden ld against the night sky. As he wheeled his bicycle away from the car nto the station, Paddy called after him,

"So long, *Scríbhneoir!*"

Through densest darkness, lit only here and there by transitory streetlamps in passing towns, or isolated cottages strewn on the darkened fields, like distant stars in the night sky, the train rattled and rolled its way to the midland station where his brother was waiting. The two men embraced.

"Welcome back to the land of the living!" Harry's brother said warmly.

"It's so great to see you…"

Epilogue

A crystal clear sky of blue arched over Droichead. Harry stood all alone in the cemetery alongside Claire's grave which appeared adequately tended. He read the white marble stone with its very simple inscription in green. Alongside the names and dates of birth and death of Claire's mother and her beatific brother, Gerard, he read her own name, with the years of her birth and death. She had been thirty-three. He had never really known, just one of the things he had never really known about her. He had come up to Droichead on the train and had walked from the station to the cemetery. He needed to hurry back to catch the last train from Dublin to Limerick and from there take a bus to Shannon where he would spend the night in the hotel at the airport. Early in the morning he would fly to Minneapolis. It wasn't easy to turn away though. He knew it wouldn't be. The minutes and then an hour and yet another hour passed as Claire held him as tightly as she ever had. He felt his love for her filling him but felt it had nowhere to go. It rose up and embraced his heart, it flooded his lungs, and filled his throat. He could not stop his grief rising with it nor the tears. He was afraid he was going to cry out in anguish, afraid he was going to fall to his knees upon the earth in which she lay. For a moment he was all and nothing but despair. Why, oh why, did life and the world do this to us? We come from nothing… We inhabit this eternal star-studded thing we call the Universe… From the depths of time we meet and for a flickering instant of life we love and lose ourselves helplessly, hopelessly, beautifully, wonderfully, in each other… And then we get torn apart. And we are left with only separation, loss, grief, heartbreak… And the nothingness, the "no more", that comes ever after. Ever after. Where the only consolation can be that in the midst of it all we did find, know, and, for however briefly, love each other. If any consolation there can ever be.

His eyes were blinded and his mouth was full of words of love he could only mumble over her, like a beaten, broken prayer, as he finally, hopelessly, helplessly, turned away.

Before he left, he threw a single white rose down upon her grave.

Oh Heaven, he hoped she was sleeping peacefully.

The End

Dublin, 1st January 2021

Printed in Great Britain
by Amazon

6515849R00145